Evelyn Innes

George Moore

CONTENTS

CHAPTER ONE
CHAPTER TWO
CHAPTER THREE
CHAPTER FOUR
CHAPTER FIVE
CHAPTER SIX
CHAPTER SEVEN
CHAPTER EIGHT
CHAPTER NINE
CHAPTER TEN
CHAPTER ELEVEN
CHAPTER TWELVE
CHAPTER THIRTEEN
CHAPTER FOURTEEN
CHAPTER FIFTEEN
CHAPTER SIXTEEN
CHAPTER SEVENTEEN
CHAPTER EIGHTEEN
CHAPTER NINETEEN
CHAPTER TWENTY
CHAPTER TWENTY-ONE
CHAPTER TWENTY-TWO
CHAPTER TWENTY-THREE
CHAPTER TWENTY-FOUR
CHAPTER TWENTY-FIVE
CHAPTER TWENTY-SIX
CHAPTER TWENTY-SEVEN
CHAPTER TWENTY-EIGHT
CHAPTER TWENTY-NINE
CHAPTER THIRTY
CHAPTER THIRTY-ONE
CHAPTER THIRTY-TWO
CHAPTER THIRTY-THREE
CHAPTER THIRTY-FOUR
CHAPTER THIRTY-FIVE
THE END

EVELYN INNES

GEORGE MOORE

First published 1898
Reprinted (Essex Library) 1929

*To
Arthur Symons and W.B. Yeats
Two contemporary writers
with whom
I am in sympathy*

CHAPTER ONE

The thin winter day had died early, and at four o'clock it was dark night in the long room in which Mr. Innes gave his concerts of early music. An Elizabethan virginal had come to him to be repaired, and he had worked all the afternoon, and when overtaken by the dusk, he had impatiently sought a candle end, lit it, and placed it so that its light fell upon the jacks.... Only one more remained to be adjusted. He picked it up, touched the quill and dropped it into its place, rapidly tuned the instrument, and ran his fingers over the keys.

Iron-grey hair hung in thick locks over his forehead, and, shining through their shadows, his eyes drew attention from the rest of his face, so that none noticed at first the small and firmly cut nose, nor the scanty growth of beard twisted to a point by a movement habitual to the weak, white hand. His face was in his eyes: they reflected the flame of faith and of mission; they were the eyes of one whom fate had thrown on an obscure wayside of dreams, the face of a dreamer and propagandist of old-time music and its instruments. He sat at the virginal, like one who loved its old design and sweet tone, in such strict keeping with the music he was playing—a piece by W. Byrd, "John, come kiss me now"—and when it was finished, his fingers strayed into another, "Nancie," by Thomas Morley. His hands moved over the keyboard softly, as if they loved it, and his thoughts, though deep in the gentle music, entertained casual admiration of the sixteenth century organ, which had lately come into his possession, and which he could see at the end of the room on a slightly raised platform. Its beautiful shape, and the shape of the old instruments, vaguely perceived, lent an enchantment to the darkness. In the corner was a viola da gamba, and against the walls a harpsichord and a clavichord.

Above the virginal on which Mr. Innes was playing there hung a portrait of a woman, and, happening to look up, a sudden memory came upon him, and he began to play an aria out of *Don Giovanni*. But he stopped before many bars, and holding the candle end high, so that he could see the face, continued the melody with his right hand. To see her lips and to strike the notes was almost like hearing her sing it again. Her voice came to him through many years, from the first evening he had heard her sing at La Scala. Then he was a young man spending a holiday in Italy, and she had made his fortune for the time by singing one of his songs. They were married in Italy, and at the end of some months they had gone to Paris and to Brussels, where Mrs. Innes had engagements to fulfil. It was in Brussels that she had lost her voice. For a long while it was believed that she might recover it, but these hopes proved illusory, and, in trying to regain what she had lost irrevocably, the money she had earned dwindled to a last few hundred pounds. The Innes had returned to London, and, with a baby-daughter, settled in Dulwich. Mr. Innes accepted the post of organist at St. Joseph's, the parish church in Southwark, and Mrs. Innes had begun her singing classes.

Her reputation as a singer favoured her, and an aptitude for teaching enabled her to maintain, for many years, a distinguished position in the musical world. Mr. Innes's abilities contributed to their success, and he might have become a famous London organist if he had devoted himself to the instrument. But one day seeing in a book the words "viola d'amore," he fancied he would like to possess an instrument with such a name. The instrument demanded the music that had been written for it. Byrd's beautiful vocal Mass had led him to Palestrina and Vittoria, and these wakened in him dreams of a sufficient choir at St. Joseph's for a revival of their works.

So when Evelyn clambered on her father's knee, it was to learn the chants that he hummed from old manuscripts and missals, and it was the contrapuntal fancies of the Elizabethan composers that he gave her to play on the virginal, or the preludes of Bach on the clavichord. Her infantile graces at these instruments were the delight and amazement of her parents. She warbled this old-time music as other children do the vulgar songs of the hour; she seemed less anxious to learn the operatic music which she heard in her mother's class-rooms, and there was a shade of uneasiness in Mrs. Innes's admiration of the beauty of Evelyn's taste; but Mr. Innes said that it was better that her first love should be for the best, and he could not help hoping that it would not be with the airs of *Lucia* and *Traviata* that she would become famous. As if in answer, the child began to hum the celebrated waltz, a moment after a beautiful Ave Maria, composed by a Fleming at the end of the fifteenth century, a quick, sobbing rhythm, expressive of naïve petulance at delay in the Virgin's intercession. Mr. Innes called it natural music—music which the modern Church abhorred and shamefully ostracised; and the conversation turned on the incurably bad taste and the musical misdeeds of a certain priest, Father Gordon, whom Mr. Innes judged to be responsible for all the bad music to be heard at St. Joseph's.

For Mr. Innes's ambition was to restore the liturgical chants of the early centuries, from John Ockeghem, the Flemish silver-smith of Louis XI., whose recreation it was to compose motets, to Thomas da Vittoria; and, after having made known the works of Palestrina and of those who gravitated around the great Roman composer, he hoped to disinter the masses of Orlando di Lasso, of Goudimel and Josquin des Près, the motets of Nannini, of Felice Anerio, of Clemens non Papa.... He would go still further back. For before this music was the plain chant or Gregorian, bequeathed to us by the early Church, coming down to her, perhaps, from Egyptian civilisation, the mother of all art and all religion, an incomparable treasure which unworthy inheritors have mutilated for centuries. It was Mr. Innes's belief that the supple, free melody of the Gregorian was lost in the shouting of operatic tenors and organ accompaniments. The tradition of its true interpretation had been lost, and the text itself, but by long study of ancient missals, Mr. Innes had penetrated the secret of the ancient notation, vague as the eyeballs of the blind, and in the absence of a choir that could read this strange alphabet of sound, he cherished a plan for an edition of these old chants, re-written by him into the ordinary notation of our day. But impassable obstacles intervened: the apathy and indifference of the Jesuits, and their fear lest such radical innovations should prove unpopular and divert the congregation of St. Joseph's elsewhere. He had abandoned hope of converting them from their error, but he was confident that reaction was preparing against the jovialities of Rossini, whose *Stabat Mater*, he said, still desecrated Good Friday, and against the erotics of M. Gounod and his suite. And this inevitable reaction Mr. Innes strove to advance by his pupils. Many became disciples and helped to preach the new musical gospel. He induced them to learn the old instruments, and among them found material for his concerts. Though a weak man in practical conduct, he was steadfast in his ideas. His concerts had begun to attract a little attention; he was receiving support from some rich amateurs, and was able to continue his propaganda under the noses of the worthy fathers in whose church he was now serving, but where he knew that one day he would be master.

But, unfortunately, Mr. Innes could only give a small part of his time to these concerts. Notwithstanding his persuasiveness, there remained on his hands some intractable pupils who would not hear of viol or harpsichord, who insisted upon being taught to play modern masses on the organ, and these he could not afford to refuse. For of late years his wife's failing health had forced her to relinquish teaching, and the burden of earning their living had fallen entirely upon him. She hoped that a long rest might improve her in health, and that in some months—six, she imagined as a sufficient interval—she would be able to undertake in full earnestness her daughter's education. To do this had become her dearest wish; for there could now be little doubt that Evelyn had inherited her voice, the same beautiful quality and fluency in vocalisation; and thinking of it, Mrs. Innes held out her hands and looked at them, striving to read in them the progress of her illness. Evelyn wondered why, just at that moment, her father had turned from the bedside overcome by sudden tears. But whoever dies, life goes on the same, our interests and necessities brook little interference. Meal-times are always fixed times, and when father and daughter met in the parlour—it was just below the room in which Mrs. Innes was dying—Evelyn asked why her mother had looked at her hands so significantly.

He said that it was thus her mother foreshadowed Violetta's death, when Armand's visit is announced to her.

In the silence which followed this explanation their souls seemed to say what their lips could not. Sympathies and perceptions hitherto dormant were awakened; he recognised in her, and she, in herself, an unsuspected inheritance. Her voice she had received from her mother, but all else came from her father. She felt his life and character stirring in her, and moved as by a new instinct, she sat by his side, holding his hand. They sat waiting for the announcement of the death which could not be delayed much longer, and each thought of the difference the passing would make in their lives! It was her death that had brought them together, that had given them a new and mutual life. And in those hours their eyes had seemed to seal a compact of love and fealty.

This was three years ago; but since Mrs. Innes's death very little had been done with Evelyn's voice. The Jesuits had spent money in increasing their choir and orchestra, and Mr. Innes was constantly rehearsing the latest novelties in religious music. All his spare time was occupied with private teaching; and discovering in his daughter a real aptitude for the lute, he had taught her that instrument, likewise the viola da gamba, for which she soon displayed even more original talent. She played both instruments at his concerts, and as several pupils offered themselves, he encouraged her to give lessons—he had made of her an excellent musician, able to write fugue and counterpoint; only the production of the voice he had neglected. Now and again, in a fit of repentance, he had insisted on her singing some scales, but his heart was not in the lesson, and it fell through.

He was suspicious that she knew she could not learn singing from him; but an avowal of his inability to teach her would necessitate some departure from his own ideas, and, like all men with a mission, Mr. Innes was deficient in moral courage, and in spite of himself he evaded all that did not coincide with the purpose of his life. He loved his daughter above everything, except his music, and the thought that he was sacrificing her to his ambition afflicted him with cruel assaults of conscience. Often he asked himself if he were capable of redeeming his promise to his dead wife, or if he shirked the uncongenial labour it entailed? And it was this tormenting question that had impelled him to light the candle, and raise it so that he could better see his wife's face.

Though an indifferent painting, the picture was elaborately like the sitter. The pointed oval of the face had been faithfully drawn, and its straight nose and small brown eyes were set characteristically in the head. Remembering a photograph of his daughter, Mr. Innes fetched it from the other end of the room, and stood with it under the portrait, so that he could compare both faces, feature by feature. Evelyn's face was rounder, her eyes were not deep-set like her mother's; they lay nearly on the surface, pools of light illuminating a very white

and flower-like complexion. The nose was short and high; the line of the chin deflected, giving an expression of wistfulness to the face in certain aspects. Her father was still bent in examination of the photograph when she entered. It was very like her, and at first sight Nature revealed only two more significant facts: her height—she was a tall girl—and a beautiful undulation in her walk, occasioned by the slight droop in her shoulders. She was dressed in dark green woollen, with a large hat to match.
"Well, darling! and how have you been getting on?"
The vague pathos of his grey face was met by the bright effusion of hers, and throwing her arms about him, she kissed him on the cheek.
"Pretty well, dear; pretty well."
"Only pretty well," she answered reproachfully. "No one has been here to interrupt you; you have had all the afternoon for finishing that virginal, and you've only been getting on 'pretty well.' But I see your necktie has come undone."
Then overlooking him from head to foot—
"Well, you have been making a day of it."
"Oh, these are my old clothes—that is glue; don't look at me—I had an accident with the glue-pot; and that's paint. Yes; I must get some new shirts, these won't hold a button any longer."
The conversation paused a few seconds, then running her finger down the keys, she said—
"But it goes admirably."
"Yes; I've finished it now; it is an exquisite instrument. I could not leave it till it was finished."
"Then what are you complaining of, darling? Has Father Gordon been here? Has he discovered any new Belgian composer, and does he want all his music to be given at St. Joseph's?"
"No; Father Gordon hasn't been here, and as for the Belgian composers, there are none left; he has discovered them all."
"Then you've been thinking about me, about my voice. That's it," she said, catching sight of her own photograph. "You've been frowning over that photograph, thinking"—her eyes went up to her mother's portrait—"all sorts of nonsense, making yourself miserable, reproaching yourself that you do not teach me to vocalise, a thing which you know nothing about, or lamenting that you are not rich enough to send me abroad, where I could be taught it." Then, with a pensive note in her voice which did not escape him, she said—
"As if there was any need to worry. I'm not twenty yet."
"No, you're not twenty yet, but you will be very soon. Time is going by."
"Well, let time go by, I don't care. I'm happy here with you, father. I wouldn't go away, even if you had the money to send me. I intend to help you make the concerts a success. Then, perhaps, I shall go abroad."
His heart went out to his daughter. He was proud of her, and her fine nature was a compensation for many disappointments. He took her in his arms and thankfully kissed her. She was touched by his emotion, and conscious that her eyes were threatening tears, she said—
"I can't stand this gloom. I must have some light. I'll go and get a lamp. Besides, it must be getting late. I wonder what kind of a dinner Margaret has got for us. I left it to her. A good one, I hope. I'm ravenous."
A few minutes after she appeared in the doorway, holding a lamp high, the light showing over her white skin and pale gold hair. "Margaret has excelled herself—boiled haddock, melted butter, a neck of mutton and a rice pudding. And I have brought back a bag of oranges. Now come, darling. You've done enough to that virginal. Run upstairs and wash your hands, and remember that the fish is getting cold."
She was waiting for him in the little back room—the lamp was on the table—and when they sat down to dinner she began the tale of her day's doings. But she hadn't got farther than the fact that they had asked her to stay to tea at Queen's Gate, when her tongue, which always

went quite as fast as her thoughts, betrayed her, and before she was aware, she had said that her pupil's sister was in delicate health and that the family was going abroad for the winter. This was equivalent to saying she had lost a pupil. So she rattled on, hoping that her father would not perceive the inference.

"There doesn't seem to be much luck about at present," he said. "That's the third pupil you've lost this month."

"It is unfortunate ... and just as I was beginning to save a little money." A moment after her voice had recovered its habitual note of cheerfulness. "Then what do you think I did? An idea struck me; I took the omnibus and went straight to St. James's Hall."

"To St. James's Hall!"

"Yes, you old darling; don't you know that M. Desjardin, the French composer, has come over to give a series of concerts. I thought I should like him to try my voice."

"You didn't see him?"

"Yes I did. When I asked for him, the clerk said, pointing to a gentleman coming downstairs, that is Monsieur Desjardin. I went straight up to him, and told him who I was, and asked him if he had ever heard of mother. Just fancy, he never had; but he seemed interested when I told him that everyone said my voice was as good as mother's. We went into the hall, and I sang to him."

"What did you sing to him?"

"'Have you seen but a white lily grow?' and 'Que vous me coûtez cher, mon coeur, pour vos plaisirs.'"

"Ah! that music must have surprised him. What did he say?"

"I don't think I sang very well, but he seemed pleased, and asked me if I knew any modern music. I said 'Very little.' He was surprised at that. But he said I had a very fine voice, and sang the old music beautifully, but that it would be impossible for me to sing modern music without ruining my voice, until I had been taught. I asked him if it would not be well to try to earn a little money by concert singing, so that I might go abroad later on. He said, 'I am glad that all my arrangements are made, otherwise I might be tempted to offer you an engagement. One engagement leads to another, and if you sing before your voice is properly placed'—'posée' was the word he used—'you will ruin it.'"

"Is that all?"

"Yes, that's all." Then, noticing the pained look that had come into her father's face, she added, "It was nice to hear that he thought well of my voice."

But she could tell what he was thinking of, and regretting her tongue's indiscretion, she tried to divert his thoughts from herself. His brooding look continued, and to remove it she had to fetch his pipe and tobacco. When he had filled it for the third time he said—

"There is the Bach and the Handel sonata waiting for us; we ought to be getting to work."

"I'm quite ready, father. I suppose I must not eat any more oranges," and she surveyed her plate full of skins.

Mr. Innes took up the lamp, Evelyn called to the servant to get another, and followed him into the music-room. The lamps were placed on the harpsichord. She lighted some candles, and in the moods and aspirations of great men they found a fairyland, and the lights disappeared from the windows opposite, leaving them still there.

The wings of the hours were light—weariness could not reach them—and at half-past eleven Mr. Innes was speaking of a beautiful motet, "O Magnum Mysterium," by Vittoria. His fingers lingered in the wailing chords, and he said—

"That is where Wagner went for his chorus of youths in the cupola. The critics haven't discovered it yet; they are still talking of Palestrina."

CHAPTER TWO

Jesuits from St. Joseph's were not infrequently seen at Mr. Innes's concerts. The worthy fathers, although they did not see their way to guaranteeing a yearly grant of money sufficient to ensure adequate performances of Palestrina's finest works, were glad to support, with occasional guineas, their organist's concerts. Painters and men of letters were attracted by them; musicians seldom. Nor did Mr. Innes encourage their presence. Musicians were of no use to him. They were, he said, divided into two classes—those who came to scoff, and those who came to steal. He did not want either sort.

The rare music interested but a handful, and the audience that had come from London shivered in remembrance of the east wind which had accompanied their journey. But this little martyrdom did not seem to be entirely without its satisfactions, and conscious of superiority, they settled themselves to listen to the few words of explanation with which Mr. Innes was accustomed to introduce the music that was going to be played. He was speaking, when he was interrupted by the servant-maid, who whispered and gave him a card: "Sir Owen Asher, Bart., 27 Berkeley Square." He left the room hurriedly, and his audience surmised from his manner that something important had happened.

Sir Owen, seemingly a tall man, certainly above the medium height, was waiting for him in the passage. His thin figure was wrapped tightly in an overcoat, most of his face was concealed in the collar, and the pale gold-coloured moustache showed in contrast to the dark brown fur. The face, wide across the forehead, acquired an accent in the pointed chin and strongly marked jaw. The straight nose was thin and well shaped in the nostrils. "An attractive man of forty" would be the criticism of a woman. Sir Owen's attractiveness concentrated in his sparkling eyes and his manner, which was at once courteous and manly. He told Mr. Innes that he had heard of his concerts that morning at the office of the *Wagnerian Review*, and Mr. Innes indulged in his habitual dream of a wealthy patron who would help him to realise his musical ambitions. Sir Owen had just bought the periodical, he intended to make it an organ of advanced musical culture, and would like to include a criticism of these concerts. Mr. Innes begged Sir Owen to come into the concert-room. But while taking off his coat, Sir Owen mentioned what he had heard regarding Mr. Innes's desire to revive the vocal masses of the sixteenth century at St. Joseph's, and the interest of this conversation delayed them a little in the passage.

The baronet's evening clothes were too well cut for those of a poet, a designer of wall paper, or a journalist, and his hands were too white and well cared for at the nails. His hair was pale brown, curling a little at the ends, and carefully brushed and looking as if it had been freshened by some faintest application of perfumed essence. Three pearl studs fastened his shirt front, and his necktie was tied in a butterfly bow. He displayed some of the nonchalant ease which wealth and position create, smiled a little on catching sight of the jersey worn by a lady who had neglected to fasten the back of her bodice, and strove to decipher the impression the faces conveyed to him. He grew aware of that flitting anxiety which is inseparable from the task of finding a daily living, and that pathos which tells of fidelity to idea and abstinence from gross pleasure. A young man, who stood apart, in a carefully studied attitude, a dark lock of hair falling over his forehead, amused him, and the young man in the chair next Sir Owen wore a threadbare coat and clumsy boots, and sat bolt upright. Sir Owen pitied him and imagined him working all day in some obscure employment, finding his life's pleasure once a week in a score by Bach. Catching sight of a priest's profile, a look of contempt appeared on his face.

He was of his class, he had lived its life and lived it still, in a measure, but from the beginning his ideas and tastes had been superior to those of a merely fashionable man. At five-and-twenty he had purchased a Gainsborough, and at thirty he had spent a large sum of money in exhuming some sonatas of Bach from the dust in which they were lying. At three-and-thirty he had wrecked the career of a fashionable soprano by inspiring her with the belief that she might become a great singer, a great artist; at five-and-thirty Bayreuth and its world of musical culture and ideas had interested him in spite of his unconquerable aversion to long hair and dirty hands. After some association with geniuses he withdrew from the art-world, confessing himself unable to bear the society of those who did not dress for dinner; but while repudiating, he continued to spy the art-world from a distance. An audience is, however, necessary to a 'cello player, and the Turf Club and the Royal Yacht Club contained not a dozen members, he said, who would recognise the Heroica Symphony if they happened to hear it, which was not likely. Lately he had declared openly that he was afraid of entering any of his clubs, lest he should be asked once more what he thought of the Spring Handicaps, and if he intended sailing the *Medusa* in the Solent this season. Nevertheless, his journey to Bayreuth could not but produce an effect. He had purchased the *Wagnerian Review*; it had led him to Mr. Innes's concerts, and he was already interested in the prospect of reviving the early music and its instruments. That this new movement should be begun in Dulwich, a suburb he would never have heard of if it had not been for its picture gallery, stimulated his curiosity.

It is the variation, not the ordinary specimen, that is most typical, for the variation contains the rule in essence, and the deviation elucidates the rule. So in his revolt against the habitual pleasures and ideas of his class, Sir Owen became more explanatory of that class than if he had acquiesced in the usual ignorance of £20,000 a year. To the ordinary eye he was merely the conventional standard of the English upper classes, but more intimate observation revealed the slight glaze of Bohemianism which natural inclination and many adventures in that land had left upon him. He listened without parade, his grey eyes following the music—they, not the head, seeming to nod to it; and when Mr. Innes approached to ask him his opinion, he sprang to his feet to tell him.

One of the pieces they had heard was a pavane for five viols and a harpsichord, composed by Ferrabosco, son of the Italian musician who had settled in Greenwich at the end of the sixteenth century. Sir Owen was extraordinarily pleased and interested, and declared the pavane to be as complete as a sonata by Bach or Beethoven; but his appreciation was suddenly interrupted by someone looking at him.

At a little distance, Evelyn stood looking at him. The moment she had seen him she had stopped, and her eyes were delighted as by a vision. Though he represented to her the completely unknown, she seemed to have known him always in her heart; she seemed to have been waiting for knowledge of this unknown, and the rumour of the future grew loud in her ears.

He raised his eyes and saw a tall, fair girl dressed in pale green. Mr. Innes introduced them. "My daughter—Sir Owen Asher."

In the little while which he took to decide whether he would take tea or coffee, he thought that something could be said for her figure, and he liked her hair, but, on the whole, he did not think he cared for her. She seemed to him an unimportant variety of what he had met before. He said he would take tea, and then he changed his mind and said he would have coffee, but Evelyn came back with a cup of tea, and perceiving her mistake, she laughed abstractedly.

"You are going to sing two songs, Miss Innes. I'm glad; I hear your voice is wonderful."

The sound of his voice conveyed a penetrating sense of his presence. It was the same happiness which the very sight of him had awakened in her, and she felt herself yielding to it as to a current. She was borne far away into mists of dream, where she seemed to live a long while. Time seemed to have ceased and the outside world to have fallen behind her. The sensation was the most delicious she had ever experienced. She hardly heard the answers that she made to his questions, and when her father called her, it was like returning after a long absence.

She sang much more beautifully than he had expected, and during the preludes and fugues and the sonatas by Bach, which finished the programme, he thought of her voice, occasionally questioning himself regarding his taste for her. Even in this short while he had come to like her better. She had beautiful teeth and hair, and he liked her figure, notwithstanding the fact that her shoulders sloped a little—perhaps because they did slope a little. He noticed, whether her eyes wandered or remained fixed, that they returned to him, and that their glance was one of interrogation, as if all depended upon him. When the concert was over he was anxious to speak to her, so that he grew impatient with the people who stopped his way. The back room was filled with musical instruments—there were two harpsichords, a clavichord and an organ, and Mr. Innes insisted on explaining these instruments to him. He seemed to Owen to pay too slight a heed to his daughter's voice. That she played the viola da gamba very well was true enough, but what sense was there in a girl like that playing an instrument? Her voice was her instrument.

When he was able to get a few words with her, he told her about Madame Savelli. There was no one else, he said, who could teach singing. She must go to France at once, and he seemed to take it for granted that she might start at the end of the week, if she only made up her mind. She did not know what answer to make, and was painfully conscious how silly she must look standing before him unable to say a word. It was no longer the same; some of the dream had been swept aside, and reality had begun to look through it. Her intense consciousness of this tall, aristocratic man frightened her. She saw the embroidered waistcoat, the slight hips, the gold moustache, and the sparkling grey eyes asked her questions to which her whole nature violently responded, and, though her feelings were inexplicable to herself, she was overcome with physical shame. Father Railston was looking at her, and the thought crossed her mind that he would not approve of Sir Owen Asher. Feeling very uncomfortable, she seized an opportunity of saying good-bye to a friend, and escaped from Sir Owen, leaving him, as she knew, under the impression that she was a little fool not worth taking further trouble about. But his ideas were different from all that she had been taught, and it would be better if she never saw him again. She did not doubt, however, that she would see him again, and when, two days after, the servant announced him and he walked into the music room, she was less surprised than her father.

The review, he said, could not go to press without an article on the concert, but to do this article he must consult Mr. Innes, for in the first piece, "La my," the viols had seemed to him out of tune. Of course this was not so—perhaps one of the players had played a wrong note; that might be the explanation. But on referring to the music, Mr. Innes discovered a better one. "From the twelfth to the fifteenth century, writers," he said, "did not consider their music as moderns do. Now we watch the effect of a chord, a combination of notes heard at the same moment, the top note of which is the tune, but the older writers used their skill in divining musical phrases which could be followed simultaneously, each one going logically its own way, irrespective of some temporary clashing. They considered their music horizontally, as the parts went on; we consider it vertically, each chord producing its impression in turn. To them all the parts were of equal importance. Their music was a purely decorative interweaving of melodies. Now we have a tune with accompanying parts."

"What a wonderful knowledge of music your father has, Miss Innes!"

"Yes, father reads old MSS. that no one else can decipher."

"These discords happened," Mr. Innes said, as he went to the harpsichord, "when a composition was based upon some old plain song melody, the notes of which could not be altered. Then the musician did not scruple to write in one of the other parts the same note altered by a sharp or flat to suit the passing requirement of the musical phrase allotted to that part. You could thus have together, say an F natural in one part and an F sharp in another. This to modern ears, not trained to understanding the meaning of the two parts, is intolerable."

While he spoke of the relative fineness of the ancient and modern ear, maintaining that the reason ancient singers could sing without an accompaniment was that they were trained to sing from the monochord, Owen considered the figure of this tall, fair girl, and wondered if she would elect to remain with her father, playing the viola da gamba in Dulwich, or bolt with a manager—that was what generally happened. Her father was a most interesting old man, a genius in his way, but just such an one as might prove his daughter's ruin. He would keep her singing the old music, perhaps marry her to a clerk, and she would be a fat, prosaic mother of three in five years.

However this might be, he, Owen, was interested in her voice, and, if he had never met Georgina, he might have liked this girl. It would be better that he should take her away than that she should go away with a manager who would rob and beat her. But, if he were to take her away, he would be tied to her; it would be like marrying her. Far better stick to married women, and he remembered his epigram of last night. It was at Lady. Ascott's dinner-party, the conversation had turned on marriage, and its necessity had been questioned. "But, of course, marriage is necessary," he had answered. "You can't have husbands without marriage, and if there were no husbands, who would look after our mistresses?" A lot of hypocrites had chosen to look shocked; Georgina had said it was a horrid remark and had hardly spoken to him all the evening; and this afternoon she had said she should not come and see him any more—she was afraid her husband suspected, her children were growing up, etc. When women cease to care for one, how importunate their consciences are! A little terror took him, and he wondered if he were about to lose Georgina, or if she were only trying to make him jealous. Perhaps he could not do better than make her jealous. For that purpose this young girl was just the thing.

Moreover, he was interested in the revival of Palestrina at St. Joseph's, and he liked Ferrabosco's pavane. He would like to have a harpsichord; even if he did not play on it much, it would be a beautiful, characteristic piece of furniture.... And it would be a good idea to ask Mr. Innes to bring all his queer instruments to Berkeley Square, and give a concert to-morrow night after his dinner-party. His friends had bored him with Hungarian bands, and the improvisations the bands had been improvising for the last ten years, and he saw no reason why he should not bore them, just for a change, with Mr. Innes.

At this moment his reflections were interrupted by Mr. Innes, who wanted to know if he did not agree with him regarding the necessity for the re-introduction of the monochord, if the sixteenth century masses were ever to be sung again properly. All this was old story to Evelyn. In a sort of dream, through a sort of mist, she saw the embroidered waistcoat and the gold moustache, and when the small, grey, smiling eyes were raised from her father's face and looked at her, a delicious sensation penetrated through the very tissues of her flesh, and she experienced the tremor of a decisive moment; and then there came again a gentle sense of delicious bewilderment and illusion.

She did not know how it would all happen, but her life seemed for the first time to have come to a definite issue. The very moment he had spoken of Madame Savelli, the great singing mistress, it was as if a light had begun in her brain, and she saw a faint horizon line; she seemed to see Paris from afar; she knew she would go there to study, and that night she had fallen asleep listening to the applause of three thousand hands.

But she did not like to stand before him, offering him first the cup of tea, then the milk and sugar, then the cake, and bread and butter. Her repugnance had nothing to do with him; it was an obscure feeling, quite incomprehensible to herself. When he looked up she answered him with a smile which she felt to be mysterious, and he perceived its mystery, for he compared it to the hesitating smile of the Monna Lisa, a print of which hung on the wall. But the remark increased her foreboding and premonition. And she was sorry for her father, who was saying that he hoped to send her abroad in the spring; that he would have done so before, but she was studying harmony with him. And she could see that Owen was bored. He was only staying on in the hope of speaking to her, but she knew that her father was not going out, so there was no chance of their having a few words together. His invitation to Mr. Innes to bring the instruments to London, and give a concert to-morrow night at Berkeley Square, he had reserved till the moment he had got up to go. Mr. Innes was taken aback. He doubted if there would be time to get the instruments to London. But Owen said that all that was necessary was a Pickford van, and that if he would say "Yes," the van and a competent staff of packers would be at Dulwich in the morning, and would take all further trouble off his hands. The question was debated. Mr. Innes thought the instruments had better go by train, and Owen could not help smiling when he said that he would arrive with the big harpsichord and Evelyn about nine or half-past.

She had two evening gowns—a pale green silk and a white. The pale green looked very nice; it had cost her three pounds. The white had nearly ruined her, but it had seemed to suit her so well that she had not been able to resist, and had paid five pounds ten, a great deal for her to spend on a dress. Its great fault was that it soiled at the least touch. She had worn it three times, and could not wear it again till it had been cleaned. It was a pity, but there was no help for it. She would have to wear the green, and to console herself she thought of the compliments she had had for it at different parties. But these seemed insignificant when she thought of the party she was going to to-night.

She had never been to Berkeley Square, and expected to be surprised. But it lay in a hollow, a dignified, secluded square, exactly as she had imagined it. Nor did the great doorway, and the carpet that stretched across the pavement for her to walk upon, surprise her, nor the lines of footmen, nor the natural grace of the wide staircase. She seemed to have seen it all before, only she could not remember where. It came back to her like a dream. She seemed to recognise the pictures of the goddesses, the Holy Families and the gold mirrors; and lifting her eyes, she saw Owen at the head of the stairs, and he smiled so familiarly, that it seemed strange to think that this was only the third time she had seen him.

He introduced her father to a fashionable musician, whose pavanes and sonatas were composed with that lack of matter and excess of erudition which delight the amateur and irritate the artist, and he walked down the rooms looking for seats where they could talk undisturbed for a few minutes. He was nervous lest Georgina should find him sitting with this girl in an intimate corner, but he did not expect her for another half-hour, and could not resist the temptation. He was curious to know how far Evelyn acquiesced in the obscure lot which her father imposed upon her, to play the viola da gamba, and sing old music, instead of singing for her own fame upon the stage. But had she a great voice? If she had, he would like to help her. The discovery of a new prima donna would be a fine feather in his cap. Above all, he was also curious to find out if she were the innocent maiden she appeared to be, or if she had had flirtations with the clerks in the neighbourhood, and he found his opportunity to speak to her on this subject in the first line of a French song she was going to sing:—

"Que vous me coûtez cher, mon coeur, pour vos plaisirs."

His appreciation of her changed every moment. Truly her eyes lit up with a beautiful light, and her remarks about the length of our payment for our pleasures revealed an apprehension which he had not credited her with. But he was alarmed at the quickness with which they had strayed to the very verge of things: From the other room they would seem very intimate, sitting on a sofa together, and he was expecting Georgina every minute. If she were to see them, it would lead to further discussion, and supply her with an excuse. But his curiosity was kindled, and while he considered how he could lead Evelyn into confidences, he saw her arm trembling through the gauze sleeve, for it seemed to her that all that was happening now had happened before. The walls covered with red pleated silk, the bracket-clocks, the brocade-covered chairs: where had she seen them? And Owen's grey eyes fixed upon her: where had she seen them? In a dream perhaps. She asked him if he had ever experienced the sensation of having already lived through a scene that was happening at the very moment. He did not seem to hear; he seemed expecting someone; and then the vision returned to her again, and she could not but think that she had known Sir Owen long ago, but how and where she could not tell. At that moment she noticed his absent-mindedness, and it was suddenly flashed upon her that he was in love with some woman and was waiting for her, and almost at the same moment she saw a tall, red-haired woman cross the further room. The woman paused in the doorway, as if looking for someone. She nodded to Owen and engaged in conversation with a group of men standing by the fireplace. Something told Evelyn that that smooth, cream-coloured neck was the woman Owen was in love with, and the sudden formality of his manner convinced her that she was right, that that was the woman he was in love with. He said that he must go and see after his other guests, and, as she expected, he went straight to the woman with the red hair. But she did not leave her friends. After shaking hands with Owen, she continued talking to them, and he was left out of the conversation.

The concert began with a sonata for the harpsichord and the viola da gamba, and then Evelyn sang her two songs. She sang for Owen, and it seemed to her that she was telling him that she was sorry that it had all happened as it had happened, and that he must go away and be happy with the woman he loved. She did not think that she sang particularly well, but Owen came and told her that she had sung charmingly, and in their eyes were strange questions and excuses, and an avowal of regret that things were not different. Slim women in delicious gowns glided up and praised her, but she did not think that they had been as much impressed by her singing as they said; distinguished men were introduced to her, and she felt she had nothing to say to them; and looking round the circle of men and women she saw Owen in the doorway, and noticed that his eyes were restless and constantly wandered in the direction of the tall woman with the red hair, who sat calmly talking to her friends, never noticing him. He seemed waiting for a look that never came; his glances were furtive and quickly withdrawn, as if he feared he was being watched. When she got up to leave, Owen came forward and spoke to her, but she barely replied, and left the room alone. Evelyn saw all this, and she was surprised when Owen came rapidly through the room and sat down by her. He was painfully absent-minded, and so nervous that he did not seem to know what he was saying: indeed, that was the only excuse she could make for his remarks. She hardly recognised this man as the man she had hitherto known. She hated all his sentiments and his ideas; she thought them horrid, and was glad when her father came to tell her it was time for her to go.

"You didn't sing well," he said, as they went home. "What was the matter with you?"

Owen and the red-haired lady seemed to fall behind this last misfortune. If she had lost her voice she was no longer herself, and as she went to her teaching she saw herself a music mistress to the end of her days.

But on Sunday morning she came down stairs singing, and Mr. Innes heard a future prima donna in her voice. Her face lit up, and she said, "Do you think so, dear. It was unlucky I sang so badly the other night. I seemed to have no voice at all."

He told her that there were times when her mother suddenly lost her voice.

"But, father, you are not fit to go out, and can't go out in that state."

"What is the matter?" and his hand went to his shirt collar.

"No, your necktie is all right. Ah! there you've untied it; I'll tie it for you. It's your coat that wants brushing."

The black frock coat which he wore on Sundays was too small for him. If he buttoned it, it wrinkled round the waist and across the chest; if he left it open, its meagre width and the shortness of the skirts (they were the fashion of more than ten years ago) made it seem ridiculous. At the elbows the cloth was shiny with long wear, and the cuffs were frayed. His hat was as antiquated as his coat. It was a mere pulp, greasy inside and brown outside; the brim was too small, it was too low in the crown, and after the severest brushing it remained rough like a blanket. Evelyn handed it back to him in despair. He thanked his daughter, put it on his head, and forgot its appearance. But in spite of shabby coat and shabbier hat, Mr. Innes remained free from suspicion of vulgarity—the sad dignity of his grey face and the dreams that haunted his eyes saved him from that.

"And whose mass are you going to play to-day?" she asked him.
"A mass by Hummel, in B; on Thursday, a mass by Dr. Gladstone; and next Sunday, Mozart's Twelfth, beloved of Father Gordon and village choirs. I wonder if he will allow the Reproaches to be sung in Holy Week? He will insist on the expense of the double choir."
"But, father, do you think that the congregation of St. Joseph's is one that would care for the refinement of Palestrina? Would you not require a cultivated West-end audience—the Oratory or Farm Street?"
"That is Sir Owen's opinion."
"I never heard him say so."
How had she come to repeat anything she had heard him say? Moreover, why had she said that she had not heard him say so? And Evelyn argued with herself until the train reached their station—it was one of those absurd little mental complications, the infinitesimal life that flourishes deep in the soul.
A little way down a side street, a few yards from the main thoroughfare, where the roads branched, the great gaunt façade of St. Joseph's pointed against a yellow sky. Its foundations had been laid and its walls built by a priest, who had collected large sums of money in America, and whose desire had been to have the largest church that could be built for the least money, in the shortest possible time. The result was the great, sprawling, grey stone building with a desolate spire, now fading into the darkness of the snow-storm. Money had run short. The church had not been completed when its founder died; then another energetic priest had raised another subscription. Doors and stained glass had been added, and, for a while, St. Joseph's had become a flourishing parish church, supported by various suburbs, and projects for the completion of its interior decoration had begun to be entertained; but while these projects were under consideration, the suburbs had acquired churches of their own, and the congregation of St. Joseph's had dwindled until it had lost all means of support, except the meagre assistance it received from the poor Irish and Italians of the neighbourhood. There had been talk of closing the church, and it would have had to be closed if the Jesuits had not accepted the mission. Another subscription had been started, but the greater part of this third subscription the Jesuits had spent upon their schools, so the fate of St. Joseph's seemed to be to remain, as someone had said, an unfinished ruin. Their resources were exhausted, and they surveyed the barren aisles, dreaming of the painting and mosaics they would put up when the promises of Father Gordon were realised. For it was understood that their fortunes should be retrieved by his musical abilities, and his competence to select the most attractive masses. Father Gordon was a type often found among amateur musicians—a man with a slight technical knowledge, a good ear, a nice voice, and absolutely no taste whatever. His natural ear was for obvious rhythm, his taste coincided with the popular taste, and as the necessity of attracting a congregation was paramount, it is easy to imagine how easily he conceded to his natural inclinations. And the arguments with which he rebutted those of his opponents were unanswerable, that whatever moved the heart to the love of God was right; that if the plain chant failed to help the soul to aspiration, we were justified in substituting Rossini's *Stabat Mater*, or whatever other musical idiom the neighbourhood craved for.
Religious rite, according to Father Gordon, should conform to the artistic taste of the congregation, and he urged, with some force, that the artistic taste of Southwark stood on quite as high a level as that of Mayfair. To get a Mayfair audience they had only to follow the taste of Southwark. And so, under his guidance, the Jesuits had increased their orchestra and employed the best tenors that could be hired. Nevertheless, their progress was slow. Father Gordon pleaded patience. The neighbourhood was unfashionable; it was difficult to persuade their friends to come so far. Mr. Innes answered that if they gave him a choir of forty-five voices—he could do nothing with less—the West-end would come at once to hear Palestrina. The distance, and the fact of the church being in a slum, he maintained, would not be in itself a drawback. Half the success of Bayreuth, he urged, is owing to its being so far off. And this

plan, too, seemed to possess some elements of success, and so the Jesuits hesitated between very divergent methods by which the same result might be attained.

A few flakes of snow were falling, and Evelyn and her father put up their umbrellas as they crossed the road to the church. Three steps led to the pointed door above which was the figure of the patron saint.

The nakedness of the unfinished and undecorated church was hidden in the twilight of the approaching storm, and Evelyn trembled as she walked up the aisle, so menacing seemed the darkness that descended from the sky. The stained glass, blackened by the smoke of the factory chimneys, let in but little light, the aisles were plunged in darkness, and kneeling in her favourite place the ineffectual gaslight seemed to her like painted flames on a dark background. The side chapels which opened on to the aisles were shut off by no ornamental screens, indeed, the only piece of decoration seemed to be the fine modern ironwork which veiled the sanctuary.

She opened her prayer book, but in the shadow of the pillar where she was kneeling there was not sufficient light for her to read, so she bent her face upon her hands, intent upon losing herself in prayer. She abased herself before her Father in Heaven; attaining once more the wonderful human moment when the creature who crouches on this rim of earth implores pardon for her trespass from the beneficent Creator of things. But to-day her devotional mood was interrupted by sudden thought and sensation of Owen's presence; she was forced to look up, and convinced that he was very near her, she sought him amid the crowd of people who sat and knelt in front of her, blackening the dusk, a vague darkness in which she could at first distinguish nothing but an occasional white plume and a bald head. But her eyes grew accustomed to the darkness, and above the uninteresting backs of middle-aged men she recognised his thin sharp shoulders. She had been compelled to look up from her prayers, and she wondered if he had been thinking of her. If so, it was very wrong of him to interrupt her at her prayers. But a sensation of pleasure arose spontaneously in her. At that moment he had to remove his hat from the chair on which he had placed it, and she noticed the gold stud links in his large shirt cuffs, the rough material of which the coat was made, and how well it lay along the thin arm. She imagined the look of vexation on the grave interesting face, and laughed a little to herself. What was the poor woman to do? She had a right to her chair. But she did look so frightened, and was visibly perturbed by the presence of so fine a gentleman. Evelyn knew the woman by sight—a curious thin and crooked creature, who wore a strange bonnet and a little black mantle, and walked up the church, her hands crossed like a doll....

No doubt he had driven all the way from Berkeley Square. She could see him leaning back in his brougham, humming various music, or plaintively thinking about the lady with the red hair, who did not care for him. Her breath caught her in the throat. That was the reason why he had come to St. Joseph's. It was all over with the red-haired lady, and it was for her that he had come to St. Joseph's! But that could not be.... She saw him moving in rich and elegant society, where everyone had a title, and the narrowness of her life compared with his dismayed her. It was impossible that he could care for her. She was remaining in Dulwich, with nothing but a few music lessons to look forward to.... But when she reached the operatic stage her life would be like his, and the vision of her future passed before her eyes—diamonds in stars, baskets of wonderful flowers, applause, and the perfume of a love story, swinging like a censer over it all.

At that moment the priests entered; mass began. She opened her prayer book, but, however firmly she fixed her thoughts in prayer, they sprang back, without her knowing it, to Owen and the red-haired woman, with the smooth, cream-coloured shoulders. Without being aware of it, she was looking at him, and it was such a delight to think of him that she could not refrain. His chair was the last on the third line from the altar rail, and she noticed that he wore patent leather shoes; the hitching of the dark grey trousers displayed a silk sock; but he suddenly uncrossed his legs, and assumed a less negligent attitude. In a sudden little melancholy she remembered how he had watched the woman with the red hair, and the determined indifference of this woman's face as she left the room. Immediately after she was amused at the way in which his face expressed his opinion of the music, and she had to admit to herself that he listened as if he understood it.

It was not until her father began to play the offertory, one of Schubert's beautiful inspirations, that she noticed the look of real delight that held the florid profile till the last note, and for some seconds after. "He certainly does love music," she thought; and when the bell rang for the Elevation, she bowed her head and became aware of the Real Presence. When it rang a second time she felt life stifle in her. When it rang a third time she again became conscious of time and place. But the sensation of awe which the accomplishment of the mystery had inspired was dissipated in the tumult of a very hideous Agnus Dei, in the voice of a certain concert singer, who seemed determined to shout down the organ. Evelyn had some difficulty in keeping her countenance, so plain was the expression of amazement upon the profile in front of her.

Then the book was carried from the right to the left side of the altar, and when the priest had read the Gospel, she began once more to ask herself the reason that had brought Sir Owen to St. Joseph's. The manner in which he genuflected before the altar told her that he was a Catholic; perhaps he had come to St. Joseph's merely to hear mass.

"I have come to see your father."

"You will find him in the organ loft.... But he'll be down presently."

And at the end of the church, in a corner out of the way of the crowd, they waited for Mr. Innes, and she learnt almost at once, from his face and the remarks that he addressed to her, that it was not for her that he had come to St. Joseph's. His carriage was waiting, he told the coachman to follow; all three tramped through the snow together to the station. In this miserable walk she learnt that he had decided to go for a trip round the world in his yacht, and expected to be away for nearly a year. As he bade them good-bye he looked at her, and his eyes seemed to say he was sorry that it was so, that he wished it were otherwise. She felt that if she had been able to ask him to stay he would have stayed; but, of course, that was impossible, and the last she saw of him was as he turned, just before getting into his brougham, to tell her father that the best critic of the *Review* should attend the concerts, and that he hoped that what he would write would bring some people of taste to hear them.

CHAPTER THREE

The name was no indication. None remembered that Dowlands was the name of Henry the Eight's favourite lute player, and there was nothing in the snug masonry to suggest an æstheticism of any kind. The dulcimers, lutes and virginals surprised the visitor coming in from the street, and he stayed his steps as he might on the threshold of a fairy land.

The villas, of which Dowlands was one, were a builder's experiment. They had been built in the hopes of attracting wealthy business West-end shopkeepers; but Dulwich had failed to become a fashionable suburb. Many had remained empty, and when Mr. Innes had entered into negotiations with the house agents, they declared themselves willing to entertain all his proposals, and finally he had acquired a lease at a greatly reduced rental.

In accordance with his and Mrs. Innes's wishes, the house had been considerably altered. Partition walls had been taken away, and practically the whole ground floor converted into class-rooms, leaving free only one little room at the back where they had their meals. During his wife's lifetime the house suited their requirements. The train service from Victoria was frequent, and on the back of their notepaper was printed a little map, whereby pupils coming and going from the station could find their way. On the second floor was Mr. Innes's workshop, where he restored the old instruments or made new ones after the old models.

There was Evelyn's bedroom—her mother had re-furnished it before she died—and she often sat there; it was, in truth, the most habitable room in the house. There was Evelyn's old nursery, now an unoccupied room; and there were two other empty rooms. She had tried to convert one into a little oratory. She had placed there a statue of the Virgin, and hung a crucifix on the wall, and bought a *prie-Dieu* and put it there. But the room was too lonely, and she found she could say her prayers more fervently by her bedside. Their one servant slept downstairs in a room behind the kitchen. So the house often had the appearance of a deserted house; and Evelyn, when she returned from London, where she went almost daily to give music lessons, often paused on the threshold, afraid to enter till her ear detected some slight sound of her servant at work. Then she cried, "Is that you, Margaret?" and she advanced cautiously, till Margaret answered, "Yes, miss."

The last summer and autumn had been the pleasantest in her life since her mother's death. Her pupils interested her—she had some six or seven. Her flow of bright talk, her eager manner, her beautiful playing of the viola da gamba, her singing of certain old songs, her mother's fame, and the hopes she entertained of one day achieving success on the stage made her a heroine among her little circle of friends. Her father was a remarkable man, but he seemed to her the most wonderful of men. It was exciting to go to London with him, to bid him good-bye at Victoria—she to her lessons, he to his—to meet him in the evenings, and in conjunction to arrange the programme of their next concert. These interests and ambitions had sufficed to fill her life, and to keep the greater ambition out of sight; and since her mother's death she had lived happily with her father, helping him in his work. But lately things had changed. Some of her pupils had gone abroad, others had married, and interest in the concerts declined. For a little while the old music had seemed as if it were going to attract sufficient attention, but already their friends had heard enough, and Mr. Innes had been compelled to postpone the next, which had been announced for the beginning of February. There would be no concert now till March, perhaps not even then; so there was nothing for her to look forward to, and the wet windy weather which swept the suburb contributed to her disheartenment. The only event of the day seemed to be her father's departure in the morning. Immediately after breakfast he tied up his music in a brown paper parcel and put his violin into its case; he spoke of missing his train, and, from the windows of the music-room, she saw him hastening down the road. She had asked him if there were any MSS. he wished copied in the British Museum; absent-mindedly he had answered "No;" and, drumming on the glass with her fingers, she wondered how the day would pass. There was nothing to do; there was nothing even to think about. She was tired of thinking that a pupil might come back—that a new pupil might at any moment knock at the door. She was tired of wondering if her father's concerts would ever pay—if the firm of music publishers with whom he was now in treaty would come to terms and enable him to give a concert in their hall, or if they would break off negotiations, as many had done before. And, more than of everything else, she was tired of thinking if her father would ever have money to send her abroad, or if she would remain in Dulwich always.

One morning, as she was returning from Dulwich, where she had gone to pay the weekly bills, she discovered that she was no longer happy. She stopped, and, with an empty heart, saw the low-lying fields with poultry pens, and the hobbled horse grazing by the broken hedge. The old village was her prison, and she longed as a bird longs. She had trundled her hoop there; she ought to love it, but she didn't, and, looking on its too familiar aspect, her aching heart asked if it would never pass from her. It seemed to her that she had not strength nor will to return home. A little further on she met the vicar. He bowed, and she wondered how he could have thought that she could care for him. Oh, to live in that Rectory with him! She pitied the young man who wore brown clothes, and whose employment in a bank prevented him from going abroad for his health. These people were well enough, but they were not for her. She seemed to see beyond London, beyond the seas, whither she could not say, and she could not quell the yearning which rose to her lips like a wave, and over them.

Formerly, when there was choir practice at St. Joseph's, she used to go there and meet her father, but lately, for some reason which she could not explain to herself, she had refrained. The thought of this church had become distasteful to her, and she returned home indifferent to everything, to music and religion alike. Her eyes turned from the pile of volumes—part of Bach's interminable works—and all the old furniture, and she stood at the window and watched the rain dripping into the patch of black garden in front of the house, surrounded by a low stone wall. The villas opposite suggested a desolation which found a parallel in her heart; the sloppy road and the pale brown sky frightened her, so menacing seemed their monotony. She knew all this suburb; it was all graven on her mind, and all that ornamental park where she must go, if it cleared a little, for her afternoon walk. She must tramp round that park once more. She strove to keep out of her mind its symmetrical walls, its stone basins, where the swans floated like white china ornaments, almost as lifeless. But worse even than these afternoons were the hours between six and eight. For very often her father was detained, and if he missed the half-past six train he had to come by the half-past seven, and in those hours of waiting the dusk grew oppressive and fearful in the music-room. Startled by a strange shadow, she crouched in her armchair, and when the feeling of dread passed she was weak from want of food. Why did her father keep her waiting? Hungry, faint and weary of life, she opened a volume of Bach; but there was no pleasure for her in the music, and if she opened a volume of songs she had neither strength nor will to persevere even through the first, and, rising from the instrument, she walked across the room, stretching her arms in a feverish despair. She had not eaten for many hours, and out of the vacuity of the stomach a dimness rose into her eyes. Pressing her eyes with her hand, she leaned against the door.

One evening she walked into the garden. The silence and damp of the earth revived her, and the sensation of the cold stone, against which she was leaning, was agreeable. Little stars speckled a mauve and misty sky, and out of the mysterious spring twilight there came a strange and ultimate yearning, a craving which nothing she had ever known could assuage. But those stars—could they tell her nothing? One, large almost as the moon itself, flamed up in the sky, and a voice within her whispered that that was her star, that it held the secret of her destiny. She gazed till her father called to her from the gate; and all that evening she could think of nothing else. The conviction flowed within her that the secret of her destiny was there; and as she lay in bed the star seemed to take a visible shape.

A face rose out of the gulf beneath her. She could not distinguish whether it was the face of man or woman; it was an idea rather than a face. The ears were turned to her for her to take the earrings, the throat was deeply curved, the lips were large and rose-red, the eyes were nearly closed, and the hair was curled close over a straight, low forehead. The face rose up to hers. She looked into the subtle eyes, and the thrill of the lips, just touching hers, awakened a sense of sin, and her eyes when they opened were frightened and weary. And as she sat up in her bed, trembling, striving vainly to separate the real from the unreal, she saw the star still shining. She hid her face in the pillow, and was only calmed by the thought that it was watching her.

She went into the garden every evening to see it rise, and a desire of worship grew up in her heart; and thinking of the daffodils, it occurred to her to lay these flowers on the wall as an offering. Even wilder thoughts passed through her brain; she could not keep them back, and more than once asked herself if she were giving way to an idolatrous intention. If so, she would have to tell the foolish story to her confessor. But she could hardly bring herself to tell him such nonsense.... If she didn't, the omission might make her confession a false one; and she was so much perplexed that it seemed to her as if the devil took the opportunity to insinuate that she might put off going to confession. This decided her. She resolved to combat the Evil One. To-day was Thursday. She would confess on Saturday, and go to Communion on Sunday.

Till quite lately her confessor had been Father Knight—a tall, spare, thin-lipped, aristocratic ecclesiastic, in whom Evelyn had expected to find a romantic personality. She had looked forward to thrilling confessions, but had been disappointed. The romance his appearance suggested was not borne out; he seemed unable to take that special interest in her which she desired; her confessions were barren of spiritual adventure, and after some hesitations her choice dropped upon Father Railston. In this selection the law of contrast played an important part. The men were very opposites. One walked erect and tall, with measured gait; the other walked according to the impulse of the moment, wearing his biretta either on one side of the head or the other. One was reserved; the other voluble in speech. One was of handsome and regular features; the other's face was plain but expressive. Evelyn had grown interested in Father Railston's dark, melancholy eyes; and his voice was a human voice vibrant with the terror and suffering of life. In listening to her sins he seemed to remember his own. She had accused herself of impatience at the circumstances which kept her at home, of even nourishing, she would not say projects, but thoughts, of escape.

"Then, my child, are you so anxious to change your present life for that of the stage?"

"Yes, Father."

"You weary of the simplicity of your present life, and sigh for the brilliancy of the stage?"

"I'm afraid I do." It was thrilling to admit so much, especially as the life of an actress was not in itself sinful. "I feel that I should die very soon if I were to hear I should never leave Dulwich."

The priest did not speak for a long while, and raising her eyes she watched his expression. It seemed to her that her confession of her desire of the world had recalled memories, and she wondered what were they.

"I am more than forty—I'm nearly fifty—and my life has passed like a dream."

He seemed about to tell her the secret of life, and had stopped. But the phrase lingered through her whole life, and eventually became part of it. "My life has passed like a dream." She did not remember what he had said after, and she had gone away wondering if life seemed to everyone like a dream when they were forty, and if his life would have seemed more real to him if he had given it to the world instead of to God? Her subsequent confessions seemed trite and commonplace. Not that Father Railston failed to listen with kind interest to her; not that he failed to divine that she was passing through a physical and spiritual crisis. His admonitions were comforting in her weariness of mind and body; but notwithstanding her affection for him, she felt that beyond that one phrase he had no influence over her. She almost felt that he was too gentle and indulgent, and the thought she would have liked a confessor who was severe, who would have inflicted heavier penances, compelled her to fast and pray, who would have listened in deeper sternness to the sins of thought which she with averted face shamefully owned to having entertained. She was disappointed that he did not warn her with the loss of her soul, that he did not invent specious expedients for her use, whereby the Evil One might be successfully checked.

One Sunday morning the servant told Mr. Innes that Miss Evelyn has left a little earlier, as she was going to Communion. She remained in church for High Mass, and when chided for such long abstinence, she smiled sadly and said that she did not think that it would do her much harm. During the following week he noticed that she hardly touched breakfast, and the only reason she gave was that she thought she would like to fast. No, she had not obtained leave from her confessor; she had not even consulted him. She, of course, knew that she was not obliged to fast, not being of age; but she was not doing any work; she had no pupils; the concert had been postponed; she thought she would like to fast. Father and daughter looked at each other; they felt that they did not understand, that there was nothing to be done, and Mr. Innes put his fiddle into its case and went to London, deeply concerned about his daughter, and utterly unable to arrive at any conclusion.

She fasted, and she broke through her fast, and as Lent drew to a close she asked her father if she might make a week's retreat in a convent at Wimbledon where she had some friends. There was no need for her at home; it would be at least change of air and she pressed him to allow her to go. He feared the influence the convent might have upon her, and admitted that his selfishness was largely accountable for this religious reaction. No doubt she wanted change, she was looking very poorly. He spoke of the sea, but who was to take her to Brighton or Margate? The convent seemed the only solution of the difficulty, and he had to consent to her departure.

The retreat was to last four days, but Evelyn begged that she might stay on till Easter Tuesday. This would give her a clear week away from home, and the improvement that this little change wrought in her was surprising. The convent had made her cheeks fair as roses, and given her back all her sunny happiness and abundant conversation. She delighted in telling her father of her week's experience. For four days she had not spoken (perhaps that was the reason she was talking so much now), and during these four days they were nearly always in chapel; but somehow it hadn't seemed long, the services were so beautiful. The nuns wore grey serge robes and head-dresses, the novices white head-dresses; what had struck her most was the expression of happy content on their faces.

"I wish, father, you had seen them come into church—their long robes and beautiful white faces. I don't think there is anything as beautiful as a nun."

The mother prioress was a small woman, with an eager manner. She looked so unimportant that Evelyn had wondered why she had been chosen, but the moment she spoke you came under the spell of her keen, grey eyes and clear voice.... Mother Philippa, the mistress of the novices, was quite different—stout and middle-aged, and she wore spectacles. She was beautiful notwithstanding; her goodness was like a soft light upon her face. ...Evelyn paused. She could not find words to describe her; at last she said—

"When she comes into the room, I always feel happy."

She could not say which she liked the better, but branched off into a description of the Carmelite who had given the retreat—strong, eagle-faced man, with thin hair drawn back from his forehead, and intense eyes. He wore sandals, and his white frock was tied with a leather belt, and every word he spoke had entered into her heart. He gave the meditations, which were held in the darkened library. They could not see each other's faces; they could only see the white figure at the end of the room.

She had had her meals in the parlour with two other ladies who had come to the convent for the retreat. They were both elderly women, and Evelyn fancied that they belonged to the grandest society. She could tell that by their voices. The one she liked best had quite white hair, and her expression was almost that of a nun. She was tall, very stout, and walked with a stick. On Easter Sunday this old lady had asked her if she would care to come into the garden with her. It was such a beautiful morning, she said, that it would do both of them good. The old lady walked very slowly with her stick. But though Evelyn thought that she must be at least a countess, she did not think she was very rich—she had probably lost her money. The black dress she wore was thin and almost threadbare, and it was a little too long for her; she held it up in her left hand as she walked—a most beautiful hand for an old woman. Both these ladies had been very kind to her; she had often walked with them in the garden—a fine old garden. There were tall, shady trees; these were sprinkled with the first tiny leaves; and the currant and raspberry bushes were all out. And there was a fishpond swarming with gold fish, and they were so tame that they took bread from the novices' hands.

The conversation had begun about the convent, and after speaking of its good sisters, the old lady, whose hair was quite white, had asked Evelyn about herself. Had she ever thought of being a nun? Evelyn had answered that she had not. She had never considered the question whether she had a vocation.... She had been brought up to believe that she was going on the stage to sing grand opera.

"It is hardly for me to advise you. But I know how dangerous the life of an opera singer is. I shall pray God that He may watch over you. Promise me always to remember our holy religion. It is the only thing we have that is worth having; all the rest passes."

"Father, we were close by the edge of the fishpond, and all the greedy fish swarmed to the surface, thinking we had come to feed them. She said, 'I cannot walk further without resting;

come, my dear, let me sit down on that bench, and do you sing me a little song, very low, so that no one shall hear you but I.' I sang her "John, come kiss me now," and she said, "My dear, you have a beautiful voice, I pray that you make good use of it."

But not in one day could all Evelyn's convent experiences be related, and it was not until the end of the week that Evelyn told how Mother Philippa, at the end of a long talk in which she had spoken to Evelyn about the impulses which had led her to embrace a religious life (she had been twenty years in this convent), had taken her upstairs to the infirmary to see Sister Bonaventure, an American girl, only twenty-one, who was dying of consumption. She lay on a couch in grey robes, her hands and face waxen white, and a smile of happy resignation on her lips and in her eyes.

"But," exclaimed Evelyn, "they told me she would die within the fortnight, so she may be dead now; if not to-day, to-morrow or after. I hadn't thought of that.... I shall never forget her, every few minutes she coughed—that horrible cough! I thought she was going to die before my eyes, but in the intervals she chattered and even laughed, and no word of complaint escaped her. She was only twenty-one ... had known nothing of life; all was unknown to her, except God, and she was going to Heaven. She seemed quite happy, yet to me it seemed the saddest sight in the world.... She'll be buried in a few days in the sunniest corner of the garden, away from the house—that is their graveyard. The mother Prioress, the founder of the convent, is buried there; a little dedicatory chapel has been built, and on the green turf, tall wooden crosses mark the graves of six nuns; next week there'll be one more cross."

The conversation paused, and Evelyn sat looking into the corner of the room, her large clear eyes wide open and fixed. Presently she said—

"Father," I've often thought I should like to be a nun."

"You a nun! And with that voice!"

She looked at him, smiling a little.

"What matter?"

"What matter! Have you not thought—but I understand; you mean that your voice is wasted here, that we shall never have the means to go abroad.... But we shall."

"Father, dear, I wasn't thinking of that. I do believe that means will be found to send me abroad to study. But what then? Shall I be happy?"

"Fame, fortune, art!"

"Those nuns have none of those things, and they are happy. As that old lady said their happiness comes from within."

"And you'll be happy with those things, as happy as they are without them. You're in a melancholy mood; come, we'll think of the work before us. I've decided that we give our concert the week after next. That will give us ten clear days."

He entered into the reasons which had induced him to give this concert. But Evelyn had heard all about the firm of musical publishers, who possibly might ask him to bring up the old instruments to London, and give a concert in a fashionable West-end hall. Seeing that she was not listening, he broke off his narrative with the remark that he had received a letter that morning from Sir Owen.

"Is he coming home? I thought he was going round the world and would not be back for a year."

"He has changed his mind. This letter was posted at Malta—a most interesting letter it is;" and while Mr. Innes read Sir Owen's account of the discovery of the musical text of an ancient hymn which had been unearthed in his presence, Evelyn wondered if he had come home for her or—the thought entered her heart with a pang—if he had come home for the red-haired woman. Mr. Innes stopped suddenly in his reading, and asked her of what she was thinking.

"Nothing, father."

"You don't seem to take any interest. The text is incomplete, and some notes have been conjecturally added by a French musician." But much more interesting to Evelyn was his account of the storm that had overtaken his yacht on the coast of Asia Minor. He had had to take his turn at the helm, all the sailors being engaged at the sails, and, with the waves breaking over him, he had kept her head to the wind for more than two hours.

"I can hardly fancy him braving the elements, can you, Evelyn?"

"I don't know, father," she said, startled by the question, for at that moment she had seen him in imagination as clearly as if he were present. She had seen him leaning against the door-post, a half-cynical, half-kindly smile floating through his gold moustache. "Do you think he will like the music you are going to give at the next concert? He is coming, I suppose?"

"It is just possible he may arrive in time; but I should hardly think so. I've written to invite him; he'll like the music; it is the most interesting programme we've had—an unpublished sonata by Bach—one of the most interesting, too. If that is not good enough for him—by the way, have you looked through that sonata?"

"No, father, but I will do so this afternoon."

And while practising the sonata, Evelyn felt as if life had begun again. The third movement of the sonata was an exquisite piece of musical colour, and, if she played it properly, he could not fail to come and congratulate her.... But he would not be here in time for the concert ... not unless he came straight through, and he would not do that after having nearly escaped shipwreck. She was sure he would not arrive in time, but the possibility that he might gave her additional interest in the sonata, and every day, all through the week, she discovered more and more surprising beauties in it.

CHAPTER FOUR

She was alone in the music-room reading a piece of music, and her back was to the door when he entered. She hardly recognised him, tired and tossed as he was by long journeying, and his grey travelling suit was like a disguise.

"Is that you, Sir Owen?... You've come back?"

"Come back, yes, I have come back. I travelled straight through from Marseilles, a pretty stiff journey.... We were nearly shipwrecked off Marseilles."

"I thought it was off the coast of Asia Minor?"

"That was another storm. We have had rough weather lately."

The music dropped from her hand, and she stood looking at him, for he stood before her like an ancient seafarer. His grey tweed suit buttoned tightly about him set off every line of his spare figure. His light brown hair was tossed all over his head, and she could not reconcile this rough traveller with the elegant fribble whom she had hitherto known as Sir Owen. But she liked him in this grey suit, dusty after long travel. He was picturesque and remote as a legend. A smile was on his lips; it showed through the frizzled moustache, and his eyes sparkled with pleasure at sight of her.

"But why did you travel straight through? You might have slept at Marseilles or Paris."

"One of these days I will tell you about the gale. I wonder I am not at the bottom of that treacherous sea; it did blow my poor old yacht about—I thought it was her last cruise; and when we got to the hotel I was handed your father's letter. As I did not want to miss the concert, I came straight through."

"You must be very fond of music."

"Yes, I am.... Music can be heard anywhere, but your voice can only be heard at Dulwich."

"Was it to hear me sing that you came back?"

She had spoken unawares, and felt that the question was a foolish one, and was trembling lest he should be inwardly laughing at her. But the earnest expression into which his little grey eyes concentrated reassured her. She seemed to lose herself a little, to drift into a sort of dream in which even he seemed to recede, and so intense and personal was her sensation that she could not follow his tale of adventure. It was an effort to listen to it at that moment, and she said—

"But you must be tired, you've not had a proper night's sleep ... for a week."

"I'm not very tired, I slept in the train, but I'm hungry. I've not had anything since ten o'clock this morning. There was no time to get anything at Victoria. I was told that the next train for Dulwich started in five minutes. I left my valet to take my trunks home; he will bring my evening clothes on here for the concert. Can you let me have a room to dress in?"

"Of course; but you must have something to eat."

"I thought of going round to the inn and having a chop."

"We had a beefsteak pudding for dinner; I wonder if you could eat beefsteak pudding?"

"There's nothing better."

"Warmed up?"

"Yes, warmed up."

"Then I may run and tell Margaret?"

"I shall be much obliged if you will."

She liked to wait upon him, and her pleasure quickened when she handed him bread or poured out ale, making it foam in the glass, for refreshment after his long journey; and when she sat opposite, her eyes fixed on him, and he told her his tale of adventure, her happy flushed face reminded him of that exquisite promise, the pink almond blossom showing through the wintry wood.

"So you didn't believe me when I said that it was to hear you sing that I came back?"

"That you renounced your trip round the world?"

"Yes, I renounced my trip round the world to hear you sing."

She did not answer, and he put the question again.

"I can understand that there might be sufficient reason for your giving up your trip round the world. I thought that perhaps—no, I cannot say—"

They had been thinking of each other, and had taken up their interest in each other at their last thoughts rather than at their last words. She was more conscious of the reason of their sudden intimacy than he was, but he too felt that they had advanced a long way in their knowledge of each other, and their intuition was so much in advance of facts that they sat looking at each other embarrassed, their words unable to keep pace with their perceptions.

Evelyn suddenly felt as if she were being borne forward, but at that moment her father entered.

"Father, Sir Owen was famishing when he arrived. He wanted to go to the inn and eat a chop, but I persuaded him to stop and have some beefsteak pudding."

"I am so glad ... you've arrived just in time, Sir Owen. The concert is to-night."

"He came straight through without stopping; he has not been home. So, father, you will never be able to say again that your concerts are not appreciated."

"Well, I don't think that you will be disappointed, Sir Owen. This is one of the most interesting programmes we have had. You remember Ferrabosco's pavane which you liked so much—"

Margaret announced the arrival of Sir Owen's valet, and while Mr. Innes begged of Sir Owen not to put himself to the trouble of dressing, Owen wondered at his own folly in yielding to a sudden caprice to see the girl. However, he did not regret; she was a prettier girl than he had thought, and her welcome was the pleasantest thing that had happened to him for many a day.

"My poor valet, I am afraid, is quite *hors de combat*. He was dreadfully ill while we were beating up against that gale, and the long train journey has about finished him. At Victoria he looked more dead than alive."

Evelyn went out to see this pale victim of sea sickness and expedition. She offered him dinner and then tea, but he said he had had all he could eat at the refreshment bars, and struggled upstairs with the portmanteau of his too exigent master.

A few of her guests had already arrived, and Evelyn was talking to Father Railston when Sir Owen came into the room.

"I shall not want you again to-night," he said, turning towards the door to speak to his valet. "Don't sit up for me, and don't call me to-morrow before ten."

She had not yet had time to speak to Owen of a dream which she had dreamed a few nights before, and in which she was much interested. She had seen him borne on the top of a huge wave, clinging to a piece of wreckage, alone in the solitary circle of the sea. But Owen, when he came downstairs dressed for the concert, looked no longer like a seafarer. He wore an embroidered waistcoat, his necktie was tied in a butterfly bow, and the three pearl studs, which she remembered, fastened the perfectly-fitting shirt. She was a little disappointed, and thought that she liked him better in the rough grey suit, with his hair tossed, just come out of his travelling cap. Now it was brushed about his ears, and it glistened as if from some application of brilliantine or other toilet essence. Now he was more prosaic, but he had been extraordinarily romantic when he ran in to see her, his grey travelling cap just snatched from his head. It was then she should have told him her dream. All this was a very faint impression, half humorous, half regretful, it passed, almost without her being aware of it, in the background of her mind. But she was keenly disappointed that he was not impressed by her dream, and was inclined to consider it in the light of a mere coincidence. In the first place, he hadn't been shipwrecked, and that she should dream of shipwreck was most natural since she knew that he had gone a-seafaring, and any gust of wind in the street was enough to excite the idea of a castaway in the unclosed cellular tissues of her brain. She did not answer, and he stood trying to force an answer from her, but she could not, nor did she wish to think that her dream was no more than a merely physiological phenomenon. But just at that moment Mr. Innes was waiting to speak to Sir Owen.

He had a great deal to say on the subject of the disgraceful neglect of the present Royal Family in not publishing the works of their single artistic ancestor, Henry VIII. Up to the present time none of his numerous writings, except one anthem played in the Chapel at Windsor, was known; the pieces that were going to be played that evening lay in MS. in the British Museum, and had probably not been heard for two, maybe three hundred years. Encouraged by Sir Owen's sympathy, he referred again, in his speech to his audience, to the indifference of the present Royal Family to art, and he added that it was strange that he should be doing at Dowlands what the Queen or the Prince of Wales should have done long ago, namely, the publication of their ancestor's work with all the prestige that their editorship or their patronage could give it.

"I must go," she said; "they are waiting for me."

She took her place among the viol players and began playing; but she had forgotten to tune her instrument, and her father stopped the performance. She looked at him, a little frightened, and laughed at her mistake. The piece they were playing was by Henry VIII., a masterpiece, Mr. Innes had declared it to be, so, to stop the performance on account of Evelyn's viola da gamba, and then to hear her play worse than he had ever heard her play before, was very disappointing.

"What is the matter? Aren't you well? I never heard you play so badly."

He hoped that she would play better in the next piece, and he besought her with a look before he signed to the players to begin. She resolved not to think of Owen, and she played so well that the next piece was applauded. Except for her father's sake she cared very little how she played; she tried to play well to please him, but she was anxious to sing well—she was singing for herself and for Owen, which was the same thing—and she sang beautifully in the King's madrigal and the two songs accompanied by the lute—"I loathe what I did love," and "My lytell pretty one," both anonymous, composed in 1520, and discovered by Mr. Innes in the British Museum. The musical interest of these two songs was slight, and Owen reflected that all Mr. Innes's discoveries at the British Museum were not of equal importance. But she had sung divinely, and he thought how he should praise her at the end of the concert.

Evelyn hoped he would tell her that she had sung better than she had sung on the fatal night of the party in Berkeley Square. This was what she wished him to say, and she wished it partly because she knew that that was what he would say. That party had not yet been spoken of, but she felt sure it would be, for it seemed a decisive point in their lives.

She was not playing in the next two pieces—fantasies for treble and tenor viols—and she sat in the background, catching glimpses of Owen between the hands and the heads of the viol players, and over the rims of their, instruments. She sat apart, not hearing a note of the music, absorbed in herself, a little exaltation afloat in her brain, her flesh glowing as in the warmth of an inward fire, her whole instinct telling her that Owen had not come back for the red-haired woman; he had gone away for her, perhaps, but he had not come back for her—of that she was sure In spite of herself, the conviction was forced upon her that the future was for her. The red-haired lady was a past which he would tell her some day, and that day she knew to be not very far distant.

The programme was divided into two parts, and after the first, there was a little interval during which tea and cake were handed round. Evelyn helped to hand them round, and when she held the cake tray to Owen, she raised her eyes and they looked at each other, and in that interval it almost seemed as if they kissed each other.

They met again at the end of the concert, and she waited anxiously for him to speak. He told her, as she expected he would, that she had sung to-night much better than she had sung at his party. But they were surrounded by people seeking their coats and umbrellas; it was impossible to speak without being overheard; he had told her that she had sung to his satisfaction; that was sufficient, and they felt that all had been said, and that they understood each other perfectly.

As she lay in bed, the thought came that he might write to her a letter asking her to meet him, to keep an appointment. But she would have to refuse, it would be wrong; but it was not wrong to think about it. He would be there before her; the moment he saw her coming his eyes would light up in a smile, and they would walk on together some little way without speaking. Then he would say, "Dearest, there will be a carriage waiting at the corner of the road"—and then? She could see his face and his tall, thin figure, she could picture it all so distinctly that it was almost the same as if it were happening. All he said, as well as all she said, kept pouring in upon her brain without a missing word, and she hugged herself in the delight of these imaginings, and the hours went by without weariness for her. She lay, her arms folded, thinking, thinking, seeing him through the darkness.

He came to see them the following day. Her father was there all the time, but to hear and see him was almost enough for her. She seemed to lose sight of everything and to be engulfed in her own joy. When he had gone away she remembered the smile which had lit up some pretty thought of her; her ears were full of his voice, and she heard the lilt that charmed her whenever she pleased. Then she asked herself the meaning of some casual remark, and her mind repeated all he had said like a phonograph. She already knew his habitual turns of speech; they had begun to appear in her own conversation, and all that was not connected with him lost interest for her. Once or twice during the week she went to bed early so that she might not fancy her father was looking at her while she thought of Owen.

Owen called at the end of the week—the *Wagnerian Review* always supplied him with sufficient excuse for a visit—but he had to spend his visit in discussing the text of a Greek hymn which he had seen disinterred in Greece. She was sorry for him, sorrier than she was for herself, for she could always find him in her thoughts.... She wondered if he could find her as vividly in his thoughts as she settled herself (the next day was Sunday) in the corner of her pew, resolved from the beginning not to hear a word of the sermon, but to think of Owen the whole time. She wanted to hear why he had left England so suddenly, and why he had returned so suddenly. She was sure that she and the red-haired lady were the cause of one or the other, and that neither was the cause of both. These two facts served for a warp upon which she could weave endless mental embroideries, tales as real as the tales of old tapestry, tales of love and jealousy, and unexpected meetings, in which she and Owen and the red-haired lady met and re-met. Whilst Father Railston was preaching, these tales flowed on and on, subtle as silk, illusive as evening tinted clouds; and it was not until she had exhausted her fancy, and Owen had made one more fruitless visit to Dulwich, that she began to scheme how she might see him alone. There was so much that they could only talk about if they were alone; and then she wanted so much to hear the story of the red-haired lady. If she did not contrive an opportunity for being with him alone, she might never hear why he had left England for a trip round the world, and had returned suddenly from the Mediterranean. She felt that, however difficult and however wrong it might be, she must find this opportunity. She thought of asking him the hour of the train by which he generally came to Dulwich, so that she might meet him in the station. Other schemes came into her mind, but she could think of nothing that was just right.

But one day, as she was running to post a letter, she saw Owen, more beautifully dressed than ever, coming toward her. Her feet and her heart stood still, for she wore her old morning gown and a pair of old house slippers. But he had already seen her and was lifting his hat, and with easy effrontery he told her that he had come to Dulwich to consult her father about the Greek hymn.

"But father is at St. Joseph's," she said, and then she stopped; and then, before she saw his smile, she knew why he had come to Dulwich so early.

The shadows of the leaves on the pavement drew pretty pattern for their feet, and they strolled meditatively through the subdued sunlight.

"Why did you stop and look so startled when you saw me?"

"Because I am so badly dressed; my old house slippers and this—"

"You look very well—dress matters nothing."

"No one would gather your opinions from your appearance."

Owen laughed, and admired the girl's wit.

"Do you want to see father very much about the Greek hymn?"

"Well," he said, and he looked at her questioningly, and not liking to tell her in so many words that he had come to Dulwich to see her, he entered into the question of the text of the hymn, which was imperfect. Many notes were missing, and had been conjecturally added by a French musician, and he had wished to consult Mr. Innes about them. So a good deal of time was wasted in conversation in which neither was interested. Before they were aware, they were at Dowlands, and with an accent of regret in her voice, which Owen noticed with pleasure, she held out her hand and said good-bye.

"Are you very busy, then, are you expecting a pupil?"

"No, I have nothing to do."

"Then why should we say good-bye? It is hardly worth while getting up so early in the morning to discuss the text of an ancient Greek hymn."

His frankness was unexpected, and it pleased her.

"No, I don't suppose it is; Greek music at eleven o'clock in the morning would be a little trying."

A delicious sense of humour lit up in her eyes, and he felt his interest in her advance a further stage.

"If you have nothing to do we might go to the picture gallery. There is a wonderful Watteau—"

"Watteau at eleven, Greek hymn at one."

But she felt, all the same, that she would give everything to go to the picture gallery with him.

"But I am not dressed, this is an old thing I wear in the morning; not that there would be many people there, only the curator and a girl copying at eleven in the morning."

"But is your father coming back at one?"

"Why do you ask?"

"Because you said Greek hymn at one. The time will pass quickly between eleven and one. You need not change your dress."

Then, with an expressive little glance which went straight to his heart, she noted his fastidious dress, the mauve necktie, the perfectly fitting morning coat buttoned across the chest, the yellow-brown trousers, and the long laced boots, half of patent and half of tan coloured leather.

"I could not walk about with you in this dress and hat, but I sha'n't keep you long."

While he waited he congratulated himself on the moment when he had determined to abandon his tour round the world, and come back to seek Evelyn Innes at Dulwich.

"She is much nicer, a hundred times more exciting than I thought. Poetry, sympathy, it is like living in a dream." He asked himself if he liked her better than Georgina, and answered himself that he did; but deep down in his heart he knew that the other woman had given him deeper and more poignant emotions, and he knit his brows, for he hated Georgina.

Owen was the first temptation in Evelyn's life, and it carried her forward with the force of a swirling river. She tried to think, but thoughts failed her, and she hooked her black cloth skirt and thrust her arms into her black cloth jacket with puffed sleeves. She opened her wardrobe, and wondered which hat he would like, chose one, and hastened downstairs.

"You've not been long ... you look very nice. Yes, that is an improvement."

His notice of her occasioned in her a little flutter of joy, a little exaltation of the senses, and she walked on without speaking, deep in her pleasure, and as the sensation died she became aware that she was very happy. The quiet silence of the Spring morning corresponded to her mood, and the rustle of last year's leaves communicated a delicious emotion which seemed to sing in the currents of her blood, and a little madness danced in her brain at the ordinary sight of nature. "This way," she said, and they turned into a lane which almost looked like country. There were hedges and fields; and the sunlight dozed amid the cows, and over the branches of the high elm the Spring was already shaking a soft green dust. There were nests in the bare boughs—whether last year's or this year's was not certain. Further on there was a stile, and she thought that she would like to lean upon it and look straight through the dim fields, gathering the meaning which they seemed to express. She wondered if Owen felt as she did, if he shared her admiration of the sunlight which fell about the stile through the woven branches, making round white spots on the roadway.

"So you were surprised to hear that I had given up my trip round the world?"

"I was surprised to hear you had given it up so that you might hear me sing."

"You think a man incapable of giving up anything for a woman?"

He was trembling, and his voice was confused; experience did not alter him; on the verge of an avowal he was nervous as a schoolboy. He watched to see if she were moved, but she did not seem to be; he waited for her to contest the point he had raised, but her reply, which was quite different, took him aback.

"You say you came back to hear me sing. Was it not for another woman that you went away?"

"Yes, but how did you know?"

"The woman with the red hair who was at your party?"

The tale of a past love affair often served Owen as a plank of transition to another. He told her the tale. It seemed to him extraordinary because it had happened to him, and it seemed to Evelyn very extraordinary because it was her first experience of the ways of love.

"Then it was she who got tired of you? Why did she get tired of you?"

"Why anything? Why did she fall in love with me?"

"Is it, then, the same thing?"

He judged it necessary to dissemble, and he advanced the theory which he always made use of on these occasions—that women were more capricious than men, that so far as his experience counted for anything, he had invariably been thrown over. The object of this theory was two-fold. It impressed his listener with an idea of his fidelity, which was essential if she were a woman. It also suggested that he had inspired a large number of caprices, thereby

he gratified his vanity and inspired hope in the lady that as a lover he would prove equal to her desire. It also helped to establish the moral atmosphere in which an intrigue might develop.
"Did you love her very much?"
"Yes, I was crazy about her. If I hadn't been, should I have rushed off in my old yacht for a tour round the world?"
He felt the light of romance fall upon him, and this, he thought, was how he ought to appear to her.
Yet he was sincere. He admired Evelyn, he thought he might like to be her lover, and he regarded their present talk as a necessary subterfuge, the habitual comedy in which we live. So, when Evelyn asked him if he still loved Georgina, he answered that he hated her, which was only partly true; and when she asked him if he would go back to her if she were to invite him, he said that nothing in the world would induce him to do so, which was wholly untrue, though he would not admit it to himself. He knew that if Georgina were to hold up her little finger he would leave Evelyn without a second thought, however foolish he might know such conduct to be.
"Why did you not marry her when she was in love with you?"
"You can love a woman very well indeed without wanting to marry her; besides, she is married. But are you sure we're going right?...Is this the way to the picture gallery?"
"Oh, the picture gallery, I had forgotten. We have passed it a long while."
They turned and went back, and, in the silence, Owen considered if he had not been too abrupt. His dealings with women had always been conducted with the same honour that characterised his dealings on the turf, but he need not have informed her so early in their acquaintanceship of his vow of celibacy. While he thought how he might retrieve his slight indiscretion, she struggled in a little crisis of soul. Owen's words, tone of voice, manner were explicit; she could not doubt that he hoped to induce her to leave her father, and she felt that she ought not to see him any more. She must see him, she must go out to walk with him, and her will fluttered like a feather in space. She remembered with a gasp that he was the only thing between herself and Dulwich, and at the same moment he decided that he could not do better than to suggest to her that her father was sacrificing her to his ambitions.
"I wonder," he said, assuming a meditative air, "what will become of you? Eventually, I mean."
"What do you think?" Her eagerness told him that he had struck the right note.
"You have grown up in an atmosphere of great music, far removed from the tendencies of our day. You have received from your father an extraordinary musical education. He has prepared you on all points but one for your career, he has not developed your voice; his ambition intervened—"
"You must not say that. Father does not allow his ambition to interfere with his duties regarding me. You only think that because you do not know him; you don't know all the difficulties he has to contend with."
Owen smiled inwardly, pleased at the perception he had shown in divining her feelings, and he congratulated himself on having sown some slight seed of discontent; and then, as if he were withdrawing, or at least attenuating, the suggestion he had thrown out, he said—
"Anyone can see that you and your father are very attached to each other."
"Can they?"
"You always like to be near him, and your favourite attitude is with your hand on his shoulder."
"So many people have noticed that. Yes, I am very fond of father. We were always very fond of each other, but now we are more like pals than father and daughter."
He encouraged her to talk of herself, to tell him the story of her childhood, and how she and her father formed this great friendship. Evelyn's story of her mother's death would have interested him if he had been able to bestow sufficient attention upon it, but the intricacy of

the intrigue he was entering upon engrossed his thoughts. There were her love of her father, her duty towards him, and her piety to be overcome. Against these three considerable influences there were her personal ambition and her love of him. A very evenly matched game, he thought, and for nothing in the world would he have missed this love adventure.
At that moment the words, "A few days later she died," caught on his ear. So he called all the sorrow and reverence he could into his eyes, sighed, and raised his eyebrows expressing such philosophic resignation in our mortal lot as might suffice to excuse a change in the conversation.
"That is the picture gallery," Evelyn said, pointing to a low brick building, almost hidden at the back of a well-kept garden. The unobtrusive doorway was covered with a massive creeper, just beginning to emerge from it's winter's rust. "Do you care to go in?" she said negligently. "You know the pictures so well, I am afraid they will bore you."
"No, I should like to see them with you."
He could see that her æsthetic taste had been absorbed by music, and that pictures meant nothing to her, but they meant a great deal to him, and, unable to resist the temptation, he said—"Let us go in for a little while, though it does seem a pity to waste this beautiful Spring day."
There was an official who took her parasol and his cane, and they were impressed by the fact of having to write their names side by side in the book—Sir Owen Asher, Evelyn Innes.
On pushing through the swing-door, they found themselves in a small room hung with the Dutch school. There were other rooms, some four or five, opening one into the other, and lighted so that the light fell sideways on to the pictures. Owen praised the architecture. It was, he said, the most perfectly-constructed little gallery he had ever seen, and he ought to know, for he had seen every gallery in Europe. But he had not been here for many years and had quite forgotten it. "A veritable radiation of masterpieces," he said, stepping aside to see one. But the girl was the greater attraction, and only half satisfied he returned to her, and when the attraction of the pictures grew irresistible he tried to engage her attention in their beauties, so that he might be allowed to enjoy them. To his surprise and pleasure the remarks he had hazarded provoked an extraordinary interest in her, and she begged of him to tell her more about the paintings. He was not without suspicion that the pictures were a secondary interest; but as it was clear that to hear him talk excited her admiration, he favoured her with all he knew regarding the Dutch school. She followed attentive as a peahen, he spreading a gorgeous tail of accumulated information. He asked if the dark background in Cuyp's picture, "The White Horse and the Riding School," was not admirable? And that old woman peeling onions in her little kitchen, painted by a modern would be realistic and vulgar; but the Dutchman knew that by light and shade the meanest subject could be made as romantic as a fairy tale. As dreamers and thinkers they did not compare with the Italians, but as painters they were equal to any. They were the first to introduce the trivialities of daily life into Art—the toil of the field, the gross pleasures of the tavern. "Look at these boors drinking; they are by Ostade. Are they not admirably drawn and painted? "Brick-making in a Landscape, by Teniers the younger." Won't you look at this? How beautiful! How interesting is its grey sky! Here are a set of pictures by Wouvermans—pictures of hawking. Here is a Brouwer, a very rare Dutch master, a very fine example too. And here is a Gerard Dow. Miss Innes, will you look at this composition? Is it not admirable? That rich curtain hung across the room, how beautifully painted, how sonorous in colour."
"Ah! she's playing a virginal!" said Evelyn, suddenly. "She is like me, playing and thinking of other things. You can see she is not thinking of the music. She is thinking ... she is thinking of the world outside."
This pleased him, and he said, "Yes, I suppose it is like your life; it is full of the same romance and mystery."
"What romance, what mystery? Tell me."

They sat down on the bench in the third room, opposite the colonnade by Watteau, to which his thoughts frequently went, while telling her how, when cruising among the Greek Islands, he had often seen her, sometimes sitting in the music-room playing the virginal, sometimes walking in the ornamental park under a wet, grey sky, a somewhat desolate figure hurrying through shadows of storm.
"How strange you should think all that. It is quite true. I often walked in that hateful park."
"You will never be able to stand another winter in Dulwich."
She raised her eyes, and he noticed with an inward glee their little frightened look.
"I thought of you in that ornamental park watching London from the crest of the hill; and I thought of London—great, unconscious London—waiting to be awakened with the chime of your voice."
She turned her head aside, overcome by his praise, and he exulted, seeing the soft rose tint mount into the whiteness of her face.
"You must not say such things to me. How you do know how to praise!"
"You don't realise how wonderful you are."
"You should not say such things, for if they are not true, I shall be so miserable."
"Of course they are true," he said, hushing his voice; and in his exultation there was a savour of cruelty. "You don't realise how wonderful your story is. As I sailed through the Greek Isles, I thought less and less of that horrid, red-haired woman; your face, dim at first, grew clearer and clearer.... All my thoughts, all things converged to you and were absorbed in you, until, one day on the deck, I felt that you were unhappy; the knowledge came, how and whence I know not; I only know that the impulse to return was irresistible. I called to the skipper, and told him to put her head about."
"Then you did think of me whilst you were away?"
Evelyn looked at him with her soft, female eyes, and meeting his keen, bright, male eyes, she drew away from him with a little dread. Immediately after, this sensation of dread gave way to a delicious joy; an irresponsible joy deep down in her heart, a joy so intimate that she was thankful to know that none could know it but herself.
Her woman's instinct told her that many women had loved him. She suspected that the little lilt in his voice, and the glance that accompanied it, were the relics of an old love affair. She hoped it was not a survival of Georgina.
"It must be nearly one o'clock. It is time for you to come to talk to father about the Greek hymn."
"Let's look at this picture first—'The Fête beneath the Colonnade'—it is one of the most beautiful things in the world."

CHAPTER FIVE

Sipping her coffee, her feet on the fender, she abandoned herself to memories of the afternoon. She had been to the Carmelite Church in Kensington, to hear the music of a new and very realistic Belgian composer; and, walking down the High Street after Mass, she and Owen had argued his artistic intentions. At the end of the High Street, he had proposed that they should walk in the Gardens. The broad walk was full of the colour of Spring and its perfume, the thick grass was like a carpet beneath their feet; they had lingered by a pond, and she had watched the little yachts, carrying each a portent of her own success or failure. The Albert Hall curved over the tops of the trees, and sheep strayed through the deep May grass in Arcadian peacefulness; but the most vivid impression was when they had come upon a lawn stretching gently to the water's edge. Owen had feared the day was too cold for sitting out, but at that moment the sun contradicted him with a broad, warm gleam. He had fetched two chairs from a pile stacked under a tree, and sitting on that lawn, swept by the shadow of softly moving trees, they had talked an hour or more. The scene came back to her as she sat looking into the fire. She saw the Spring, easily victorious amid the low bushes, capturing the rough branches of the elms one by one, and the distant slopes of the park, grey like a piece of faded tapestry. And as in a tapestry, the ducks came through the mist in long, pulsing flight, and when the day cleared the pea fowl were seen across the water, sunning themselves on the high branches. While watching the spectacle of the Spring, Owen had talked to Evelyn about herself, and now their entire conversation floated back, transposed into a higher key.

"I want your life to be a great success."

"Do you think anyone's life can be that?"

"That is a long discussion; if we seek the bottom of things, none is less futile than another. But what passes for success, wealth and renown, are easily within your reach.... If it be too much trouble to raise your hand, let me shake the branches, and they'll fall into your lap."

"I wonder if they would seem as precious to me when I had got them as they do now. Once I did not know what it was to despond, but I lost my pupils last winter, and everything seemed hopeless. I am not vain or egotistic; I do not pine for applause and wealth, but I should like to sing.... I've heard so much about my voice that I'm curious to know what people will think of it."

"Once I was afraid that you were without ambition, and were content to live unknown, a little suburban legend, a suburban might-have-been."

"That was long ago.... I've been thinking about myself a great deal lately. Something seems always crying within me, 'You're wasting your life; you must become a great singer and shine like a star in the world.'"

"That is the voice of vocation speaking within you, a voice that may not be disobeyed. It is what the swallows feel when the time for departure has come."

"Ah, yes, what the swallows feel."

"A yearning for that which one has never known, for distant places, for the sunshine which instinct tells us we must breathe."

"Oh, yes, that is it. I used to feel all that in the afternoons in that ornamental park. I used to stop in my walk, for I seemed to see far away, to perceive dimly as in a dream, another country."

"And since I came back have you wished to go away?"

"No ... for you come to see me, and when I go out with you I'm amused."

"I'm afraid I do little to amuse you."

"You do a great deal—you lend me books. I never cared to read, now I'm very fond of reading—and I think more."

"Of what do you think?"

"You see, I never met anyone like you before. You've travelled; you've seen everything; you know everything and everyone. When you come I seem to see in you all the grand world of fashion."

"Which you used to see far away as in a dream?"

"No, the world of fashion I did not think of till I saw you. Since you came back I have thought of it a little. You seem to express it somehow in your look and dress; and the men who nodded to you in Piccadilly, and the women who bowed to you, all wore the same look, and when they spoke they seemed to know all about you—where you were last summer, and where you are going to spend this autumn. Their friends are your friends; you're all like one family."

"You're very observant. I never noticed the things you speak of, but no doubt it is so. But society is ready to receive you; society, believe me, is most anxious for you."

After some pause she heard him say—

"But you must not delay to go abroad and study."

"Tell me, do you think the concerts will ever pay?"

"No, not in the sense of your requirements. Evelyn, since you ask me, I must speak the truth. Those concerts may come to pay their expenses, with a little over, but it is the veriest delusion to imagine that they will bring enough money to take you and your father abroad. Moreover, your father would have to resign his position at St. Joseph's, where he is required; there his mission is. It is painful for me to tell you these things, but I cannot see you waste your life."
"What you say is quite true.... I've known it all along."
"Only you have shut your eyes to it."
"Yes, that's it."
"Don't look so frightened, Evelyn. It was better that you should be brought face to face with the truth. You'll have to go abroad and study."
"And my father! Don't advise me to leave him. I couldn't do that."
"Why make my task more difficult than it is? I wish to be honest. I should speak just the same, believe me, if your father were present. Is not our first duty towards ourselves? The rest is vague and uncertain, the development of our own faculties is, after all, that which is most sure.... I'm uttering no paradox when I say that we serve others best by considering our own interests. Let us suppose that you sacrifice yourself, that you dedicate your life to your father, that you do all that conventional morality says you should do. You look after his house, you sing at his concerts, you give music lessons. Ten, fifteen years pass, and then, remembering what might have been, but what is no longer possible, you forgive him, and he, overcome with remorse for the wrong he did you, sinks into the grave broken-hearted."
"I should at least have the satisfaction of knowing that I had done my duty."
"Words, Evelyn, words. Take your life into your keeping, go abroad and study, come back a great success."
"He would never forgive me."
"You do not think so.... Evelyn, you do not believe that."
"But even if I wished to leave home, I could not. Where should I get the money? You have not thought what it would cost."
"Have you forgotten the knight that came to release the sleeping beauty of the woods from her bondage? Fifteen hundred or two thousand pounds would be ample. I can easily afford it."
"But I cannot afford to accept it. Father would not allow me."
"You can pay it all back."
"Yes, I could do that. But why don't you offer to help father instead?"
"Why are you what you are? Why am I interested in you?"
"If I went abroad to study, I should not see you again for a long while—two years."
"I could go to Paris."
She did not remember what answer she had made, if she had made any answer, but as she leaned forward and stirred the fire, she saw his hands, their strength and comeliness, the kindliness of his eyes. She was not sure that he was fond of, but she thought that she could make him like her. At that moment he seemed to take her in his arms and kiss her, and the illusion was so vivid that she was taken in an instant's swoon, and shuddered through her entire flesh. When her thoughts returned she found herself thinking of a volume of verses which had come to be mentioned as they walked through the Gardens. He had told her of the author, a Persian poet who had lived in a rose-garden a thousand years ago. He had compared life to a rose, an exquisite flower to be caught in the hand and enjoyed for a passionate moment, and had recited many of the verses, and she had listened, enchanted by the rapid interchange of sorrow, and gladness, and lofty resignation before the inevitable. Often it seemed as if her own soul were speaking in the verses. "So do not refuse to accept the flowers and fruit that hang in reach of your hands, for to-morrow you may be where there are none.... The caravan will have reached the nothing it set out from.... Surely the potter will not toss to hell the pots he marred in the making." She started from her reverie, and suddenly grew aware of his very words, "However we may strive to catch a glimpse of to-morrow, we

must fall back on to-day as the only solid ground we have to stand on, though it be slipping momentarily from under our feet." She recalled the intonation of his sigh as he spoke of the inscrutable nature of things, and she wondered if he, too, with all his friends and possessions, was unhappy. She seemed to have exhausted her thoughts about him, and in the silence of her mind, her self came up for consideration.... Owen intended to ask her to go away with him; but he did not intend to marry her. It was shocking to think that he could be so wicked, and then with a thrill of pleasure that it would be much more exciting to run away with him than to be married to him by Father Railston. But how very wicked of her to think such things, and she was frightened to find that she could not think differently; and with sensations of an elopement clattering in her brain, she sat still striving to restrain her thoughts.

CHAPTER SIX

On leaving her at Victoria, he had walked down the Buckingham Palace Road, not quite knowing where he was going. Suddenly an idea struck him. He put up his stick, stopped a hansom, and drove to Georgina; for he was curious to see what impression she would make upon him. He spent an hour with her, and returned to Berkeley Square to dine alone. He was sure that he cared no more for Georgina, that she was less than nothing to him. He dismissed her from his thoughts, and fixed them on Evelyn. He had said he would send her a book. It stood next to his hand, on the shelf by the round table where he wrote his articles. After dinner, he would walk from the dining-room into the library, take down the volume and pack it up, leaving orders that it should be sent off by the first post.

When man ceased to capture women, he reflected, man invented art whereby he might win them. The first melody blown through a reed pipe was surely intended for woman's ears. The first verses were composed in a like intention. Afterwards man began to take an interest in art for its own sake.... Women, having no necessity for art, have not been artists. The idea amused him, and he remembered that while Evelyn's romantic eyes and gold hair were sufficient to win his regard, he had availed himself of a dozen devices to tempt her. Suddenly his face grew grave, and he asked himself how this flirtation was to end. As a sufficient excuse for seeing her he was taking music lessons; he wrote to her every other day and often sent her books and music. They had met in London.... He had been observed walking with her, and at Lady Ascott's lunch the conversation had suddenly turned on a tall girl with gold hair and an undulating walk. Pointed observations had been made.... Lady Lovedale had looked none too well pleased. He didn't wish to be cynical, but he did want to know whether he was going to fall in love?... They had now arrived at that point when love-making or an interruption in their intimacy was imperative. He did not regret having offered her the money to go abroad to study, it was well he should have done so, but he should not have said, "But *I'll* go to see you in Paris." She was a clever girl, and knew as well as he how such adventures must end.... She was a religious girl, a devout Catholic, and as he had himself been brought up in that religion, he knew how it restrained the sexual passion or fashioned it in the mould of its dogma. But we are animals first, we are religious animals afterwards. Religious defences must yield before the pressure of the more original instinct, unless, indeed, hers was a merely sexual conscience. The lowest forms of Anglicanism are reduced to perceiving conscience nowhere except in sex. The Catholic was more concerned with matters of faith. Not in France, Italy or Spain did Catholicism enter so largely into the private life of the individual as it did in England. The foreign, or to be more exact, the native Catholic had worn the yoke till it fitted loose on his shoulders. His was a more eclectic Christianity; he took what suited him and left the rest. But in England Romanism had never shaken itself free from the Anglican conscience. The convert never acquired the humanities of Rome, and in addition the lover had to contend against the confessional. But in Evelyn's case he could set against the confessional the delirium of success, the joy of art, the passion of emulation, jealousy and ambition, and last, but far from least, the ache of her own passionate body. Remembering the fear and humility with which he had been used to approach the priest, and the terror of eternal fire in which he had waited for him to pronounce absolution, Owen paused to think how far such belief was from him now. Yet he had once believed—in a way. He wondered at the survival of such a belief in the nineteenth century, and asked himself if confession were not inveterate in man. The artist in his studio, the writer in his study, strive to tell their soul's secret; the peasant throws himself at the feet of the priest, for, like them, he would unburden himself of that terrible weight of inwardness which is man. Is not the most mendacious mistress often taken with the desire of confession ... the wish to reveal herself? Upon this bed rock of human nature the confessional has been built. And Owen admired the humanity of Rome. Rome was terribly human. No Church, he reflected, was so human. Her doctrine may seem at times quaint, medieval, even gross, but when tested by the only test that can be applied, power to reach to human needs, and administer consolation to the greatest number, the most obtuse-minded cannot fail to see that Rome easily distances her rivals. Her dogma and ceremonial are alike conceived in extraordinary sympathy with man's common nature.... Our lives are enveloped in mystery, the scientist concedes that, and the woof of which the stuff of life is woven is shot through with many a thread of unknown origin, untraceable to any earthly shuttle. There is a mystery, and in the elucidation of that mystery man never tires; the Sovereign Pontiff and the humblest crystal gazer are engaged in the same adventure. The mystery is so intense, and lives so intimately in all, that Rome dared to come forward with a complete explanation. And her necessarily perfunctory explanation she drapes in a ritual so magnificent, that even the philosopher ceases to question, and pauses abashed by the grandeur of the symbolism. High Mass in its own home, under the arches of a Gothic cathedral, appealed alike to the loftiest and humblest intelligence. Owen paused to think if there was not something vulgar in the parade of the Mass. A simple prayer breathed by a burdened heart in secret awaked a more immediate and intimate response in him. That was Anglicanism. Perhaps he preferred Anglicanism. The truth was, he was deficient in the religious instinct.

Awaking from his reverie, he raised himself from the mantelpiece against which he was leaning. Never had he thought so brilliantly, and he regretted that no magical stenographer should be there to register his thoughts as they passed. But they were gone.... Resuming his position against the mantelpiece, he continued his interrupted train of thoughts.

There would be the priest's interdiction ... unless, indeed, he could win Evelyn to agnosticism. In his own case he could imagine a sort of religious agnosticism. But is a woman capable of such a serene contemplation and comprehension of the mystery, which perforce we must admit envelops us, and which often seems charged with murmurs, recollections and warnings of the under world? Does not woman need the grosser aid of dogma to raise her sensual nature out of complete abjection? But all this was very metaphysical. The probability was that Evelyn would lead the life of the ordinary prima donna until she was fifty, that she would then retire to a suburb in receipt of a handsome income, and having nothing to do, she would begin to think again of the state of her soul. The line of her chin deflected; some would call it a weak chin, but he had observed the same in men of genius—her father, for instance. None could be more resolute than he in the pursuance of his ideas. The mother's thin, stubborn mouth must find expression somewhere in her daughter. But where? Evelyn's mouth was thin and it drooped at the ends.... But she was only twenty; at five-and-twenty, at thirty, she might be possessed by new ideas, new passions.... The moment we look into life and examine the weft a little, what a mystery it becomes, how occult the design, and out of what impenetrable darkness the shuttle passes, weaving a strange pattern, harmonious in a way, and yet deducible to none of our laws! This little adventure, the little fact of his becoming Evelyn's lover, was sown with every eventuality.... If, instead of his winning her to agnosticism, she should win him to Rome! They then would have to separate or marry, otherwise they would burn in hell for ever.

But he would never be fool enough as to accept such a story as that again. That God should concern himself at all in our affairs was strange enough, that he should do so seemed little creditable to him, but that he should manage us to the extent of the mere registration of a cohabitation in the parish books was—. Owen flung out his arms in an admirable gesture of despair, and crossed the room. After a while he returned to the fireplace calmer, and he considered the question anew. By no means did he deny the existence of conscience; his own was particularly exact on certain points. In money matters he believed himself to be absolutely straight. He had never even sold a friend a horse knowing it to be unsound; and he had always avoided—no, not making love to his friends' wives (to whose wives are you to make love if not to your friends'?)—he had avoided making women unhappy. But much more than in morals his conscience found expression in art. That Evelyn should use her voice except for the interpretation of masterpieces would shock him quite as much as an elopement would shock the worthy Fathers of St. Joseph's. He smiled at his thoughts, and remembered that it was through fear of not making a woman happy that he had not married. He hated unhappiness. His wish had always been to see people happy. Was not that why he wished to go away with Evelyn? A particularly foolish woman had once told him that she liked going out hunting because she liked to see people amused.... He did not pretend to such altruism as hers, and he remembered how he used to watch for her at the window as she came across the square with her dog. But Evelyn was quite different. He could not have her to luncheon or tea, and send her back to her father. Somehow, it would not seem fair to her. No; he must break with her, or they must go away together. Which was it to be? Mrs. Hartrick had written three times that week! And there was Lady Lovedale. She had promised to come to tea on Friday. Was he going to renounce the list, or was he going to put all his eggs in one basket? The list promised much agreeable intercourse, but it was wholly lacking in unexpectedness. He had been through it all before, and knew how each story would end. In mutual indifference or in a tiff because he wearied of accompanying her to all racecourses and all theatres. Another would pretend that her husband was jealous, and that she daren't come to see him any more. But Evelyn would be quite different. In her case, he could not see further than driving to Charing Cross and getting into the mail train for Paris. She was worth the list, not a doubt of it. If he were only sure that he loved her, he would not hesitate. He was interested in her, he admired her, but did he love her? A genuine passion alone would make an elopement excusable.

One of his moralities was that a man who did not love his mistress was a beast, and that a man who loved a woman who wasn't, was a fool. Another was that although every man of the world knew a *liaison* would not last for ever, he should not begin one unless it seemed as if it were going to. In other words, you should not be able to see the end before you began. But he had never even kissed Evelyn, and it was impossible even to guess, even approximately, if you were going to like a girl before you had kissed her. There could be no harm in kissing her. Then, if he was sure he loved her, they might go away together. Of course, there were hypocrites who would say that he had seduced her, that he had ruined her, robbed Mr. Innes of his only daughter. But he was not concerned with conventional, but with real morality. If he did not go away with her, what would happen? He had told her the truth in the park that morning, and he believed every word he had said.... If she did not leave her father she would learn to hate him. It was terrible to think of, but it was so, and nothing could change it. He tried to recall his exact words, and easily imagined her father stricken with remorse, and Evelyn looking across the table, hating him in spite of herself. But if he could persuade her to leave him for two years he would engage to bring her back a great singer. And what an interest it would be to watch the development of that voice, surely the most beautiful soprano he had ever heard! She might begin with "Margaret" and "Norma," if she liked, for in singing these popular operas she would acquire the whole of her voice, and also the great reputation which should precede and herald the final stage of her career. "Isolde," "Brunnhilde," "Kundry," Wagner's finest works, had remained unsung—they en merely howled. Evelyn should be the first to sing them. His eyes glowed with subdued passion as he thought of an afternoon, some three years hence, in the great theatre planned by the master himself, when he should see her rush in as the Witch Kundry. The marvellous evocation of Arabia flashed upon him.... Would he ever hear her sing it?... Yes, if she would consent to go away with him he would hear her sing it. But would she go away with him? Her love of her father, and her religion, might prevent her.... She might not even care for him.... She might be thinking of marrying him. Was it possible that she was such a fool! What good would it do her to marry him? She could not go on the stage as Lady Asher. Lady Asher as Kundry! Could anything be more grotesque? How beset life was with difficulties! Without her vocation she was no longer the Evelyn Innes he was in love with.... Someone else, a pretty, interesting girl, the daughter of a suburban organist. To marry her now would be to ruin her. But he might marry her five or six years hence, for there was no reason why she should continue singing "Isolde" and "Brunnhilde" till she had no shred of voice left. When she had established a standard she would have achieved her mission, then it would be for others to maintain the standard. In the full blaze of her glory she might become Lady Asher. He would have to end his life somehow, that way as well as another. Five years are a long while—anything might happen. She might leave him for someone else ... anything—anything—anything might happen. It was impossible to divine the turn human lives would take. The simple fact of his elopement contained a dozen different stories in germ. Each would find opportunities of development; they would struggle for mastery; which would succeed?... Keep women you couldn't; he had long ago found out that. Marry them, and they came to hate the way you walked across the room; remain their lover, and they jilted you at the end of six months. He had hardly ever heard of a *liaison* lasting more than a year or eighteen months, and Evelyn would meet all the nicest men in Europe. All Europe would be his rival—really it would be better to give her up.... She was the kind of woman who, if she once let herself go, would play the devil. Turning from the fire he looked into the glass.... He admitted to eight-and-thirty, he was forty—a very well-preserved forty. There were times when he did not look more than five-and-thirty. His hair was paler than it used to be; it was growing a little thin on the forehead, otherwise he was the same as when he was five-and-twenty. But he was forty, and a man of forty cannot marry a prima donna of twenty. Five pleasant years they might have together, five delicious years; it were vain to expect more. But he would not get her to go away with him under a promise of marriage; all such deception he held to be as dishonourable as cheating at cards. So in their next interview it would have to be suggested that there could be no question of marriage, at least for the present. At the same time he would have her understand that he intended to shirk no responsibility. But if he were to tire of her! That was another possibility, and a hateful one; he would prefer that she should jilt him. Perhaps it would be better to give her up, and throw his fate in with the list. But he was tired of country houses, with or without a *liaison*, and felt that he could not go through another season's hunting; he had no horses that suited him, and didn't seem to be able to find any. To go abroad with Evelyn, watch over the cultivation of her voice, see her fame rising, that was his mission! The only question to decide was whether he was in love with her. He would not hesitate a moment if he were only sure of that. He thought of the women he knew. Georgina was the first to come up in his mind. He had been to see her, and had come away at a loss to understand what he had ever seen in her. She had struck him as vulgar and middle-class, sly, with a taste for intrigue. He remembered that was how she had struck him when he first saw her. But if anyone had described her as vulgar and middle-class six months ago. Good heavens!

CHAPTER SEVEN

The day grew too fine, as he said, for false notes, so the music lesson was abandoned, and they went to sit in the garden behind the picture gallery, a green sward with high walls covered with creeper, and at one end a great cedar with a seat built about the trunk; a quiet place rife with songs of birds, and unfrequented save by them. They had taken with them Omar's verses, and Evelyn hoped that he would talk to her about them, for the garden of the Persian poet she felt to be separated only by a wicket from theirs. But Owen did not respond to her humour. He was prepense to argue about the difficulties of her life, and of the urgent necessity of vanquishing these.

He had noticed, he said, as they sat in the park, that she had a weak face. Her thoughts were far away; he had caught her face, as it were, napping, and had seen through it to the root of her being. The conclusion at which he had arrived was that she was not capable of leading an independent life.

"Am I not right? Isn't it so?"

"You think that because I don't leave father and go abroad."

"You might go abroad and lead a dependent life; you might stay at home and lead an independent life."

He asked her what offers of marriage she had had.

One was from the Vicar, a widower, a man of fifty, the other from a young man in a solicitor's office. She did not care for either, and had not entertained their proposals for a second.

"If you marry anyone, it must be a duke. Life is a battle; society will get the better of us unless we get the better of society. Everyone must realise that—every young man, every young woman. We must conquer or be conquered."

Society, he argued, did not require a chaperon from her; society would, indeed, resent a chaperon if she were to appear with one. Society not only granted her freedom, but demanded that she should exercise it. As a freelance she would be taken notice of, as a respectable, marriageable girl she would be passed over. The cradle and the masterpiece were irreconcilable ideals. He drew an amusing picture of the prima donna's husband, the fellow who waits with a scarf ready to wind it round the throat of his musical instrument; the fellow who is always on the watch lest someone should walk off with his means of subsistence. Evelyn listened because she liked to hear him talk; she knew that he was trying to influence her with argument, but it was he himself who was influencing her, she dreaded his presence, not his argument.

She got up and walked across the sward; and as they returned through the flowery village street, the faint May breeze shed the white chestnut bloom about their feet. It seemed to him better to say nothing; there are times when silence is more potent than speech. They were walking under the trees of the old Dulwich street, and so charming were the hedge-hidden gardens, and the eighteenth-century houses with white porticoes, that Owen could not but think Dulwich at that moment seemed the natural nativity of the young girl's career. A few moments after they were at Dowlands. She was trembling, and had no strength of will to refuse to ask him in. She would have had the strength if she had not been obliged to give him her hand. She had tried to bid him good-bye without giving her hand, and had not succeeded, and while he held her hand her lips said the words without her knowing it. She spoke unconsciously, and did not know what she had said till she had said it.

And while they waited for tea, Evelyn lay back in a wicker chair thinking. He had said that life without love was a desert, and many times the conversation trembled on the edge of a personal avowal, and now he was playing love music out of "Tristan" on the harpsichord. The gnawing, creeping sensuality of the phrase brought little shudders into her flesh; all life seemed dissolved into a dim tremor and rustling of blood; vague colour floated into her eyes,

and there were moments when she could hardly restrain herself from jumping to her feet and begging of him to stop.... The servant brought in the tea, and she thought she would feel better when the music ceased. But neither did the silence nor the tea help her. He sat opposite her, his eyes fixed upon her, that half-kindly, half-cynical face of his showing through the gold of his moustache. He seemed to know that she could not follow the conversation, and seemed determined to drive the malady that was devouring her to a head. He continued to speak of the motive of the love call, how it is interwoven with the hunting fanfare; when the fanfare dies in the twilight, how it is then heard in the dark loneliness of the garden. She heard him speak of the handkerchief motive, of thirty violins playing three notes in ever precipitated rhythm, until we feel that the world reels behind the woman, that only one thing exists for her—Tristan. A giddiness gathered in Evelyn's brain, and she fell back in her chair, slightly to the left side, and letting her hand slip towards him, said, with a beseeching look—
"I cannot go on talking, I am too tired."
It seemed as if she were going to faint, and this made it easy and natural for him to take her hand, to put his arm about her, and then to whisper—
"Evelyn, dear, what is the matter?"
She opened her eyes; their look was sufficient answer.
"Dearest Evelyn," he said; and bending over, he kissed her on the cheek.
"This is very foolish of me," she said, and throwing her arm about his neck, she kissed him on the mouth. "But you are fond of me?" she said impulsively, laying her hand on his shoulder. It was a movement full of affectionate intimacy.
"Yes," he said, moving her face again towards him. "I love you, I've always loved you."
"No," she said, "you didn't, not always; I know when you began to care for me."
"When?"
"When you returned from Greece, at the moment when you said you wanted me to like you. Is it not true?"
Owen dared not tell her that it was at the moment of kissing her that he had really begun to love her. In that moment he had entered into her atmosphere; it was fragrant as a flower, and it had decided him to use every effort to become her lover.
"No," she said, "you must not kiss me again."
She got up from the low wicker chair; he followed her, and they sat close together on two low seats. He put his arm round her and said—
"I love to kiss you.... Why do you turn away your head?"
"Because it is wrong; I shall be miserable to-night."
"You don't think wrong to kiss me?"
"Yes, I do."
Then turning her face to his, she kissed him.
"Who taught you to kiss like that?"
"No one, I never kissed anyone before—father, of course. You know what I mean."
"She'll be an adorable mistress," he thought, "and in four years the greatest singer in England. I shall get very fond of her. I like her very much as it is, and when she gets over her religious scruples—when I've reformed her—she'll be enchanting. It is lucky she met me; without me she'd have come to nothing."
She asked him what he was thinking about, and he answered of the happiness he had begun to feel was in store for them.
"What happiness?" she asked; and he answered—
"The happiness of seeing each other constantly—the happiness of lovers. Now we must see each other more often."
"How often? Every day?"
He wondered what was the exact colour of her eyes, and he pressed her to answer. At last she said—

"You cannot come here oftener than you do at present. I'm deceiving father about these lessons. What will you do if he asks you to play to him? What excuse will you give? You daren't attempt the simplest exercise, you haven't got over the difference of the bowing; you'd play false notes all the time."

"Yes," he said; "I've not made much progress, have I?"

"No, you haven't; but that isn't my fault."

"But the days I don't see you seem so long!"

"Do you think they do not seem long to me? I've nothing to think about but you."

"Then, on your weariest days, come and see me. We can always see each other in Berkeley Square. Send me a wire saying you are coming."

"I could not come to see you," she said, still looking at him fixedly; "you know that I could not.... Then why do you ask me?"

"Because I want you."

"You know that I'd like to come."

"Then, if you do, you'll come. I don't believe in temptations that we don't yield to."

"I suppose that the temptation that we yield to is the temptation?"

"Of course. But, Evelyn, you are not going to waste your life in Dulwich. Come and see me to-morrow and, if you like, we'll decide."

"On what?"

"You know what I mean, dearest."

"Yes, I think I do," she said, smiling at once sadly and ardently; "but I'm afraid it wouldn't succeed. I'm not the kind of woman to play the part to advantage."

"I'm very fond of you, and I think you're very fond of me."

"You don't think about it—you know I am."

"Then why did you say you would not come and see me?"

"I did not say so. But something tells me that if I did go away with you it would not succeed."

"Why do you think that?"

"I don't know. Something whispers that it wouldn't succeed. All my people were good people—my mother, my grandmother, my aunts. I never had a relative against whom anything could be said, so I don't know why I am what I am. For I'm only half good. It is you who make me bad, Owen; it isn't nice of you." She flung her arms about him, and then recoiled from him in a sudden revulsion of feeling.

"When you go away I shall be miserable; I shall repent of all this ... I'm horrid." She covered her face in her hands. "I didn't know I was like this."

A moment after she reached out her hand to him saying—

"You're not angry with me? I can't help it if I'm like this. I should like to go and see you; it would be so much to me. But I must not. But why mustn't I?"

"I know no reason, except that you don't care for me."

"But you know that isn't so."

"Come, dearest, be reasonable. You're not going to stop here all your life playing the viola da gamba. The hour of departure has come," he said, perceiving her very thought; "be reasonable, come and see me to-morrow. Come to lunch, and I'll arrange. You know that you—"

"Yes, I believe that," she said, in response to a change which had come into her appreciation.

"But can I trust myself? Suppose I did go away, and repented and left you. Where should I go? I could not come back here. Father would forgive me, I daresay, but I could not come back here."

"'Repented,' Those are fairy tales," he said lifting her gold hair from her ear and kissing it. "A woman does not leave the man who adores her."

"You told me they often did."

"How funny you are.... They do sometimes, but not because they repent."

Her head was on his shoulder, and she stood looking at him a long while without speaking.

"Then you do love me, dearest? Tell me so again."
Kissing her gently on the mouth and eyes, he answered—
"You know very well that I do. Come and see me to-morrow. Say you will, for I must go now."
"Go now!"
"Do you know what time it is? It is past seven."
She followed him to the gate of the little garden. The lamps were lighted far away in the suburbs. Again he asked her to come and see him.
"I cannot to-morrow; to-morrow will be Sunday."
His footsteps echoed through the chill twilight, and seeing a thin moon afloat like a feather in the sky, she thought of Omar's moon, that used to seek the lovers in their garden, and that one evening sought one of them in vain.

CHAPTER EIGHT

There was no other place except the picture gallery where they could see each other alone. But the dignity of Velasquez and the opulence of Rubens distracted their thoughts, and they were ill at ease on a backless seat in front of a masterpiece. Owen regretted the Hobbema; it was less aggressive than the colonnade. A sun-lit clearing in a wood and a water mill raised no moral question. He turned his eyes from the dancers, but however he resisted them, their frivolous life found its way into the conversation. They were the wise ones, he said. They lived for art and love, and what else was there in life? A few sonatas, a few operas, a few pictures, a few books, and a love story; we had always to come back to that in the end. He spoke with conviction, his only insincerity being the alteration of a plural into a singular. But no, he did not think he had lied; he had spoken what seemed to him the truth at the present moment. Had he used the singular instead of the plural a fortnight ago, he would have lied, but within the last week his feelings for Evelyn had changed. If she had broken with him a week ago, he would have found easy consolation in the list, but now it was not women, but a woman that he desired. A mere sexual curiosity, and the artistic desire to save a beautiful voice from being wasted, had given way to a more personal emotion in which affection was beginning. Looking at him, thinking over what he had just said, unable to stifle the hope that those women in the picture were the wise ones, she heard life calling her. The art call and the love call, subtly interwoven, were modulated now on the violins now on the flutes of an invisible orchestra. At the same moment his immeshed senses, like greedy fish, swam hither and thither, perplexed and terrified, finding no way of escape, and he dreaded lest he had lost his balance and fallen into the net he had cast so often. He had begun to see that she was afraid of the sin, and not at all of him. She had never asked him if he would always love her—that she seemed to take for granted—and he had, or fancied he had, begun to feel that he would never cease to love her. He looked into the future far enough to see that it would be she who would tire of him, and that another would appear two or three years hence who would appeal to her sensual imagination just as he did to-day. She would strive to resist it, she would argue with herself, but the enticing illusion would draw her as in a silken net. He was now engaged in the destruction of her moral scruples—in other words, making the way easy for his successor.

They were in the gallery alone, and, taking her hand, he considered in detail the trouble this *liaison* would bring in its train. He no longer doubted that she would go abroad with him sooner or later. He hoped it would be sooner, for he had begun to perceive the absurdity of his visits to Dulwich. The question was whether she was worth an exile in a foreign country. He would have to devote himself to her and to her interests. She would have a chaperon. There would be no use in their openly living together—that he could not stand. But at that moment the exquisite happiness of seeing her every day, coming into the room where she was reading or singing, and kissing her as he leaned over her chair affectionately, as a matter of course, deriving his enjoyment from the prescriptive right to do so, and then talking to her about ordinary affairs of life, came upon him suddenly like a vision; and this imagined life was so intense that for one moment it was equivalent to the reality. He saw himself taking her home from the theatre at night in the brougham. In the next instant they were in the train going to Bayreuth. In the next he saw her as Kundry rush on to the stage. He felt that, whatever it cost him, that was the life he must obtain. He felt that he could not live if he did not acquire it, and so intense was the vision that, unable to endure its torment, he got up and proposed they should go into the garden and sit under the cedar.

They were alone in the garden as they were in the gallery, but lovers are averse to open spaces, and Owen felt that their appearance coincided too closely with that of lovers in many popular engravings. He hoped he was not observed, and regretted he had often spoken of the picture gallery to his friends. An unlucky chance might bring one of them down.

It was in this garden, amid the scent and colour of May, that the most beautiful part of their love story was woven. It was in this garden that they talked about love and happiness, and the mystery of the attraction of one person to another, and whilst listening to him, a poignant memory of the afternoon when he had first kissed her often crossed her mind. Little faintnesses took her in the eyes and heart. Their voices broke, and it seemed that they could not continue to talk any longer of life and art. It was in this garden that they forgot each other. Their thoughts wandered far away, and then, when one called the other's attention, he or she relinquished scenes and sensations and came back appearing suddenly like someone out of a mist. Each asked the other what he or she had been dreaming. Once he told her his dream. It was of a villa in the middle of a large garden surrounded by chestnut trees and planted with rhododendrons. In this villa there dwelt a great singer whose name was a glory in the world, and to this villa there came very often a tall, thin, ugly man, and, seeing the beautiful singer walking with him, the folk wondered how she could love him.

It was a sort of delicious death, a swooning ecstasy, an absorption of her individuality in his. Just as the spring gradually displaced the winter by a new branch of blossom, and in that corner of the garden by the winsome mauve of a lilac bush, without her knowing it his ideas caught root in her. New thoughts and perceptions were in growth within her, and every day she discovered the new where she had been accustomed to meet the familiar idea. She seemed to be slipping out of herself as out of a soft, white garment, unconsciously, without any effort on her part.

Very often they discussed whether sacrifice of self is not the first of the sins against life. "That is the sin," he said, "that cries loudest to Nature for vengeance. To discover our best gift from Nature, and to cultivate that gift, is the first law of life." If she could not accept this theory of life as valid and justifiable, she had at least begun to consider it. Another of Owen's ideas that interested her was his theory of beauty. He said that he could not accept the ordinary statement that a woman was beautiful and stupid. Beauty and stupidity could not exist in the same face, stupidity being the ugliest thing on earth; and he contended that two-thirds of human beauty were the illumination of matter by the intelligence, and but one-third proportion and delicacy of line. After some hesitation, he admitted that at first he had been disappointed in her, but now everything about her was an enchantment, and when she was not present, he lived in memories of her. He spoke without emphasis, almost as if he were speaking to himself, and she could not answer for delight.

Her father was vaguely conscious of some change in his daughter, and when one day he heard her singing "Faust," he was perplexed; and when she argued that it was a beautiful and human aspiration, he looked at her as if he had never seen her before. He asked her how she had come to think such a thing, and was perplexed by her embarrassments. She was sorry for her liking for Gounod's melodies. It seemed to alienate them; they seemed to have drifted apart. She saw a silently widening distance, as if two ships were moving away. One day he asked her if she were going to communion next Sunday. She answered that she did not think so, and sat thinking a long while, for she had become suddenly aware that she was not as pious as she used to be. She did not think that Owen's arguments had touched her faith, but she no longer felt the same interest in religion; and in thinking over this change, which seemed so independent of her own will, she grew pensive and perplexed. Her melancholy was a sort of voluptuous meditation. She was conscious all the while of Owen's presence. It was as if he were standing by her, and she felt that he must be thinking of her.

He had often spoken of going away with her; she had smiled plaintively, never regarding an elopement as possible. But one evening her father had gone to dine with a certain Roman prelate who believed in the advantage to the Catholic Church of a musical reformation. And she had gone to meet Owen, who had driven from London. They had walked two hours in the lanes, and when she got home she ran to her room and undressed hurriedly, thinking how delightful it would be to lie awake in the dark and remember it all. And feeling the cool sheets about her she folded her arms and abandoned herself to every recollection. Her imagination, heightened as by a drug, enabled her to see the white, dusty road and the sickly, yellow moon rising through the branches. Again she was standing by him, her arms were on his neck; again they stood looking into the vague distance, seeing the broken paling in the moonlight. There were his eyes and hands and lips to think about, and when she had exhausted these memories, others sprang upon her. It was in the very centre of her being that she was thinking of the moment when she had spied his horse's head over the hill top. She had recognised his silhouette against the sky. He had whipped up the horse, he had thrown the reins to the groom, he had sprung from the step. The evening was then lighted by the sunset, and as the sky darkened, their love had seemed to grow brighter. In comparison with this last meeting, all past meetings seemed shadowy and unreal. She had never loved him before, and if her smile had dwindled when he asked her to come away with him, she had liked to hear him say the dogcart was waiting at the inn. But when they stood by the stile where cattle were breathing softly, and the moon shone over the sheepfold like a shepherd's lantern, her love had grown wilful, and she had liked to say that she would go away with him. She knew not whether she could fulfil her promise, but it had been a joy to give it. They had walked slowly towards Dulwich, the groom had brought round the dog-cart; Owen had asked her once more to get in. Oh, to drive away with him through the night! "Owen, it is impossible," she said; "I cannot, at least not now. But I will one day very soon, sooner perhaps than you think." He had driven away, and, standing on the moon-whitened road, she had watched the white dust whirl about the wheels.

One of the difficulties in the indulgence of these voluptuous meditations was that they necessitated the omission of her evening prayers. She could not kneel by her bedside and pray to God to deliver her from evil, all the while nourishing in her heart the intention of abandoning herself to the thought of Owen the moment she got into bed. Nor did the omission of her evening prayers quite solve the difficulty, for when she could think no more of Owen, the fear of God returned. She dared not go to sleep, and lay terrified, dreading the devil in every corner of the room. Lest she might die in her sleep and be summoned before the judgment seat, she lay awake as long as she could.

When she fell asleep she dreamed of the stage when the world was won, and when it seemed she had only to stretch her hands to the sky to take the stars. But in the midst of her triumph she perceived that she could no longer sing the music the world required; a new music was drumming in her ears, drowning the old music, a music written in a melancholy mode, and played on invisible harps. Owen told her it was madness to listen, and she strove to close her ears against it. In great trouble of mind she awoke; it was only a dream, and she had not lost her voice. She lay back upon the pillow and tried to recall the music which she had heard on the invisible harps, but already it was forgotten; it faded from her brain like mist from the surface of a mere. But the humour that the dream had created endured after the dream was dead. She felt no longer as she had felt over night, and lay in a sort of obtuse sensibility of conscience. She got up and dressed, her mind still clouded and sullen, and her prayers were said in a sort of middle state between fervour and indifference. Her father attributed her mood to the old cause; several times he was on the point of speaking, and she held him for the moment by the lappet of his coat and looked affectionately into his face. But something told her that if she were to confide her trouble to anyone, she would lose the power she had acquired over herself. Something told her that all the strength on her side was reposed in the secrecy of the combat. If it were known, she could imagine herself saying—

"Well, nothing matters now; let us go away, Owen."

He was coming to see her between eleven and twelve—at the very time he knew her father would be away from home, and this very fact stimulated her ethical perception. Her manner was in accordance with her mood, and the moment he entered he saw that something had happened, that she was no longer the same Evelyn from whom he had parted a couple of nights before.

"Well, I can see you have changed your mind; so we are not going away together. Evelyn, dear, is it not so? Tell me."

He was a little ashamed of his hypocrisy, for, as he had driven home in the dogcart, the adventure he was engaged in had appeared to him under every disagreeable aspect. He could not but think that the truth of the story would leak out, and he could hear all the women he knew speaking of Evelyn as a girl he had picked up in the suburbs—an organist's daughter. He had thought again of the responsibility that going away with this girl imposed upon him, and he had come to the conclusion that it would be wiser to drop the whole thing and get out of it while there was time. That night, as he lay in bed, he saw himself telling people how many operas she knew; and the tales of her successes in Vienna and Naples.... But he need not always be with her, she would have a chaperon; and he had fallen asleep thinking which among his friends would undertake the task for him. In the morning he had awakened in the same nervous indecision, and had gone to Dulwich disheartened, provoked at his own folly. It therefore happened that her refusal to go away with him coincided exactly with his humour. So all that was necessary was a mere polite attempt to persuade her that she was sacrificing her career, but without too much insistence on the point; a promise to call again soon; then a letter saying he was unwell, or was going to Paris or to Riversdale. A month after they could meet at a concert, but he must be careful not to be alone with her, and very soon the incident—after all, he had only kissed her—would be forgotten. But as he sat face to face with her, all his carefully considered plans seemed to drop behind him in ruins, and he doubted if he would be able to deny himself the pleasure of taking her away. That is to say, if he could induce her to go, which no longer seemed very sure. She might be one of those women in whom the sense of sin was so obdurate that they could not but remain virtuous.

But of what was she thinking? he asked himself; and he scanned the yielding face, reading the struggle in a sudden suppressed look or nervous twitching of the lips.

"Dearest Evelyn, I love you. Life would be nothing without you."

"Owen, I am very fond of you, but there would be no use in my going away with you. I should be miserable. I know I am not the kind of woman who would play the part."

Her words roused new doubts. It would be useless to go away with her if she were to be miserable all the while. He did not want to make anyone miserable; he wanted to make people happy. He indulged in a moment of complacent self-admiration, and then reflected that this adventure would cost a great deal of time and money, and if he were really to get nothing out of it but tears and repentance, he had better take her at her word, bid her good-bye, and write to-morrow saying he was called away to Riversdale on business.

"But you are not cross with me? You will come to see me all the same?"

He wondered if she were tortured with as many different and opposing desires as he was. Perhaps not, and he watched her tender, truthful eyes. In her truthful nature, filled full of passion and conscience, there was no place for any slightest calculation. But he was mistrustful, and asked himself if all this resistance was a blind to induce him to marry her. If he thought that, he would drop her at once. This suspicion was lost sight of in a sudden lighting of her hair, caused by a slight turning of her head. Beyond doubt she was a fresh and delicious thing, and if he did not take her, someone else would, and then he would curse his indecision; and if she had a great voice, he would for ever regret he had not taken her when he could get her. If he did not take her now, the chance was gone for ever. She was the adventure he had dreamed all his life. At last it had come to him, perhaps through the sheer force of his desire, and now, should he refrain from the dream, or should he dream it? He saw the exquisite sensual life that awaited him and her in Paris. He saw her, pale and pathetic, and thought of her eager eyes and lips.

Evelyn sat crestfallen and repentant, but her melancholy was a pretty, smiling melancholy, and her voice had not quite lost the sparkle and savour of wit. She regretted her sin, admitted her culpability, and he was forced to admit that sorrow and virtue sat becomingly upon her. Her mood was in a measure contagious, and he talked gently and gaily about herself, and the day when the world would listen to her with delight and approbation. But while he talked, he was like a man on the rack. He was dragged from different sides, and the questioner was at his ear.

Hitherto he had never compromised himself in his relations with women. As he had often said of himself, he had inspired no great passion, but a multitude of caprices. But now he had begun to feel that it is one love and not twenty that makes a life memorable, he wished to redeem his life from intrigues, and here was the very chance he was waiting for. But habit had rendered him cowardly, and this seduction frightened him almost as much as marriage had done. To go away with her, he felt, was equivalent to marrying her. His life would never be the same again. The list would be lost to him for ever, no more lists for him; he would be known as the man who lived with—lived with whom? A girl picked up in the suburbs, and sang rather prettily. If she were a great singer he would not mind, but he could not stand a mediocre singer about whom he would have to talk continual nonsense: conspiracies that were in continual progress against her at Covent Garden, etc. He had heard all that sort of thing before.... What should he do? He must make up his mind. It might be as well if he were to ask her to come to his house; then in some three or four months he would be able to see if she were worth the great sacrifice he was going to make for her.

Her hand lay on her knees. He knew that he should not take it, but it lay on her knees so plaintively, that in spite of all his resistance he took it and examined it. It did not strike him as a particularly beautiful hand. It was long and white, and exceedingly flexible. It was large, and the finger-tips were pointed. The palms curved voluptuously, but the slender fingers closed and opened with a virile movement which suggested active and spontaneous impulses. In taking her hand and caressing it, he knew he was prejudicing his chances of escape, and fearing the hand he held in his might never let him go again, he said—

"If your destiny should be to play the viola da gamba in Dulwich, and mine to set forth again on my trip round the world."

In an instant, in a rapid succession of scenes, the horrible winter she had spent in Dulwich passed before her eyes. She saw herself stopping at the corner of a street, and looking at a certain tree and the slope of a certain house, and asking herself if her life would go on for ever, if there would be no change. She saw herself star-gazing, with daffodils for offerings in her hands; and the memory of the hungry hours when she waited for her father to come home to dinner was so vivid, that she thought she felt the same wearying pain and the exhausting yearning behind her eyes, and that feeling as if she wanted to go mad. No; she could not endure it again, and she cried plaintively, falling slightly forward—

"Owen, don't make things more difficult than they are. Why is it wrong for me to go away with you? I don't do any harm to anyone. God is merciful after all."

"If I were to marry you, you could not go on the stage; you would have to live at Riversdale and look after your children."

"But I don't want children. I want to sing."

"And I want you to sing. No one but husbands have children, exception the stage and in novels."

"It would be much more exciting to run away together, than to be married by the Vicar. It is very wicked to say these things. It is you who make me wicked."

A mist blinded her eyes, and a sickness seemed instilled in her very blood, and in a dubious faintness she was conscious of his lips. He hardly heard the words he uttered, so loud was the clatter of his thoughts, and he seemed to see the trail of his destiny unwinding itself from the distaff in the hands of Fate. He was frightened, and an impulse strove to force him to his feet, and hence, with a rapid good-bye, to the door. But instead, he leaned forth his hands, he sought her, but she shrank away, and turning her face from him, she said—

"Owen, you must not kiss me."

Again he might choose between sailing the *Medusa* in search of adventure, or crossing the Channel in the mail packet in search of art.

"Will you come away with me?" he said. His heart sank, and he thought of the Rubicon.

"You don't mean this very instant? I could not go away without seeing father."

"Why not? You don't intend to tell him you are going away with me?"

"No; it is not the sort of thing one generally tells one's father, but—I cannot go away with you now—"

"When will you come?"

"Owen, don't press me for an answer. I don't know."

"The way of escape is still open to me," he thought; but he could not resist the temptation that this girl's face and voice presented to his imagination.

CHAPTER NINE

She sat in the music-room thinking, asking herself what use it would be to meet him in Berkeley Square unless to go away with him to Paris. She sat engrossed in her emotion; it was like looking into water where weeds are carried by a current out of the dim depths into the light of day. In a pensive atmosphere, a quiet daylight, his motives were revealed to her. She was in the humour to look at things sympathetically, and she understood that for him to run away with her entailed as much sacrifice on his part as on hers. It meant a giving up of his friends, pursuits and habits of life. There were sacrifices to be made by him as well as by her, and she smiled a little sadly as she thought of the differences of their several renunciations. She was asked to surrender her peace of mind, he his worldly pleasure. Often the sensation was almost physical; it rose up like a hand and seemed to sweep her heart clear, and at the same moment a voice said—It is not right. Owen had argued with her, but she could not quench the feeling that it was not right, and yet, when he asked her to explain, she could give no other reason except that it was forbidden by the Church.

Each thought that very little was asked from the other. To him her conscience seemed a slight forfeit, and worldly pleasure seemed very little to her. She thought that she would readily forfeit this world for him.... But eternity was her forfeit; even that she might sacrifice if she were sure her conscience would not trouble her in this world. She followed her conscience like a river; it fluttered along full of unexpected eddies and picturesque shallows, and there were pools so deep that she could not see to the bottom.

Suddenly the vision changed. She was no longer in Dulwich with her father. She saw railway trains and steamboats, and then the faint outline of the coast of France. Her foreboding was so clear and distinct that she could not doubt that Owen was the future that awaited her. The presentiment filled her with delight and fear, and both sensations were mingled at the same moment in her heart as she rose from her chair. She stood rigid as a visionary; then, hoping she would not be disturbed, she sank back into her chair and allowed her thoughts their will.

She followed the course of the journey to France, and at every moment the sensation grew more exquisite. She heard him say what she wished him to say, and she saw the white villa in its garden planted with rhododendrons and chestnut trees in flower. The mild spring air, faint with perfume, dilated her nostrils, and her eyes drank in the soft colour of the light shadows passing over the delicate grass and the light shadows moving among the trees. She lay back in her chair, her eyes fixed on a distant corner of the room, and her life went by, clear and surprising as pictures seen in a crystal. When she grew weary of the villa, she saw herself on the stage, and heard her own voice singing as she wished to sing. Nor did she foresee any break in the lulling enchantment of her life of music and love. She knew that Owen did not love her at present, but she never doubted that she could get him to love her, and once he loved her it seemed to her that he must always love her. What she had heard and read in books concerning the treachery of men, she remembered, but she was not influenced, for it did not seem to her that any such things were to happen to her. She closed her eyes so that she might drink more deeply of the vision, so that she might bring it more clearly before her. Like aspects seen on a misty river, it was as beautiful shadows of things rather than the things themselves. The meditation grew voluptuous, and as she saw him come into her room and take her in his arms, her conscience warned her that she should cease to indulge in these thoughts; but it was impossible to check them, and she dreamed on and on in kisses and tendernesses of speech.

That afternoon she was going to have tea with some friends, and as she paused to pin her hat before the glass, she remembered that if Owen were right, and that there was no future life, the only life that she was sure of would be wasted. Then she would endure the burden of life for naught; she would not have attained its recompense; the calamity would be irreparable; it would be just as if she had not lived at all. Thought succeeded thought in instantaneous succession, contradicting and refuting each other. No, her life would not be wasted, it would be an example to others, it was in renunciation that we rose above the animal and attained spiritual existence. At that moment it seemed to her that she could renounce everything but love. Could she renounce her art? But her art was not a merely personal sacrifice. In the renunciation of her art she was denying a great gift that had been given to her by Nature, that had come she knew not whence nor how, but clearly for exercise and for the admiration of the world. It therefore could not have been given to her to hide or to waste; she would be held responsible for it. Her voice was one of her responsibilities; not to cultivate her voice would be a sort of suicide. This seemed quite clear to her, and she reflected, and with some personal satisfaction, that she had incurred duties toward herself. Right and wrong, as Owen said, was a question of time and place. What was right here was wrong there, but oneself was the one certain thing, and to remain with her father meant the abandonment of herself.... She wanted herself! Ah, she wanted to live, and how well she knew that she was not living, and could never live, in Dulwich. The nuns! Strange were their renunciations! For they yielded the present moment, which Owen and a Persian poet called our one possession. She seemed to see them fading in a pathetic decadence, falling like etiolated flowers, and their holy simplicities seemed merely pathetic.

And in the exaltation of her resolution to live, her soul melted again into Owen's kisses, and she drew herself together, and the spasm was so intense and penetrating that to overcome it she walked across the room stretching her arms. It seemed to her more than impossible that she could endure Dulwich any longer. The life of love and art tore at her heart; always she saw Owen offering her love, fame, wealth; his hands were full of gifts; he seemed to drop them at her feet, and taking her in his arms, his lips closed upon hers, and her life seemed to run down like the last struggling sand in a glass.

Besides this personal desire there was in her brain a strange alienation. Paris rose up before her, and Italy, and they were so vague that she hardly knew whether they were remembrances or dreams, and she was compelled by a force so exterior to herself that she looked round frightened, as if she believed she would find someone at her elbow. She did not seem to be alone, there seemed to be others in the room, presences from which she could not escape; she could not see them, but she felt them about her, and as she sought them with fearing eyes, voices seemed speaking inside her, and it was with extreme terror that she heard the proposal that she was to be one of God's virgins. The hell which opened on the other side of Owen ceased to frighten her. The devils waiting there for her soul grew less substantial, and thoughts and things seemed to converge more and more, to draw together and become one. She was aware of the hallucination in her brain, but could not repress it, nor all sorts of rapid questions and arguments. Suddenly a voice reminded her that if she were going to abandon the life of the soul for the life of the flesh, that she should accept the flesh wholly, and not subvert its intentions. She should become the mother of children. Life was concerned more intimately with children than with her art. But somehow it did not seem the same renunciation, and she stood perplexed before the enigma of her conscience.

She looked round the room, dreading and half believing in some diabolic influence at her elbow, but perceiving nothing, an ungovernable impulse took her, and her steps strayed to the door, in the desire and almost in the intention of going to London. But if she went there, how would she explain her visit?... Owen would understand; but if he were not in, she could not wait until he came in. She paused to consider the look of pleasure that would come upon his face when he came in and found her there. There would be just one look, and they would throw themselves into each other's arms. She was about to rush away, having forgotten all else but him, when she remembered her father. If she were to go now she must leave a letter for him explaining—telling him the story. And who would play the viola da gamba at his concerts? and there would be no one to see that he had his meals.

Was she or was she not going away with Owen to Paris on Thursday night? The agonising question continued at every moment to present itself. Whatever she was doing or saying, she was always conscious of it, and as the time drew near, with every hour, it seemed to approach and menace her. She seemed to feel it beating like a neuralgic pain behind her eyes; and though she laughed and talked a great deal, her father noticed that her animation was strained and nervous, and he noticed, too, that in no part of their conversation was she ever entirely with him, and he wondered what were the sights and scenes he faintly discerned in her changing eyes.

On getting up on Wednesday morning, she remembered that the best train from Dulwich was at three o'clock, and she asked herself why she had thought of this train, and that she should have thought of it seemed to her like an omen. Her father sat opposite, looking at her across the table. It was all so clear in her mind that she was ashamed to sit thinking these things, for thinking as clearly as she was thinking seemed equivalent to accomplishment; and the difference between what she thought and what she said was so repulsive to her that she was on the point of flinging herself at his feet several times.

There were times when the temptation seemed to have left her, when she smiled at her own weakness and folly; and having reproved herself sufficiently, she thought of other things. It seemed to her extraordinary why she should argue and trouble about a thing which she really had no intention of doing. But at that moment her heart told her that this was not so, that she would go to meet Owen in Berkeley Square, and she was again taken with an extraordinary inward trembling.

Our actions obey an unknown law, implicit in ourselves, but which does not conform to our logic. So we very often succeed in proving to ourselves that a certain course is the proper one for us to follow, in preference to another course, but, when it comes for us to act, we do not act as we intended, and we ascribe the discrepancy between what we think and what we do to a deficiency of will power. Man dares not admit that he acts according to his instincts, that his instincts are his destiny.

We make up our mind to change our conduct in certain matters, but we go on acting just the same; and in spite of every reason, Evelyn was still undecided whether she should go to meet Sir Owen. It was quite clear that it was wrong for her to go, and it seemed all settled in her mind; but at the bottom of her heart something over which she had no kind of control told her that in the end nothing could prevent her from going to meet him. She stopped, amazed and terrified, asking herself why she was going to do a thing which she seemed no longer even to desire.

In the afternoon some girl friends came to see her. She played and sang and talked to them, but they, too, noticed that she was never really with them, and her friends could see that she saw and heard things invisible and inaudible to them. In the middle of some trifling chatter—whether one colour or another was likely to be fashionable in the coming season—she had to put her hand in her pocket for her handkerchief, and happened to meet the key of the square, and it brought back to her in a moment the entire drama of her destiny. Was she going to take the three o'clock train to London, or to remain in Dulwich with her father? She thought that she would not mind whatever happened, if she only knew what would happen. Either lot seemed better to her than the uncertainty. She rattled on, talking with fictitious gaiety about the colour of bonnets and a party at which Julia had sung, not even hearing what she was saying. Wednesday evening passed with an inward vision so intense that all the outer world had receded from her, she was like one alone in a desert, and she ate without tasting, saw without seeing what she looked at, spoke without knowing what she was saying, heard without hearing what was said to her, and moved without knowing where she was going.

On Thursday morning the obsession of her destiny took all colour from her cheek, and her eyes were nervous.

"What is it, my girl?" Her father said, taking her hand, and the music he was tying up dropped on the floor. "Tell me, Evelyn; something, I can see, is the matter."

It was like the breaking of a spring. Something seemed to give way within her, and slipping on her knees, she threw her arms about him.

"I am very unhappy. I wish I were dead."

He strove to raise her from her knees, but the attitude expressed her feelings, and she remained, leaning her face against him. Nor could he coax any information from her. At last she said, raising her tearful eyes—

"If I were to leave you, father, you would never forgive me? But I am your only daughter, and you would forgive me; whatever happened, we should always love one another?"

"But why should you leave me?"

"But if I loved someone? I don't mean as I love you. I could never love anyone so tenderly; I mean quite differently. Don't make me say more. I am so ashamed of myself."

"You are in love with him?"

"Yes, and he has asked me to go away with him." And as she answered, she wondered at the quickness with which her father had guessed that it was Owen. He was such a clever man; the moment his thoughts were diverted from his music, he understood things as well as the most worldly, and she felt that he would understand her, that she must open her heart to him. "If I don't go away with him I shall die, or kill myself, or go mad. It is terrible to have to tell you these things, father, I know, but I must. I was ill when he went away to Greece, you remember. It was nothing but love of him."

"Did he not ask you to marry him?"

"No, he will never marry anyone."

"And that made no difference to you?"

"Oh, father, don't be angry, don't think me horrid. You are looking at me as if you never saw me before. I know I ought to have been angry when he asked me to go away with him, but somehow I wasn't. I don't know that I even wanted him to marry me. I want to go away and be a great singer, and he is not more to blame than I am. I can't tell lies. What is the use of telling lies? If I were to tell you anything else, it would be untrue."

"But are you going away with him?"

"I don't know. Not if I can help it;" and at that moment her eyes went to the portrait of her mother.

"You lost your mother very early, and I have neglected you. She ought to be here to protect you."

"No, no, father; she would not understand me as well as you do."

"So you are glad that she is not here?"

Evelyn nodded, and then she said—

"If he were to go away and I were left here again, I don't know what would become of me. It isn't my fault, father; I can't help it."

"I did not know that you were like this. Your mother—"

"Ah I mother and I are quite different. I am more like you, father. You can't blame me; you have been in love with women—with mother, at least—and ought to understand."

"Evelyn ... these are subjects that cannot be discussed between us."

The eyes of the mother watched them, and there was something in her cold, distant glance which went to their hearts, but they could not interpret its meaning.

"I either had to go away, father, telling you nothing, or I had to tell you everything."

"I will go to Sir Owen."

"No, father, you mustn't. Promise me you won't. I have trusted you, and you mustn't make me regret my trust. This is my secret." He was frightened by the strange light that appeared in her eyes, and he felt that an appeal to Owen would be like throwing oil on a flame. "You mustn't go to Sir Owen; you have promised you won't. I don't know what would happen if you did."

His daughter's confession had frightened him, and he knew not what answer to make to her. When the depths find voice we stand aghast, knowing neither ourselves nor those whom we have lived with always. He was caught in the very den of his being, and seemed at every moment to be turning over a leaf of his past life.

"If you had only patience, Evelyn—ah! you have heard what I am going to say so often, but I don't blame your incredulity. That was why I did not tell you before."

"What has happened?" she asked eagerly; for she, too, wished for a lull in this stress of emotion.

"Well," he said, "Monsignor Mostyn, the great Roman prelate, who has just arrived from Rome, and is staying with the Jesuits, shares all my views regarding the necessity of a musical reformation. He believes that a revival of Palestrina and Vittoria would be of great use to the Catholic cause in England. He says that he can secure the special intervention of the Pope, and, what is much more important, he will subscribe largely, and has no doubt that sufficient money can be collected."

Evelyn listened, smiling through her sorrow, like a bird when the rain has ceased for a moment, and she asked questions, anxious to delay the inevitable return to her own unhappy condition. She was interested in the luck that had come to her father, and was sorry that her conduct had clouded or spoilt it. At last a feeling of shame came upon them that at such a time they should be engaged in speaking of such singularly irrelevant topics. She could see that the same thought had come upon him, and she noticed his trim, square figure, and the old blue jacket which she had known so many years, as he walked up and down the room. He was getting very grey lately, and when she returned he might be quite white.

"Oh, father, father," she exclaimed, covering her face with her hands, "how unhappy I am."

"I shall send a telegram to Monsignor saying I can't see him this morning."

"Ah! you have to see him this morning;" and she did not know whether she was glad or sorry. Perhaps she was more frightened than either, for the appointment left her quite free to go to London by the three o'clock train.

"I can't leave you alone."

"Darling, if I had wanted to deceive you, I should have told you nothing; and, however you were to watch me, I could always get away if I chose."

She was right, he could not keep her by force, he could do nothing; shame prevented him from appealing to her affection for him, for it was in his interest she should stay. After all, Sir

Owen will make a great singer of her. The thought had come and gone before he was aware, and to atone for this involuntary thought he spoke to her about her religion.

"I used to be religious," she said, "but I am religious no longer. I can hardly say my prayers now. I said them last night, but this morning I couldn't."

He passed his hand across his eyes, and said—

"It seems all like a bad dream."

He felt that he ought to stay with her, and at the same time he felt that she was right; that his intervention would be unavailing, for the struggle resided in herself. But if she should learn from Sir Owen to forget him; if he were to lose her altogether; if she should never return? The thought of such a calamity was the rudest blow of all, and the possibility of her going away for a time, shocking as it was, seemed almost light beside it. He struggled against these thoughts, for he hated and was ashamed of them. They came into his mind unasked, and he hoped that they represented nothing of his real feeling. Suddenly his face changed, he remembered his passion for her mother. He had suffered what Evelyn was suffering now. She had divined it by some instinct; true, they were very much like each other. Nothing would have kept him from Gertrude. But all that was so long ago. Good God! It was not the same thing, and at the very same moment he regretted that it was not a music lesson he was going to, for an appointment with Monsignor introduced a personal interest, and if he were not to stay by her, it would seem that he was indifferent to what became of her.

"No, Evelyn, I shan't go; I will stay here, I will stay by you."

"But I don't know that I am going away with Sir Owen."

"You said just now that you were."

"Did I say so? Father, you must keep your appointment with Monsignor, and you must say nothing to Owen if you should meet him; you promise me that? It rests with me, father, it is all in the heart."

He stood looking at her, twisting his beard into a point, and while she wondered whether he would go or stay, she admired the delicacy of his hand.

"Think of the disgrace you will bring upon me, and just at the time, too, when Monsignor is beginning to see that a really great choir in London—

"Then, father, you do think that my going away will prejudice him against you?"

"I don't say that. I mean that this time seems less—Of course you cannot go. It is very shocking that we should be discussing the subject together."

A sudden fortitude came upon her, and a sudden desire to sacrifice herself to her father.

"Then, father, I shall stay. I will do nothing that will interfere with your work."

"My dearest child, it is not for me—it is yourself—"

She threw herself into his arms, begging him to forgive her. She wanted to stay with him. She loved him better than her voice, better than anything in the world. He did not answer, and when she raised her eyes she caught a slight look of doubt upon his face, and wondered what it could mean. At the very moment she had determined to stay with him, and forfeit her love and her art for his sake, a keen sense of his responsibility towards her was borne in upon him, and the feeling within him crushed like a stone that he could never do anything for her, nor anything else except, perchance, achieve that reformation of Church music upon which his heart was set. He understood in that instant that she was sacrificing all her life to his, and he feared the sacrifice she was making, and anticipated in some measure the remorse he would suffer. But he dared not think that she had better go and achieve her destiny in the only way that was open to her. He urged himself to believe that she was acting rightly, it was impossible for him to hold any other opinion. The thoughts that came upon him he strove to think were merely nervous accidents, and he forced himself to accept the irresponsibility of the sacrifice. He wished not to be selfish, but, however he acted, he always seemed to be acting in his own interest. Since she had promised him not to go away with Sir Owen, he was quite free to keep his appointment with Monsignor, and he gathered up his music, and then he let it fall again, fearing that she would interpret his action to mean that he was glad to get away.

She besought him to go; she said she was tired and wanted to lie down, and all the while he spoke she was tortured with an uncertainty as to whether she was speaking the truth or not; and he had not been gone many minutes when she remembered that she had not told him that Owen had asked her to meet him that very afternoon in Berkeley Square, and that the key of the square lay in her pocket. Like one with outstretched hands, striving to feel her way in the dark, she sought to discover in her soul whether she had deliberately suppressed or accidentally omitted the fact of her appointment with Owen. It might be that the conversation had taken a sudden turn, at the moment she was about to tell him, for the thought had crossed her mind that she ought to tell him. Then she seemed to lose count of everything, and was unable to distinguish truth from falsehood.

To increase her difficulties, she remembered that she had betrayed Owen's confidence. She could not quite admit to herself that she had a right to tell her father that it was he. But he had guessed it.... It seemed impossible to do right. Perhaps there was no right and no wrong, as Owen said; and a wish rose from the bottom of her heart that it might be so, and then she feared she had been guilty of blasphemy. Perhaps she should warn Owen of her indiscretion, and she thought of herself going to London for this purpose, and smiled as she detected the deception which she was trying to practise on herself.

There was nothing for her to do in the house, and when she had walked an hour in the ornamental park, she strayed into the picture gallery, and stood a long time looking at the Dutch lady who was playing the virginal, and whose life passed peacefully apparently without any emotion, in a silent house amid rich furniture. But she was soon drawn to the Watteau, where a rich evening hushes about a beautiful carven colonnade, under which the court is seated; where gallants wear deep crimson and azure cloaks, and the ladies striped gowns of dainty refinement; where all the rows are full of amorous intrigue, and vows are being pleaded, and mandolines are playing; where a fountain sings in the garden and dancers perform their pavane or minuet, the lady holding out her striped skirt, and the gentleman bowing to her with a deference that seems a little mocking. An hour of pensive attitudes and whispered confidences, and over every fan a face wonders if there is truth in love.

"It is strange," Evelyn thought, "how one woman lives in obscurity, and another in admiration and success. That woman playing the virginal is not ugly; if she were dressed like these seated under the colonnade, she would be quite as pretty; but she is not as clever, Owen would say, or she wouldn't be playing the virginal in a village. It is strange how I remember everything he says."

She thought of herself as the lady in the centre, the one that looked like the queen, and to whom a tall young man in a lovely cloak was being introduced, and then imagined herself one of the less important ladies who, for the sake of her beautiful voice, would be surrounded and admired by all men; she would create bitter jealousies and annoy a number of women, which, however, she would endeavour to overcome by giving back to them the several lovers whom she did not want for herself.

The life in this picture would be hers if she took the three o'clock train and went to Berkeley Square. The life in the other picture would be hers if she remained in Dulwich.

Only one more hour remained between her and the moment when she would be getting into the train, and on going out of the gallery her senses all seemed awake at the same moment; she saw and felt and heard with equal distinctness, and she seemed to be walking automatically, to be moving forward as if on wheels. She met a friend on her way home, but it was like talking to one across a river or gulf; she wondered what she had said, and hardly heard, on account of the tumult within her, what was being said to her. When she got home, she noticed that she did not take off her hat; and she ate her lunch without tasting it. Her thoughts were loud as the clock which ticked out the last minutes she was to remain at home, and trying not to hear them, she turned to the Monna Lisa, wondering what Owen meant when he had said that the hesitating smile in the picture was like her smile. Her thoughts ran on ticking in her brain like the clock in the corner of a room, and though she would have given anything to stop thinking, she could not.

Every moment the agony of anxiety and nervousness increased, and it was almost a relief when the clock pointed to the time when she would have to go to the station. She looked round the room, a great despair mounted into her eyes, and she walked quickly out of the house. As she went down the street she tried to think that she was going to Owen to tell him she had told her father that she was resolved to give him up. It seemed no longer difficult to do this, for, on looking into her mind, she could discover neither desire nor love, nor any wish to see him. She was only conscious of a nervous agitation which she could not control, and through this waking nightmare she walked steadily, thinking with extraordinary clearness. In the railway carriage the passengers noticed her pallor, and they wondered what her trouble was, and at Victoria the omnibus conductor just saved her from being run over. The omnibus jogged on, stopping now and then for people to get in and out, and Evelyn wondered at the extraordinary mechanism of life, and she took note of everyone's peculiarities, wondering what were their business and desires, and wondering also at the conductor's voice crying out the different parts of the town the omnibus would pass through.

"This is Berkeley Street, miss, if you are getting out here."

She waited a few minutes at the corner, and then wandered down the street, asking herself if it was yet too late to turn back.

The sun glanced through the foliage, and glittered on the cockades of the coachmen and on the shining hides of the horses. It was the height of the season, and the young beauties of the year, and the fashionable beauties of the last decade, lay back, sunning themselves under the shade of their parasols. The carriages came round the square close to the curb, under the waving branches, and, waiting for an opportunity to cross, Evelyn's eyes followed an unusually beautiful carriage, drawn by a pair of chestnut horses. She did not see the lady's face, but she wore a yellow dress, and the irises in her bonnet nodded over the hood of the carriage. This lady, graceful and idle, seemed to mean something, but what? Evelyn thought of the picture of the colonnade in the gallery.

The men to whom the stately servants opened the doors wore long frock coats pinched at the waist, and they swung their canes and carried their thick, yellow gloves in their hands. They were all like Owen. They all lived as he lived, for pleasure; they were all here for the season, for balls and dinner parties, for love-making and the opera.

"They are the people," Evelyn thought, "who will pay thousands to hear me sing. They are the people who will invite me to their houses. If my voice is cultivated, if I ever go abroad."

She ran across the street and walked under the branches until she came to a gate. But why not go straight to the house? She did not know.... She was at the gate, and the square looked green and cool. The gate swung to and closed with a snap; but she had the key and could leave when she liked, and worn out with various fears she walked aimlessly about the grass plots. There was no one in the square, so if he were watching for her he could not fail to see her. Once more a puerile hope crossed her mind fitfully, that perhaps it would be as well if he failed to see her. But no, since she had gone so far she was determined to go on to the end, and before this determination, her spirits revived, and she waited for him to come to her. But for shyness she did not dare to look round, and the minutes she walked under the shady trees were very delightful, for she was penetrated with an intimate conviction that she would not be disappointed. And one of the moments of her life that fixed itself most vividly on her mind was when she saw Owen coming towards her through the trees. He was so tall and thin, and walked so gracefully; there was something in his walk that delighted her; it seemed to her that it was like the long, soft stride of a cat.

"I am glad you have come," he said.

But she could not answer. A moment afterwards he said, and she noticed that his voice trembled, "You are coming in to tea?"

Again she did not answer, and thinking it safer to take things for granted, he walked towards the gate. He was at the point of saying, "That is my house," but he checked himself, thinking that silence was safer than speech. He could not get the gate open, and while he wrenched at the lock, he dreaded that delay might give her time to change her mind. But Evelyn was now quite determined. Her brain seemed to effervesce and her blood to bubble with joy, a triumphant happiness filled her, for no doubt remained that she was going to Paris to-night.
"Let us have tea as soon as possible, and tell Stanley to bring the brougham round at once."
"Why did you order the brougham?"
"Are you not—? I thought—"
The brilliancy of her eyes answered him, and he took her hands.
"Then you are coming with me to Paris?"
"Yes, if you like, Owen, anywhere.... But let me kiss you."
And she stood in a beautiful, amorous attitude, her arm thrown about his neck, her eyes aflame.
"The brougham will be round in half an hour. There is a train at six to Dover. It gets there at nine. So we shall have time to dine at the Lord Warden, and get on board the boat before the mail arrives."
"But I have no clothes."
"The night is fine; we shall have a lovely crossing; you will only want a shawl and a rug.... But what are you thinking of? You don't regret?"
His eyes were tenderer than hers. She perceived in their grey lights a tenderness, as affection which seemed in contradiction to his nature as she had hitherto understood it. Even the thought flashed dimly in the background of her mind that his love was truer than hers; his cynicism, which had often frightened her, seemed to have vanished; indeed, there was something different in him from the man she had hitherto known—a difference which was rendered evident by the accent with which he said—
"Dearest Evelyn, this is the happiest moment of my life. I have spent two terrible days wondering if you would come."
"Did you, dear? Did you think of me? Are you fond of me?"
He pressed her hand, and with one look answered her question, and she saw the streets flash past her—for they were in the brougham driving to Charing Cross. There was still the danger of meeting Mr. Innes at the station; but the danger was slight. She knew of no business that would take him to Charing Cross, and they were thankful the train did not start from Victoria. Owen called to his coachman to hasten. They had wasted, he said, too much time over the tea-table, and might miss the train. But they did not miss it, and through the heat of the long, summer afternoon the slow train jogged peacefully through the beautiful undulations of the southern counties. The sky was quiet gold and torquoise blue, and far away were ruby tinted clouds. A peaceful light floated over the hillsides and dozed in the hollows, and the happiness of the world seemed eternal. Deep, cool shadows filled the copses, and the green corn was a foot high in the fields, and every gate and hedgerow wore a picturesque aspect. Evelyn and Owen sat opposite each other, talking in whispers, for they were not alone; they had not been in time to secure a private carriage. The delight that filled their hearts was tender as the light in the valleys and the hill sides. But Evelyn's feelings were the more boisterous, for she was entering into life, whereas Owen thought he was at last within reach of the ideal he had sought from the beginning of his life.
This feeling, which was very present in his mind, appeared somehow through his eyes and in his manner, and even through the tumult of her emotions she was vaguely aware that he was even nicer than she had thought. She had never loved him so much as now; and again the thought passed that she had not known him before, and far down in her happiness she wondered which was the true man.

CHAPTER TEN

From Dover they telegraphed to Mr. Innes—"Your daughter is safe. She has gone abroad to study singing;" and at midnight they were on board the boat. The night was strangely calm and blue; a little mist was about, and they stood watching the circle of light which the vessel shed upon the water, moving ever onwards, with darkness before and after.
"Dearest, what are you thinking of?"
"Of father. He has received our message by now. Poor dad, he won't sleep to-night. To-morrow they will all have the news, and on Sunday in church they will 'be talking about it.'"
"But your voice would have been wasted. Your father would have reproached himself; he would think he had sacrificed you to his music."
"Which wouldn't be true."
"True or false, he'd think it. Besides, it would be true in a measure."
Evelyn told Owen of her interview with her father that morning, and he said—
"You acted nobly."
"Nobly? Owen!"
"There was nobility in your conduct."
"He'll be so lonely, so lonely. And," she exclaimed, clasping her hands, "who will play the viola da gamba?"
"When I bring you back a great singer ... there'll be substantial consolation in that."
"But he won't close his eyes to-night, and he'll miss me at breakfast and at dinner—his poor dinner all by himself."
"But you don't want to go back to him? You love me as much as your father?"
They pressed each other's hands, and, striving to see through the blue hollow of the night, they thought of the adventure of the voyage they had undertaken. Spectral ships loomed up and vanished in the spectral stillness; and only within the little circle of light could they perceive the waves over which they floated. The moon drifted, and a few stars showed through the white wrack. Whither were their lives striving? She had thought that her life in Dulwich must endure for ever, but it had passed from her like a dream; it had snapped suddenly, and she floated on another voyage, and still the same mystery encircled her as before. She knew that Owen loved her. This was the little circle of life in which she lived, and beyond it she might imagine any story she pleased.
Her thoughts reverted to the Eastern dreamer, and she realised that she was living through the tragedy which he had written about a thousand years ago in his rose garden. She might imagine what she pleased—that she was going to become a great singer, that artistic success was the harbour whither she steered, but in truth she did not know. She could not believe such an end to be her destiny. Then what was her destiny? All she had ever known was behind her, had floated into the darkness as easily as those spectral ships; her religion, her father, her home, all had vanished, and all she knew was that she was sailing through the darkness without them. Seen for a moment in the light of the high moon, and then in shrouded blue light, a great ship came and went, and Evelyn clung to the arm of her lover. He folded the rough shawl he had bought at Charing Cross about her shoulders. The lights of Calais harbour grew larger, the foghorn snorted, the vessel veered, and there was preparation on board; the crowd thickened, and as the night grew fainter they saw between the dawn and the silvery moon the long low sandhills of the French coast. The vessel veered and entered the harbour, and as she churned alongside the windy piers, the mystery with which a moonlit sea had filled their hearts passed, and they were taken in an access of happiness; and they cried to each other for sheer joy as they struggled up the gangway.
They were in France! their life of love was before them! He could hardly take his eyes off the delicious girl; and soon two or three waiters attended at her first meal, her first acquaintance

with French food and wine! Owen was known on the line, and the obsequiousness shown to him flattered her, and it was thrilling to read his name on the window of their carriage. Her foot was on the footboard, and seeing the empty carriage the thought struck her, "We shall be alone; he'll be able to kiss me." And, her heart beating with fear and delight, she got in and sat speechless in a corner.

As the train moved out of the station he took her hand, and said that he hoped they would be very happy together. She looked at him, and in her eyes there was a little questioning, almost cynical look, which perplexed him. The part he had to play was a difficult one, and on board the boat, in the pauses of their conversation, he had felt that his future influence over Evelyn depended upon his conduct during the forthcoming week. This foresight had its origin in his temperament. It was his temperament to suggest and to lead, and as he talked to her of Madame Savelli, the great singing mistress, and Lady Duckle, a lady whom he hoped to induce to come to Paris to chaperon her, he saw the hotel sitting-room at the moment when the waiter, having brought in the coffee, and delayed his departure as long as he possibly could, would finally close the door. Nervousness dilated her eyes, and his thoughts were often far from his words. He often had to catch his breath, and he quailed before the dread interrogation which often looked out of her eyes. They had passed Boulogne, and through the dawn, vague as an opal, appeared a low range of hills, and as these receded, the landscape flattened out into a bleak, morose plain.

What lives were lived yonder in that low grange, crouching under the five melancholy poplars? An hour later father and son would go forth in that treacherous quaking boat, lying amid the sedge, and cast their net into one of those black pools. But these pictures of primeval simplicities which the landscape evoked were not in accord with a journey toward love and pleasure. Evelyn and Owen did not dare to contrast their lives with those of the Picardy peasants, and that they should see not roses and sunshine, but a broken and abandoned boat amid the sedge, and mournful hills faintly outlined against the heavy, lowering sky seemed to them significant. They watched the filmy, diffused, opal light of the dawn, and they were filled with nervous expectation. The man who appeared at the end of the plain in his primitive guise of a shepherd driving his flock towards the hard thin grass of the uplands seemed menacing and hostile. His tall felt hat seemed like a helmet in the dusk, his crook like a lance, and Owen understood that the dawn was the end of the truce, that the battle with Nature was about to begin again. At that moment she was thinking that if she had done wrong in leaving home, the sin was worth all the scruples she might endure, and she rejoiced that she endured none. He folded her in his rug. The train seemed to stop, and the names of the stations sounded dim in her ears. Her perceptions rose and sank, and, as they sank, the villa engarlanded, of which Owen had spoken, seemed there. Its gates, though unbarred, were impassable. She thought she was shaking them, but when she opened her eyes it was Owen telling her that they had passed the fortifications, that they were in Paris.

He had brought with him only his dressing-bag, so they were not detained at the Customs. His valet was following with the rest of his luggage, and as soon as she had had a few hours' sleep, he would take her to different shops. She clung on to his arm. Paris seemed very cold and cheerless, and she did not like the tall, haggard houses, nor the slattern waiter arranging chairs in front of an early café, nor the humble servant clattering down the pavement in wooden shoes. She saw these things with tired eyes, and she was dimly aware of a decrepit carriage drawn by two decrepit horses, and then of a great hotel built about a courtyard. She heard Owen arguing about rooms, but it seemed to her that a room where there was a bed was all that she desired.

But the blank hotel bedroom, so formal and cheerless, frightened her, and it seemed to her that she could not undress and climb into that high bed, and she had no clothes—not even a nightgown. The chambermaid brought her a cup of chocolate, and when she had drunk it she fell asleep, seeing the wood fire burning, and thinking how tired she was.

It was the chambermaid knocking. It was time for her to get up, and Owen had sent her a brush and comb. She could only wash her face with the corner of a damp towel. Her stockings were full of dust; her chemise was like a rag—all, she reflected, the discomforts of an elopement. As she brushed out her hair with Owen's brush, she wondered what he could see to like in her. She admired his discretion in not coming to her room. But really, this hotel seemed as unlikely a place for love-making as the gloomy plain of Picardy.

She was pinning on her hat when he knocked. He told her that he had been promised some nice rooms on the second floor later in the day, and they went to breakfast at Voisin's. The rest of the day was spent getting in and out of cabs.

They took the shops as they came. The first was a boot and shoe maker, and in a few moments between four and five hundred francs had been spent. This seemed to Evelyn an unheard-of extravagance. Tea-gowns at five hundred and six hundred francs apiece were a joy to behold and a delicacy to touch. The discovery that every petticoat cost fifty francs seriously alarmed her. They visited the bonnet shop later in the afternoon. By that time she had grown hardened, and it seemed almost natural to pay two hundred francs for a hat. Two of her dresses were bought ready made. A saleswoman held out the skirt of a flowered silk, which she was to wear that night at the opera; another stood by, waiting for her and Owen to approve of the stockings she held in her hands. Some were open-work and embroidered, and the cheapest were fifteen francs a pair. It had to be decided whether these should be upheld by suspenders or by garters. Owen's taste was for garters, and the choice of a pair filled them with a pleasurable embarrassment. In the next shop—it was a glove shop—as she was about to consult him regarding the number of buttons, she remembered, in a sudden moment of painful realisation, the end for which they had met. She turned pale, and the words caught in her throat. Fortunately, his eyes were turned from her, and he perceived nothing of the nervous agitation which consumed her; but on leaving the shop, a little way down the street, when she had recovered herself sufficiently to observe him, she perceived that he was suffering from the same agitation. He seemed unable to fix his attention upon the present moment. He seemed to have wandered far afield, and when with an effort he returned from the ever nearing future, he seemed like a man coming out of another atmosphere—out of a mist!

At six they were back at their hotel, surveying the sitting-rooms, already littered with cardboard boxes. But he hurried her off to the Rue de la Paix, saying that she must have some jewels. Trays of diamonds, rubies, emeralds and pearls were presented to her for choice.

"You're not looking," he said, feigning surprise. "You take no interest in jewels; aren't you well?"

"Yes, dearest; but I'm bewildered."

When they returned to the hotel, the gown she was to wear that night at the opera had arrived. "It must have cost twenty pounds, and I usen't to spend much more than that in a whole year on my clothes."

Neither cared to go to the opera; but half-past ten seemed to him quite a proper time for them to return home, and for this makeshift propriety he was so bored with "Lohengrin" that he never saw it afterwards with the old pleasure; and Evelyn's glances told of the wasted hours. While Elsa sang her dream, he realised the depth of his folly. If something were to happen? If they were to find Mr. Innes waiting at the door of the hotel? If he were robbed of her, it would serve him right. The aria in the second act was beautifully sung, and it helped them to forget; but with the rather rough chorus of men in the second half of the second act, their nervous boredom began again, and Evelyn's face was explicit.

"You're tired, Evelyn; you're too tired to listen."

"Yes, I'm tired, let's go; give me my cloak."

"I don't care much for the nuptial music," he remarked accidentally; and then, feeling obliged to take advantage of the slip of the tongue, he said, "Lohengrin and Elsa are in the bridal chamber in the next act."

He felt her hand tremble on his arm.

"In two years hence you'll be singing here.... But you don't answer."

"Owen, dear, I'm thinking of you now."

Her answer was a delicious flattery, and he hurried her to the carriage. The moment his arm was about her she leaned over him, and when their lips parted he uttered a little cry. But in the middle of the sitting-room she stopped and faced him, barring the way. He took her cloak from her shoulders.

"Owen, dear, if anything should happen."

But it was not till the third night that they entered into the full possession of their delight. Every night after seemed more exquisite than the last, like sunset skies, as beautiful and as unrememberable. She could recall only the moment when from the threshold he looked back, nodded a good-night, and then told her he would call her when it was time to get up. Then in a happy weariness she closed her eyes; and when they opened she closed them quickly, and curled herself into dreams and thoughts of Owen.

They were going to the races, and he would come and tell her when it was time to get up. She hoped this would not be till she had dreamed to the end of her dream. But her eyes opened, and she saw him in his dressing gown with blue facings standing in the middle of the room watching her. His little smile was in his eyes; they seemed to say, So there you are; I haven't lost you.

"You're the loveliest thing," he said, "in God's earth."

"Dearest Owen, I'm very fond of you;" and there was a plaintive and amorous cry in her voice which found echo in the movement with which she threw herself into her lover's arms, and laid her head upon his shoulder.

"I've never seen such a hand, it is like a spray of fern; and those eyes—look at me, Eve."

"Why do you call me Eve? No one ever called me Eve before."

"Sometimes they are as green as sea water, at other times they are grey or nearly grey, most often they are hazel green. And your feet are like hands, and your ankle—see, I can span it between forefinger and thumb.... Your hair is faint, like flowers. Your throat is too thick, you have the real singer's throat; thousands of pounds lie hidden in that whiteness, which is mine—the whiteness, not the gold."

"How you know how to praise, Owen!"

"I love that sweet indecision of chin."

"A retreating chin means want of character."

"You have not what I call a retreating chin, the line merely deflects. Nothing more unlovable than a firm chin. It means a hard, unimaginative nature. Eve, you're adorable. Where should I find a sweetheart equal to you?"

"That isn't the way I want you to love me."

"Isn't it? Are you sure of that?"

"I don't know—perhaps not. But why do you make me say these things?"

She held his face between her hands, and moved aside his moustache with her lips.... Suddenly freeing herself from his embraces, she said, "I don't want to kiss you any more. Let's talk."

"Dearest, do you know what time is it? You must get up and dress yourself. It is past nine o'clock. We are going to the races. I'll send you the chambermaid. You promise me to get up?"

It was these little authoritative airs that enchanted her remembrance of him; and while the chambermaid poured out her bath she thought of the gown she was going to wear. She knew that she had some pink silk stockings to match it, but it took her a long while to find them. She opened all the wrong boxes. "It's extraordinary," she thought, "how long it takes one to dress sometimes; all one's things get wrong." And when hooking the skirt she suddenly remembered she had no parasol suitable to the gown. It was Sunday; it would be impossible to buy one. There was nothing for it but to send for Owen. If there was anything wrong with her gown he would give her no peace. He wished her to wear a flower-embroidered dress, but her fancy was set on a pale yellow muslin, and it amused her to get cross with him and to send him out of the room; but when the door closed she was moved to run after him. The grave question as to what she would wear dispelled other thoughts. She must be serious; and to please him she decided she would wear the gown he liked, and as she fixed the hat that went with it she admired the contrast of its purple with her rich hair. Owen was always right. She had never thought that she could look so well, and it was a happy moment when he took her by both hands and said—

"Dearest, you are delicious—quite delicious. You'll be the prettiest woman at Longchamps to-day."

She asked for tea, but he said they were in France, and must conform to French taste. When Marie Antoinette was informed that the people wanted bread, etc., Evelyn thought Marie Antoinette must have been a cruel woman. But she liked chocolate and the brioche, and henceforth they were brought to her bedside, and in a Sèvres service, a present from Owen.

"When they had finished the little meal he rang for writing material, and said—

"Now, my dear Evelyn, you must write to your father."

"*Must* I? What shall I say? Oh, Owen, I cannot write. If I did, father would come over here, and then—"

"I'll tell you what to say. I'll dictate the letter you ought to write. You need not give him any address, but you must let him know you're well, and why you intend to remain abroad. It is by relieving his mind on these subjects that you'll save yourself from the vexation of his hunting you up here.... Come, now," he said, noticing the agonised and bewildered look on Evelyn's face, "this is the only disagreeable hour in the day—you must put up with it. Here is the pen. Now write—

"'My DEAR FATHER,—I should be happy in Paris, very happy, if it were not for the knowledge of the grief that my flight must have occasioned you. Of course I have acted very wrongly, very wickedly—'"

"But," said Evelyn, "you told me I was acting rightly, that to do otherwise would be madness."

"Yes, and I only told you the truth. But in writing to your father you must adopt the conventional tone. There's no use in trying to persuade your father you did right.... I don't know, though. Scratch out 'I have acted wrongly and very wickedly,' and write—

"'I will not ask you to think that I have acted otherwise than wrongly, for, of course, as a father you can hold no other opinion, but being also a clever man, an artist, you will perhaps be inclined to admit that my wrong-doing is not so irreparable a wrong-doing as it might have been in other and easily imagined circumstances.'" Full stop.

"You've got that—'so irreparable a wrong-doing as it might have been in other and easily imagined circumstances'?"

"Yes."

"'Father dear, you know that if I had remained in Dulwich my voice would have been wasted, not through my fault or yours, but through the fault of circumstances.'"

"You have got circumstances a few lines higher up, so put 'through the fault of fate.'"

"Father will never believe that I wrote this letter."

"That doesn't matter—the truth is the truth from whoever it comes."

"'We should have gone on deceiving ourselves, or trying to deceive ourselves, hoping as soon as the concerts paid that I should go abroad with a proper chaperon. You know, father dear, how we used to talk, both knowing well that no such thing could be. The years would have slipped by, and at five-and-thirty, when it would have been too late, I should have found myself exactly where I was when mother died. You would have reproached yourself, you would have suffered remorse, we should have both been miserable; whereas now I hope that we shall both be happy. You will bring about a revival of Palestrina, and I shall sing opera. Be reasonable, father, and remember that it had to be. Write to me if you can; to hear from you will make me very happy. But do not try to seek me out and endeavour to induce me to return home. Any meeting between us now would merely mean intolerable suffering to both of us, and it would serve no purpose whatever. A little later, when I have succeeded, when I am a great singer, I will come and see you, that is to say if you will see me. Meanwhile; for a year or two we had better not meet, but I'll write constantly, and shall look forward to your letters. Again, my dear father, I beseech you to be reasonable; everything will come right in the end. I will not conceal from you the fact that Sir Owen Asher advised me to this step. He is very fond of me, and is determined to help me in every way. When he brings me back to England a great singer, he hopes you will try to look on his fault with as much leniency as may be. He asks me to warn you against speaking of him in connection with me, for any accusation brought against him will injure me. He intends to provide me with a proper chaperon. I need not mention her name; suffice it to say that she is a very grand lady, so appearances will be preserved. No one need know anything for certain if you do not tell them. If you will promise to do this, I will send the name of the lady with whom I am going to live. You can say that I am living with her; her name will be a sufficient cloak—everyone will be satisfied. Interference can be productive of no good, remember that; let things take their natural course, and they will come right in the end. If you decide to do as I ask you, write at once to me, and address your letter to 31 Rue Faubourg St Honore, care of Monsieur Blanco.—Always, dear father, Your affectionate daughter,—EVELYN INNES.'"

"How clever you are," she said, looking up. "You have written just the kind of letter that will influence father. I have lived with father all my life, and yet I couldn't have known how to write that letter. How did you think of it?"

"I've put the case truthfully, haven't I? Now, do you copy out that letter and address it; meanwhile I'll go round to Voisin's and order breakfast. Try to have it finished by the time I get back. We'll post it on our way."

She promised that she would do so, but instead sat a long while with the letter in her hands. It was so unlike herself that she could not bring herself to send it. It would not satisfy her father, he would sooner receive something from her own familiar heart, and, obeying a sudden impulse, she wrote—

"My DARLING,—What must you think of me, I wonder! that I am an ungrateful girl? I hope not. I don't think you would be so unjust as to think such things of me. I have been very wicked, but I have always loved you, father, and never more than now; and had anything in the world been able to stop me, it would have been my love of you. But, father dear, it was just as I told you; I was determined to resist the temptation if I could, but when the time came I could not. I did my best, indeed I did. I went through agony after agony after you left, and in the end I had to go whether I desired it or not. I could not have stopped in Dulwich any longer; if I had I should have died, and then you would have lost me altogether. You would not have liked to see me pine away, grow white, and lie coughing on the sofa like poor mother. No, you would not. It would have killed you. You remember how ill I was last Easter when he was away in the Mediterranean, darling. We've always been pals, we've always told each other everything, we never had any secrets, and never shall. I should have died if I hadn't gone away. Now I've told you everything—isn't that so?—and when I come back a great success, you'll come and hear me sing. My success would mean very little if you were not there. I would sooner see your dear, darling face in a box than any crowned head in Europe. If I were only sure that you would forgive me. Everything else will turn out right. Owen will be good to me, I shall get on; I have little fear on that score. If I could only know that you were not too lonely, that you were not grieving too much. I shall write to Margaret and beg her to look after you. But she is very careless, and the grocer often puts down things in his book that we never had. A couple of years, and then we shall see each other again. Do you think, darling, you can live all that time without me? I must try to live that time without you. It will be hard to do so, I shall miss you dreadfully, so if you could manage to write to me, not too cross a letter, it would make a great deal of difference. Of course, you are thinking of the disgrace I have brought on you. There need be none. Owen is going to provide me with a chaperon—a lady, he says, in the best society. I will send you her name next week, as soon as Owen hears from her. He may hear to-morrow, and if you say that I'm living with her, no one will know anything. It is deceitful, I know; I told Owen so, but he says that we are not obliged to take the whole world into our confidence. I don't like it, but I suppose if one does the things one must put up with the consequences. Now, I must say good-bye. I've expressed myself badly, but you'll know what I mean—that I love you very dearly, that I hope you'll forgive me, and be glad to see me when I come back, that I shall always be,—Your affectionate daughter,—EVELYN."

She put the letter into an envelope, and was addressing it when Owen came into the room.

"Have you copied the letter, dear?"

She looked at him inquiringly, and he wondered at her embarrassment.

"No," she said, "I have written quite a different letter. Yours was very clever, of course, but it was not like me. I've written a stupid little letter, but one which will please father better."

"I daresay you're right. If your father suspected the letter was dictated by me he would resent it."

"That's just what I thought."

"Let me see the letter you have written."

"No; don't look at it. I'd rather you didn't."

"Why, dearest? Because there's something about me in it?"

"No, indeed. I would not write anything about you that I wouldn't show you. No; what I don't want you to see is about myself."

"About yourself! Well, as you like, don't show me anything you don't want to."

"But I don't like to have secrets from you, Owen; I hate secrets."

"One of these days you'll tell me what you've written. I'm quite satisfied." He raised her face and kissed her tenderly, and she felt that she loved him better for his well-assumed indifference. Then they went downstairs, and she admired her dress in the long glasses on the landings. She listened to his French as he asked for a stamp. The courtyard was full of sunlight and carriages. The pages pushed open the glass doors for them to pass, and, tingling with health and all the happiness and enchantment of love, she walked by his side under the arcade—glad when, in walking, they came against each other—swinging her parasol pensively, wondering what happy word to say, a little perplexed that she should have a secret from him, and all the while healthily hungry. Suddenly she recognised the street as the one where they had dined on Friday night. He pushed open a white-painted door, and it seemed to her that all the white-aproned waiters advanced to meet her; and the one who drew the table forward that she might pass seemed to fully appreciate the honour of serving them. A number of *hors d'oeuvres* were placed before her, but she only ate bread and butter and a radish, until Owen insisted on her trying the *filets d'anchois*—the very ones she was originally most averse from. The sole was cooked very elaborately in a rich brown sauce. The tiny chicken which followed it was first shown to her in a tin saucepan; then the waiter took it away and carved it at a side table. She enjoyed the melon which, for her sake, ended instead of beginning the meal, as Owen said it should.

An Englishman, a friend of Owen's, sat at the next table, and she could see he regretted that Owen had not introduced him. Most of his conversation seemed designed for that end, and when they got up to go, his eyes surely said, "Well, I wish that he had introduced us; I think we should have got on together." And the eyes of the young man who sat at the opposite table said, as plain as any words, "I'd have given anything to have been introduced! Shall we ever meet again?"

So her exit was very thrilling; and no sooner were they on the pavement than another surprise was in store for her.

A smart coachman touched his hat, and Owen stepped back for her to get into the victoria.

"But this is not our carriage?"

"You did not think we were going to the Lonchamps in a *fiacre*, did you? This is your carriage—I bought these horses yesterday for you."

"You bought this carriage and these horses for me, Owen?"

"Yes, dear, I did; don't let's waste time. *Aux courses!*"

"Owen, dear, I cannot accept such a present. I appreciate your kindness, but you will not ask me to accept this carriage and horses."

"Why not?"

Evelyn thought for some time before answering.

"It would only make people think that I was an amateur. The fine clothes you have bought me I shall not be able to wear, except when I want you to think me nice. I shall have to learn Italian, of which I don't know a word, and French, of which I know very little."

Owen looked at her, at once pleased and surprised.

"You're quite right," he said; "this carriage and these horses are unsuitable to your present circumstances. The chestnuts took my fancy ... however, I haven't paid for them. I'll send them back for the present; they, or a pair like them, will come in all right later on."

After a slight pause she said—

"I do not want to run into your debt more than I can help. If my voice develops, if it be all you think it is, I shall be able to go on the stage in a year, at latest in a year and a half from now. My mother was paid three and four hundred a week. Unless I fail altogether, I shall have no difficulty in paying you back the money you so generously lent me."

"But why do you want to cost me nothing?"

"I don't know. Why shouldn't I pay you back? If I succeed I shall have plenty of money; if I don't, I daresay you'll overlook the debt. Owen, dear, how enchanting it is to be with you in Paris, to wear these beautiful dresses, to drive in this carriage, to see those lovely horses, and to wonder what the races will be like. You're not disappointed in me? I'm as nice as you thought I'd be?"

"Yes; you're a great deal nicer. I was afraid at one time you might be a bore; scruples of conscience aren't very interesting. But somehow in your case they don't seem to matter."

"I do try to keep them to myself. There's no use in inflicting one's personal worries on others. I am all one thing or all the other. When I'm with you, I'm afraid I'm all the other."

He had always known that he could "make something of her," as he used to put it to himself, but she exceeded his expectations; she certainly was an admirable mistress. Her scruples did not bore him; they were, indeed, a novelty and an excitement which he would not willingly be without. Moreover, she was so intelligent he had not yet heard her make a stupid remark. She had always been interested in the right things; and, excited by her admiration of the wooden balconies—the metal lanterns hanging from them, the vases standing on the steps leading to the porticoes, he attempted a reading of these villas.

"How plain is this paganism," he said. "Seeing them, we cannot but think of their deep feather beds, the savoury omelettes made of new-laid eggs served at mid-day, and followed by juicy beefsteaks cooked in the best butter. Those villas are not only typical of Passy, but of France; their excellent life ascends from the peasant's cottage; they are the result of agriculture, which is the original loveliness. All that springs from agriculture must be beautiful, just as all that springs from commerce must be vile. Manchester is the ugliest place on the earth, and the money of every individual cotton spinner serves to multiply the original ugliness—the house he builds, the pictures he buys. Isn't that so?"

"I can't say, dear; I have never been to Manchester. But how can you think of such things?"

"Don't you like those villas? I love them, and their comfort is secure; its root is in the earth, the only thing we are sure of. There is more pagan of life and sentiment in France than elsewhere. Would you not like to have a Passy villa? Would you not like to live here?"

"One of these days I may buy one, then you shall come to breakfast, and I'll give you an omelette and a beefsteak. For the present, I shall have to put up with something less expensive. I must be near my music lessons. Thanks all the same, dearest."

She sought a reason for the expression of thoughtfulness which had suddenly come over his face.

"I don't know how it is, but I never see Paris without thinking of Balzac. You don't know Balzac; one of these days you must read him. The moment I begin to notice Paris, I think, feel, see and speak Balzac. That dark woman yonder, with her scornful face, fills my mind with Balzacian phrases—the celebrated courtesan, celebrated for her diamonds and her vices, and so on. The little woman in the next carriage, the Princess de Saxeville, would delight him. He would devote an entire page to the description of her coat of arms—three azure panels, and so on. And I should read it, for Balzac made all the world beautiful, even snobbery. All interesting people are Balzacians. The moment I know that a man is an admirer of Balzac, a sort of Freemasonry is established between us, and I am interested in him, as I should be in a man who had loved a woman whom I had loved."

"But I shouldn't like a woman because I knew that you had loved her."

"You are a woman; but men who have loved the same woman will seek each other from the ends of the earth, and will take an intense pleasure in their recollections. I don't know whether that aphorism is to be found in Balzac; if not, it is an accident that prevented him from writing it, for it is quite Balzacian—only he would give it a turn, an air of philosophic distinction to which it would be useless for me to pretend."

"I wonder if I should like him. Tell me about him."

"You would be more likely than most women to appreciate him. Supposing you put the matter to the test. You would not accept these horses, maybe you will not refuse a humbler present—an edition of Balzac. There's a very good one in fifty-two volumes."

"So many as that?"

"Yes; and not one too many—each is a masterpiece. In this enormous work there are something like two thousand characters, and these appear in some books in principal, in other books in subordinate, parts. Balzac speaks of them as we should of real people. A young lady is going to the opera and to a ball afterwards, and he says—

"'It is easy to imagine her delight and expectation, for was she not going to meet the delicious Duchesse de la Maufregneuse, and her friend the celebrated Madame d'Espard, Coralis, Lucien de Rubempré and Rastignac.'

"These people are only mentioned in the *Mémoires de deux jeunes Mariées*. But they are heroes and heroines in other books, in *Les Secrets de la Princesse de Cadignan*, *Le Père Goriot*, and *Les Illusions Perdues*." Before you even begin to know Balzac, you must have read at least twenty volumes. There is a vulgarity about those who don't know Balzac; we, his worshippers, recognise in each other a refinement of sense and a peculiar comprehension of life. We are beings apart; we are branded with the seal of that great mind. You should hear us talk among ourselves. Everyone knows that Popinot is the sublime hero of *L'Interdiction*, but for the moment some feeble Balzacian does not remember the other books he appears in, and is ashamed to ask.... But I'm boring you."

"No, no; I love to listen. It is more interesting than any play."

Owen looked at her questioningly, as if he doubted the flattery, which, at the bottom of his heart, he knew to be quite sincere.

"You cannot understand Paris until you have read Balzac. Balzac discovered Paris; he created Paris. You remember just now what I said of those villas? I was thinking at the moment of Balzac. For he begins one story by a reading of the human characteristics to be perceived in its streets. He says that there are mean streets, and streets that are merely honest; there are young streets about whose morality the public has not yet formed any opinion; there are murderous streets—streets older than the oldest hags; streets that we may esteem—clean streets, work-a-day streets and commercial streets. Some streets, he says, begin well and end badly. The Rue Montmartre, for instance, has a fine head, but it ends in the tail of a fish. How good that is. You don't know the Rue Montmartre? I'll point it out next time we're that way. But you know the Rue de la Paix?"

"Yes; what does that mean?"

"The Rue de la Paix, he says, is a large street, and a grand street, but it certainly doesn't awaken the gracious and noble thoughts that the Rue Royale suggests to every sensitive mind; nor has it the dignity of the Place Vendôme. The Place de la Bourse, he says, is in the daytime babble and prostitution, but at night it is beautiful. At two o'clock in the morning, by moonlight, it is a dream of old Greece."

"I don't see much in that. What you said about the villas was quite as good."

Fearing that the conversation lacked a familiar and personal interest, he sought a transition, an idea by which he could connect it with Evelyn herself. With this object he called her attention to two young men who, he pretended, reminded him of Rastignac and Morny. That woman in the mail phaeton was an incipient Madame Marneffe; that dark woman now looking at them with ardent, amorous eyes might be an Esther.

"We're all creatures of Balzac's imagination. You," he said, turning a little so that he might see her better, "are intensely Balzacian."

"Do I remind you of one of his characters?" Evelyn became more keenly interested. "Which one?"

"You are more like a character he might have painted than anyone I can think of in the Human Comedy. He certainly would have been interested in your temperament. But I can't think which of his women is like you. You are more like the adorable Lucien; that is to say, up to the present."

"Who was Lucien?"

"He was the young poet whom all Paris fell in love with. He came up to Paris with a married woman; I think they came from Angouleme. I haven't read *Lost Illusions* for twenty years. She and he were the stars in the society of some provincial town, but when they arrived in Paris each thought the other very common and countrified. He compares her with Madame d'Espard; she compares him with Rastignac; Balzac completes the picture with a touch of pure genius—'They forgot that six months would transform them both into exquisite Parisians.' How good that is, what wonderful insight into life!"

"And do they become Parisians?"

"Yes, and then they both regret that they broke off—"

"Could they not begin it again?"

"No; it is rarely that a *liaison* can be begun again—life is too hurried. We may not go back; the past may never become the present—ghosts come between."

"Then if I broke it off with you, or you broke it off with me, it would be for ever?"

"Do not let us discuss such unpleasant possibilities;" and he continued to search the *Human Comedy* for a woman resembling Evelyn. "You are essentially Balzacian—all interesting things are—but I cannot remember any woman in the *Human Comedy* like you—Honorine, perhaps."

"What does she do?"

"She's a married woman who has left her husband for a lover who very soon deserts her. Her husband tries in vain to love other women, but his wife holds his affections and he makes every effort to win her back. The story is mainly an account of these efforts."

"Does he succeed?"

"Yes. Honorine goes back to her husband, but it cost her her life. She cannot live with a man she doesn't love. That is the point of the story."

"I wonder why that should remind you of me?"

"There is something delicate, rare, and mystical about you both. But I can't say I place *Honorine* very high among Balzac's works. There are beautiful touches in it, but I think he failed to realise the type. You are more virile, more real to me than Honorine. No; on the whole, Balzac has not done you. He perceived you dimly. If he had lived it might, it certainly would, have been otherwise. There is, of course, the Duchesse Langeais. There is something of you in her; but she is no more than a brilliant sketch, no better than Honorine. There is Eugene Grandet. But no; Balzac never painted your portrait."

Like all good talkers, he knew how to delude his listeners into the belief that they were taking an important part in the conversation. He allowed them to speak, he solicited their opinions, and listened as if they awakened the keenest interest in him; he developed what they had vaguely suggested. He paused before their remarks, he tempted his listener into personal appreciations and sudden revelations of character. He addressed an intimate vanity and became the inspiration of every choice, and in a mysterious reticulation of emotions, tastes and ideas, life itself seemed to converge to his ultimate authority. And having induced recognition of the wisdom of his wishes, he knew how to make his yoke agreeable to bear; it never galled the back that bore it, it lay upon it soft as a silken gown. Evelyn enjoyed the gentle imposition of his will. Obedience became a delight, and in its intellectual sloth life floated as in an opium dream without end, dissolving as the sunset dissolves in various modulations. Obedience is a divine sensualism; it is the sensualism of the saints; its lassitudes are animated with deep pauses and thrills of love and worship. We lift our eyes, and a great joy fills our hearts, and we sink away into blisses of remote consciousness. The delights of obedience are the highest felicities of love, and these Evelyn had begun to experience. She had ascended already into this happy nowhere. She was aware of him, and a little of the brilliant goal whither he was leading her. She was the instrument, he was the hand that played upon it, and all that had happened from hour to hour in their mutual existence revealed in some new and unexpected way his mastery over life. She had seen great ladies bowing to him, smiling upon him in a way that told their intention to get him away from her. She had heard scraps of his conversation with the French and English noblemen who had stopped to speak to him; and now, as Owen was getting into the victoria, after a brief visit to some great lady who had sent her footman to fetch him, a man, who looked to Evelyn like a sort of superior groom, came breathless to their carriage. He had only just heard that Owen was on the course. He was the great English trainer from Chantilly, and had tried Armide II. to win with a stone more on his back than he had to carry.

"That is the horse," and Owen pointed to a big chestnut. "The third horse—orange and white sleeves, black cap ... they are going now for the preliminary canter. We shall have just time to back him. There is a Pari Mutuel a little way down the course; or shall we back the horse in the ring? No, it is too late to get across the course. The Pari Mutuel will do. Isn't the racecourse like an English lawn, like an overgrown croquet ground? and the horses go round by these plantations."

It was not fashionable, he admitted, for a lady to leave her carriage, but no one knew her. It did not matter, and the spectacle amused her. But there was only time to catch a glimpse of beautiful toilettes, actresses and princesses, and the young men standing on the steps of the carriages. Owen whispered the names of the most celebrated, and told her she should know them when she was on the stage. At present it would be better for her to live quietly—unknown; her lessons would take all her time. He talked as he hastened her towards where a crowd had collected. She saw what looked like a small omnibus, with a man distributing tickets. Owen took five louis out of her purse and handed them to the man, who in return handed her a ticket. They would see the race better from their carriage, but it was pleasanter to stroll about the warm grass and admire the little woods which surrounded this elegant pleasure-ground, the white painted stands with all their flags flying on the blue summer air, the glitter of the carriages, the colour of the parasols, the bright jackets and caps of the jockeys, the rhythmical movement of the horses. Some sailed along with their heads low, others bounded, their heads high in the air. While Owen watched Evelyn's pleasure, his face expressed a cynical good humour. He was glad she was pleased, and he was flattered that he was influencing her. No longer was she wasting her life, the one life which she had to live. He was proud of his disciple, and he delighted in her astonishment, when, having made sure that Armide II. had won, he led her back to the Pari Mutuel, and, bidding her hold out her hands, saw that forty louis were poured into them.

Then Evelyn could not believe that she was in her waking senses, and it took some time to explain to her how she had won so much money; and when she asked why all the poor people did not come and do likewise, since it was so easy, Owen said that he had had more sport seeing her win five and thirty louis than he had when he won the gold cup at Ascot. It almost inclined him to go in for racing again. Evelyn could not understand the circumstance and, still explaining the odds, he told the coachman that they would not wait for the last race. He had tied her forty louis into her pocket-handkerchief, and feeling the weight of the gold in her hand she leant back in the victoria, lost in the bright, penetrating happiness of that summer evening. Paris, graceful and indolent—Paris returning through a whirl of wheels, through pleasure-grounds, green swards and long, shining roads—instilled a fever of desire into the blood, and the soul cried that life should be made wholly of such light distraction.

The wistful light seemed to breathe all vulgarity from the procession of pleasure-seekers returning from the races. An aspect of vision stole over the scene. Owen pointed to the group of pines by the lake's edge, to the gondola-like boat moving through the pink stillness; and the cloud in the water, he said, was more beautiful than the cloud in heaven. He spoke of the tea-house on the island, of the shade of the trees, of the lush grass, of the chatter of the nursemaids and ducks. He proposed, and she accepted, that they should go there to-morrow. The secret of their lips floated into their eyes, its echoes drifted through their souls like a faint strain played on violins; and neither spoke for fear of losing one of the faint vibrations. Evelyn settled her embroidered gown over her feet as the carriage swept around the Arc de Triomphe.

"That is our rose garden," he said, pointing to Paris, which lay below them glittering in the evening light, "You remember that I used to read you Omar?"

"Yes, I remember. Not three days ago, yet it seems far away."

"But you do not regret—you would not go back?"

"I could not if I would."

"It has been a charming day, hasn't it?"

"Yes."

"And it isn't over yet. I have ordered dinner at the Café des Ambassadeurs. I've got a table on the balcony. The balcony overlooks the garden, and the stage is at the end of the garden, so we shall see the performance as we dine. The comic songs, the can-can dancers and the acrobats will be a change after Wagner. I hope you'll like the dinner."

He took a card from his pocket and read the menu.

"There is no place in Paris where you get a better *petite marmite* than the Ambassadeurs. I have ordered, you see, *filets de volaille, pointes d'asperges*. The *filets de volaille* are the backs of the chickens, the tit-bits; the rest—the legs and the wings—go to make the stock; that is why the *marmite* is so good. *Timbale de homard à l'Americaine* is served with a brown sauce garnished with rice. You ought to find it excellent. If we were in autumn I should have ordered a pheasant *Sauvaroff*. A bird being impossible, I allowed myself to be advised by the head waiter. He assured me they have some very special legs of lamb; they have just received them from Normandy; you will not recognise it as the stringy, tasteless thing that in England we know as leg of lamb. *Soufflé au paprike*—this *soufflé* is seasoned not with red pepper, which would produce an intolerable thirst, nor with ordinary pepper, which would be arid and tasteless, but with an intermediate pepper which will just give a zest to the last glass of champagne. There is a *parfait*—that comes before the *soufflé* of course. I don't think we can do much better."

CHAPTER ELEVEN

The appointment had been made, and he was coming back at half-past three to take her to Madame Savelli, the great singing mistress, and at four her fate would be decided. She would then learn beyond cavil or doubt if she had, or was likely to acquire, sufficient voice for grand opera. So much Madame Savelli would know for certain, though she could not predict success. So many things were required, and to fail in one was to fail.... Owen expected Isolde and Brunnhilde, and she was to achieve in these parts something which had not been achieved. She was to sing them; hitherto, according to Owen, they had been merely howled. Other triumphs were but preparatory to this ultimate triumph, and if she fell short of his ideal, he would take no further interest in her voice. However well she might sing Margaret, he would not really care; as for Lucia and Violetta, it would be his amiability that would keep him in the stalls. To-day her fate was to be decided. If Madame Savelli were to say that she had no voice—she couldn't very well say that, but she might say that she had only a nice voice, which, if properly trained, could be heard to advantage in a drawing-room—then what was she to do? She couldn't live with Owen as his kept mistress; in that case she would be no better than the women she had seen at the races. She grew suddenly pale. What was she to do? The choice lay between drowning herself and going back to her father.

Only yesterday she had received such a kind letter from him, offering to forgive everything if she would come back. So like her dear, unpractical dad to ask her to go back and suffer all the disgrace without having attained the end for which she had left home. If, as Owen had said, she went back with the finest soprano voice in Europe, and an engagement to sing at Covent Garden at a salary of £400 a week, the world would close its ears to scandal, the world would deny that any violation of its rules had been committed; but to return after an escapade of a week in Paris would be ruin. So, at Owen's persuasion, she had written a letter to her father explaining why she could not return. But her inability to obey her father did not detract from the fear which her disobedience caused her. She thought of the old man whom she loved so well grieving his heart out and thinking her, whom he loved so dearly, cruel and ungrateful. But what could she do? Go back and bring disgrace upon herself and upon her father? Ah, if she had known beforehand the suffering she was enduring, she did not think she would ever have gone away with Owen. It was all wrong, very wrong, and she had merited this punishment by her own grievous fault.... Lady Duckle was coming that evening—the woman whom she was going to live with—an unfortunate day for her to arrive; if Madame Savelli thought that she, Evelyn, had no voice to speak of, the secret could not be kept from her. Lady Duckle would know her for a poor little fool who had been wheedled from her home, and on the pretext that she was to become the greatest singer in Europe. It was all horrid.

And when Owen returned he found Evelyn in tears. But with his scrupulous tact he avoided any allusion to her grief, and while she bathed her eyes she thanked him in her heart for this. Her father would have fretted and fussed and maddened her with questions, but Owen cheered her with sanguine smiles and seemed to look forward to her success as a natural sequence, any interruption to which it would be idle to anticipate; and he cleverly drew her thoughts from doubt in her own ability into consideration of the music she was going to sing. She suggested the jewel song in "Faust," or the waltz in "Romeo and Juliet." But he was of the opinion that she had better sing the music she was in the habit of singing; for choice, one of Purcell's songs, the "Epithalamium," or the song from the "Indian Queen."

"Savelli doesn't know the music; it will interest her. The other things she hears every day of her life."

"But I haven't the music—I don't know the accompaniments."

"The music is here."

"It is very thoughtful of you."

"Henceforth it must be my business to be thoughtful."

They descended the hotel staircase very slowly, seeing themselves in the tall mirrors on the landings. The bright courtyard glittered through the glass verandah; it was full of carriages.

Owen signed to his coachman. They got into the victoria, and a moment after were passing through the streets, turning in and out. But not a word did they speak, for the poison of doubt had entered into his, as it had into her, soul. He had begun to ask himself if he was mistaken—if she had really this wonderful voice, or if it only existed in his imagination? True it was that everyone who had heard her sing thought the same; but the last time he had heard her, had not her voice sounded a little thin? He had doubts, too, about her power of passionate interpretation.... She had a beautiful voice—there could be no doubt on that point—but a beautiful voice might be heard to a very great disadvantage on the stage. Moreover, could she sing florid music? Of course, the "Epithalamium" she was going to sing was as florid as it could be. Purcell had suited it to his own singing.... A woman did not always sing to an orchestra as well as to a single instrument. That was only when the singer was an insufficient musician. Evelyn was an excellent musician.... If a woman had the loveliest voice, and was as great a musician as Wagner himself, it would profit her nothing if she had not the strength to stand the wear and tear of rehearsals. He looked at Evelyn, and calculated her physical strength. She was a rather tall and strongly-built girl, but the Wagnerian bosom was wanting. He had always considered a large bosom to be a dreadful deformity. A bosom should be an indication, a hint; a positive statement he viewed with abhorrence. And he paused to think if he would be willing to forego his natural and cultured taste in female beauty and accept those extravagant growths of flesh if they could be proved to be musical necessities. But Evelyn was by no means flat-chested ... and he remembered certain curves and plenitudes with satisfaction. Then, catching sight of Evelyn's frightened face, he forced himself to invent conversation. That was the Madeleine, a fine building, in a way; and the boulevard they had just entered was the Boulevard Malesherbes, which was called after a celebrated French lawyer. The name Haussmann recalled the Second Empire, and he ransacked his memory for anecdotes. But soon his conversation grew stilted—even painful. He could continue it no longer, and, taking her hand, he assured her that, if she did not sing well, she should come to Madame Savelli again. Evelyn's face lighted up, and she said that what had frightened her was the finality of the decision—a few minutes in which she might not be able to sing at all. Owen reproved her. How could she think that he would permit such a barbarism? It really did not matter a brass button whether she sang well or ill on this particular day; if she did not do herself justice, another appointment should be made. He had money enough to hire Madame Savelli to listen to her for the next six months, if it were required.

He was truly sorry for her. Poor little girl! it really was a dreadful ordeal. Yet he had never seen her look better. What a difference dressing her had made! Her manner, too, had improved. That was the influence of his society. By degrees, he'd get rid of all her absurd ideas. But he sorely wished that Madame Savelli's verdict would prove him right—not for his sake—it didn't matter to him—such teeth, such hands, such skin, such eyes and hair! Voice or no voice, he had certainly got the most charming mistress in Europe! But, if she did happen to have a great voice it would make matters so much better for them. He had plenty of money—twenty thousand lying idle—but it was better that she should earn money. It would save her reputation ... in every way it would be better. If she had a voice, and were a success, this *liaison* would be one of the most successful things in his life. If he were wrong, they'd have to get on as best they could, but he didn't think that he could be altogether mistaken.

The door was opened by a footman in livery, and they ascended half-a-dozen steps into the house. Then, off a wide passage, a door was opened, and they found themselves in a great saloon with polished oak floor. There was hardly any furniture—three or four chairs, some benches against the walls and a grand piano. The mantelpiece was covered with photographs, and there were life-sized photographs in frames on the walls. Owen pointed to one of a somewhat stout woman in evening-dress, and he whispered an illustrious name.

A moment after madame entered.

She was of medium height, thin and somewhat flat-chested. Her hair was iron-grey, and the face was marked with patches of vivid colouring. The mouth was a long, determined line, and the lines of the hips asserted themselves beneath the black silk dress. She glanced quickly at Evelyn as she went towards Sir Owen.

"This is the young lady of whom you spoke to me?"

"Yes, madame, it is she. Let me introduce you. Madame Savelli—Miss Evelyn Innes."

"Does mademoiselle wish to sing as a professional or as an amateur?"

The question was addressed at once to Evelyn and to Owen, and, while Evelyn hesitated with the French words, Owen answered—

"Mademoiselle will be guided by your advice."

"They all say that; however, we shall see. Will mademoiselle sing to me? Does mademoiselle speak French?"

"Yes, a little," Evelyn replied, timidly.

"Oh, very good. Has mademoiselle studied music?"

"Yes; my father is a musician, but he only cares for the very early music, and I have hardly ever touched a piano, but I play the harpsichord.... My instrument is the viola da gamba."

"The harpsichord and the viola da gamba! That is very interesting, but"—and Madame Savelli laughed good-naturedly—"unfortunately we have no harpsichord here, nor yet a spinet only the humble piano."

"Miss Innes will be quite satisfied with your piano, Madame Savelli."

"Now, Sir Owen, I will not have you get cross with me. I must always have my little pleasantry. Does he get cross with you like that, Miss Innes?"

"I didn't get cross with you, Madame Savelli."

"You wanted to, but I would not let you—and because I regretted I had not a harpsichord, only a humble piano! Mademoiselle knows, I suppose, all the church songs. I only know operas.... You see, Sir Owen, you cannot silence me; I will have my little pleasantry. I only know opera, and have nothing but the humble piano. But, joking apart, mademoiselle wants to study serious opera."

"Yes; mademoiselle intends to study for the stage, not for the church."

"Then I will teach her."

"You have three classes here. Mademoiselle would like to go into the opera class."

"In the opera class I How you do go on, Sir Owen! If mademoiselle can go into the opera class next year, I shall be more than satisfied, astonished."

"Perhaps you'll be able to say better if mademoiselle will be able to go into the opera class when you have heard her sing."

"But I know, my dear Sir Owen, that is impossible. You don't believe me. Well, I am prepared to be surprised. It matters not to me. Mademoiselle can go into the opera class in three months if she is sufficiently advanced. Will mademoiselle sing to me? Are these her songs?" Madame Savelli took the music out of Sir Owen's hands. "I can see that this music would sound better on the harpsichord or the spinet.... Now, Sir Owen, I see you are getting angry again."

"I'm not angry, Madame Savelli—no one could be angry with you—only mademoiselle is rather nervous."

"Then perhaps my pleasantry was inexpedient. Let me see—this is it, isn't it?" she said, running her fingers through the first bars.... "But perhaps you would like to accompany mademoiselle?"

"Which would you like, Evelyn?"

"You, dear; I should be too nervous with Madame Savelli."

Owen explained, and madame gave him her place at the piano with alacrity, and took a seat far away by the fireplace. Evelyn sang Purcell's beautiful wedding song, full of roulades, grave pauses and long-sustained notes, and when she had finished Owen signed to madame not to speak. "Now, the song from the 'Indian Queen.' You sang capitally," he whispered to Evelyn. And, thus encouraged, she poured all her soul and all the pure melody of her voice into this music, at once religious and voluptuous, seemingly the rapture of a nun that remembrance has overtaken and for the moment overpowered. When she had done, Madame Savelli jumped from her chair, and seizing her by both hands said,—

"If you'll stop with me for a year, I'll make something wonderful of you."

Then without another word she ran out of the room, leaving the door open behind her, and a few moments after they heard her calling on the stairs to her husband.

"Come down at once; come down, I've found a star."

"Then she thinks I've a good voice?"

"I should think so indeed. She won't get over the start you've given her for the next six months."

"Are you sure, Owen? Are you sure she's not laughing at us?"

"Laughing at us? She's calling for her husband to come down. She's shouting to him that she's found a star."

Then the joy that rose up in Evelyn's heart blinded her eyes so that she could not see, and she seemed to lose sense of what was happening. It was as if she were going to swoon.

"I have told her," Madame Savelli said to her husband, who followed her into the room, "that, if she will remain a year with me, I'll make something wonderful of her. And you will stay with me, my dear...."

Owen thought that this was the moment to mention the fact that Evelyn was the daughter of the famous Madame Innes.

Monsieur Savelli raised his bushy eyebrows.

"I knew your mother, mademoiselle. If you have a voice like hers—"

"In a year, if she will remain with me, she will have twice the voice her mother had. Mademoiselle must go into the opera class at once."

"I thought you said that such a thing could not be; that no pupil of yours had ever gone straight into the opera class?"

Madame Savelli's grey eyes laughed.

"Ah! I was mistaken.... I had forgotten that all the other classes are full. There is no room for Miss Innes in the other classes. It is against all precedence; it will create much jealousy, but it can't be helped. She must go straight into the opera class. When will mademoiselle begin? The sooner the better."

"Next Monday. Will that be soon enough?"

"On Monday I'll begin to teach her the *rôle* of Marguerite. Such a thing was never heard of; but then mademoiselle's voice is one such as one never hears."

Turning to her husband, she said—

"You see my husband is looking at me. Yes, you are looking at me. You think I have gone mad, but he'll not think I've gone mad when he hears mademoiselle sing. Will mademoiselle be so kind?"

Evelyn felt she could not sing again, and, turning suddenly away, she walked to the window and watched the cabs going by. She heard Owen ask Madame and Monsieur Savelli to excuse her. He said that madame's praise had proved too much for her; that her nerves had given way. Then he came over and spoke to her gently. She looked at him through her tears; but she could not trust herself to speak, nor yet to walk across the room and bid Monsieur and Madame Savelli good-bye. She felt she must die of shame or happiness, and plucked at Owen's sleeve. She was glad to get out of that room; and the moments seemed like years. They could not speak in the glaring of the street. But fortunately their way was through the park, and when they passed under the shade of some overhanging boughs, she looked at him.

"Well, little girl, what do you think? Everything is all right now. It happened even better than I expected."

She wiped away her tears.

"How foolish I am to cry like this. But I could not bear it; my nerves gave way. It was so sudden. I'm afraid those people will think me a little fool. But you don't know, Owen, what I have suffered these last few days. I don't want to worry you, but there were times when I thought I couldn't stand it any longer. I thought that God might punish me by taking my voice from me. Just fancy if I had not been able to sing at all! It would have made you look a fool. You would have hated me for that; but now, even if I should lose my voice between this and next Monday.... Did I sing well, Owen? Did I sing as well as ever you heard me sing?"

"I've heard you sing better, but you sang well enough to convince Savelli that you'll have the finest voice in Europe by this time next year. That's good enough for you, isn't it? You don't want any more, do you?"

"No, no, half that would do, half that; I only want to know that it is all true." Tears again rose to her eyes. "I mean," she said, laughing, "that I want to know that I am sitting by you in the carriage; that Madame Savelli has heard me sing; that she said that I should be a great singer. Did she say that?"

"Yes, she said you would be a great singer."

"Then why does it not seem true? But nothing seems true, not even Paris. It all seems like a dazzling, scattered dream, like spots of light, and every moment I fear that it will pass away, and that I shall wake up and find myself in Dulwich; that I shall see my viola da gamba standing in the corner; that a rap at the front door will tell me that a pupil has come for a lesson."

"Do you remember the lessons that you gave me on the viola da gamba?"

She looked at him beseechingly.

"Then it is true. I suppose it is true, but I wish I could feel this life to be true."

She looked up and saw the clouds moving across the sky; she looked down and saw the people passing along the streets.

"In a few days, in a few weeks, this life will seem quite real. But, if you cannot bear the present, how will you bear the success that is to come?"

"When I was a tiny girl, the other girls used to say, 'Evey, dear, do make that funny noise in your throat,' and that was my trill. But since mother's death everything went wrong; it seemed that I would never get out of Dulwich. I never should have if it had not been for you. I had ceased to believe that I had a voice."

"In that throat there are thousands of pounds."

Evelyn put her hand to her throat to assure herself that it was still on her shoulders.

"I wonder, I wonder. To think that in a year—in a year and a half—I shall be singing on the stage! They will throw me bouquets, I suppose?"

"Oh, yes, you need have no fear about that; this park would not suffice to grow all the flowers that will be thrown at your feet."

"It seems impossible that I—poor, miserable I—should be moving towards such splendour. I wonder if I shall ever get there, and, if I do get there, if I shall be able to live through it. I cannot yet see myself the great singer you describe. Yet I suppose it is all quite certain."

"Quite certain."

"Then why can't I imagine it?"

"We cannot imagine ourselves in other than our present circumstances; the most commonplace future is as unimaginable as the most extravagant."

"I suppose that is so."

The carriage stopped at the Continental, and he asked her what she would like to do. It was just five.

"Come and have a cup of tea in the Rue Cambon."

She consented, and, after tea, he said, standing with one foot on the carriage step—

"If you'll allow me to advise you, you will go for a drive in the Bois by yourself. I want to see some pictures."

"May I not come?"

"Certainly, if you like, but I don't think you could give your attention to pictures; you're thinking of yourself, and you want to be alone with yourself—nothing else would interest you."

A pretty flush of shame came into her cheeks. He had seen to the bottom of her heart, and discovered that of which she herself was not aware. But, now that he had told her, she knew that she did want to be alone—not alone in a room, but alone among a great number of people. A drive in the Bois would be a truly delicious indulgence of her egotism. The Champs Elysées floated about her happiness, the Avenue du Bois de Boulogne seemed to stretch out and to lead to the theatre of her glory; and, looking at the lake, its groups of pines, its gondola-like boats, she recalled, and with little thrills of pleasure, the exact words that madame had used—

"If you will stay a year with me, I'll make something wonderful of you." "Was there ever such happiness? Can it be true? Then I am wonderful—perhaps the most wonderful person here. Those women, however haughty they may look, what are they to me? I am wonderful. With not one would I change places, for I am going to be something wonderful." And the word sang sweeter in her ears than the violins in "Lohengrin." ... "Owen loves me. I have the nicest lover in the world. All this good fortune has happened to me. Oh, to me! If father could only know. But Owen thinks that will be all right. Father will forgive me when I come back the wonderful singer that I am—that I shall be.... If anyone could hear me, they would think I was mad. I can't help it.... She'll make something wonderful of me, and father will forgive me everything. We always loved each other. We've always been pals, dear dad. Oh, how I wish he had heard Madame Savelli say, 'If you will stop with me a year, I'll make something wonderful of you!' I will write to him ... it will cheer him up."

Then, seeing the poplars that lined the avenue, beautiful and tall in the evening, she thought of Owen. He had said they were the trees of the evening. She had not understood, and he had explained that we only see poplars in the sunset; they appear with the bats and the first stars.

"How clever he is, and he is my lover! It is dreadfully wicked, but I wonder what Madame Savelli said to her husband about my voice. She meant all she said; there can be no doubt about that."

Catching sight of some passing faces, Evelyn thought how, in two little years, at this very hour, the same people would be returning from the Bois to hear her sing—what? Elsa? Elizabeth? Margaret? She imagined herself in these parts, and sang fragments of the music as it floated into her mind. She was impelled to extravagance. She would have liked to stand up in her carriage and sing aloud, nothing seemed to matter, until she remembered that she must not make a fool of herself before Lady Duckle. And that she might walk the fever out of her blood, she called to the coachman to stop, and she walked down the Champs Elysées rapidly, not pausing to take breath till she reached the Place de la Concorde; and she almost ran the rest of the way, so that she might not be late for dinner. When she entered the hotel, she came suddenly upon Owen on the verandah. He was sitting there engaged in conversation with an elderly woman—a woman of about fifty, who, catching sight of her, whispered something to him.

"Evelyn.... This is Lady Duckle."

"Sir Owen has been telling me, Miss Innes, what Madame Savelli said about your voice. I do not know how to congratulate you. I suppose such a thing has not happened before." And her small, grey eyes gazed in envious wonderment, as if seeking to understand how such extraordinary good fortune should have befallen the tall, fair girl who stood blushing and embarrassed in her happiness. Owen drew a chair forward.

"Sit down, Evelyn, you look tired."

"No, I'm not tired ... but I walked from the Arc de Triomphe."

"Walked! Why did you walk?"

Evelyn did not answer, and Lady Duckle said—

"Sir Owen tells me that you'll surely succeed in singing Wagner—that I shall be converted."

"Lady Duckle is a heretic."

"No, my dear Owen, I'm not a heretic, for I recognise the greatness of the music, and I could hear it with pleasure if it were confined to the orchestra, but I can find no pleasure in listening to a voice trying to accompany a hundred instruments. I heard 'Lohengrin' last season. I was in Mrs. Ayre's box—a charming woman—her husband is an American, but he never comes to London. I presented her at the last Drawing-Room. She had a supper party afterwards, and when she asked me what I'd have to eat, I said, 'Nothing with wings' ... Oh, that swan!"
Her grey hair was drawn up and elaborately arranged, and Evelyn noticed three diamond rings and an emerald ring on her fat, white fingers. There had been moments she said, when she had thought the people on the stage were making fun of them—"such booing!"—they had all shouted themselves hoarse—such wandering from key to key.
"Hoping, I suppose, that in the end they'd hit off the right ones. And that trick of going up in fifths. And then they go up in fifths on the half notes. I said if they do that again, I'll leave the theatre."
Evelyn could see that Owen liked Lady Duckle, and her conversation, which at first might have seemed extravagant and a little foolish, was illuminated with knowledge and a vague sense of humour which was captivating. Her story of how she had met Rossini in her early youth, and the praise he had bestowed on her voice, and his intention of writing an opera for her, seemed fanciful enough, but every now and then some slight detail inspired the suspicion that there was perhaps more truth in what she was saying than appeared at first hearing.
"Why did he not write the opera, Olive?"
"It was just as he was ill, when he lived in Rue Monsieur. And he said he was afraid he was not equal to writing down so many notes. Poor old man! I can still see him sitting in his arm-chair."
She seemed to have been on terms of friendship with the most celebrated men of the time. Her little book entitled *Souvenirs of Some Great Composers* was alluded to, and Owen mentioned that at that time she was the great Parisian beauty.
"But instead of going on the stage, I married Lord Duckle."
And this early mistake she seemed to consider as sufficient explanation for all subsequent misfortunes. Evelyn wondered what these might be, and Owen said—
"The most celebrated singers are glad to sing at Lady Duckle's afternoons; no reputation is considered complete till it has received her sanction."
"That is going too far, Owen; but it is true that nearly all the great singers have been heard at my house."
Owen begged Evelyn to get ready for dinner, and as she stood waiting for the lift, she saw him resume confidential conversation with Lady Duckle. They were, she knew, making preparations for her future life, and this was the woman she was going to live with for the next few years! The thought gave her pause. She dried her hands and hastened downstairs. They were still talking in the verandah just as she had left them. Owen signed to the coachman and told him to drive to Durand's. They were dining in a private room, and during dinner the conversation constantly harked back to the success that Evelyn had achieved that afternoon. Owen told the story in well-turned sentences. His eyes were generally fixed on Lady Duckle, and Evelyn sat listening and feeling, as Owen intended she should feel, like the heroine of a fairy tale. She laughed nervously when, imitating Madame Savelli's accent, he described how she had said, "If you'll stop with me for a year, I'll make something wonderful of you." Lady Duckle leaned across the table, glancing from time to time at Evelyn, as if to assure herself that she was still in the presence of this extraordinary person, and murmured something about having the honour of assisting at what she was sure would be a great career.
Owen noticed that Evelyn seemed preoccupied, and did not respond very eagerly to Lady Duckle's advances. He wondered if she suspected him of having been Lady Duckle's lover.... Evelyn was thinking entirely of Lady Duckle herself, trying to divine the real woman that was behind all this talk of great men and social notabilities. One phrase let drop seemed to let in some light on the mystery. Talking of her, Lady Duckle said that it was only necessary to

know what road we wanted to walk in to succeed, and instantly Lady Duckle appeared to her as one who had never selected a road. She seemed to have walked a little way on all roads, and her face expressed a life of many wanderings, straying from place to place. There was nothing as she said, worth doing that she had not done, but she had clearly accomplished nothing. As she watched her she feared, though she could not say what she feared. At bottom it was a suspicion of the deteriorating influence that Lady Duckle would exercise, must exercise, upon her—for were they not going to live together for years? And this companionship would be necessarily based on subterfuge and deceit. She would have to talk to her of her friendship for Owen. She could never speak of Owen to Lady Duckle as her lover. But as Evelyn listened to this pleasant, garrulous woman talking, and talking very well, about music and literature, she could not but feel that she liked her, and that her easy humour and want of principle would make life comfortable and careless. She was not a saint; she could not expect a saint to chaperon her; nor did she want a saint. At that moment her spirits rose. She wanted Owen, and she loved him the more for the tact he had shown in finding Lady Duckle for her. She accepted the good lady's faults with reckless enthusiasm, and when they got back to the hotel she took the first occasion to whisper that she liked Lady Duckle and was sure they'd get on very well together.

"Owen, dear, I'm so happy, I don't know what to do with myself. I did enjoy my drive to the Bois. I never was so happy and I don't seem to be enjoying myself enough; I should like to sit up all night to think of it."

"There's no reason why you shouldn't."

"Only I should feel tired in the morning.... Are you coming to my room?"

"Unless you want me not to. Do you want me to come?"

"Do I look as if I didn't?"

"Your eyes are shining like stars. It is worth while taking trouble to make you happy. You do enjoy it so.... We'll go upstairs now. We can't talk here, Lady Duckle is coming back. Leave your door ajar."

"You don't think she suspects?"

"It doesn't matter what people suspect, the essential is that they shouldn't know. I've lots to tell you. I've arranged everything with Lady Duckle."

"I was just telling Miss Innes that in three years she'll probably be singing at the Opera House. In a year or a year and a half she'll have learnt all that Savelli can teach her. Isn't that so?"

The question was discussed for a while, and then Lady Duckle mentioned that it was getting late. It was an embarrassing moment when Owen stopped the lift and they bade her good-night. She was on the third, they were on the second floor. As Evelyn went down the passage, Owen stood to watch her sloping shoulders; they seemed to him like those of an old miniature. When she turned the corner a blankness came over him; things seemed to recede and he was strangely alone with himself as he strolled into his room. But standing before the glass, his heart was swollen with a great pride. He remarked in his eyes the strange, enigmatic look which he admired in Titian and Vandyke, and he thought of himself as a principle—as a force; he wondered if he were an evil influence, and lost himself in moody meditations concerning the mystery of the attractions he presented to women. But suddenly he remembered that in a few minutes she would be in his arms, and he closed his eyes as if to delight more deeply in the joy that she presented to his imagination. So intense was his desire that he could not believe that he was her lover, that he was going to her room, and that nothing could deprive him of this delight. Why should such rare delight happen to him? He did not know. What matter, since it was happening? She was his. It was like holding the rarest jewel in the world in the hollow of his hand.

That she was at that moment preparing to receive him brought a little dizziness into his eyes, and compelled him to tear off his necktie. Then, vaguely, like one in a dream, he began to undress, very slowly, for she had told him to wait a quarter of an hour before coming to her room. He examined his thin waist as he tied himself in blue silk pyjamas, and he paused to admire his long, straight feet before slipping them into a pair of black velvet slippers. He turned to glance at his watch, and to kill the last five minutes of the prescribed time he thought of Evelyn's scruples. She would have to read certain books—Darwin and Huxley he relied upon, and he reposed considerable faith in Herbert Spencer. But there were books of a lighter kind, and their influence he believed to be not less insidious. He took one out of his portmanteau—the book which he said, had influenced him more than any other. It opened at his favourite passage—

'I am a man of the Homeric time; the world in which I live is not mine, and I know nothing of the society which surrounds me. I am as pagan as Alcibiades or as Phidias.... I never gathered on Golgotha the flowers of the Passion, and the deep stream which flowed from from the side of the Crucified and made a red girdle round the world never bathed me in its tide. I believe earth to be as beautiful as heaven, and I think that precision of form is virtue. Spirituality is not my strong point; I love a statue better than a phantom.' ... He could remember no further; he glanced at the text and was about to lay the book down, when, on second thoughts, he decided to take it with him.

Her door was ajar; he pushed it open and then stopped for moment, surprised at his good fortune. And he never forgot that instant's impression of her body's beauty. But before he could snatch the long gauze wrapper from her, she had slipped her arm through the sleeves, and, joyous as a sunlit morning hour, she came forward and threw herself into his arms. Even then he could not believe that some evil accident would not rob him of her. He said some words to that effect, and often tried to recall her answer to them; he was only sure that it was exquisitely characteristic of her, as were all her answers—as her answer was that very evening when he told her that he would have to go to London at the end of the week.

"But only for some days. You don't think that I shall be changed? You're not afraid that I shall love you less?"

"No; I was not thinking of you, dear. I know that you'll not be changed; I was thinking that I might be."

He withdrew the arm that was round her, and, raising himself upon his elbow, he looked at her.

"You've told me more about yourself in that single phrase than if you had been talking an hour."

"Dearest Owen, let me kiss you."

It seemed to them wonderful that they should be permitted to kiss each other so eagerly, and it sometimes was a still more intense rapture to lie in each other's arms and talk to each other. The dawn surprised them still talking, and it seemed to them as if nothing had been said. He was explaining his plans for her life. They were, he thought, going to live abroad for five, six, or seven years. Then Evelyn would go to London, to sing, preceded by an extraordinary reputation. But the first thing to do was to get a house in Paris.

"We cannot stop at this hotel; we must have a house. I have heard of a charming hotel in the Rue Balzac."

"In the Rue Balzac! Is there a street called after him? Is it on account of the name you want me to live there?"

"No; I don't think so, but perhaps the name had something to do with it—one never knows. But I always liked the street."

"Which of his books is it like?"

"*Les Secrets de la Princesse de Cadignan*"

They laughed and kissed each other.

"At the bottom of the street is the Avenue de Friedland; the tram passes there, and it will take you straight to Madame Savelli's."

The sparrows had begun to shrill in the courtyard, and their eyes ached with sleep.

"Five or six years—you'll be at the height of your fame. They will pass only too quickly," he added.

He was thinking what his age would be then. "And when they have passed, it will seem like a dream."

"Like a dream," she repeated, and she laid her face on the pillow where his had lain.

CHAPTER TWELVE

As she lay between sleeping and waking, she strove to grasp the haunting, fugitive idea, but shadows of sleep fell, and in her dream there appeared two Tristans, a fair and a dark. When the shadows were lifted and she thought with an awakening brain, she smiled at the absurdity, and, striving to get close to her idea, to grip it about its very loins, she asked herself how much of her own life she could express in the part, for she always acted one side of her character. Her pious girlhood found expression in the Elizabeth, and what she termed the other side of her character she was going to put on the stage in the character of Isolde. Again sleep thickened, and she found it impossible to follow her idea. It eluded her; she could not grasp it. It turned to a dream, a dream which she could not understand even while she dreamed it. But as she awaked, she uttered a cry. It happened to be the note she had to sing when the curtain goes up and Isolde lies on the couch yearning for Tristan, for assuagement of the fever which consumes her. All other actresses had striven to portray an Irish princess, or what they believed an Irish princess might be. But she cared nothing for the Irish princess, and a great deal for the physical and mental distress of a woman sick with love.

Her power of recalling her sensations was so intense, that in her warm bed she lived again the long, aching evenings of the long winter in Dulwich, before she went away with Owen. She saw again the Spring twilight in the scrap of black garden, where she used to stand watching the stars. She remembered the dread craving to worship them, the anguish of remorse and fear on her bed, her visions of distant countries and the gleam of eyes which looked at her through the dead of night. How miserable she had been in that time—in those months. She had wanted to sing, and she could not, and she had wanted—she had not known what was the matter with her. That feeling (how well she remembered it!) as if she wanted to go mad! And all those lightnesses of the brain she could introduce in the opening scene—the very opening cry was one of them. And with these two themes she thought she could create an Isolde more intense than the Isolde of the fat women whom she had seen walking about the stage, lifting their arms and trying to look like sculpture.

No one whom she had seen had attempted to differentiate between Isolde before she drinks and after she has drunk the love potion, and, to avoid this mistake, she felt that she would only have to be true to herself. After the love potion had been drunk, the moment of her life to put on the stage was its moment of highest sexual exaltation. Which was that? There were so many, she smiled in her doze. Perhaps the most wonderful day of her life was the day Madame Savelli had said, "If you'll stay with me for a year, I'll make something wonderful of you." She recalled the drive in the Bois, and she saw again the greensward, the poplars, and the stream of carriages. She had hardly been able so resist springing up in the carriage and singing to the people; she had wanted to tell them what Madame Savelli had said. She had wished to cry to them, "In two years all you people will be going to the opera to hear me." What had stopped her was the dread that it might not happen. But it had happened! That was the evening she had met Olive. She could see the exact spot. Although Olive had only just arrived, she had been up to her room and put on a pair of slippers. They had dined at a café, and all through dinner she had longed to be alone with Owen, and after dinner the time had seemed so long. Before going up in the lift he had asked her if he might come to her room. In a quarter of an hour, she had said, but he had come sooner than she expected, and she remembered slipping her arm into a gauze wrapper. How she had flung herself into his arms! That was the moment of her life to put upon the stage when she and Tristan look at each other after drinking the love potion.

In the second act Tristan lives through her. She is the will to live; and if she ultimately consents to follow him into the shadowy land, it is for love of him. But of his desire for death she understands nothing; all through the duet it is she who desires to quench this desire with kisses. That was her conception of women's mission, and that was her own life with Owen; it was her love that compelled him to live down his despondencies. So her Isolde would have an intense and a personal life that no Isolde had had before. And in holding up her own soul to view, she would hold up the universal soul, and people would be afraid to turn their heads lest they should catch each other's eyes. But was not a portrayal of sexual passion such as she intended very sinful? It could not fail to suggest sinful thoughts.... She could not help what folk thought—that was their affair. She had turned her back upon all such scruples, and this last one she contemptuously picked up and tossed aside like a briar.

Her eyes opened and she gazed sleepily into the twilight of mauve curtains, and dreaded her maid's knock. "It must be nearly eight," she thought, and she strove to pick up the thread of her lost thoughts. But a sharp rap at her door awakened her, and a tall, spare figure crossed the room. As the maid was about to draw the curtains, Evelyn cried to her—

"Oh, wait a moment, Herat.... I'm so tired. I didn't get to bed till two o'clock."

"Mademoiselle forgets that she told me to awaken her very early. Mademoiselle said she wanted to go for a long drive to the other end of London before she went to rehearsal."

Merat's logic seemed a little severe for eight o'clock in the morning, and Evelyn believed that her conception of Isolde had suffered from the interruption.

"Then I am not to draw the curtains? Mademoiselle will sleep a little longer. I will return when it is time for mademoiselle to go to rehearsal."

"Did you say it was half-past eight, Merat?"

"Yes, mademoiselle. The coachman is not quite sure of the way, and will have to ask it. This will delay him."

"Oh, yes, I know.... But I must sleep a little longer."

"Then mademoiselle will not get up. I will take mademoiselle's chocolate away."

"No, I'll have my chocolate," Evelyn said, rousing herself. "Merat, you are very insistent."

"What is one to do? Mademoiselle specially ordered me to wake her.... Mademoiselle said that—"

"I know what I said. I'll see how I feel when I have had my chocolate. The coachman had better get a map and look out the way upon it."

She lay back on the pillow and regretted she had come to England. There was no reason why she should not have thrown over this engagement. It wouldn't have been the first. Owen had always told her that money ought never to tempt her to do anything she didn't like. He had persuaded her to accept this engagement, though he knew that she did not want to sing in London. How often before had she not refused, and with his approbation? But then his pleasure was involved in the refusal or the acceptance of the engagement. He did not mind her throwing over a valuable offer to sing if he wanted her to go yachting with him. Men were so selfish. She smiled, for she knew she was acting a little comedy with herself. "But, quite seriously, I am annoyed with Owen. The London engagement—no, of course, I could not go on refusing to sing in London." She was annoyed with him because he had dissuaded her from doing what her instinct had told her was the right thing to do. She had wished to go to her father the moment she set foot in England, and beg his forgiveness. When they had arrived at Victoria, she had said that she would like to take the train to Dulwich. There happened to be one waiting. But they had had a rough crossing; she was very tired, and he had suggested she should postpone her visit to the next day. But next day her humour was different. She knew quite well that the sooner she went the easier it would be for her to press her father to forgive her, to entrap him into reconciliation. She had imagined that she could entrap her father into forgiving her by throwing herself into his arms, or with the mere phrase, "Father, I've come to ask you how I sing." But she had not been able to overcome her aversion to going to Dulwich, and every time the question presented itself a look of distress came into her face. "If I only knew what he would say when he sees me. If the first word were over—the 'entrance,'" she added, with a smile.

It was hopeless to argue with her, so Owen said that if she did not go before the end of the week it would be better to postpone her visit until after her first appearance.

"But supposing I fail. I never cared for my Margaret. Besides, it was mother's great part. He'll think me as bad an artist as I have been a bad daughter. Owen, dear, have patience with me, I know I'm very weak, but I dread a face of stone."

Neither spoke for a long while. Then she said, "If I had only gone to him last year. You remember he had written me a nice letter, but instead I went away yachting; you wanted to go to Greece."

"Evelyn, don't lay the blame on me; you wanted to go too.... I hope that when you do see your father you will say that it was not all my fault."

"That what was not your fault, dear?"

"Well—I mean that it was not all my fault that we went away together. You know that I always liked your father. I was interested in his ideas; I do not want him to think too badly of me. You will say something in my favour. After all, I haven't treated you badly. If I didn't marry you, it was because—"

"Dearest Owen, you've been very good to me."

He felt that to ask her again to go to see her father would only distress her. He said instead—

"I hear a great deal about your father's choir. It appears to be quite the fashion to hear high mass at St. Joseph's."

"Father always said that Palestrina would draw all London, if properly given. Last Sunday he gave a mass by Vittoria; I longed to go. He'll never forgive me for not going to hear his choir. It is strange that we both should have succeeded—he with Palestrina, I with Wagner."

"Yes, it is strange.... But you promise me that you'll go and see him as soon as you've sung Margaret—the following day."

"Yes, dear, I promise you I'll do that."

"You'll send him a box for the first night?"

"He wouldn't sit in a box. If he went at all, it would be in some obscure place where he would not be seen."

"You had better send him a box, a stall and a dress circle, then he can take his choice.... But perhaps you had better not send. His presence among the audience would only make you nervous."

"No, on the contrary, his presence would make me sing."

For whatever reason she had certainly sung and acted with exceptional force and genius, and Margaret was at once lifted out of the obscurity into which it was slipping and took rank with her Elizabeth and her Elsa. As they drove home together in the brougham after the performance, Owen assured her that she had infused a life and meaning into the part, and that henceforth her reading would have to be "adopted."

"I wonder if father was there? He was not in the box. Did you look in the stalls?"

"Yes, but he was not there. You'll go and see him to-morrow."

"No, not to-morrow, dear."

"Why not to-morrow?"

"Because I want him to see the papers. He may not have been in the theatre; on Thursday night is Lady Ascott's ball; then on Friday—I'll go and see father on Friday. I'll try to summon courage. But there is a rehearsal of 'Tannhäuser' on Friday."

And so that she might not be too tired on Friday morning, Owen insisted on her leaving the ball-room at two o'clock, and their last words, as he left her on her doorstep, were that she would go to Dulwich before she went to rehearsal. But in the warmth of her bed, not occupied long enough to restore to the body the strength of which a ball-room had robbed it, her resolution waned, and her brain, weak from insufficient sleep, shrank from the prospect of a long drive and a face of stone at the end of it. She sat moodily sipping her chocolate and *brioche*.

"You were at the opera last night, Merat. Was Mademoiselle Helbrun a success?"

"No, mademoiselle, I'm afraid not."

"Ah!" Evelyn put down her cup and looked at her maid. "I'm sorry, but I thought she wouldn't succeed in London. She was coldly received, was she?"

"Yes, mademoiselle."

"I'm sorry, for she's a true artist."

"She has not the passion of mademoiselle."

A little look of pleasure lit up Evelyn's face.

"She is a charming singer. I can't think how she could have failed. Did you hear any reason given?"

"Yes, mademoiselle, I met Mr. Ulick Dean."

"What did he say? He'd know."

"He said that Mademoiselle Helbrun's was the true reading of the part. But 'Carmen' had lately been turned into a *femme de la balle*, and, of course, since the public had tasted realism it wanted more. I thought Mademoiselle Helbrun rather cold. But then I'm one of the public. Mademoiselle has not yet told me what I am to tell the coachman."

"You do not listen to me, Merat," Evelyn answered in a sudden access of ill humour. "Instead of accepting the answer I choose to give, you stop there in the intention of obtaining the answer which seems to you the most suitable. I told you to tell the coachman that he was to get a map and acquaint himself with the way to Dulwich."

And to bring the interview to a close, she told Merat to take away the chocolate tray, and took up one of the scores which lay on a small table by the bedside—"Tannhäuser" and "Tristan and Isolde." It would bore her to look at Elizabeth again; she knew it all. She chose Tristan instead, and began reading the second act at the place where Isolde, ignoring Brangäne's advice, signals to Tristan with the handkerchief. She glanced down the lines, hearing the motive on the 'cellos, then, in precipitated rhythm, taken up by the violins. When the emotion has reached breaking point, Tristan rushes into Isolde's arms, and the frantic happiness of the lovers is depicted in short, hurried phrases. The score slipped from her hands and her thoughts ran in reminiscence of a similar scene which she had endured in Venice nearly four years ago. She had not seen Owen for two months, and was expecting him every hour. The old walls of the palace, the black and watchful pictures, the watery odours and echoes from the canal had frightened and exhausted her. The persecution of passion in her brain and the fever of passion afloat in her blood waxed, and the minutes became each a separate torture. There was only one lamp. She had watched it, fearing every moment lest it should go out.... She had cast a frightened glance round the room, and it was the spectre of life that her exalted imagination saw, and her natural eyes a strange ascension of the moon. The moon rose out of a sullen sky, and its reflection trailed down the lagoon. Hardly any stars were visible, and everything was extraordinarily still. The houses leaned heavily forward and Evelyn feared she might go mad, and it was through this phantom world of lagoon and autumn mist that a gondola glided. This time her heart told her with a loud cry that he had come, and she had stood in the shadowy room waiting for him, her brain on fire. The emotion of that night came to her at will, and lying in her warm bed she considered the meeting of Tristan and Isolde in the garden, and the duet on the bank of sultry flowers. Like Tristan and Isolde, she and Owen had struggled to find expression for their emotion, but, not having music, it had lain cramped up in their hearts, and their kisses were vain to express it. She found it in these swift irregularities of rhythm, replying to every change of motion, and every change of key cried back some pang of the heart.

This scene in the second act was certainly one of the most difficult—at least to her—and the one in which she most despaired of excelling. It suddenly occurred to her that she might study it with Ulick Dean. She had met him at rehearsal, and had been much interested in him.

He had sent her six melodies—strange, old-world rhythms, recalling in a way the Gregorian she used to read in childhood in the missals, yet modulated as unintermittently as Wagner; the same chromatic scale and yet a haunting of the antique rhythm in the melody. Ulick knew her father; he had said, "Mr. Innes is my greatest friend." He loved her father, she could see that, but she had not dared to question him. Talking to Owen was like the sunshine—the earth and only the earth was visible—whereas talking to Ulick was like the twilight through which the stars were shining. Dreams were to him the true realities; externals he accepted as other people accepted dreams—with diffidence. Evelyn laughed, much amused by herself and Ulick, and she laughed as she thought of his fixed and averted look as he related the tales of bards and warriors. Every now and then his dark eyes would light up with gleams of sunny humour; he probably believed that the legends contained certain eternal truths, and these he was shaping into operas. He was the most interesting young man she had met this long while. He had been about to tell her why he had recanted his Wagnerian faith when they had been interrupted by Owen.... She could conceive nothing more interesting than the recantation by a man of genius of the ideas that had first inspired him. His opera had been accepted, and would be produced if she undertook the principal part. Why should she not? They could both help each other. Truly, he was the person with whom she could study Isolde, and she imagined the flood of new light he would throw upon it. Her head drowsed on the pillow, and she dreamed the wonderful things he would tell her. But as she drowsed she thought of the article he had written about her Margaret, and it was the desire to read it again that awoke her. Stretching out her hand, she took it from the table at her bedside and began reading. He liked the dull green dress she wore in the first act; and the long braids of golden hair which he admired were her own. He had mentioned them and the dark velvet cape, which he could not remember whether she wore or carried. As a matter of fact, she carried it on her arm. His forgetfulness on this point seemed to her charming, and she smiled with pleasure. He said that she made good use of the cape in the next act, and she was glad that he had perceived that.

Like every other Margaret, her prayer-book was in her hand when she first met Faust; but she dropped it as she saw him, and while she shyly and sweetly sang that she was neither a lady nor a beauty, she stooped and with some embarrassment picked up the book. She passed on, and did not stop to utter a mechanical cry when she saw Mephistopheles, and then run away. She hesitated a moment; Mephistopheles was not in sight, but Faust was just behind her, and over the face of Margaret flashed the thought, "What a charming—what a lovely young man! I think I'll stop a little longer, and possibly he'll say something more. But no—after all—perhaps I'd better not," and, with a little sigh of regret, she turned and went, at first quietly and then more quickly, as though fearful of being tempted to change her mind.

In the garden scene, she sang the first bars of the music absent-mindedly, dusting and folding her little cape, stopping when it was only half folded to stand forgetful a moment, her eyes far off, gazing back into the preceding act. Awaking with a little start, she went to her spinning-wheel, and, with her back to the audience, arranged the spindle and the flax. Then stopping in her work and standing in thought, she half hummed, half sang the song "Le Roi de Thulé." Not till she had nearly finished did she sit down and spin, and then only for a moment, as though too restless and disturbed for work that afternoon.

Evelyn was glad that Ulick had remarked that the jewels were not "the ropes of pearls we are accustomed to, but strange, mediæval jewels, long, heavy earrings and girdles and broad bracelets." Owen had given her these. She remembered how she had put them on, just as Ulick said, with the joy of a child and the musical glee of a bird. "She laughed out the jewel song," he said, "with real laughter, returning lightly across the stage;" and he said that they had "wondered what was this lovely music which they had never heard before!" And when she placed the jewels back, she did so lingeringly, regretfully, slowly, one by one, even forgetting the earrings, perhaps purposely, till just before she entered the house.

"In the duet with Faust," he said, "we were drawn by that lovely voice as in a silken net, and life had for us but one meaning—the rapture of love."

"Has it got any other meaning?" Evelyn paused a moment to think. She was afraid that it had long ceased to have any other meaning for her. But love did not seem to play a large part in Ulick's life. Yet that last sentence—to write like that he must feel like that. She wondered, and then continued reading his article.

She was glad that he had noticed that when she fainted at the sight of Mephistopheles, she slowly revived as the curtain was falling and pointed to the place where he had been, seeing him again in her over-wrought brain. This she did think was a good idea, and, as he said, "seemed to accomplish something."

He thought her idea for her entrance in the following act exceedingly well imagined, for, instead of coming on neatly dressed and smiling like the other Margarets, she came down the steps of the church with her dress and hair disordered, in the arms of two women, walking with difficulty, only half recovered from her fainting fit. "It is by ideas like this," he said, "that the singer carried forward the story, and made it seem like a real scene that was happening before our eyes. And after her brother had cursed Margaret, when he falls back dead, Miss Innes retreats, getting away from the body, half mad, half afraid. She did not rush immediately to him, as has been the operatic custom, kneel down, and, with one arm leaning heavily on Valentine's stomach, look up in the flies. Miss Innes, after backing far away from him, slowly returned, as if impelled to do so against her will, and, standing over the body, looked at it with curiosity, repulsion, terror; and then she burst into a whispered laugh, which communicated a feeling of real horror to the audience.

"In the last act, madness was tangled in her hair, and in her wide-open eyes were read the workings of her insane brain, and her every movement expressed the pathos of madness; her lovely voice told its sad tale without losing any of its sweetness and beauty. The pathos of the little souvenir phrases was almost unbearable, and the tragic power of the finish was extraordinary in a voice of such rare distinction and fluid utterance. Her singing and acting went hand in hand, twin sisters, equal and indivisible, and when the great moment in the trio came, she stepped forward and with an inspired intensity lifted her quivering hands above her head in a sort of mad ecstasy, and sang out the note clear and true, yet throbbing with emotion."

The paper slid from Evelyn's hand. She could see from Ulick's description of her acting that she had acted very well; if she had not, he could not have written like that. But her acting only seemed extraordinary when she read about it. It was all so natural to her. She simply went on the stage, and once she was on the stage she could not do otherwise. She could not tell why she did things. Her acting was so much a part of herself that she could not think of it as an art at all; it was merely a medium through which she was able to re-live past phases of her life, or to exhibit her present life in a more intense and concentrated form. The dropping of the book was quite true; she had dropped a piece of music when she first saw Owen, and the omission of the scream was natural to her. She felt sure that she would not have seen Mephistopheles just then; she would have been too busy thinking of the young man. But she thought that she might take a little credit for her entrance in the third act. Somehow her predecessors had not seen that it was absurd to come smiling and tripping out of church, where she had seen Mephistopheles. She read the lines describing her power to depict madness. But even in the mad scenes she was not conscious of having invented anything. She had had sensations of madness—she supposed everyone had—and she threw herself into those sensations, intensifying them, giving them more prominence on the stage than they had had in her own personal life.

Many had thought her a greater actress than a singer; and she had been advised to dispense with her voice and challenge a verdict on her speaking voice in one of Shakespeare's plays. Owen would have liked her to risk the adventure, but she dared not. It would seem a wanton insult to her voice. She had imagined that it might leave her as an offended spirit might leave its local habitation. Her Margaret had been accepted in Italy, so she must sing it as well as she acted it. But when she had asked the Marquis d'Albazzi if she sang it as well as her mother, he had said, "Mademoiselle, the singers of my day were as exquisite flutes, and the singers of your day give emotions that no flute could give me," and when she had told him that she was going to be so bold as to attempt Norma, he had raised his eyebrows a little and said, "Mademoiselle will sing it according to the fashion of to-day; we cannot compare the present with the past." Ah! *Ce vieux marquis était très fin.* And her father would think the same; never would he admit that she could sing like her mother. But Ulick had said—and no doubt he had already read Ulick's article—that she had rescued the opera from the grave into which it was gliding. None of them liked it for itself. Her father spoke indulgently about it because her mother had sung it. Ulick praised it because he was tired of hearing Wagner praised, and she liked it because her first success had been made in it.

These morning hours, how delicious they were! to roll over in one's silk nightgown, to feel it tighten round one's limbs and to think how easily success had come. Madame Savelli had taught her eight operas in ten months, and she had sung Margaret in Brussels—a very thin performance, no doubt, but she had always been a success. Ulick would not have thought much of her first Margaret. Almost all the points he admired she had since added. She had learnt the art of being herself on the stage. That was all she had learnt, and she very much doubted if there was anything else to learn. If Nature gives one a personality worth exhibiting, the art of acting is to get as much of one's personality into the part as possible. That was the A B C and the X Y Z of the art of acting. She had always found that when she was acting herself, she was acting something that had not been acted before. She did not compare her Margaret with her Elizabeth. With Margaret she was back in the schoolroom. Still she thought that Ulick was right; she had got a new thrill out of it. Her Margaret was unpublished, but her Elizabeth was three times as real. There was no comparison; not even in Isolde could she be more true to herself. Her Elizabeth was a side of her life that now only existed on the stage. Brunnhilde was her best part, for into it she poured all her joy of life, all her love of the blue sky with great white clouds floating, all her enthusiasm for life and for the hero who came to awaken her to life and to love. In Brunnhilde and Elizabeth all the humanity she represented—and she thought she was a fairly human person—was on the stage. But Elsa? That was the one part she was dissatisfied with. There were people who liked her Elsa. Oh, her Elsa had been greatly praised. Perhaps she was mistaken, but at the bottom of her heart she could not but feel that her Elsa was a failure. The truth was that she had never understood the story. It began beautifully, the beginning was wonderful—the maiden whom everyone was persecuting, who would be put to death if some knight did not come to her aid. She could sing the dream—that she understood. Then the silver-clad knight who comes from afar, down the winding river, past thorpe and town, to release her from those who were plotting against her. But afterwards? This knight who wanted to marry her, and who would not tell his name. What did it mean? And the celebrated duet in the nuptial chamber—what did it mean? It was beautiful music—but what did it mean? Could anyone tell her? She had often asked, but no one had ever been able to tell her.

She knew very well the meaning of the duet, when Siegfried adventures through the fire-surrounded mountain and wakes Brunnhilde with a kiss. That duet meant the joy of life, the rapture of awakening to the adventure of life, the delight of the swirling current of ephemeral things. And the duet that she was going to sing; she knew what that meant too. It meant the desire to possess. Desire finding a barrier to complete possession in the flesh would break off the fleshly lease, and enter the great darkness where alone was union and rest.

But she could not discover the idea in the "Lohengrin" duet? Senta she understood, and she thought she understood Kundry. She had not yet begun to study the part. But Elsa? Suddenly the thought that, if she was going to Dulwich, she must get up, struck her like a spur, and she sprang out of bed, and laying her finger on the electric bell she kept the button pressed till Merat arrived breathless.

"Merat, I shall get up at once; prepare my bath, and tell the coachman I shall be ready to start in twenty minutes."

"Twenty minutes? Mademoiselle is joking."

"No, I am not ... in twenty minutes—half-an-hour at the most."

"It would be impossible for me to dress you in less than three-quarters of an hour."

"I shall be dressed in half-an-hour. Go and tell the coachman at once; I shall have had my bath when you return."

Her dressing was accomplished amid curt phrases. "It doesn't matter, that will do.... I can't afford to waste time.... Come, Merat, try to get on with my hair."

And while Merat buttoned her boots, she buttoned her gloves. She wore a grey, tailor-made dress and a blue veil tied round a black hat with ostrich feathers. Escaping from her maid's hands, she ran downstairs. But the dining-room door opened, and Lady Duckle intervened.

"My dear girl, you really cannot go out before you have had something to eat."

"I cannot stay; I'll get something at the theatre."

"Do eat a cutlet, it will not take a moment ... a mouthful of omelette. Think of your voice."

There were engravings after Morland on the walls, and the silver on the breakfast-table was Queen Anne—the little round tea urn Owen and Evelyn had picked up the other day in a suburban shop; the horses, whose glittering red hides could be seen through the window, had been bought last Saturday at Tattersall's. Evelyn went to the window to admire them, and Lady Duckle's thoughts turned to the coachman.

"He sent in just now to ask for a map of London. It appears he doesn't know the way, yet, when I took up his references, I was assured that he knew London perfectly."

"Dulwich is very little known; it is at least five miles from here."

"Oh, Dulwich!... you're going there?"

"Yes, I ought to have gone the day after we arrived in London. ... I wanted to; I've been thinking of it all the time, and the longer I put it off the more difficult it will become."

"That is true."

"I thought I would drive there to-day before I went to rehearsal."

"Why choose a day on which you have a rehearsal?"

"Only because I've put it off so often. Something always happens to prevent me. I must see my father."

"Have you written to him?"

"No, but I sent him a paper containing an account of the first night. I thought he might have written to me about it, or he might have come to see me. He must know that I am dying to see him."

"I think it would be better for you to go to see him in the first instance."

Lady Duckle meant Evelyn to understand that it would not be well to risk anything that might bring about a meeting between Sir Owen and Mr. Innes. But she did not dare to be more explicit. Owen had forbidden any discussion of his relations with Evelyn.

"Of course it would be nice for you to see your father. But you should, I think, go to him; surely that is the proper course."

"We've written to each other from time to time, but not lately—not since we went to Greece.... I've neglected my correspondence."

Tears rose to Evelyn's eyes, and Lady Duckle was sorely tempted to lead her into confidences. But Owen's counsels prevailed; she dissembled, saying that she knew how Evelyn loved her father, and how nice it would be for her to see him again after such a long absence.

"I dare say he'll forgive me, but there'll be reproaches. I don't think there's anyone who hates a scene more than I do."

"I haven't lived with you five years without having found out that. But in avoiding a disagreeable scene we are often preparing one more disagreeable."

"That is true.... I think I'll go to Dulwich."

"Shall you have time?... You're not in the first act."

"Dulwich is not six miles from here. We can drive there easily in three-quarters of an hour. And three-quarters of an hour to get back. They won't begin to rehearse the second act before one. It is a little after ten now."

"Then good-bye."

Lady Duckle followed her to the front door and stood for a moment to admire the beauty of the morning. The chestnut horses pawed the ground restlessly, excited by the scent of the lilac which a wilful little breeze carried up from Hamilton Place. Every passing hansom was full of flowered silks, and the pale laburnum gold hung in loose tassels out of quaint garden inlets. The verandahed balconies seemed to hang lower than ever, and they were all hung and burdened with flowers. And of all these eighteenth century houses, Evelyn's was the cosiest, and the elder of the two men, who, from the opposite pavement, stood watching the prima donna stroking the quivering nostrils of her almost thoroughbred chestnuts with her white-gloved hand, could easily imagine her in her pretty drawing-room standing beside a cabinet filled with Worcester and old Battersea china, for he knew Owen's taste and was certain the Louis XVI. marble clock would be well chosen, and he would have bet five-and-twenty-pounds that there were some Watteau and Gainsborough drawings on the walls.

"Owen is doing the thing well. Those horses must have cost four hundred. I know how much the Boucher drawing cost."

"How do you know there is a Boucher drawing?"

"Because we bid against each other for it at Christie's. A woman lying on her stomach, drawn very freely, very simply—quite a large drawing—just the thing for such a room as hers is, amid chintz and eighteenth century inlaid or painted tables."

"I wonder where she is going. Perhaps to see him."

"At ten o'clock in the morning! More likely that she will call at her dressmaker's on her way to rehearsal. She is to sing Elizabeth to-morrow night." And while discussing her singing, the elder man asked himself if he had ever had a mistress that would compare with her. "She isn't by any means a beautiful woman," he said, "but she's the sort of woman that if one did catch on to it would be for a long while."

The young man pitied Evelyn's misfortune of so elderly an admirer as Owen. It seemed to him impossible that she could like a man who must be over forty, and the thought saddened him that he might never possess so desirable a mistress.

"I wonder of she's faithful to him?"

"Faithful to him, after six years of *liaison!*"

"But, my dear Frank, we know you don't believe that any woman is straight. How do you know that he is her lover? Very often—"

"My dear Cyril, because you meet her at a ball at Lady Ascott's, and because she has lived with that Lady Duckle—an old thing who used to present the daughters of ironmongers at Court for a consideration—above all, because you want her yourself, you are ready to believe anything. I never did meet anyone who could deceive himself with the same ease. Besides, I know all about her. It's quite an extraordinary story."

"How did he pick her up?"

"I'll tell you presently. She's got into her carriage; we shall be able to see if she rouges as she passes."

Evelyn had noticed the men as she stood trying to explain as much of the way as she could to her somewhat obtuse coachman. Her bow was gracious as the chestnuts swept the light carriage by them; the young man pleased her fancy for the moment, and she tried to recall the few words they had exchanged as she left the ball. The elder man was a friend of Owen's. But his face was suddenly blotted from her mind. For if her father were to refuse to see her, if he were to cast her off for good and all, what would she do? Her life would be unendurable; she would go mad, mad as Margaret. But the picture did not frighten her, she knew it was fictitious; and looking into her soul for the truth, she saw the trees in the Green Park and the chimney pots of Walsingham House, and she realised that the nearest future is enveloped in obscurity. She had always dreaded the journey to London; she had been warned against London, and ever since she had consented to come she had been ill at ease and nervous—of what she did not know—of someone behind her, of someone lurking round her. She argued that she would not have had those feelings if there was not a reason. When she had them, something always happened to her, and nothing could convince her that London was not the turning-point in her fortune. The carriage seemed to be going very fast; they were already in Victoria Street; she cried to the coachman not to drive so fast, he answered that he must drive at that pace if he was to get there by eleven.... Surely her father would not refuse to see her. He could not, he would not take her by the shoulders and turn her out of the house—the house she had known all her life. Oh, good heavens! if he did, what would happen afterwards? She could not go back to Owen and sing operas at Covent Garden, and her soul wailed like a child and a deadly terror of her father came upon her. It might be her destiny never to speak to him again! That fate had been the fate of other women. Why should it not be hers? He might not send for her when he was dying, and if she were dying he might not come to her; and after death, would she see him? Would they then be reconciled? If she did not see her father in this world, she would never see him, for she had promised Owen to believe in oblivion, and she thought she did believe in nothing; but she felt now that she must say her prayers, she must pray that her father might forgive her. It might be absurd, but she felt that a prayer would ease her mind. It was dreadfully hypocritical to pray to a God one didn't believe in. There was no sense in it, nor was there much sense in much else one did.... She had promised Owen not to pray, and it was a sort of blasphemy to say prayers and lead a life of sin. She did not like to break her promise to Owen. She must make up her mind.... Her father might be at St. Joseph's! and it was with a sense of refreshing delight that she called the coachman and gave the order. The chestnuts were prancing like greyhounds amid heavy drays and clumsy, bear-like horses; the coachman was trying to hold them in and to understand the policeman, who shouted the way to him from the edge of the pavement.

CHAPTER THIRTEEN

But she ought not to go to St. Joseph's. She had promised Owen to avoid churches, priests—all that reminded her of religion. He had begged that until she was firm in her agnosticism she should not expose herself to influences which could but result in mental distress, and without any practical issue unless to separate them. She had escaped once; next time he might find it more difficult to win her back. How kind he was. He had not said a word about his own suffering.
It had happened nearly three years ago in Florence, and an accident had brought it all about. One afternoon she was walking in the streets; she could still see the deep cornices showing distinct against the sky; she was admiring them when suddenly a church appeared; she could not tell how it was, but she had been propelled to enter.... A feeling which had arisen out of her heart, a sort of yearning—that was it. The church was almost empty; how restful it had seemed that afternoon, the rough plastered walls and the two figures of the nuns absorbed in prayer. Her heart had begun to ache, and her daily life with its riches and glories had seemed to concern her no longer. It was as if the light had changed, and she had become suddenly aware of her real self. A tall cross stood oddly placed between the arches; she had not seen it at first, but as her eyes rested upon it she had been drawn into wistful communion with her dying Redeemer. And all that had seemed false suddenly became true, and she had left the church overcome with remorse. That night her door was closed to Owen; she had pleaded indisposition, unable for some shame to speak the truth. On the next day and the day after the desire of forgiveness had sent her to the church and then to the priest, but the priest had refused her absolution till she separated from her lover. She had felt that she must obey. She

had written a note—she could not think of it now—so cruel did it seem, yet at the time it had seemed quite natural. It was not until the next day, and the day after was worse still, that she began to plumb the depths of her own unhappiness; every day it seemed to grow deeper. She could not keep him out of her mind. She used to sit and try to do needlework in the hotel sitting-room. But how often had she had to put it down and to walk to the window to hide her tears? As the time drew near for her to go to the theatre, she had to vow not to cry again till she got home. He was always in his box—once she had nearly broken down, and, pitying her, he came no more. But not to see him at all was worse than the pain of seeing him. That empty box! And all through the night she thought of him in his hotel, only a street or two distant. She could not go through it again, nor could she think what would have happened if they had not met. Something had prompted her to go out one afternoon; she was weak with weeping and sick with love, and, feeling that there are burdens beyond our strength, she had walked with her eyes steadily fixed before her ... and somehow she was not surprised when she saw him coming towards her. He joined her quite naturally, as if by appointment, and they had walked on, instinctively finding their way out of the crowd. They had walked on and on, now and then exchanging remarks, waiting for a full explanation, wondering what form it would take. Cypresses and campanili defined themselves in the landscape as the evening advanced. Further on the country flattened out; there were urban gardens and dusty little vineyards. They had sat on a bench; above them was a statue of the Virgin; she remembered noticing it; it reminded her of her scapular, but nothing had mattered to her then but Owen. He said—
"Well Evelyn, when is all this nonsense going to cease?"
"I don't know, Owen; I'm very unhappy."
The sense of reconciliation which overtook her was too delicious to be resisted, and she remembered how all the way home she had longed for the moment when she would throw herself into his arms. He had not reproved her nor reproached her; he had merely forgiven her the pain she had caused him. There were sounds of children's voices in the air and a glow of light upon the roofs. Their talk had been gentle and philosophic; she had listened eagerly, and had promised to shun influences which made her uselessly unhappy. And he had promised her that in time to come she would surely succeed in freeing herself from the tentacles of this church, and that the day would come when she would watch the Mass as she would some childish sport. "Though," he added, smiling, "it is doubtful if anyone can see his own rocking-horse without experiencing a desire to mount it." Nearly three years had passed since that time in Florence, and she was now going to put the strength of her agnosticism to the test.
"They have not built a new entrance," she remarked to herself, as the coachman reined up the chestnuts before the meagre steps. "But alterations are being made," she thought, catching sight of some scaffolding. As she stepped out of her carriage she remembered that her dress and horses could not fail to suggest Owen's money to her father. She paused, and then hoped he would remember that she was getting three hundred pounds a week, and could pay for her carriage and gowns herself. And, smiling at the idea of dressing herself in a humble frock suitable for reconciliation, she entered the church hurriedly. She did not care to meet him in open daylight, in the presence of her servants. The church would be a better place. He could not say much to her in church, and she thought she would like to meet him suddenly face to face; then there would be no time for explanations, and he could not refuse to speak to her. Looking round she saw that Mass was in progress at one of the side altars. The acolyte had just changed the book from the left to the right, and the congregation of about a dozen had risen for the reading of the Gospel. She knew that her father was not among them. She must have known all the while that he was not in church. If he were at St. Joseph's, he would be in the practising room. She might go round and ask for him ... and run the risk of meeting one of the priests! They were men of tact, and would refrain from unpleasant allusions. But they knew she was on the stage, that she had not been back since she had left home; they could

not but suspect; however they might speak, she could not avoid reading meanings, which very likely were not intended, into their words.... And she would see the practising room full of faces, and her father, already angry at the interruption, opening the door to her. It would be worse than meeting him in the street. No, she would not seek him in the practising room—then where—Dulwich? Perhaps, but not to-day. She would wait in the church and see if the Elevation compelled her to bow her head.

And in this intention she took a seat in full view of the altar where the priest was saying Mass. Every shape and every colour of this church, its slightest characteristics, brought back an impression of long ago; the very wording of her childish thoughts was suddenly remembered; and she felt, whether she believed or disbelieved, that it was pleasant to kneel where she knelt when she was a little girl. It was touching to see the poor folk pray. The poor Irish and Italians—especially the Irish—how simple they were; it was all real to them, however false it may have become to her. Her eyes wandered among the little congregation; only one she recognised—the strangely thin and crooked lady who, as far back as she could remember, used to walk up the aisle, her hands crossed in front of her like a wooden doll's. She had not altered at all; she wore the same battered black bonnet. This lonely lady had always been a subject of curiosity to Evelyn. She remembered how she used to invent houses for her to live in and suitable friends and evenings at home. The day that Owen came to St. Joseph's before he went away on his yacht to the Mediterranean, he had put his hat on this lady's chair, and she had had to ask him to remove it. How frightened she had looked, and he not too well pleased at having to sit beside her. That was six years ago, and Evelyn thought how much had happened to her in that time—a great deal to her and very little to that poor woman in the black bonnet. She must have some little income on which she lived in a room with wax fruit in the window. Every morning and evening she was at St. Joseph's. The church was her one distraction; it was her theatre, the theatre certainly of all her thoughts.

But at that moment the new choir-loft caught Evelyn's eye, and she imagined the melodious choirs answering each other from opposite sides. No doubt her father had insisted on the addition, so that such antiphonal music as the Reproaches might be given. Some rich carpets had been laid down, some painting and cleaning had been done, and the fashionable names on the front seats reminded her of the Grand Circle at Covent Garden. Evidently the frequentation of St. Joseph's was much the same as the theatres. The congregation was attracted by the choirs, and, when these were silenced, the worship shrank into the mumbled prayers of a few Irish and Italians. Evelyn wondered if the poor lady could distinguish between her father's music and Father Gordon's. The only music she heard was the ceaseless music of her devout soul.

Was it not strange that the paper she had sent her father containing an account of her success in the part of Margaret contained also an account of his choir? They had both succeeded. The old music had made St. Joseph's a fashionable church. So far she knew, and despite her strange terror of their first meeting, she longed to hear him tell her how he had overcome the opposition of Father Gordon.

The Gospel ended, the little congregation sat down, and Evelyn reflected how much more difficult belief was to her than to the slightly-deformed woman in front of her. The doctrine that a merciful God has prepared a place of eternal torment for his erring creatures is hard enough to credit. She didn't think she could ever believe that again; or that God had sent his Son on earth to expiate on the cross the sins which he and his Father in conjunction with the Holy Ghost had fated them to commit; or that bread and wine becomes, at the bidding of the priest, the creator of all the stars we see at midnight. True that she believed these doctrines no longer, but, unfortunately, this advancement brought her no nearer to the solution of the question directly affecting her life. Owen encouraged her to persevere in her agnosticism. "Old instincts," he said, "are not conquered at once. You must be patient. The Scotch were converted about three or four hundred years after Christ. Christianity is therefore fourteen hundred years old, whereas the seed of agnosticism has been sown but a few years; give it time to catch root." She had laughed, his wit amused her, but our feelings are—well, they are ours, and we cannot separate ourselves from them. They are certain, though everything else is uncertain, and when she looked into her mind (she tried to avoid doing so as much as possible, but she could not always help herself) something told her that the present was but a passing stage. Often it seemed to her that she was like one out on a picnic—she was amused—she would be sorry when it ended; but she could not feel that it was to last. Other women were at home in their lives; she was not in hers. We all have a life that is more natural for us to live than any other; we all have a mission of some sort to accomplish, and the happiest are those whose lives correspond to their convictions. Even Owen's love did not quite compensate her for the lack of agreement between her outer and inner life.

All this they had argued a hundred times, but their points of view were so different. Once, however, she thought she had made him understand. She had said, "If you don't understand religion, you understand art. Well, then, imagine a man who wants to paint pictures; give him a palace to live in; place every pleasure at his call, imposing only one condition—that he is not to paint. His appetites may detain him in the palace for a while, but sooner or later he will cry out, 'All these pleasures are nothing to me; what I want is to paint pictures.'" She could see that the parable had convinced him, or nearly. He had said he was afraid she was hopeless. But a moment after, drawing her toward him with quiet, masterful arm, and speaking with that hard voice that could become so soft, it had seemed as if heaven suddenly melted away, and his kisses were worth every sacrifice.

That was the worst of it. She was neither one thing nor the other. She desired two lives diametrically opposed to each other, consequently she would never be happy. But she was happy. She had everything; she could think of nothing that she wanted that she had not got: it was really too ridiculous for her to pretend to herself that she was not happy. So long as she had believed in religion she had not been happy, but now she believed no longer—she was happy. It was strange, however, that a church always brought the old feeling back again, and her thoughts paused, and in a silent awe of soul she asked herself if, at the bottom of her soul, she still disbelieved in God. But it was so silly to believe the story of the Virgin—think of it.... As Owen said, in no mythology was there anything more ridiculous. Nevertheless, she did not convince herself that the dim, vague, unquiet sensation which rankled in her was not a still unextirpated germ of the original faith. She tried to think it was not a religious feeling but the result of the terrible interview still hanging over her, the dread that her father might not forgive her. She tried to look into her mind to discover the impulse which had compelled her to turn from her intention and come to this church. She remembered the uncontrollable desire to say a prayer: that she could have resisted, but the moment after she had remembered that perhaps it was too late to find her father at home. But had she really hoped to find him at St. Joseph's, or had she used the pretext to deceive herself? She could not tell. But if religion was not true, if she did not believe, how was it that she had always thought it wrong to live with a man to whom she was not married? There was no use pretending, she never had quite got a haunting scruple on that point out of her mind.

There could be but two reasons, he had insisted, for the maintenance of the matrimonial idea—the preservation of the race, and the belief that cohabitation without matrimony is an offence against God. But the race is antecedent to matrimony, and if there be no resurrection, there can be no religion.... If there be no personal God who manages our affairs and summons to everlasting bliss or torment, the matter is not worth thinking about—at least not to a Catholic. Pious agnosticism is a bauble unworthy to tempt anyone who has been brought up a Catholic. A Catholic remains a Catholic, or else becomes a frank agnostic. Only weak-minded Protestants run to that slender shelter—morality without God. "But why are you like this?" he had said, fixing his eyes.... "I think I see. Your father comes of a long line of Scotch Protestants; he became a Catholic so that he might marry your mother. Your scruples must be a Protestant heredity. I wonder if it is so? In no other way can I account for the fact that although you no longer believe in a resurrection, you cling fast to the doctrine which declares it wrong for two people, both free, to live together, unless they register their cohabitation in the parish books. Our reason is our own. Our feelings we inherit. You are enslaved to your Scotch ancestors; you are a slave to the superstitions of your grandmother and your grand-aunts; you obey them."

"But do we not inherit our reason just as much as we inherit our feelings?"

They had argued that point. She could not remember what his argument was, but she remembered that she had held her ground, that he had complimented her, not forgetting, however, to take the credit of the improvement in her intellectual equipment to himself, which was indeed no more than just. She would have been nothing without him. How he had altered her! She had come to think and feel like him. She often caught herself saying exactly what he would say in certain circumstances, and having heard him say how odours affected him, she had tried to acquire a like sensibility. Unconsciously she had assimilated a great deal. That little trick of his, using his eyes a certain way, that knowing little glance of his had become habitual to her. She had met men who were more profound, never anyone whose mind was more alert, more amusing and sufficient for every occasion. She sentimentalised a moment, and then remembered further similarities. They now ate the same dishes, and no longer had need to consult each other before ordering dinner. In their first week in Paris she had learnt to look forward to chocolate in the morning before she got up, and this taste was endeared to her, for it reminded her of him. In the picture galleries she had always tried to pick out the pictures he would like. If they could not decide how a passage should be sung, or were in doubt regarding the attitude and gesture best fitted to carry on a dramatic action, she had noticed that, if they separated so that they might arrive at individual conclusions, they almost always happened upon the same. To each other they now affected not to know from whom a certain quaint notion had come—clearly it had been inspired by him, but which had first expressed it was not sure—that the three great type operas were "Tristan and Isolde," the "Barber of Seville," and "La Belle Hélène." Nor were they sure which had first suggested that in the last week of her stage career she should appear in all three parts. Evelyn Innes, as La Belle Hélène, would set musical London by the ears.

She had often wondered whether, by having absorbed so much of Owen's character, she had proved herself deficient in character. Owen maintained, on the contrary, that the sign of genius is the power of recognising and assimilating that which is necessary to the development of oneself. He mentioned Goethe's life, which he said was but the tale of a long assimilation of ideas. The narrow, barren soul is narrow and barren because it cannot acquire. We come into the world with nothing in our own right except the capacity for the acquisition of ideas. We cannot invent ideas; we can only gather some of those in circulation since the beginning of the world. We endow them with the colour and form of our time, and, if that colour and form be of supreme quality, the work is preserved as representative of a period in the history of civilisation; a name may or may not be attached to each specimen. Genius is merely the power of assimilation; only the fool imagines he invents. Owen would go still further. He maintained that if the circumstances of a man's life admitted the acquisition of only one set of ideas, his work was thin; but if, on the contrary, circumstances threw him in the way of a new set of ideas, a set of ideas different from the first set, yet sufficiently near for the same brain to assimilate, then the work produced by that brain would be endowed with richer colour; or, in severer form, the idea was, he said, to a work of art what salt is to meat—it preserved works of art against the corrupting action of time.

How they had talked! how they had discussed things! They had talked about everything, and she remembered all he said, as she recalled the arguments he had used. The scene of this last conversation passed and repassed in vanishing gleams—Bopart on the Rhine. They had stopped there on their way to Bayreuth, where she was going to sing Elsa. The maidens and their gold, the fire-surrounding Brunnhilde, the death of the hero, the end of the legends: these she knew, but of "Parsifal" she knew nothing—the story or the music. The time was propitious for him to tell it. The flame of the candle burnt in the still midnight, and she had listened with bated breath. She could see Owen leaning forward, telling the story, and she could even see her own listening face as he related how the poor fool rises through sanctification of faith and repudiation of doubt, how he heals the sick king with the sacred spear and becomes himself the high priest of the Grail. It had seemed to Evelyn that she had been carried beyond the limits of earthly things. The thrill and shiver of the dead man's genius haunted the liquid ripple of the river; the moment was ecstatic; the deep, windless night was full of the haunting ripple of the Rhine. And she remembered how she had clasped her hands ... her very words came back to her....

"It is wonderful ... and we are listening to the Rhine; we shall never forget this midnight."

At that moment the Sanctus bell rang, and she remembered why she had stayed in church. She wished to discover what remnant, tatter or shred of her early faith still clung about her. She wished to put her agnosticism to the test. She wondered if at the moment of consecration she would be compelled to bow her head. The bell rang again.... She grew tremulous with expectation. She strove to refrain, but her head bowed a little, and her thoughts expanded into prayer; she was not sure that she actually prayed, for her thoughts did not divide into explicit words or phrases. There certainly followed a beautiful softening of her whole being, the bitterness of life extinguished; divine eyes seemed bent upon her, and she was in the midst of mercy, peace and love; and daring no longer to think she did not believe, she sat rapt till Mass was ended.

CHAPTER FOURTEEN

Still under the sweet influence of the church and the ceremony she got into her carriage. But the mystery engendered in her soul seemed to fade and die in the sunshine; she could almost perceive it going out like a gentle, evanescent mist on the surface of a pool; she remembered that she would very likely meet Ulick at rehearsal, and could find out from him how her father would be likely to receive her visit. Ulick seemed the solution of the difficulty—only he might tell her that her father did not wish to see her. She did not think he would say that, and the swing of her carriage and her thoughts went to the same rhythm until the carriage stopped before the stage door of Covent Garden Theatre.

As she ascended the stairs the swing door was pushed open. The pilgrims' song drifted through it, and she knew that they had begun the overture. She crossed a stage in indescribable disorder. Scene-shifters were calling to each other, and there was an incessant hammering in the flies. "We might as well rehearse in a barn with the threshing-machine going all the while," Evelyn thought. She had to pass down a long passage to get to the stalls, and, finding herself in inky darkness, she grew nervous, though she knew well enough whither it led. At last she perceived a little light, and, following it for a while, she happened to stumble into one of the boxes, and there she sat and indulged in angry comments on the negligence of English operatic management.

Through the grey twilight of the auditorium she could see heads and hands, and shapes of musical instruments. The conductor's grey hair was combed back over his high forehead. He swung a lean body to the right and left. Suddenly he sprang up in his seat, and, looking in the direction of certain instruments, he brought down his stick determinedly, and, having obtained the effect he desired, his beat swung leisurely for a while.... "'Cellos, crescendo," he cried. "Ah, *mon Dieu!* Ta-ra-la-la-la! Now, gentlemen, number twenty-five, please."

For a few bars the stick swung automatically, striking the harmonium as it descended. "'Cellos, a sudden piano on the accent, and then no accent whatever. Ta-ra-ta-ta-ta!"

At the back of the stalls the poor Italian chorus had gathered like a herd, not daring to sit in seats, the hire of which for a few hours equalled their weekly wages. But the English girls, whose musical tastes had compelled them from their suburban homes, had no such scruples.

Confident of the cleanliness of their skirts and hats, they sat in the best stalls, their scores on their knees. One happened to look up as Evelyn entered. She whispered to her neighbours, and immediately after the row was discussing Bayreuth and Evelyn Innes.

Meanwhile, the pilgrims' song grew more strenuous, until at last the trombones proclaimed, in unconquerable tones, Tannhäuser's abjuration of sensual life, and at that moment the tall, spare figure of Mr. Hermann Goetze, the manager, appeared in the doorway leading to the stalls. He was with his apparitor and satellite, Mr. Wheeler, a foppish little man, who seemed pleased at being in confidential conversation with his great chief. Catching sight of Evelyn in the box just above his eyes, he smiled and bowed obsequiously. A sudden thought seemed to strike him, and Evelyn said to herself, "He's coming to talk with me about the Brangäne. I hope he has done what I told him, and engaged Helbrun for the part."

At the same moment it flashed across her mind that Mademoiselle Helbrun's unsuccessful appearance in "Carmen" might cause Mr. Harmann Goetze to propose someone else. She hoped that this was not so, for she could not consent to sing Isolde to anyone but Helbrun's Brangäne, and it was in this resolute, almost aggressive, frame of mind that she received the manager.

"How do you do, Mr. Hermann Goetze? Well, I hope you succeeded in inducing Mademoiselle Helbrun to play Brangäne?"

"I have not had a moment, Miss Innes. I have not seen Mademoiselle Helbrun since last night. You will be sorry to hear that her Carmen was not considered a success.... Do you think—"

"There is no finer artist than Mademoiselle Helbrun. If you do not engage her—"

Mr. Hermann Goetze took his handkerchief from his pocket, and, upon inquiry, she learnt that he was suffering from toothache. Mr. Wheeler advised different remedies, but Mr. Hermann Goetze did not believe in remedies. There was nothing for it but to have it out. Evelyn suggested her dentist, and Mr. Hermann Goetze apologised for this interruption in the conversation. He begged of her not to think of him, and they entered into the difficult question of salary. He told her that Mademoiselle Helbrun would ask eighty pounds a performance, and such heavy salary added to the four hundred pounds a performance he was paying for the Tristan and Isolde would—But so intense was the pain from his tooth at this moment that he could not finish the sentence. A little alarmed, Evelyn waited until the spasm had ended, and when the manager's composure was somewhat restored, she spoke of the change and stress of emotion, often expressed in isolated notes and vehement declamation, and she reminded the poor man of Brangäne's long song in which she endeavours to appease Isolde. Mr. Hermann Goetze looked at her out of pain-stricken eyes, and said he was listening. She assured him that the melodious effect would be lost if Brangäne could not sing the long-drawn phrases in a single breath. But she stopped suddenly, perceiving that an æsthetic discussion was impossible with a man who was in violent pain. Mr. Wheeler proposed to go to the chemist for a remedy. Mr. Hermann Goetze shook his head; he had tried all remedies in vain; the dentist was the only resort, and he promised to go to Evelyn's when the rehearsal was over, and he retired from the box, holding his handkerchief to his face. When he got on to the stage, Evelyn was glad to see that he was a little better, and was able to give some directions regarding the stage management. She was genuinely sorry for him, for she had had toothache herself. Nevertheless, it was unfortunate that they had not been able to settle about Mademoiselle Helbrun's engagement. She pondered how this might be effected; perhaps, after rehearsal, Mr. Hermann Goetze might be feeling better, or she might ask him to dinner. As she considered the question, her eyes wandered over the auditorium in quest of Ulick Dean.

She spied him sitting in the far corner, and wondered when he would look in her direction, and then remembering what he had said about the transmission of thought between sympathetic affinities, she sought to reach him with hers. She closed her eyes so that she might concentrate her will sufficiently for it to penetrate his brain. She sat tense with her desire, her hands clenched for more than a minute, but he did not answer to her will, and its tension relaxed in spite of herself. "He sits there listening to the music as if he had never heard a note of it before. Why does he not come to me?" As if in answer, Ulick got out of his stall and walked toward the entrance, seemingly in the intention of leaving the theatre. Evelyn felt that she must speak to him, and she was about to call to one of the chorus and ask him to tell Mr. Dean that she wanted to speak to him, but a vague inquietude seemed to awaken in him, and he seemed uncertain whether to go or stay, and he looked round the theatre as if seeking someone. He looked several times in the direction of Evelyn's box without seeing her, and she was at last obliged to wave her hand. Then the dream upon his face vanished, and his eyes lit up, and his nod was the nod of one whose soul is full of interesting story.

He had one of those long Irish faces, all in a straight line, with flat, slightly hollow cheeks, and a long chin. It was clean shaven, and a heavy lock of black hair was always falling over his eyes. It was his eyes that gave its sombre ecstatic character to his face. They were large, dark, deeply set, singularly shaped, and they seemed to smoulder like fires in caves, leaping and sinking out of the darkness. He was a tall, thin young man, and he wore a black jacket and a large, blue necktie, tied with the ends hanging loose over his coat. Evelyn received him effusively, stretching both hands to him and telling him she was so glad he had come. She said she was delighted with his melodies, and would sing them as soon as she got an occasion. But he did not seem as pleased as he should have done; and sitting, his eyes fixed on the floor—now and then he muttered a word of thanks. His silence embarrassed her, and she felt suddenly that the talk which she had been looking forward to would be a failure, and she almost wished him out of her box. Neither had spoken for some time, and, to break an awkward silence, she said that she had been that morning at St. Joseph's. He looked up; their eyes met unexpectedly, and she seemed to read an impertinence in his eyes; they seemed to say, "I wonder how you dared go there!" But his words contradicted the idea which she thought she had read in his eyes. He asked her at once eagerly and sympathetically, if she had seen her father. No, he was not there, and, growing suddenly shy, she sought to change the conversation.

"You are not a Roman Catholic, I think.... I know you were born a Catholic, but from something you said the other day I was led to think that you did not believe."

"I cannot think what I could have said to give you such an idea. Most people reproach me for believing too much."

"The other day you spoke of the ancient gods Angus and Lir, and the great mother Dana, as of real gods."

"Of course I spoke of them as real gods; I am a Celt, and they are real gods to me."

Now his face had lighted up, and in clear, harmonious voice he was arguing that the gods of a nation cannot die to that nation until it be incorporated and lost in another nation.

"I don't see how you reconcile Angus and Lir with Christianity, that is all."

"But I don't try to reconcile them; they do not need reconciliation; all the gods are part of one faith."

"But what do you believe ... seriously?"

"Everything except Atheism, and unthinking contentment. I believe in Christianity, but I am not so foolish as to limit myself to Christianity; I look upon Christianity as part of the truth, but not the whole truth. There is a continuous revelation: before Christ Buddha, before Buddha Krishna, who was crucified in mid-heaven, and the Gods of my race live too."

She longed to ask Ulick so many questions that she could not frame one, so far had the idea of a continuous revelation carried her beyond the limits of her habitual thoughts; and while she was trying to think out his meaning in one direction, she lost a great deal of what he said subsequently, and her face wore an eager, puzzled and disappointed look. That she should have been the subject of this young man's thoughts, that she should have suggested his opera of Grania, and that he should have at last succeeded, by means of an old photograph, in imagining some sort of image of her, flattered her inmost vanity, and with still brightening eyes she hoped that he was not disappointed in her.

"When did you begin to write opera? You must come to see me. You will tell me about your opera, and we will go through the music."

"Will you let me play my music to you?"

"Yes, I shall be delighted."

At that moment she remarked that Ulick's teeth were almost the most beautiful she had ever seen, and that they shone like snow in his dark face.

"Some afternoon at the end of the week. We're friends—I feel that we are. You are father's friend; you were his friend when I was away. Tell me if he missed me very much. Tell me about him. I have been longing to ask you all the time. What is he doing? I have heard about his choir. He has got some wonderful treble voices."

"He is very busy now rehearsing the 'Missa Brevis.' It will be given next Sunday. It will be splendidly done ... You ought to come to hear it."

"I should like to, of course, but I am not certain that I shall not be able to go to St. Joseph's next Sunday. How did you and father become acquainted?"

"Through an article I wrote about the music of St. Joseph's. Mr. Innes said that it was written by a musician, and he wrote to the paper."

"Asking you to come to see him?"

"Yes. Your father was the first friend I made in London."

"And that was some years ago?"

"About four years ago. I had come over from Ireland with a few pounds in my pocket, and a portmanteau full of music, which I soon found no one wanted."

"You had written music before you had met father?"

"Yes, I was organist at St. Patrick's in Dublin for nearly three years. There's no one like your father, Miss Innes."

"No one, is there?" she replied enthusiastically. "There's no one like him. I'm so glad you are friends. You see him nearly every day, and you show him all your music." Then after a pause, she said, "Tell me, did he miss me very much?"

"Yes, he missed you, of course. But he felt that you were not wholly to blame."

"And you took my place. I can see it all. It was father and son, instead of father and daughter. How well you must have got on together. What talks you must have had."

The silence was confidential, and though they both were thinking of Mr. Innes, they seemed to become intimately aware of each other.

"But may I venture to advise you?"

"Yes. What?"

"I'm sure you ought to go and see him, or at least write to him saying you'd like to see him."

"I know—I know—I must go. He'll forgive me; he must forgive me. But I wish it were over. I'm afraid you think me very cowardly. You will not say you have seen me. You promise me to say nothing."

Ulick gave her the required promise, and she asked him again to come to see her.

"I want you," she said, "to go through Isolde's music with me."

"Do you think I can tell you anything about the music you don't know already?"

"Yes, I think you can. You tell me things about myself that I did not know. I hardly knew that I acted as you describe in Margaret. I hope I did, for I seemed very good in your article. I read it over again this morning in bed. But tell me, did father come?"

"You must not press me to answer that question. My advice to you is to go and see your father. He will tell you what he thought of your singing if he came here.... The act is over," he said suddenly, and he seemed glad of the interruption. "I wonder what your Elizabeth will be like?"

"What do you think?"

"You're a clever woman; you will no doubt arrive at a very logical and clear conception of the part, but—"

"But we cannot act what is not in us. Is that what you were going to say?"

"Something like that."

"You think I shall arrive at a logical and clear conception. Is that the way you think I arrived at my Margaret? Did it look like that? I may play the part of Elizabeth badly, but I sha'n't play it as you think I shall. This frock is against me. I've a mind to send you away."

CHAPTER FIFTEEN

Instead of rushing wildly from side to side according to custom, she advanced timidly, absorbed in deep memory; at every glance her face expressed a recollection; she seemed to alternate between a vague dread and an unconquerable delight; she seemed like a dim sky filled with an inner radiance, but for a time it seemed uncertain which would prevail—sunlight or shadow. But, like the sunlight, joy burst forth, scattering uncertainty and alarm, illuminating life from end to end; and her emotion vented itself in cries of April melody, and all the barren stage seemed in flower about her; she stood like a bird on a branch singing the spring time. And she sang every note with the same ease, each was equally round and clear, but what delighted Ulick was the perfect dramatic expression of her singing. It seemed to him that he was really listening to a very young girl who had just heard of the return of a man whom she had loved or might have loved. A bud last night slept close curled in virginal strictness, with the morning light it awoke a rose. But the core of the rose is still hidden from the light, only the outer leaves know it, and so Elizabeth is pure in her first aspiration; she rejoices as the lark rejoices in the sky, without desiring to possess the sky. Ulick could not explain to himself the obsession of this singing; he was thrall to the sensation of a staid German princess of the tenth century, and the wearing of a large hat with ostrich feathers, and tied with a blue veil, hindered no whit of it. And the tailor-made dress and six years of *liaison* with Owen Asher was no let to the mediæval virgin formulated in antique custom. In the duet with Tannhäuser she was benign and forgiving, the divine penitent who, having no sins of her own to do penance for, does penance for the sins of others.

It was then that Ulick began to understand the secret of Evelyn's acting; in Elizabeth she had gone back to the Dulwich days before she knew Asher, and was acting what she then felt and thought. She believed she was living again with her father, and so intense was her conviction that it evoked the externals. Even her age vanished; she was but eighteen, a virgin whose sole reality has been her father and her châtelaine, and whose vision of the world was, till now, a mere decoration—sentinels on the drawbridge, hunters assembling on the hillside, pictures hardly more real to her than those she weaves on her tapestry loom.

Ulick leaned out of the box and applauded; he dared even to cry encore, and, following suit, the musicians laid aside their instruments and, standing up in the orchestra, applauded with him. The conductor tapped approval with his stick on the little harmonium, the chorus at the back cried encore. It was a curious scene; these folk, whose one idea at rehearsal is to get it over as soon as possible, conniving at their own retention in the theatre.

The applause of her fellow artistes delighted her; she bowed to the orchestra, and, turning to the chorus, said that she would be pleased to sing the duet again if they did not mind the delay; and coming down the stage and standing in front of the box, she said to Ulick—

"Well, are you satisfied?... Is that your idea of Elizabeth?"

"So far as we have gone, yes, but I shall not know if your Elizabeth is my Elizabeth until I have heard the end of the act."

Turning to Mr. Hermann Goetze, she said—

"Mr. Dean has very distinct ideas how this part should be played."

"Mr. Dean," answered the manager, laughing, "would not go to Bayreuth three years ago because they played 'Tannhäuser.' But one evening he took the score down to read the new music, and to his surprise he found that it was the old that interested him. Mr. Dean is always making discoveries; he discovers all my singers after he has heard them."

"And Mr. Hermann Goetze discovers his singers before *he* has heard them," cried Ulick.

Mr. Hermann Goetze looked for a moment as if he were going to get angry, but remembering that Dean was critic to an important weekly, he laughed and put his handkerchief to his jaw, and Evelyn went up the stage to meet the Landgrave—her father—and she sang a duet with him. As soon as it was concluded, the introduction to the march brought the first courtiers and pages on the stage, and with the first strains of the march the assembly, which had been invited to witness the competitions, was seated in the circular benches ranged round the throne of the Landgrave and his daughter.

Having consulted with his stage manager and superintended some alterations in the stage arrangements, Mr. Hermann Goetze, whose toothache seemed a little better again, left the stage, and coming into the box where Ulick was sitting, he sat beside him and affected some interest in his opinion regarding the grouping, for it had occurred to him that if Evelyn should take a fancy to this young man nothing was more likely than that she should ask to have his opera produced. With the plot and some of the music he was already vaguely acquainted; and he had gathered, in a general way, that Ulick Dean was considered to be a man of talent. The British public might demand a new opera, and there had been some talk of Celtic genius in the newspapers lately. Dean's "Grania" might make an admirable diversion in the Wagnerian repertoire—only it must not be too anti-Wagnerian. Mr. Goetze prided himself on being in the movement. Now, if Evelyn Innes would sing the title *rôle*, "Grania" was the very thing he wanted. And in such a frame of mind, he listened to Ulick Dean. He was glad that "Grania" was based on a legend; Wagner had shown that an opera could not be written except on a legendary basis. The Irish legends were just the thing the public was prepared to take an interest in. But there was one thing he feared—that there were no motives.

"Tell me more about the music? It is not like the opera you showed me a year or two ago in which instead of motives certain instruments introduce the characters? There is nothing Gregorian about this new work, is there?"

"Nothing," Ulick answered, smiling contemptuously—nothing recognisable to uneducated ears."

"Plenty of chromatic writing?"

"Yes, I think I can assure you that there is plenty of modulation, some unresolved dissonances. I suppose that that is what you want. Alas, there are not many motives."

"Ah!"

Ulick waited to be asked if he could not introduce some. But at that moment Tannhäuser's avowal of the joys he had experienced with Venus in Mount Horsel had shocked the Landgrave's pious court. The dames and the wives of the burgesses had hastened away, leaving their husbands to avenge the affront offered to their modesty. The knights drew their swords; it was the moment when Elizabeth runs down the steps of the throne and demands mercy from her father for the man she loves. The idea of this scene was very dear to Ulick, and his whole attention was fixed on Evelyn.

He was only attracted by essential ideas, and the mysterious expectancy of the virgin awaiting the approach of the man she loves was surely the essential spirit of life—the ultimate meaning of things. The comedy of existence, the habit of life worn in different ages of the world had no interest for him; it was the essential that he sought and wished to put upon the stage—the striving and yearning, and then the inevitable acceptation of the burden of life; in other words, the entrance into the life of resignation. That was what he sought in his own operas, and from this ideal he had never wavered; all other art but this essential art was indifferent to him. It was no longer the beautiful writing of Wagner's later works that attracted him; he deemed this one to be, perhaps, the finest, being the sincerest, and "Parsifal" the worst, being the most hypocritical. Elizabeth was the essential penitent, she who does penance not for herself, she has committed no sin, but the sublime penitent who does penance for the sins of others. Not for a moment could he admit the penitence of Kundry. In her there was merely the external aspect. "Parsifal" was to Ulick a revolting hypocrisy, and Kundry the blot on Wagner's life. In the first act she is a sort of wild witch, not very explicit to any intelligence that probes below the surface. In the second, she is a courtesan with black diamonds. In the third, she wears the coarse habit of a penitent, and her waist is tied with a cord; but her repentance goes no further than these exterior signs. She says no word, and Ulick could not accept the descriptive music as sufficient explanation of her repentance, even if it were sincere, which it was not, and he spoke derisively of the amorous cries to be heard at every moment in the orchestra, while she is dragging herself to Parsifal's feet. Elizabeth's prayer was to him a perfect expression of a penitent soul. Kundry, he pointed out, had no such prayer, and he derisively sang the cries of amorous desire. The character of Parsifal he could admit even less than the character of Kundry. As he would say in discussion, "If I am to discuss an artistic question, I must go to the very heart of it. Now, if we ask ourselves what Siegfried did, the answer is, that he forged the sword, killed the dragon and released Brunnhilde. But if, in like manner, we ask ourselves what Parsifal did, is not the answer, that he killed a swan and refused a kiss and with many morbid, suggestive and disagreeable remarks? These are the facts," he would say; "confute them who may, explain them who can!" And if it were urged, as it often was, that in Parsifal Wagner desired the very opposite to what he had in Siegfried, the Parsifal is opposed to Siegfried as Hamlet is opposed to Othello, Ulick eagerly accepted the challenge, and like one sure of his adversary's life, began the attack.

Wagner had been all his life dreaming of an opera with a subjective hero. Christ first and then Buddha had suggested themselves as likely subjects. He had gone so far as to make sketches for both heroes, but both subjects had been rejected as unpractical, and he had fallen back on a pretty mediæval myth, and had shot into a pretty mediæval myth all the material he had accumulated for the other dramas, whose heroes were veritable heroes, men who had accomplished great things, men who had preached great doctrines and whose lives were symbols of their doctrines. The result of pouring this old wine into the new bottle was to burst the bottle.

In neither Christ nor Buddha did the question of sex arise, and that was the reason that Wagner eventually rejected both. He was as full of sex—mysterious, sub-conscious sex—as Rossetti himself. In Christ's life there is the Magdalen, but how naturally harmonious, how implicit in the idea, are their relations, how concentric; but how excentric (using the word in its grammatical sense) are the relations of Parsifal to Kundry.... A redeemer is chaste, but he does not speak of his chastity nor does he think of it; he passes the question by. The figure of Christ is so noble, that whether God or man or both, it seems to us in harmony that the Magdalen should bathe his feet and wipe them with her hair, but the introduction of the same incident into "Parsifal" revolts. As Parsifal merely killed a swan and refused to be kissed—the other preached a doctrine in which beauty and wisdom touch the highest point, and his life was an exemplification of his doctrine of non-resistance—"Take ye and eat, for this is my body, and this is my blood."

In "Parsifal" there was only the second act which he could admire without enormous reservations. The writing in the chorus of the "Flower Maidens" was, of course, irresistible—little cries, meaningless by themselves, but, when brought together, they created an enchanted garden, marvellous and seductive. But it was the duet that followed that compelled his admiration. Music hardly ever more than a recitative, hardly ever breaking into an air, and yet so beautiful! There the notes merely served to lift the words, to impregnate them with more terrible and subtle meaning; and the subdued harmonies enfolded them in an atmosphere, a sensual mood; and in this music we sink into depths of soul and float upon sullen and mysterious tides of life—those which roll beneath the phase of life which we call existence. But the vulgarly vaunted Good Friday music did not deceive him; at the second or third time of hearing he had perceived its insincerity. It was very beautiful music, but in such a situation sincerity was essential. The airs of this mock redeemer were truly unbearable, and the abjection of Kundry before this stuffed Christ revolted him. But the obtusely religious could not fail to be moved; the appeal of the chaste kiss, with little sexual cries all the while in the orchestra, could not but stir the vulgar heart to infinite delight, and the art was so dexterously beautiful that the intelligent were deceived. The artiste and the vulgarian held each other's hands for the first time; they gasped a mutual wonder at their own perception and their unsuspected nobility of soul. "Parsifal," he declared, with true Celtic love of exaggeration, "to be the oiliest flattery ever poured down the open throat of a liquorish humanity."

As he spoke such sentences his face would light up with malicious humour, and he was so interested in the subject he discussed that his listener was forced to follow him. It was only in such moments of artistic discussion that his real soul floated up to the surface, and he, as it were, achieved himself. He knew, too, how to play with his listener, to wheedle and beguile him, for after a particularly aggressive phrase he would drop into a minor key, and his criticism would suddenly become serious and illuminative. To him "Parsifal" was a fresco, a decoration painted by a man whose true genius it was to reveal the most intimate secrets of the soul, to tell the enigmatic soul of longing as Leonardo da Vinci had done. But he had been led from the true path of his genius into the false one of a rivalry with Veronese. Only where Wagner is confiding a soul's secret is he interesting, and in "Tannhäuser," in this first flower of his dramatic and musical genius, he had perhaps told the story of his own soul more truly, more sincerely than elsewhere. To do that was the highest art. Sooner or later the sublimest imaginations pale before the simple telling of a personal truth, for the most personal truth is likewise the most universal. "Tannhäuser" is the story of humanity, for what is the human story if it isn't the pursuit of an ideal?

And this essential and primal truth Evelyn revealed to him and the very spirit and sense of maidenhood, the centre and receptacle of life, the mysterious secret of things, the awful moment when the whisper of the will to live is heard in matter, the will which there is no denying, the surrender of matter, the awaking of consciousness in things. And united to the eternal idea of generation, he perceived the congenital idea which in remotest time seems to have sprung from it—that life is sin and must be atoned for by prayer. Evelyn's interpretation revealed his deepest ideas to himself, and at last he seemed to stand at the heart of life.

Suddenly his rapture was broken through; the singer had stopped the orchestra.

"You have cut some of the music, I see," she said, addressing the conductor.

"Only the usual cut, Miss Innes."

"About twenty pages, I should think."

The conductor counted them.

"Eighteen."

"Miss Innes, that cut has been accepted everywhere—Munich, Berlin, Wiesbaden—everywhere except Bayreuth."

"But, Mr. Hermann Goetze, my agreement with you is that the operas I sing in are to be performed in their entirety."

"In their entirety; that is to say, well—taken literally, I suppose—that the phrase 'In their entirety' could be held to mean without cuts; but surely, regarding this particular cut—I may say that I spoke to Sir Owen about it, and he agreed with me that it was impossible to get people into the theatre in London before half-past seven."

"But, Mr. Hermann Goetze, your agreement is with me, not with Sir Owen Asher."

"Quite so, Miss Innes, but—"

"If people don't care sufficiently for art to dine half-an-hour earlier, they had better stay away."

"But you see, Miss Innes, you're not in the first act; there are the other artistes to consider. The 'Venusberg' will be sung to empty benches if you insist."

It seemed for a moment as if Mr. Hermann Goetze was going to have his way; and Ulick, while praying that she might remain firm, recognised how adroitly Hermann Goetze had contrived to place her in a false position regarding her fellow artistes.

"I am quite willing to throw up the part; I can only sing the opera as it is written."

The conductor suggested a less decisive cut to Evelyn, and Mr. Hermann Goetze walked up and down the stage, overtaken by toothache. His agony was so complete that Evelyn's harshness yielded. She went to him, and, her hand laid commiseratingly on his arm, she begged him to go at once to the dentist.

Then some of the musicians said that they could hardly read the music, so effectually had they scratched it out.

"If the musicians cannot play the music, we had better go home," said Evelyn.

"But the opera is announced for to-morrow night," Mr. Hermann Goetze replied dolefully.

Mr. Wheeler suggested that they might go on with the rehearsal; the cut could be discussed afterwards. Groups formed, everyone had a different opinion. At last the conductor took up his stick and cried, "Number 105, please."

"They are going back," thought Ulick; "she held her ground capitally. She has more strength of character than I thought. But Hermann Goetze has upset her; she won't be able to sing."

And it was as he expected; she could not recapture her lost inspiration; mood, Ulick could see, was the foundation and the keystone of her art.

"No," she said, "I sang it horribly, I am all out of sorts, I don't feel what I am singing, and when the mood is not upon me, I am atrocious. What annoyed me was his attributing such selfishness to me, and such vulgar selfishness, too—"

"However, you had your way about the cut."

"Yes, they'll have to sing the whole of the finale. But I am sorry about his tooth; I know that it is dreadful pain."

Ulick told an amusing story how he had once called on Hermann Goetze to ask if he had read the book of his opera.

"He'd just gone into an adjoining room to fetch a clothes-brush—he had taken off his coat to brush it—but the moment he saw me, he whipped out his handkerchief and said that he must go to the dentist."

"And when I asked him to engage Helbrun to sing Brangäne, and give her eighty pounds a week if she wouldn't sing it for less, he whipped out his handkerchief as you say, and asked me if I knew a dentist."

"The idea of Wagner without cuts always brings on a violent attack," and Ulick imitated so well the expression of agony that had come into the manager's face that Evelyn exploded with laughter. She begged Ulick to desist.

"I shan't be able to sing at all. But I have not told you of my make up. I don't look at all pretty; the ugly curls I wear come from an old German print, and the staid, modest gown. But it is very provoking; I was singing well till that fiend began to argue. Don't make me laugh again."

He became very grave.

"I can only think of the joy you gave me."

His praise brightened her face, and she listened.

"I cannot tell you now what I feel; perhaps I shall never find words to express what I feel about your Elizabeth. I shall be writing about it next week, and shall have to try."

"Do tell me now. You liked it better than my Margaret?"

Ulick shrugged his shoulders contemptuously, and they looked in each other's eyes, and could hardly speak, so extraordinary was their recognition of each other; it was so intense that they could hardly help laughing, so strange it seemed that they should never have met before, or should have been separated for such a long time. It really seemed to them as if they had known each other from all eternity.

"How can you act Elizabeth, she is so different from what you are?"

"Is she?"
Her pale blue eyes seemed to open a little wider, and she looked at him searchingly. He could not keep back the words that rose to his tongue.
"You mean that your dead life now lives in Elizabeth."
"Yes, I suppose that that is it."
They asked each other whether any part of one's nature is ever really dead.
A few moments after the pilgrims were heard singing, and Evelyn would have to go on the stage. She pressed her hands against her forehead, ridding herself by an effort of will of her present individuality. The strenuous chant of the pilgrims grew louder, the procession approached, and as it passed across the stage Elizabeth sought for Tannhäuser, but he was not among them. So her last earthly hope has perished, and she throws herself on her knees at the foot of the wayside cross. And it was the anguish of her soul that called forth that high note, a G repeated three times; and it seemed to Ulick that she seemed to throw herself upon that note, that reiterated note, as if she would reach God's ears with it and force him to listen to her. In the religious, almost Gregorian, strain her voice was pure as a little child, but when she spoke of her renunciation and the music grew more chromatic, her voice filled with colour—her sex appeared in it; and when the music returned to the peace of the religious strain, her voice grew blanched and faded like a nun's voice. Henceforth her life will be lived beyond this world, and as she walked up the stage, the flutes and clarionets seemed to lead her straight to God; they seemed to depict a narrow, shining path, shining and ascending till it disappeared amid the light of the stars.
"Well," she said, "did I sing it to your satisfaction?"
"You're an astonishing artiste."
"No, that's just what I am not. I go on the stage and act; I couldn't tell you how I do it; I am conscious of no rule."
"And the music?"
"The music the same. I have often been told that I might act Shakespeare, but without music I could not express myself. Words without music would seem barren; I never try to sing, I try to express myself. But you'll see, my father won't think much of my singing. He'll compare me to mother, and always to my disadvantage. I cannot phrase like her."
"But you can; your phrasing is perfection. It is the very emotion—"
"Father won't think so; if he only thought well of my singing he would forgive me."
"How unaffected you are; in hearing you speak one hears your very soul."
"Do you? But tell me, is he very incensed? Shall I meet a face of stone?"
"He is incensed, no doubt, but he must forgive you. But every day's delay will make it more difficult."
"I know, I know."
"You cannot go to-morrow?"
"Why not?"
"To-morrow you sing this opera. Go on Saturday; you'll be sure to find him on Saturday afternoon. He has a rehearsal in the morning and will be at home about four in the afternoon."
As they walked through the scenery she said, "You'll come to see me," and she reminded him of his promise to go through the Isolde music with her.
"Mind, you have promised," she said as she got into her carriage.
"You'll not forget Saturday afternoon," he said as he shook hands.
She nodded and put up her umbrella, for it was beginning to rain.

CHAPTER SIXTEEN

Evelyn found Owen waiting for her. As soon as she came into the room he said, "Well, have you seen your father?"

She was not expecting him, and it was disagreeable to admit that she had not been to Dulwich. So she said that she had thought to find her father at St. Joseph's.

"But how did you know he was not at home if you did not go to Dulwich?"

"My gracious, Owen, how you do question me! Now, perhaps you would like to know which of the priests told me."

She walked to the window and stood with her left hand in the pocket of her jacket, and he feared that the irritation he had involuntarily caused her would interfere with his projects for the afternoon. There passed in his eyes that look of absorption in an object which marks the end of a long love affair—a look charged with remembrance, and wistful as an autumn day. The earth has grown weary of the sun and turns herself into the shadow, eager for rest. The sun has been too ardent a lover. But the gaze of the sun upon the receding earth is fonder than his look when she raised herself to his bright face. So in Owen's autumn-haunted eyes there was dread of the chances which he knew were accumulating against him—enemies, he divined, were gathering in the background; and how he might guard her, keep her for himself, became a daily inquisition. Nothing had happened to lead him to think that his possession was endangered, his fear proceeded from an instinct, which he could not subdue, that she was gliding from him; he wrestled with the intangible, and, striving to subordinate instinct to reason, he often refrained from kissing her; he imitated the indifference which in other times he could not dissimulate when the women who had really loved him besought him with tears. But there was no long gain-saying of the delight of telling her that he loved her, and when his aching heart forced him to question her regarding the truth of her feelings towards him, she merely told him that she loved him as much as ever, and the answer, instead of being a relief, was additional fuel upon the torturing flame of his uncertainty.

Ever since their rupture and reconciliation in Florence, their relations had been so uncertain that Owen often wondered if he were her lover. Whether the reason for these periods of restraint was virtue or indifference he could never be quite sure. He believed that she always retained her conscience, but he could not forget that her love had once been sufficient compensation for what she suffered from it. "The stage has not altered her," he thought, "time has but nourished her idiosyncrasies." He had been hoping for one of her sudden and violent returnings to her former self, but such thing would not happen to-day, and hardly knowing what reply to make, he asked if she were free to come to look at some furniture. She mentioned several engagements, adding that he had made her too many presents already.

She spoke of the rehearsal at considerable length, omitting, somehow, to speak of Ulick, and after lunch she seemed restless and proposed to go out at once.

As they drove off to see the Sheraton sideboard, he asked her if she had seen Ulick Dean. To her great annoyance she said she had not, and this falsehood spoilt her afternoon for her. She could not discover why she had told this lie. The memory rankled in her and continued to take her unaware. She was tempted to confess the truth to Owen; the very words she thought she should use rose up in her mind several times. "I told you a lie. I don't know why I did, for there was absolutely no reason why I should have said that I had not seen Ulick Dean." On Saturday the annoyance which this lie had caused in her was as keen as ever: and it was not until she had got into her carriage and was driving to Dulwich that her consciousness of it died in the importance of her interview with her father.

In comparing her present attitude of mind with that of last Thursday, she was glad to notice that to-day she could not think that her father would not forgive her. Her talk on the subject with Ulick had reassured her. He would not have been so insistent if he had not been sure that her father would forgive her in the end. But there would be recriminations, and at the very thought of them she felt her courage sink, and she asked herself why he should make her miserable if he was going to forgive her in the end. Her plans were to talk to him about his choir, and, if that did not succeed, to throw herself on her knees. She remembered how she had thrown herself on her knees on the morning of the afternoon she had gone away. And since then she had thrown herself at his feet many times—every time she sang in the "Valkyrie." The scene in which Wotan confides all his troubles and forebodings to Brunnhilde had never been different from the long talks she and her father used to drop into in the dim evenings in Dulwich. She had cheered him when he came home depressed after a talk with the impossible Father Gordon, as she had since cheered Wotan in his deep brooding over the doom of the gods predicted by Wala, when the dusky foe of love should beget a son in hate. Wotan had always been her father; Palestrina, Walhalla, and the stupid Jesuits, what were they? She had often tried to work out the allegory. It never came out quite right, but she always felt sure in setting down Father Gordon as Alberich. The scene in the third act, when she throws herself at Wotan's feet and begs his forgiveness (the music and the words together surged upon her brain), was the scene that now awaited her. She had at last come to this long-anticipated scene; and the fictitious scene she had acted as she was now going to act the real scene. True that Wotan forgave Brunnhilde after putting her to sleep on the fire-surrounded rock, where she should remain till a pure hero should come to release her. A nervous smile curled her lip for a moment; she trembled in her very entrails, and as they passed down the long, mean streets of Camberwell her thoughts frittered out in all sorts of trivial observation and reflection. She wondered if the mother who called down the narrow alley had ever been in love, if she had ever deceived her husband, if her father had reproved her about the young man she kept company with. The milkman presented to her strained mind some sort of problem, and the sight of the railway embankment told her she was nearing Dulwich. Then she saw the cedar at the top of the hill, whither she had once walked to meet Owen. ... Now it was London nearly all the way to Dulwich.

But when they entered the familiar village street she was surprised at her dislike of it; even the chestnut trees, beautiful with white bloom, were distasteful to her, and life seemed contemptible beneath them. In Dulwich there was no surprise—life there was a sheeted phantom, it evoked a hundred dead Evelyns, and she felt she would rather live in any ghostly graveyard than in Dulwich. Her very knowledge of the place was an irritation to her, and she was pleased when she saw a house which had been built since she had been away. But every one of the fields she knew well, and the sight of every tree recalled a dead day, a dead event. That road to the right led to the picture gallery, and at the cross road she had been nearly run over by a waggon while trundling a hoop. But eyesight hardly helped her in Dulwich; she had only to think, to see it. The slates of a certain house told her that another minute would bring her to her father's door, and before the carriage turned the corner she foresaw the patch of black garden. But if her father were at home he might refuse to see her, and she was not certain if she should force her way past the servant or return home quietly. The entire dialogue of the scene between her and Margaret passed through her mind, and the very intonation of their voices. But it was not Margaret who opened the door to her.

"This way, miss, please."

"No, I'll wait in the music-room."

"Mr. Innes won't have no one wait there in his absence. Will you come into the parlour?"

"No, I think I'll wait in the music-room. I'm Miss Innes; Mr. Innes is my father."

"What, miss, are you the great singer?"

"I suppose I am."

"Do you know, miss, something told me that you was. The moment I saw the carriage, I said, "Here she is; this is her for certain." Will you come this way, miss? I'll run and get the key."

"And who was it," Evelyn said, "that told you I was a singer?"

"Lor'! miss, didn't half Dulwich go to hear you sing at the opera?"

"Did you?"

"No, I didn't go, Miss, but I heard Mr. Dean and your father talking of you. I've read about you in the papers; only this morning there was a long piece."

"If father talks of me he'll forgive me," thought Evelyn. The girl's wonderment made her smile, and she said—

"But you've not told me your name."

"My name is Agnes, miss."

"Have you been long with my father? When I left, Margaret—"

"Ah! she's dead, miss. I came to your father the day after the funeral."

Evelyn walked up the room, overcome by the eternal absence of something which had hitherto been part of her life. For Margaret took her back to the time her mother was alive; farther back still—to the very beginning of her life. She had always reckoned on Margaret.... So Margaret was dead. Margaret would never know of this meeting. Margaret might have helped her. Poor Margaret! At that moment she caught sight of her mother's eyes. They seemed to watch her; she seemed to know all about Owen, and afraid of the haunting, reproving look, Evelyn studied the long oval face and the small brown eyes so unlike hers. One thing only she had inherited from her mother—her voice. She had certainly not inherited her conduct from her mother; her mother was one of the few great artistes against whom nothing could be said. Her mother was a good woman.... What did she think of her daughter? And seeing her cold, narrow face, she feared her mother would regard her conduct even more severely than her father.... "But if she had lived I should have had no occasion to go away with Owen." She wondered. At the bottom of her heart she knew that Owen was as much as anything else a necessity in her life.... She moved about the room and wished the hands of the clock could be advanced a couple of hours, for then the terrible scene with her father would be over. If he could only forgive her at once, and not make her miserable with reproaches, they could have such a pleasant evening.

In this room her past life was blown about her like spray about a rock. She remembered the days when she went to London with her father to give lessons; the miserable winter when she lost her pupils.... How she had waited in this room for her father to come back to dinner; the faintness of those hungry hours; worse still, that yearning for love. She must have died if she had not gone away. If it had to happen all over again she must act as she had acted. How well she remembered the moment when she felt that her life in Dulwich had become impossible. She was coming from the village where she had been paying some bills, and looking up she had suddenly seen the angle of a house and a bare tree, and she could still hear the voice which had spoken out of her very soul. "Shall I never get away from this place?" it had cried. "Shall I go on doing these daily tasks for ever?" The strange, vehement agony of the voice had frightened her.... At that moment her eyes were attracted by a sort of harpsichord. "One of father's experiments," she said, running her fingers over the keys. "A sort of cross between a harpsichord and a virginal; up here the intonation is that of a virginal."

"I forgot to ask you miss"—Evelyn turned from the window, startled; it was Agnes who had come back—"if you was going to stop for dinner, for there's very little in the house, only a bit of cold beef. I should be ashamed to put it on the table, miss; I'm sure you couldn't eat it. Master don't think what he eats; he's always thinking of his music. I hope you aren't like that, miss?"

"So he doesn't eat much. How is my father looking, Agnes?"

"Middling, miss. He varies about a good bit; he's gone rather thin lately."

"Is he lonely, do you think ... in the evenings?"

"No, miss; I don't hear him say nothing about being lonely. For the last couple of years he never did more than come home to sleep and his meals, and he'd spend the evenings copying out the music."

"And off again early in the morning?"

"That's it, miss, with his music tied up in a brown paper parcel. Sometimes Mr. Dean comes and helps him to write the music."

"Ah!... but I'm sorry he doesn't eat better."

"He eats better when Mr. Dean's here. They has a nice little dinner together. Now he's taken up with that 'ere instrument, the harpy chord, they's making. He's comin' home to-night to finish it; he says he can't get it finished nohow—that they's always something more to do to it."

"I wonder if we could get a nice dinner for him this evening?"

"Well, miss, you see there's no shops to speak of about here. You know that as well as I do."

"I wonder what your cooking is like?"

"I don't know, miss; p'r'aps it wouldn't suit you, but I've been always praised for my cooking."

"I could send for some things; my coachman could fetch them from town."

"Then there's to-morrow to be thought about if you're stopping here. I tell you we don't keep much in the house."

"Is my father coming home to dinner?"

"I can't say for certain, miss, only that he said 'e'd be 'ome early to finish the harpy chord. 'E might have 'is dinner out and come 'ome directly after, but I shouldn't think that was likely."

"You can cook a chicken, Agnes?"

"Lor'! yes, miss."

"And a sole?"

"Yes, miss; but in ordering, miss, you must think of to-morrow. You won't like to have a nice dinner to-night and a bit of hashed mutton to-morrow."

"I'll order sufficient. You've got no wine, I suppose?"

"No, we've no wine, miss, only draught beer."

"I'll tell my coachman to go and fetch the things at once."

When she returned to the music-room, Agnes asked her if she was going to stop the night.

"Because I should have to get your rooms ready, miss."

"That I can't tell, Agnes.... I don't think so.... You won't tell my father I'm here when you let him in?... I want it to be a surprise."

"I won't say nothing, miss. I'll leave him to find it out."

Evelyn felt that the girl must have guessed her story, must have perceived in her the repentant daughter—the erring daughter returned home. Everything pointed to that fact. Well, it couldn't be helped if she had.

"If my father will only forgive me; if that first dreadful scene were only over, we could have an enchanting evening together."

She was too nervous to seek out a volume of Bach and let her fingers run over the keys; she played anything that came into her head, sometimes she stopped to listen. At last there came a knock, and her heart told her it was his. In another moment he would be in the room. But seeing her he stopped, and, without a word, he went to a table and began untying a parcel of music.

"Father, I've come to see you.... You don't answer. Father, are you not going to speak to me? I've been longing to see you, and now—"

"If you had wanted to see me, you'd have come a month ago."

"I was not in London a month ago."

"Well, three weeks ago."

"I ought to have done so, but I had no courage. I could only see you looking at me as you are looking now. Forgive me, father.... I'm your only daughter; she's full of failings, but she has never ceased to love you."

He sat at the table fumbling with the string that had tied the parcel he had brought in, and she stood looking at him, unable to speak. She seemed to have said all there was to say, and wished she could throw herself at his feet; but she could not, something held her back. She prayed for tears, but her eyes remained dry; her mouth was dry, and a flame seemed to burn behind her eyes. She could only think that this might be the last time she would see him. The silence seemed a great while. She repeated her words, "I had not the courage to come before."

At the sound of her voice she remembered that she must speak to him at once of his choir, and so take their thoughts from painful reminiscence.

"I went to St. Joseph's on Thursday, but you weren't there. You gave Vittoria's mass last Sunday. I started to go, but I had to turn back."

She had not gone to hear her father's choir, because she could not resist Lady Ascott's invitation, and no more than the invitation could she resist the lie; she had striven against it, but in spite of herself it had forced itself through her lips, and now her father seemed to have some inkling of the truth, for he said—

"If you had cared to hear my choir you'd have gone. You needn't have seen me, whereas I was obliged—"

Evelyn guessed that he had been to the opera. "How good of him to have gone to hear me," she thought. She hated herself for having accepted Lady Ascott's invitation, and the desire to ask him what he thought of her voice seemed to her an intolerable selfishness.

"What were you going to say, father?"

"Nothing.... I'm glad you didn't come."

"Wasn't it well sung?" and she was seized with nervousness, and instead of speaking to him about his basses as she had intended, she asked him about the trebles.

"They are the worst part of the choir. That contrapuntal music can only be sung by those who can sing at sight. The piano has destroyed the modern ear. I daresay it has spoilt your ear."

"My ear is all right, I think."

"I hope it is better than your heart."

Evelyn's face grew quite still, as if it were frozen, and seeing the pain he had caused her he was moved to take her in his arms and forgive her straight away. He might have done so, but she turned, and passing her hand across her eyes she went to the harpsichord. She played one of the little Elizabethan songs, "John, come kiss me now." Then an old French song tempted her voice by its very appropriateness to the situation—"*Que vous me coûtez cher, mon coeur, pour vos plaisirs.*" But there was a knot in her throat, she could not sing, she could hardly speak. She endeavoured to lead her father into conversation, hoping he might forget her conduct until it was too late for him to withdraw into resentment. She could see that the instrument she was playing on he had made himself. In some special intention it was filled with levers and stops, the use of which was not quite apparent to her; and she could see by the expression on his face that he was annoyed by her want of knowledge of the technicalities of the instrument. So she purposely exaggerated her ignorance.

He fell into the trap and going to her he said, "You are not making use of the levers."

"Oh, am I not?" she said innocently. "What is this instrument—a virginal or a harpsichord?"

"It is a harpsichord, but the intonation is that of a virginal. I made it this winter. The volume of sound from the old harpsichord is not sufficient in a large theatre, that is why the harpsichord music in 'Don Juan' has to be played on the fiddles."

He stopped speaking and she pressed him in vain to explain the instrument. She went on playing.

"The levers," he said at last, "are above your knees. Raise your knees."

She pretended not to understand.

"Let me show you." He seated himself at the instrument. "You see the volume of sound I obtain, and all the while I do not alter the treble."

"Yes, yes, and the sonority of the instrument is double that of the old harpsichord. It would be heard all over Covent Garden."

She could see that the remark pleased him. "I'll sing 'Zerline' if you'll play it."

"You couldn't sing 'Zerline,' it isn't in your voice."

"You don't know what my voice is like."

"Evelyn, I wonder how you can expect me to forgive you; I wonder how I can speak to you. Have you forgotten how you went away leaving me to bear the shame, the disgrace?"

"I have come to beg forgiveness, not to excuse myself. But I wrote to you from Paris that I was going to live with Lady Duckle, and that you were to say that I had gone abroad to study singing."

"I'm astonished, Evelyn, that you can speak so lightly."

"I do not think lightly of my conduct, if you knew the miserable days it has cost me. Reproach me as you will about my neglect toward you, but as far as the world is concerned there has been no disgrace."

"You would have gone all the same; you only thought of yourself. Brought up as you have been, a Catholic—"

"My sins, father, lie between God and myself. What I come for is to beg forgiveness for the wrong I did you."

He did not answer, but he seemed to acquiesce, and it was a relief to her to feel that it was not the moral question that divided them; convention had forced him to lay some stress upon it, but clearly what rankled in his heart, and prevented him from taking her in his arms, was a jealous, purely human feud. This she felt she could throw herself against and overpower.

"Father, you must forgive me, we are all in all to each other; nothing can change that. Ever since mother's death—you remember when the nurse told us all was over—ever since I've felt that we were in some strange way dependent on each other. Our love for each other is the one unalterable thing. My music you taught me; the first songs I sang were at your concerts, and now that we have both succeeded—you with Palestrina, and I with Wagner—we must needs be aliens. Father, can't you see that that can never be? if you don't you do not love me as I do you. You're still thinking that I left you. Of course, it was very wrong, but has that changed anything? Father, tell me, tell me, unless you want to kill me, that you do not believe that I love you less."

The wonder of the scene she was acting—she never admitted she acted; she lived through scenes, whether fictitious or real—quickened in her; it was the long-expected scene, the scene in the third act of the "Valkyrie" which she had always played while divining the true scene which she would be called upon to play one day. It seemed to her that she stood on the verge of all her future—the mystery of the abyss gathered behind her eyes; she threw herself at her father's feet, and the celebrated phrase, so plaintive, so full of intercession, broke from her lips, "Was the rebel act so full of shame that her rebellion is so shamefully scourged? Was my offence so deep in disgrace that thou dost plan so deep a disgrace for me? Was this my crime so dark with dishonour that it henceforth robs me of all honour? Oh tell me, father; look in mine eyes." She heard the swelling harmony, every chord, the note that gave her the note she was to sing. She was carried down like a drowning one into a dim world of sub-conscious being; and in this half life all that was most true in her seemed to rise like a star and shine forth, while all that was circumstantial and ephemeral seemed to fall away. She was conscious of the purification of self; she seemed to see herself white and bowed and penitent. She experienced a great happiness in becoming humble and simple again.... But she did not know if the transformation which was taking place in her was an abiding or a passing thing. She knew she was expressing all that was most deep in her nature, and yet she had acted all that she now believed to be reality on the stage many times. It seemed as true then as it did now—more true; for she was less self-conscious in the fictitious than in the real scene.

She knelt at her father's or at Wotan's feet—she could not distinguish; all limitations had been razed. She was *the* daughter at *the* father's feet. She knelt like the Magdalen. The position had always been natural to her, and habit had made it inveterate; there she bemoaned the difficulties of life, the passion which had cast her down and which seemed to forbid her an ideal. She caught her father's hand and pressed it against her cheek. She knew she was doing these things, yet she could not do otherwise; tears fell upon his hand, and the grief she expressed was so intense that he could not restrain his tears. But if she raised her face and saw his tears, his position as a stern father was compromised! She could only think of her own grief; the grief and regret of many years absorbed her; she was so lost in it that she expected him to answer her in Wotan's own music; she even smiled in her grief at her expectation, and continued the music of her intercession. And it was not until he asked her why she was singing Wagner that she raised her face. That he should not know, jarred and spoilt the harmony of the scene as she had conceived it, and it was not till he repeated his question that she told him.

"Because I've never sung it without thinking of you, father. That is why I sang it so well. I knew it all before. It tore at my heart strings. I knew that one day it would come to this."

"So every time before was but a rehearsal."

She rose to her feet.

"Why are you so cruel? It is you who are acting, not I. I mean what I say—you don't. Why make me miserable? You know that you must forgive me. You can't put me out of doors, so what is the use in arguing about my faults? I am like that ... you must take me as I am, and perhaps you would not have cared for me half as much if I had been different."

"Evelyn, how can you speak like that? You shock me very much."

She regretted her indiscretion, and feared she had raised the moral question; but the taunt that it was he and not she that was acting had sunk into his heart, and the truth of it overcame him. It was he who had been acting. He had pretended an anger which he did not feel, and it was quite true that, whatever she did, he could not really feel anger against her. She was shrined in his heart, the dream of his whole life. He could feel anger against himself, but not against her. She was right. He must forgive her, for how could he live without her? Into what dissimulation he had been foolishly ensnared! In these convictions which broke like rockets in his heart and brain, spreading a strange illumination in much darkness, he saw her beauty and sex idealised, and in the vision were the eyes and pallor of the dead wife, and all the yearning and aspiration of his own life seemed reflected back in this fair, oval face, lit with luminous, eager eyes, and in the tangle of gold hair fallen about her ears, and thrown back hastily with long fingers; and the wonder of her sex in the world seemed to shed a light on distant horizons, and he understood the strangeness of the common event of father and daughter standing face to face, divided, or seemingly divided, by the mystery of the passion of which all things are made. His own sins were remembered. They fell like soft fire breaking in a dark sky, and his last sensation in the whirl of complex, diffused and passing sensations was the thrill of terror at the little while remaining to him wherein he might love her. A few years at most! His eyes told her what was happening in his heart, and with that beautiful movement of rapture so natural to her, she threw herself into his arms.

"I knew, father, dear, that you'd forgive me in the end. It was impossible to think of two like us living and dying in alienation. I should have killed myself, and you, dear, you would have died of grief. But I dreaded this first meeting. I had thought of it too much, and, as I told you, I had acted it so often."

"Have I been so severe with you, Evelyn, that you should dread me?"

"No, darling, but, of course, I've behaved—there's no use talking about it any more. But you could never have been really in doubt that a lover could ever change my love for you. Owen— I mustn't speak about him, only I wish you to understand that I've never ceased to think of you. I've never been really happy, and I'm sure you've been miserable about me often enough; but now we may be happy. 'Winter storms wane in the winsome May.' You know the *Lied* in the first act of the 'Valkyrie'? And now that we're friends, I suppose you'll come and hear me. Tell me about your choir." She paused a moment, and then said, "My first thought was for you on landing in England. There was a train waiting at Victoria, but we'd had a bad crossing, and I felt so ill that I couldn't go. Next day I was nervous. I had not the courage, and he proposed that I should wait till I had sung Margaret. So much depended on the success of my first appearance. He was afraid that if I had had a scene with you I might break down."

"Wotan, you say, forgives Brunnhilde, but doesn't he put her to sleep on a fire-surrounded rock?"

"He puts her to sleep on the rock, but it is she who asks for flames to protect her from the unworthy. Wotan grants her request, and Brunnhilde throws herself enraptured into his arms. 'Let the coward shun Brunnhilde's rock—for but one shall win—the bride who is freer than I, the god!'"

"Oh, that's it, is it? Then with what flames shall I surround you?"

"I don't know, I've often wondered; the flame of a promise—a promise never to leave you again, father. I can promise no more."

"I want no other promise."

The eyes of the portrait were fixed on them, and they wondered what would be the words of the dead woman if she could speak.

Agnes announced that the coachman had returned.

"Father, I've lots of things to see to. I'm going to stop to dinner if you'll let me."

"I'm afraid, Evelyn—Agnes—"

"You need not trouble about the dinner—Agnes and I will see to that. We have made all necessary arrangements."

"Is that your carriage?... You've got a fine pair of horses. Well, one can't be Evelyn Innes for nothing. But if you're stopping to dinner, you'd better stop the night. I'm giving the 'Missa Brevis' to-morrow. I'm giving it in honour of Monsignor Mostyn. It was he who helped me to overcome Father Gordon."

"You shall tell me all about Monsignor after dinner."

He walked about the room, unwittingly singing the *Lied*, "Winter storms wane in the winsome May," and he stopped before the harpsichord, thinking he saw her still there. And his thoughts sailed on, vagrant as clouds in a Spring breeze. She had come back, his most wonderful daughter had come back.

He turned from his wife's portrait, fearing the thought that her joy on their daughter's return might be sparer than his. But unpleasant thoughts fell from him, and happiness sang in his brain like spring-awakened water-courses, and the scent in his nostrils was of young leaves and flowers, and his very flesh was happy as the warm, loosening earth in spring. "'Winter storms,'" he sang, "'wane in the winsome May; with tender radiance sparkles the spring.' I must hear her sing that; I must hear her intercede at Wotan's feet!" His eyes filled with happy tears, and he put questions aside. She was coming to-morrow to hear his choir. And what would she think of it? A shadow passed across his face. If he had known she was coming, he'd have taken more trouble with those altos; he'd have kept them another hour.... Then, taken with a sudden craving to see her, he went to the door and called to her.

"Evelyn."

"Yes, father."

"You are stopping to-night?"

"Yes, but I can't stop to speak with you now—I'm busy with Agnes."

She was deep in discussion with Agnes regarding the sole. Agnes thought she knew how to prepare it with bread crumbs, but both were equally uncertain how the melted butter was to be made. There was no cookery-book in the house, and it seemed as if the fish would have to be eaten with plain butter until it occurred to Agnes that she might borrow a cookery-book next door. It seemed to Evelyn that she had never seen a finer sole, so fat and firm; it really would be a pity if they did not succeed in making the melted butter. When Agnes came back with the book, Evelyn read out the directions, and was surprised how hard it was to understand. In the end it was Agnes who explained it to her. The chicken presented some difficulties. It was of an odd size, and Agnes was not sure whether it would take half-an-hour or three-quarters to cook. Evelyn studied the white bird, felt the cold, clammy flesh, and inclined to forty minutes. Agnes thought that would be enough if she could get her oven hot enough. She began by raking out the flues, and Evelyn had to stand back to avoid the soot. She stood, her eyes fixed on the fire, interested in the draught and the dissolution of every piece of coal in the flame. It seemed to Evelyn that the fire was drawing beautifully, and she appealed to Agnes, who only seemed fairly satisfied. It was doing pretty well, but she had never liked that oven; one was never sure of it. Margaret used to put a piece of paper over the chicken to prevent it burning, but Agnes said there was no danger of it burning; the oven never could get hot enough for that. But the oven, as Agnes had said, was a tricky one, and when she took the chicken out to baste it, it seemed a little scorched. So Evelyn insisted on a piece of paper. Agnes said that it would delay the cooking of the chicken, and attributed the scorching to the quantity of coal which Miss Innes would keep adding. If she put any more on she would not be answerable that the chimney would not catch fire. Every seven or eight minutes the chicken was taken out to be basted. The bluey-whitey look of the flesh which Evelyn had disliked had disappeared; the chicken was acquiring a rich brown colour which she much admired, and if it had not been for Agnes, who told her the dinner would be delayed till eight o'clock, she would have had the chicken out every five minutes, so much did she enjoy pouring the rich, bubbling juice over the plump back.

"Father! Father, dinner is ready! I've got a sole and a chicken. The sole is a beauty; Agnes says she never saw a fresher one."

"And where did all these things come from?"

"I sent my coachman for them. Now sit down and let me help you. I cooked the dinner myself." Feeling that Agnes's eye was upon her, she added, "Agnes and I—I helped Agnes. We made the melted butter from the recipe in the cookery-book next door. I do hope it is a success."

"I see you've got champagne, too."

"But I don't know how you're to get the bottle open, miss; we've no champagne nippers."

After some conjecturing the wires were twisted off with a kitchen fork. Evelyn kept her eyes on her father's plate, and begged to be allowed to help him again, and she delighted in filling up his glass with wine; and though she longed to ask him if he had been to hear her sing, she did not allude to herself, but induced him to talk of his victories over Father Gordon. This story of clerical jealousy and ignorance was intensely interesting to the old man, and she humoured him to the top of his bent.

"But it would all have come to nothing if it had not been for Monsignor Mostyn."

She fetched him his pipe and tobacco. "And who is Monsignor Mostyn?" she asked, dreading a long tale in which she could feel on interest at all. She watched him filling his pipe, working the tobacco down with his little finger nail. She thought she could see he was thinking of something different, and to her great joy he said—

"Well, your Margaret is very good; better than I expected—I am speaking of the singing; of course, as acting it was superb."

"Oh, father! do tell me? So you went after all? I sent you a box and a stall, but you were in neither. In what part of the theatre were you?"

"In the upper boxes; I did not want to dress." She leaned across the table with brightening eyes. "For a dramatic soprano you sing that light music with extraordinary ease and fluency."

"Did I sing it as well as mother?"

"Oh, my dear, it was quite different. Your mother's art was in her phrasing and in the ideal appearance she presented."

"And didn't I present an ideal appearance?"

"It's like this, Evelyn. The Margaret of Gounod and his librettist is not a real person, but a sort of keepsake beauty who sings keepsake music. I assume that you don't think much of the music; brought up as you have been on the Old Masters, you couldn't. Well, the question is whether parts designed in such an intention should be played in the like intention, or if they should be made living creations of flesh and blood, worked up by the power of the actress into something as near to the Wagner ideal as possible. I admire your Margaret; it was a wonderful performance, but—"

"But what, father?"

"It made me wish to see you in Elizabeth and Brunnhilde. I was very sorry I couldn't get to London last night."

"You'd like my Elizabeth better. Margaret is the only part of the old lot that I now sing. I daresay you're right. I'll limit myself for the future to the Wagner repertoire."

"I think you'd do well. Your genius is essentially in dramatic expression. 'Carmen,' for instance, is better as Galli Marié used to play it than as you would play it. 'Carmen' is a conventional type—all art is convention of one kind or another, and each demands its own interpretation. But I hope you don't sing that horrid music."

"You don't like 'Carmen'?"

Mr. Innes shrugged his shoulders contemptuously.

"'Faust' is better than that. Gounod follows—at a distance, of course—but he follows the tradition of Haydn and Mozart. 'Carmen' is merely Gounod and Wagner. I hope you've not forgotten my teaching; as I've always said, music ended with Beethoven and began again with Wagner."

"Did you see Ulick Dean's article?"

"Yes, he wrote to me last night about your Elizabeth. He says there never was anything heard like it on the stage."

"Did he say that? Show me the letter. What else did he say?"

"It was only a note. I destroyed it. He just said what I told you. But he's a bit mad about that opera. He's been talking to me about it all the winter, saying that the character had never been acted; apparently it has been now. Though for my part I think Brunnhilde or Isolde would suit you better."

The mention of Isolde caused them to avoid looking at each other, and Evelyn asked her father to tell her about Ulick—how they became acquainted and how much they saw of each other. But to tell her when he made Ulick's acquaintance would be to allude to the time when Evelyn left home. So his account of their friendship was cursory and perfunctory, and he asked Evelyn suddenly if Ulick had shown her his opera.

"Grania?"

"No, not 'Grania.' He has not finished 'Grania,' but 'Connla and the Fairy Maiden.' Written," he added, "entirely on the old lines. Come into the music-room and you shall see."

He took up the lamp; Evelyn called Agnes to get another. The lamps were placed upon the harpsichord; she lighted some candles, and, just as in old times, they lost themselves in dreams and visions. This time it was in a faint Celtic haze; a vision of silver mist and distant mountain and mere. It was on the heights of Uisnech that Connla heard the fairy calling him to the Plain of Pleasure, Moy Mell, where Boadag is king. And King Cond, seeing his son about to be taken from him, summoned Coran the priest and bade him chant his spells toward the spot whence the fairy's voice was heard. The fairy could not resist the spell of the priest, but she threw Connla an apple and for a whole month he ate nothing but that. But as he ate, it grew again, and always kept whole. And all the while there grew within him a mighty yearning and longing after the maiden he had seen. And when the last day of the month of waiting came, Connla stood by the side of the king, his father, on the Plain of Aromin, and again he saw the maiden come towards him, and again she spoke to him—

"'Tis no lofty seat on which Connla sits among short-lived mortals awaiting fearful death, but now the folk of life, the ever-living living ones, beg and bid thee come to Moy Mell, the Plain of Pleasure, for they have learnt to know thee."

When Cond the king observed that since the maiden came Connla his son spake to none that spake to him, then Cond of the hundred fights said to him—

"Is it to thy mind what the woman says, my son?"

"'Tis hard on me; I love my folk above all things, but a great longing seizes me for the maiden."

106

"The waves of the ocean are not so strong as the waves of thy longing; come with me in my currah, the straight gliding, the crystal boat, and we shall soon reach the Plain of Pleasure, where Boadag is king."

King Cond and all his court saw Connla spring into the boat, and he and the fairy maiden glided over the bright sea, towards the setting sun, away and away, and they were seen no more, nor did anyone know where they went to.

"My dear father, manuscript, and at sight, words and music!"

"Come—begin."

"Give me the chord."

He looked at her in astonishment.

"Won't you give me the keynote?"

"In the key of E flat," he answered sternly.

She began. "Is that right?"

"Yes, that's right. You see that you can still sing at sight. I don't suppose you find many prima donnas who can."

With her arm on his shoulder they sat together, playing and singing the music with which Ulick had interpreted the tale of "Connla and the Fairy Maiden."

"You see," he said, "he has invented a new system of orchestration; as a matter of fact, we worked it out together, but that's neither here nor there. In some respects it is not unlike Wagner; the vocal music is mostly recitative, but now and then there is nearly an air, and yet it isn't new, for it is how it would have been written about 1500. You see," he said, turning over the pages of the full score, "each character is allotted a different set of instruments as accompaniment; in this way you get astonishing colour contrasts. For instance, the priest is accompanied by a chest of six viols; *i.e.*, two trebles, two tenors, two basses. King Cond is accompanied by a set of six cromornes, like the viols of various sizes. The Fairy Maiden has a set of six flutes or recorders, the smallest of which is eight inches long, the biggest quite six feet. Connla is accompanied by a group of oboes; and another character is allotted three lutes with an arch lute, another a pair of virginals, another a regal, another a set of six sackbuts and trumpets. See how all the instruments are used in the overture and in the dances, of which there are plenty, Pavans, Galliards, Allemaines. But look here, this is most important: even in the instrumental pieces the instruments are not to be mixed, as in modern orchestra, but used in groups, always distinct, like patches of colour in impressionist pictures."

"I like this," and she hummed through the fairy's luring of Connla to embark with her. "But I could not give an opinion of the orchestration without hearing it, it is all so new."

"We haven't succeeded yet in getting together sufficient old instruments to provide an orchestra."

"But, father, do you think such orchestration realisable in modern music? I see very little Wagner in it; it is more like Caccini or Monteverde. There can be very little real life in a parody."

"No, but it isn't parody, that's just what it isn't, for it is natural to him to write in this style. What he writes in the modern style is as common as anyone else. This is his natural language." In support of the validity of his argument that a return to the original sources of an art is possible without loss of originality, he instanced the Pre-Raphaelite Brotherhood. The most beautiful pictures, and the most original pictures Millais had ever painted were those that he painted while he was attempting to revive the methods of Van Eyck, and the language of Shakespeare was much more archaic than that of any of his contemporaries. "But explanations are useless. I tried to explain to Father Gordon that Palestrina was one of the greatest of musicians, but he never understood. Monsignor Mostyn and I understood each other at once. I said Palestrina, he said Vittoria—I don't know which suggested the immense advantage that a revival of the true music of the Catholic would be in making converts to Rome. You don't like Ulick's music; there's nothing more to be said."

"But I do like it, father. How impatient you are! And because I don't understand an entire æstheticism in five minutes, which you and Ulick Dean have been cooking for the last three years, I am a fool, quite as stupid as Father Gordon."

Mr. Innes laughed, and when he put his arm round her and kissed her she was happy again. The hours went lightly by as if enchanted, and it was midnight when he closed the harpsichord and they went upstairs. Neither spoke; they were thinking of the old times which apparently had come back to them. On the landing she said—

"We've had a nice evening after all. Good-night, father. I know my room."

"Good-night," he said. "You'll find all your things; nothing has been changed."

Agnes had laid one of her old nightgowns on the bed, and there was her *prie-dieu*, and on the chest of drawers the score of Tristan which Owen had given her six years ago. She had come back to sing it. How extraordinary it all was! She seemed to have drifted like a piece of seaweed; she lived in the present though it sank beneath her like a wave. The past she saw dimly, the future not at all; and sitting by her window she was moved by vague impulses towards infinity. She grew aware of her own littleness and the vastness overhead—that great unending enigma represented to her understanding by a tint of blue washed over by a milky tint. Owen had told her that there were twenty million suns in the milky way, and that around every one numerous planets revolved. This earth was but a small planet, and its sun a third-rate sun. On this speck of earth a being had awakened to a consciousness of the glittering riddle above his head, but he would die in the same ignorance of its meaning as a rabbit. The secret of the celestial plan she would never know. One day she would slip out of consciousness of it; life would never beckon her again; but the vast plan which she now perceived would continue to revolve, progressing towards an end which no man, though the world were to continue for a hundred million years, would ever know.

Her brain seemed to melt in the moonlight, and from the enigma of the skies her thoughts turned to the enigma of her own individuality. She was aware that she lived. She was aware that some things were right, that some things were wrong. She was aware of the strange fortune that had lured her, that had chosen her out of millions. What did it mean? It must mean something, just as those stars must mean something—but what?

Opposite to her window there was an open space; it was full of mist and moonlight; the lights of a distant street looked across it. She too had said, "'Tis hard upon me, I love my folk above all things, but a great longing seizes me." That story is the story of human life. What is human life but a longing for something beyond us, for something we shall not attain? Again she wondered what her end must be. She must end somehow, and was it not strange that she could no more answer that simple question than she could the sublime question which the moon and stars propounded.... That breathless, glittering peace, was it not wonderful? It seemed to beckon and allure, and her soul yearned for that peace as Connla's had for the maiden. Death only could give that peace. Did the Fairy Maiden mean death? Did the plains of the Ever Living, which the Fairy Maiden had promised Connla on the condition of his following her, lie behind those specks of light?

But what end should she choose for herself if the choice were left to her—to come back to Dulwich and live with her father? She might do that—but when her father died? Then she hoped that she might die. But she might outlive him for thirty years—Evelyn Innes, an old woman, talking to the few friends who came to see her, of the days when Wagner was triumphant, of her reading of "Isolde." Some such end as that would be hers. Or she might end as Lady Asher. She might, but she did not think she would. Owen seemed to think more of marriage now than he used to. He had always said they would be married when she retired from the stage. But why should she retire from the stage? If he had wanted to marry her he should have asked her at first. She did not know what she was going to do. No one knew what they were going to do. They simply went on living. That moonlight was melting her brain away. She drew down the blinds, and she fell asleep thinking of her father's choir and the beautiful "Missa Brevis" which she was going to hear to-morrow.

CHAPTER SEVENTEEN

As they went to church, he told her about Monsignor Mostyn. Evelyn remembered that the very day she went away, he had had an appointment with the prelate, and while trying to recall the words he had used at the time—how Monsignor believed that a revival of Palestrina would advance the Catholic cause in England—she heard her father say that no one except Monsignor could have succeeded in so difficult an enterprise as the reformation of church music in England.

The organ is a Protestant instrument, and in organ music the London churches do very well; the Protestant congregations are, musically, more enlightened; the flattest degradation is found among the English Catholics, and he instanced the Oratory as an extraordinary disgrace to a civilised country, relating how he had heard the great Mass of Pope Marcellus given there by an operatic choir of twenty singers. In the West-end are apathy and fashionable vulgarity, and it was at St. Joseph's, Southwark, that the Church had had restored to her all her own beautiful music. Monsignor had begun by coming forward with a subscription of one thousand pounds a year, and by such *largesse* he had confounded the intractable Jesuits and vanquished Father Gordon. The poor man who had predicted ruin now viewed the magnificent congregation with a sullen face. "He has a nice voice, too, that's the strange part of it; I could have taught him, but he is too proud to admit he was wrong." However, *bon gré mal gré*, Father Gordon had had to submit to Monsignor. When Monsignor makes up his mind, things have to be done. If a thousand pounds had not been enough, he would have given two thousand pounds; Monsignor was rich, but he was also tactful, and did not rely entirely on his money. He had come to St. Joseph's with the Pope's written request in his hand that St. Joseph's should attempt a revival of the truly Catholic music, if sufficient money could be obtained for the choir. So there was no gainsaying, the Jesuits had had to submit, for if they had again objected to the expense, Monsignor would come forward with a subscription of two thousand a year. He could not have afforded to pay so much for more than a limited number of years, "but he and I felt that it was only necessary to start the thing for it to succeed."

Mr. Innes told his daughter of Monsignor's social influence; Monsignor had the command of any amount of money. There is always the money, the difficulty is to obtain the will that can direct the money. Monsignor was the will. He was all-powerful in Rome. He spent his winters and springs in Rome, and no one thought of going to Rome without calling on him. It was through him that the Pope kept in touch with the English Catholics. He had a confessional at St. Joseph's, and he was *au mieux* with the Jesuits. It was the influence of Monsignor that had given Palestrina his present vogue. But a revival of Palestrina was in the air; through him the inevitable reaction against Wagner was making itself felt. Monsignor had made all the rich Catholics understand that it was their duty to support the unique experiment which some poor Jesuits in Southwark were making, and the fact that he had come forward with a subscription of one thousand a year enabled him to ask his friends for their money. He had told Mr. Innes that a dinner party which did not produce a subscriber he looked upon as a dinner wasted. Monsignor knew how to carry a thing through; his influence was extraordinary; he could get people to do what he wanted.

Evelyn and her father had so much to say that it did not seem as if they ever would find time to say it in. There was the story to tell of the construction of the vast choir and the difficulties he had experienced in teaching his singers to read at sight, for, as she knew, contrapuntal music cannot be sung except by singers who can sing unaccompanied. The trebles and the altos were of course the great difficulty; the boys often burst into tears; they said they preferred to die rather than endure his discipline. He was often sorry for them, for he knew

that the perfect singing of this contrapuntal music was almost impossible except by *castrati*. But he was able to communicate his enthusiasm; he told them stories of how the ancient choirs used to sing Palestrina's masses without a rehearsal, how the ancient choirs used to compete one against the other, singing music they had never seen against men in the opposite organ loft whom they did not even know. He was full of such stories; they served to fire the boys' enthusiasm, and to change dislike into an inspiration. He had hypnotised them into a love of Palestrina, and when they went home their parents had told him that the boys were always talking about the ancient music, and that they sat up at night reading motets. He had told them that they would abandon all foolish pastimes for Palestrina, and they had in a measure; instead of batting and bowling, their ambition became sight singing. Once a spirit of emulation is inspired, great things are accomplished. There had been some beautiful singing at St. Joseph's. Three months ago he believed that his choir would have compared with some of the sixteenth century choirs. Mr. Innes told an instructive story of how he had lost a most extraordinary treble, the best he had ever had. No, he had not lost his voice; a casual word had done the mischief. The boy had happened to tell his mother that Mr. Innes had said that he would give up cricket for Palestrina, and she, being a fool, had laughed at him. Her laughter had ruined the boy; he had refused to sing any more; he had become a dissipated young rascal, up to every mischief. Unfortunately, before he left he had influenced other boys; many had to be sent away as useless; and it was only now that his choir was beginning to recover from this egregious calamity. But though the difficulty of the trebles and the altos was always the difficulty of his choir, it no longer seemed insuperable. With the large amount of money at his disposal, he could afford to pay almost any amount of money for a good treble or alto, so every boy in London who showed signs of a voice was brought to him. But in three or four years a boy's voice breaks, and the task of finding another to take his place has to be undertaken. Very often this is impossible; there are times when there are no voices. The present time was such a one, and he fumed at the foolish woman whose casual word had broken up his choir three months ago, bemoaning that such a calamity should have happened just before Monsignor's return from Rome. It was for that reason he was giving the "Missa Brevis," a small work easily done. He declared he would give fifty pounds to recall his choir of three months ago, just for Evelyn and Monsignor to hear it. Evelyn easily believed that he would, and as they parted inside the church she said—
"I wish I could take the place of the naughty boy."
A look of hope came into his eyes, but it died away in an instant, and she watched his despondent back as he went towards the choir loft.
The influence of Monsignor had worked great changes at St. Joseph's—the very atmosphere of the church was different, the sensation was one of culture and refinement, instead of that acrid poverty. From the altar rail to the middle of the aisle the church was crowded—in the free as well as in the paying parts. From the altar rails to the middle of the aisle there were chairs for the ease of the subscribers, and for those who were willing to pay a fee of two shillings. In front of each chair was a comfortable kneeling place, and slender, gloved hands held prayer-books bound in morocco, and under fashionable hats, filled with bright beads and shadowy feathers, veiled faces were bent in dainty prayer. Among these Evelyn picked out a number of her friends. There were Lady Ascott, who missed no musical entertainment of whatever kind, even when it took place in church, and Lady Gremaldin, who thought she was listening to Wagner when she was thinking of the tenor whom she would take away to supper in her brougham after the performance.... Evelyn caught sight of a painter or two and a man of letters who used to come to her father's concerts. Suddenly she saw Ulick standing close by her; he had not seen her, and was looking for a seat. Catching sight of her, he came and sat in the chair next to hers. Almost at the same moment the acolytes led the procession from the sacristy. They were followed by the sub-deacon, the deacon and the priest who was to sing the Mass. When the Mass began the choir broke forth, singing the Introit.

The practice of singing in church proceeds from the idea that, in the exaltation of prayer, the soul, having reached the last limit obtainable by mere words, demands an extended expression, and finds it in song. The earliest form of music, the plain chant or Gregorian, is sung in unison, for it was intended to be sung by the whole congregation, but as only a few in every congregation are musicians, the idea of a choir could not fail to suggest itself; and, once the idea of a choir accepted, part writing followed, and the vocal masses of the sixteenth century were the result. Then the art of religious music had gone as far as it could, and the next step, the introduction of an accompanying instrument, was decadence.

The "Missa Brevis" is one of the most exquisite of the master's minor works. It is written for four voices, and with the large choir at his command, Mr. Innes was able to put eight to ten voices on a part; and hearing voices darting, voices soaring, voices floating, weaving an audible embroidery, Evelyn felt the vanity of accompaniment instruments. Upon the ancient chant the new harmonies blossomed like roses on an old gnarled stem, and when on the ninth bar of the "Kyrie" the tenors softly separated from the sustained chord of the other parts, the effect was as of magic. Evelyn lifted her eyes and saw her dear father conducting with calm skill.

She had heard the Mass in Rome, and remembered the beautiful phrase which opens the "Kyrie" and which is the essence of the first part of that movement. But the altos had not the true alto quality; they were trebles singing in the lower register of their voices. Leaning towards her, Ulick whispered, "The altos are not quite in tune." She had heard nothing wrong, but, seeing that he was convinced, she resolved to submit the matter to her father's decision. She had every confidence in the accuracy of her ear; but last night her father had said that the modern musical ear was not nearly so fine as the ancient, trained to the exact intervals of the monochord, instead of the coarse approximation of the keyboard.

She remembered that when she had heard the Mass in Rome there was a moment when she had longed for the sweet concord of a pure third. Now, when it came at the end of the first note of the basses, Ulick said, "It is as sharp as that of an ordinary piano." It had not seemed so to her, and she wondered if her ear had deteriorated, if the corrupting influence of modern chromatic music had been too strong, if she had lost her ear in the Wagner drama. The coarse intonation was more obvious in the "Christe Eleison," sung by four solo voices, than in the "Kyrie," sung by the full choir; and she did catch a slight equivocation, and the discovery tended to make her doubt Ulick's assertion that the altos were wrong in the "Kyrie," for, if she heard right in one place, why did she not hear right in another? The leading treble had a hard, unsympathetic voice, which did not suit the florid passages occurring three times on the second syllable of the word Eleison. He hammered them instead of singing them tenderly, with just the sense of a caress in the voice.

But outside of such extreme criticism, in the audience of the ordinary musical ear, the beautiful "Missa Brevis" was as well given as it could be given in modern times, and Evelyn was, of course, anxious to see the great prelate to whose energetic influence the revival of this music was owing, the man who had helped to make her dear father's life a satisfaction to him. It was just slipping into disappointment when the prelate had come to save it. This was why Evelyn was so interested in him—why she was already attracted toward him. It was for this reason she was sitting in one of the front chairs, near to where Monsignor would have to pass on his way to the pulpit. He was to preach that Sunday at St. Joseph's.... He passed close to her, and she had a clear view of his thin, hard, handsome face, dark in colour and severe as a piece of mediæval wood carving; a head small and narrow across the temples, as if it had been squeezed. The eyes were bright brown, and fixed; the nose long and straight, with clear-cut nostrils. She noticed the thin, mobile mouth and the swift look in the keen eyes—in that look he seemed to gather an exact notion of the congregation he was about to address.

Already Evelyn trembled inwardly. The silence was quick with possibility; anything might happen—he might even publicly reprove her from the pulpit, and to strengthen her nerves against this influence, she compared the present tension to that which gathered her audience together as one man when the moment approached for her to come on the stage. All were listening, as if she were going to sing; it remained to be seen if the effect of his preaching equalled that of her singing. She was curious to see.

"I say unto you, that likewise joy shall be in heaven over one sinner that repenteth, more than over ninety and nine just persons, which need no repentance." In introducing this text he declared it to be one of the most beautiful and hopeful in Scripture. Was it the sweet, clear voice that lured the different minds and led them, as it were, in leash? Or was it that slow, deliberate, persuasive manner? Or was it the benedictive and essentially Christian creed which he preached that disengaged the weight from every soul, allowing each to breathe an easier and sweeter breath? To one and all it seemed as if they were listening to the voice of their own souls, rather than that of a living man whom they did not know, and who did not know them. The preacher's voice and words were as the voices they heard speaking from the bottom of their souls in moments of strange collectedness. And as if aware of the spiritual life he had awakened, the preacher leaned over the pulpit and paused, as if watching the effect of his will upon the congregation. The hush trembled into intensity when he said, "Yes, and not only in heaven, but on earth as well, there shall be joy when a sinner repents. This can be verified, not in public places where men seek wealth, fame and pleasure—there, there shall be only scorn and sneers—but in the sanctuary of every heart; there is no one, I take it, who has not at some moment repented." Instantly Evelyn remembered Florence. Had her repentance there been a joy or a pain? She had not persevered. At that moment she heard the preacher ask if the most painful moments of our lives were the result of our having followed the doctrine of Jesus or the doctrine of the world? He instanced the gambler and the libertine, who willingly confess themselves unhappy, but who, he asked, ever heard of the good man saying he was unhappy? The tedium of life the good man never knows. Men have been known to regret the money they spent on themselves, but who has ever regretted the money he has spent in charity? But even success cannot save the gambler and libertine from the tedium of existence, and when the preacher said, "These men dare not be alone," Evelyn thought of Owen, and of her constant efforts to keep him amused, distracted; and when the preacher said it was impossible for the sinner to abstract himself, to enter into his consciousness without hearing it reprove him, Evelyn thought of herself. The preacher made no distinctions; all men, he said, when they are sincere with themselves, are aware of the difference between good and evil living. When they listen the voice is always audible; even those who purposely close their ears often hear it. For this voice cannot be wholly silenced; it can be stifled for a while, but it can be no more abolished than the sound of the sea from the shell. "As a shell, man is murmurous with morality."

Of the rest of the sermon Evelyn heard very little.... It was the phrase that if we look into our lives we shall find that our most painful moments are due to our having followed the doctrine of the world instead of the doctrine of Christ that touched Evelyn. It seemed to explain things in herself which she had never understood. It told her why she was not happy. ... Happy she had never been, and she had never understood why. Because she had been leading a life that was opposed to what she deemed to be essentially right. How very simple, and yet she had never quite apprehended it before; she had striven to close her ears, but she had never succeeded. Why? Because that whisper can be no more abolished than the murmur of the sea from the shell. How true! That murmur had never died out of her ears; she had been able to stifle it for a while—she had never been able to abolish it—and what convincing proof this was of the existence of God!

Disprove it you couldn't, for it was part of one's senses—the very evidence on which the materialists rely to prove that beyond this world there is nothing. Yet what a flagrant contradiction her conduct was to the murmur of spiritual existence. And that was why she was not happy. That was why she would never be happy till she reformed.... But the preacher spoke as if it were easy for all who wished it to change their lives. How was she to change her life? Her life was settled and determined for her ever since the day she went away with Owen.

If she sent Owen away again the same thing would happen; she would take him back. She could not remain on the stage without a lover; she would take another before a month was out. It was no use for her to deceive herself! That is what she would do. To sing Isolde and live a chaste life, she did not believe it to be possible—and she sat helpless, hearing vaguely the Credo, her attention so distracted that she was only half aware of its beauty. She noticed that the "Et incarnatus est" was inadequately rendered, but that she expected. It would require the strange, immortal voices she had heard in Rome. But the vigour with which the basses led the "Et resurrexit" was such that the other parts could not choose but follow. She felt thankful to them; they dissipated her painful personal reverie. Yes, the basses were the best part of the choir; among them she recognised two of her father's oldest pupils; she had known them as boys singing alto—beautiful voices they had been, and were not less beautiful now. But if she desired to reform her life, how was she to begin? She knew what the priest would tell her. He would say, send away your lover; but to send him away in the plenitude of her success would be odious. He was unhappy; he was ill; he needed her sorely. His mother's health was a great anxiety to him, and if, on the top of all, she were to announce that she intended leaving him, he would break down altogether. She owed everything to him. No, not even for the sake of her immortal soul would she do anything that would give him pain. But he had been anxious to marry her for some time. Would she make him a good wife? She was fond of him; she would do anything for him. She had travelled hundreds of miles to see him when he was ill, and the other night she could not sleep because she feared he was unhappy about his mother's health. She would marry him if he asked her. On that point she was certain. Refuse Owen? Not for anything that could be offered her; nothing would change her from that. Nothing! Her resolve was taken. No, it was not taken; it was there in her heart.
And at the moment when the Elevation bell rang she decided not only to accept Owen if he asked her, but to use all her influence to induce him to ask her. This seemed to her equivalent to a resolution to reform her life, and, happier in mind, she bowed her head, and as a very unworthy Catholic, but still a Catholic, and feeling no longer as an alien and an outcast, she assisted at the mystery of the Mass. She even ventured to offer up a vague prayer, and when the dread interval was over, she remembered that her father had spoken to her of the second "Agnus Dei" as an especially beautiful number. It was for five voices; exquisitely prayerful it seemed to her. With devout insistence the theme is reiterated by the two soprani, then the voices are woven together, and the simile that rose up in her mind was the pious image of fingers interlaced in prayer.
The first thrill, the first impression of the music over, she applied herself to the dissection of it, so that she might be able to discuss it with Ulick and her father afterwards. This beautiful melody, apparently so free, was so exquisitely contrived that it contained within itself descant and harmony. She knew it well; it is a strict canon in unison, and she had heard it sung by two grey-haired men in the Papal choir in Rome, soprano voices of a rarer and more radiant timbre than any woman's sexful voice, and subtle, and, in some complex way, hardly of the earth at all—voices in which no accent of sex transpired, abstract voices aloof from any stress of passion, undistressed by any longing, even for God. They were not human voices, and, hearing them, Evelyn had imagined angels bearing tall lilies in their hands, standing on wan heights of celestial landscape, singing their clear silver music.
These men had sung this "Agnus Dei" as perhaps it never would be sung again, but she knew the boy treble to be incapable of singing this canon properly, so she could hardly resist the impulse to run up to the choir loft and tell her father breathlessly that she would take his place. She smiled at the consternation such an act would occasion. Even if she could get to the choir loft without being noticed, she could not sing this music, her voice was full of sex, and this music required the strange sexless timbre of the voices she had heard in Rome. But the boy sang better than she anticipated; his voice was wanting in strength and firmness; she listened, anxious to help him, perplexed that she could not.
The last Gospel was then read, and she followed Ulick out of church.

CHAPTER EIGHTEEN

On getting outside the church, they were surprised to find that it had been raining. The shower had laid the dust, freshened the air, and upon the sky there was a beautiful flowerlike bloom; the white clouds hung in the blue air uplifting fugitive palace and tower, and when Evelyn and Ulick looked into this mysterious cloudland, their hearts overflowed with an intense joy.

She opened her parasol, and told him that her father was lunching with the Jesuits. But he and she were going to dine together at Dowlands; and after dinner they were not to forget to practise the Bach sonata which was in the programme for the evening concert. She thought of the long day before them, and with mixed wonderment and pleasure of how much better they would know each other at the end of the day. She wanted to know how he thought and felt about things; and it seemed to her that he could tell her all that she yearned to know, though what this was she did not know herself.

There were strange hills and valleys and fabulous prospects in the great white cloud which hung at the end of the suburban street, and it seemed to her that she would like to wander with him there among the white dells, and to stand with him upon the high pinnacles. She was happy in an infinite cloudland while he told her of her father's struggle to obtain mastery in St. Joseph's. But she experienced a passing pang of regret that she had not been present to witness the first struggles of the reformation.

She was interested in the part that Ulick had played in it. He told her how almost every week he had written an article developing some new phase of the subject, and Evelyn told him how her father had told her of the extraordinary ingenuity and energy with which he had continued the propaganda from week to week. When her father was called away to negotiate some financial difficulty, Ulick had taken charge of the rehearsals. Mr. Innes had told Evelyn that Ulick had displayed an unselfish devotion, and she added that he had been to her father what Liszt had been to Wagner, and while paying this compliment she looked at him in admiration, thanking him with her eyes. Had it not been for him, her father might have died of want of appreciation, killed by Father Gordon's obstinacy.

"But you came to him," she said, speaking unwillingly, "when I selfishly left him."

Ulick would not concede that he was worthy of any distinction in the victory of the old music; it would have achieved its legitimate triumph without his aid. He had merely done his duty like any private soldier in the ranks. But from first to last all had depended upon Monsignor. Mr. Innes had shown more energy and practical intelligence than anyone, not excepting Evelyn herself, would have credited him with; he had interested many people by his enthusiasm, but nevertheless he had remained what he was—a man of ideas rather than of practice, and without Monsignor the reformation would have come to naught. Evelyn was strangely interested to know what Ulick thought of Monsignor, and she waited eager for him to speak. She would have liked to hear him enthusiastic, but he said that Monsignor was no more than an Oxford don with a taste for dogma and for a cardinal's hat. He was not a man of ideas, but a man that would do well in an election or a strike. He was what folk call "a leader of men," and Ulick held that power over the passing moment was a sign of inferiority. Shakespeare and Shelley and Blake had never participated in any movement; they were the movement itself, they were the centres of things. Christ, too, had failed to lead men, he was far too much above them; but St. Paul, the man of inferior ideas, had succeeded where Christ had failed. Mostyn, he maintained, was much more interested in dogma than in religion; he abhorred mysticism, and believed in organisation. He considered his Church from the point of view of a trades union. An unspiritual man, one much more interested in theology than in God—an able shepherd with an instinct for lost sheep whose fixed and commonplace ideas gave him command over weak and exalted natures, natures which were frequently much more spiritual than his own. Evelyn listened, amused, though she could not think of Monsignor quite as Ulick did. Monsignor had said that if we ask ourselves to what our unhappiness is attributable, we find that it is attributable to having followed the way of the world instead of the way of Christ.

It seemed to her impossible that a man of inferior intelligence such as Ulick described could think so clearly. She reminded Ulick of these very sentences which had so greatly moved her, and it flattered her to hear him admit it, that the idea which had so greatly struck her was penetrating and far-reaching, but he denied that it was possible that it could be Monsignor's own. It was something he had got out of a book, and seeing the effect that could be made of it, he had introduced it into his sermon. In support of this opinion, he said that all the rest of the sermon was sententious commonplace about the soul, and obedience to the Church.

"But you will be able to judge for yourself. He is coming to the concert to-night."

"Then I must have a dress to wear, I suppose he would like me to wear sackcloth. But I am going to wear a pretty pink silk, which I hope you will like. Call that hansom, please."

It was amusing to watch her write the note, hear her explain to the cabman: if he brought back the right dress he was to get a sovereign. It was amusing to stroll on through the naked Sunday streets, talking of the music they had just heard and of Monsignor, to find suddenly that they had lost their way and could see no one to direct them. These little incidents served to enhance their happiness. They were nearly of the same age, and were conscious of it; a generation is but a large family, united by ties of impulse and idea. Evelyn had been brought up and had lived outside of the influence of her own generation. Now it was flashed upon her for the first time, and under the spell of its instincts she ran down the steps to the railway and jumped into the moving train. Owen would have forbidden her this little recklessness, but Ulick accepted it as natural, and they sat opposite each other, their thoughts lost in the rustle and confusion of their blood. She was conscious of a delicious inward throbbing, and she liked the smooth young face, the colour of old ivory, and the dark, fixed eyes into which she could not look without trembling; they changed, lighting up and clouding as his thought came and went. She found an attraction in his occasional absent-mindedness, and wondered of what he was thinking. Looking into his eyes, she was aware of a mystery half understood, and she could not but feel that this enigma, this mystery, was essential to her. Her life seemed to depend upon it; she seemed to have come upon the secret at last.

It was amusing to walk home to dinner together this bright summer's day, and to tell this young man, to whose intervention it pleased her to think that she owed her reconciliation to her father, how it was by pretending not to understand the new harpsichord that she had inveigled her father into speaking to her.... But it was only one o'clock—an hour still remained before dinner would be ready at Dowlands, and they were glad to dream it under the delicious chestnut trees. She sat intent, moving the tiny bloom from side to side with her parasol, thinking of her father. Suddenly she told Ulick of the Wotan and Brunnhilde scene, which she had always played, while thinking of the real scene that one day awaited her at her father's feet, and this scene she had at last acted, if you could call reality acting. She was dimly aware of the old Dulwich street, and that she had once trundled her hoop there, and the humble motion of life beneath the chestnut trees, the loitering of stout housewives and husbands in Sunday clothes, the spare figures of spinsters who lived in the damp houses which lay at the back of the choked gardens was accepted as a suitable background for her happiness. Her joy seemed to dilate in the morning, in the fluttering sensation of the sunshine, of summer already begun in the distant fields. Inspired by the scene, Ulick began to hum the old English air, "Summer is a-coming in," and without raising her eyes from the chestnut blooms that fell incessantly on the pavement, Evelyn said—"That monk had a beautiful dream."

And for a while they thought of that monk at Reading composing for his innocent recreation that beautiful piece of music; they hummed it together, thinking of his quiet monastery, and it seemed to them that it would be a beautiful thing if life were over, if it might pass away, as that monk's life had passed, in peace, in aspiration whether of prayer or of art. Thinking of the music she had heard over night, that she had hummed through and that her father had played on the harpsichord, she said—"And you, too, had a beautiful dream when you wrote 'Connla and the Fairy Maiden'?"

"Ah, your father showed it to you; you hadn't told me."

Then, absorbed in his idea, never speaking for effect, stripping himself of every adventitious pleasure in the service of his idea, he told her of the change that had come upon his æstheticism in the last year. He had been organist for three years at St. Patrick's, and since then had been interested in the modes, the abandoned modes in which the plain chant is written. These modes were the beginning of music, the original source; in them were written, no doubt, the songs and dances of the folk who died two, three, four, five thousand years ago, but none of this music had been preserved, only the religious chants of this distant period of art have come down to us, and from this accident his sprung the belief that the early modes are only capable of expressing religious emotion. But the gayest rhythms can be written in these modes as easily as in the ordinary major and minor scales. It was thought, too, that the modes did not lend themselves to modulation, but by long study of them Ulick had discovered how they may be submitted to the science of modulation.

"I see," Evelyn replied pensively. "The first line written in one of the ancient modes, and underneath the melody, chromatic harmonies."

"No, that would be horrible," Ulick cried, like a dog whose tail has been trodden upon. "That is the infamous modern practice. I seek the harmony in the sentiment of the melody I am writing, in the tonality of the mode I am writing."

And then, little by little, they entered the perilous question of the ancient modes. There were several, and three were as distinctive and as rich sources of melody and harmony as the ordinary major scale, for modern music limited itself to the major scale, the minor scale being a dependency. The major and minor modes or scales had sufficed for two or three centuries of music, but the time of their exhaustion was approaching, and the musicians of the future would have to return to the older scales. He refused to admit that they did not lend themselves to modulation, and he answered, when Evelyn suggested that the introduction of a sharp or a flat was likely to alter the character of the ancient scales, that she must not judge the ancient scales by what had already been written in them; it was nowise his intention to imitate the character of the plain chant melodies; she must not confuse the sentiment of these melodies with the modes in which they were written. It might be that in adding a sharp or a flat the musician destroyed the character of the mode which he was leaving and that of the mode he was passing into, but that proved nothing except his want of skill. His opera was written not only in the three ancient modes, but also in the ordinary major and minor scales, and he believed that he had enlarged the limits of musical expression.

He was not the first young man she had met with schemes for writing original music. So far as she was capable of judging, his practice was better than his theory. But his music was not the origin of her interest for him. What really interested her were his beliefs; her personal interest in him had really begun when he had said that he believed in a continuous revelation. Of this revelation he had argued that Christ was only a part. These ideas, which she heard for the first time, especially interested her. Owen's agnosticism had given her freedom and command of this world, but it had made a great loneliness in her life which Owen was no longer able to fill. Life seemed a desert without some form of belief, and notwithstanding her success, her life was often intolerably lonely. She had often thought of the world's flowers and fruits as mere semblance of things without true reality, and what seemed a bountiful garden, a mere hard, dry, brilliant desert. It was only at certain moments, of course, that she thought these things, but sometimes these thoughts quite unexpectedly came upon her, and she could no longer conceal from herself the fact that she was lonely in her soul, and that she was growing lonelier. She was wearying a little of all the visible world, beginning to hunger for the invisible, from which she had closed her eyes so long, but which, for all that, had never become wholly darkened to her.

Hearing Ulick speak of foreseeing and divinations by the stars was, too, like sweet rain in a dying land; and as they returned to Dowlands, she spoke to him of Moy Mell where Boadag is king, of the Plain of the Ever Living, of Connla and the Fairy Maiden gliding in the crystal boat over the Western Sea, and during dinner she longed to ask him if he believed in a future life.

It was difficult for her, who had never spoken on such subjects before, to disentangle his philosophy, and it was not until he said that we must not believe as religionists do, that one day the invisible shall become the visible, that she began to understand him. Such doctrine, he said, is paltry and materialistic, worthy of the theologian and the agnostic. We must rather, he said, seek to raise and purify our natures, so that we may see more of the spiritual element which resides in things, and which is visible to all in a greater or less degree as they put aside their grosser nature and attain step by step to a higher point of vision. She had always imagined there was nothing between the materialism of Owen and the theology of Monsignor. Ulick's ideas were quite new to her; they appealed to her imagination, and she thought she could listen for ever, and was disappointed when he reminded her that she must practise the Bach sonata for the evening's concert.

It did not, however, detain them long, for she found to her great pleasure that she had not lost nearly as much of her playing as she thought.

The evening lengthened out into long, clear hours and thoughts of the green lanes; and to escape from hauntings of Owen—the music-room it seemed still to hold echoes of his voice—she asked him to walk out with her. They wandered in the cloudless evening. They sauntered past the picture gallery, and the fact that she was walking with this strange and somewhat ambiguous young man provoked her to think of herself and him as a couple from that politely wanton assembly which had collected at eventide to watch a pavane danced beneath the beauty of a Renaissance colonnade, and to accentuate the resemblance Evelyn fluttered her parasol and said, pointing across the yellow meadows—

"Look at those idle clouds, the afternoon is falling asleep."

She walked for some time touched with the sentiment that the evening landscape inspired, a little uncertain whether he would like to talk further about his spiritual nature, and whether she should rest contented with what she knew on that subject. "It is only curiosity, but I wonder how he would make love—how he'd begin? I wonder if he cares for women?" It was some time before she could get Ulick to talk of himself; he seemed to strive to change the conversation back to artistic questions. He seemed absorbed in himself; it seemed difficult to awaken him out of his absent-mindedness. At last he spoke suddenly, as was his habit, and she learned that the scene of his first love-making was a beautiful Normandy park. He was more explicit about the park than the lady, and he seemed to lay special stress on the fact that the great saloon in the castle was hung with a faded tapestry. The story seemed to Evelyn a little obscure, but she gathered that Ulick had been tragically separated from her, whether by the intervention of another woman or through his own fault did not seem clear. The story was vague as a legend, and Evelyn was not certain that Ulick had not invented the park and the tapestries as characteristic decorations of a love story as it should happen to him, if it did happen.

Love as a theme did not seem to suit him; he seemed to fade from her; he was only real when he spoke of his ideas, and a fleeting comparison between him and herself passed across her mind. She remembered that she was no longer truly herself except when speaking of sexual emotion. Everything else had begun to seem to her trivial, trite and uninteresting. She could no longer take an interest in ordinary topics of conversation. If a man was not going to make love to her, she soon began to lose interest.... A long sequence of possibilities rose in her mind, and died away in the distance like flights of birds. Suddenly she began to sing, and they had a long and interesting talk about her rendering of Isolde in the first act. For a moment the love potion seemed as if it would carry the conversation back to their individual experiences of the essential passion; but they drifted instead into a discussion regarding the practice of sorcery in the middle ages. She was surprised to learn that she was not only a believer, but was apparently an adept in all the esoteric arts. But the subject being quite new to her, she followed with difficulty his account of a very successful evocation of the spirit of a mediæval alchemist, a Fleming of the fourteenth century, and wonder often interrupted her attention. She could not reconcile herself to the belief that he was serious in all he said, and he often spoke of the Kabbala, which apparently was the secret ritual of a sect of which he was a member, perhaps a priest. Between whiles she thought of the indignation with which Owen would hear such beliefs. Then tempted as by the edge of an abyss, she admired Ulick's strange appearance, which helped to make his story credible. She could no longer disbelieve, so simply did he tell his tales, his white teeth showing, and his dark eyes rapidly brightening and clouding as he mentioned different spells and their effects. But so illusive were his narratives that she never quite understood; he seemed always a little ahead of her; she often had to pause to consider his meaning, and when she had grasped it, he was speaking of something else, and she had missed the links. To understand him better she attempted to argue with him, and he told her of the incredible explanation that Charcot, the eminent hypnotist, had had to fall back upon in order to account materialistically for some of his hypnotic experiments, and she was forced to admit that the spiritualistic explanation was the easier to believe.

She was most interested when he spoke of the College of Adepts and the Rosicrucians. Life as he spoke seemed to become intense and exalted, and the invisible seemed on the point of becoming visible when he told her how the brotherhood greeted each other with, "Man is God, and son of God, and there is no God but man." He repeated all he could remember of their terrible oath. The College of Adepts, she learned, was the antithesis of the monastery. The monastery is passive spirituality, the College of Adepts is active spirituality; the monastery abases itself before God, the Adepts seek to become as gods. "There is a spiritual stream," he said, "that flows behind the circumstance of history, and they claim that all religions are but vulgarisations of their doctrine. The Adept, by conquering passion and ignorance, attains a mastery over change, and so prolongs his life beyond any human limit."

She begged Ulick not to forget to bring the book of magic which contained the oath of the Rosicrucians.

It was now after eight, and they returned home, watching the white mists creeping up the blue fields. The sky was lucent as a crystal, and the purple would not die out of the west until nearly midnight. Evelyn would have liked to have stayed with him in the twilight, for as the landscape darkened, his strange figure grew symbolic, and his words, whether by beauty of verbal expression or the manner with which they were spoken, seemed to bring the unseen world nearer. The outside world seemed to slip back, to become subordinate as earth becomes subordinate to the sky when the stars come. Evelyn felt the life of the flesh in which Owen had placed her fall from her; it became dissipated; her life rose to the head, and looking into the mists she seemed to discover the life that haunts in the dark. It seemed to whisper and beckon her.

Her father was in the music-room when they returned, and at sight of him she forgot Ulick and his enchantments.

"Father, dear, I am so proud of you." Standing by him, her hand on his shoulder, she said, "Your choir is wonderful, dear. Palestrina has been heard in London at last!"

She told him that she had heard the Mass in Rome, but had been disappointed in the papal choir, and she explained why she preferred his reading to that of the Roman musician. But he would not be consoled, and when he mentioned that the altos were out of tune, Ulick looked at Evelyn.

"Father, dear, Ulick and I have had an argument about the altos. He says they were wrong in the Kyrie. Were they?"

"Of course they were, but the piano has spoilt your ear. What was I saying last night?"

He took down a violin to test his daughter's ear, and the results of the examination were humiliating to her.

According to Mr. Innes, Bach was the last composer who had distinguished between A sharp and B flat. The very principle of Wagner's music is the identification of the two notes.

She ran out of the room, saying that she must change her dress, and Mr. Innes looked at Ulick interrogatively. He seemed a little confused, and hoped he had not hurt her feelings, and Ulick assured him that to-morrow she would tell the incident in the theatre, that she would be the first to see the humour of it. The news that she was staying at Dowlands, and the presumption that she would sing at the concert, had brought many a priest from St. Joseph's, and all the painters, men of letters, and designers of stained glass, and all the old pupils, the viol players, and the madrigal singers, and when Evelyn came downstairs in her pink frock, she was surrounded by her old friends.

"Do come, girls; can you come on Thursday night? I'll send you seats. It would be such a pleasure to me to sing to you, but not to-night; to-night I want to be like old times. I am going to play the viola da gamba."

"But you used to sing Elizabethan songs in old times."

"Yes, but father thinks I have lost my ear; I shall not sing to-night."

Ulick laughed outright; the others looked at Evelyn amazed and a little perplexed, and the consumptive man who wore brown clothes and who had asked her to marry him came forward to congratulate her. But while talking to him, her eyes were attracted by the tall, spare ecclesiastic who stood talking to her father. She thought vaguely of Ulick's depreciation. In spite of herself she felt herself gravitating towards him. Several times she nearly broke off the conversation with the consumptive man: her feet seemed to acquire a will of their own. But when her eyes and thought returned to the consumptive man, her heart filled with plaintive terror, for she could not help thinking of the little space he had to live, and how soon the earth would be over him. She met in his eyes a clear, plaintive look, in which she seemed to catch sight of his pathetic soul. She seemed to be aware of it, almost in contact with it, and through the eyes she divined the thought passing there, and it was painful to her to think that it was of her health and success he was thinking. She could see how cruelly she reminded him of his folly in asking her to marry him, and she was quite sure that he was thinking now how very lucky for her it was that she had refused him. Pictures were formulating, she could see, in his poor mind of how different her life would have been in the home he had to offer her, and all this seemed to her so infinitely pathetic that she forgot Ulick, Monsignor and everything else. Her father called her.

"Evelyn," he said, "let me introduce you to Monsignor."

The sight of a priest always shocked her; the austere face and the reserved manner, the hard yet kind eyes, that appearance of frequentation of the other world, at least of the hither side of this, impressed her, and she trembled before him as she had trembled six years ago when she met Owen in the same room. And when the concert was over, when she lay in bed, she wondered. She asked herself how it was that a little ordinary conversation about church singing—Palestrina, plain chant, the papal choir, and the rest of it—should have impressed her so vividly, should have excited her so much that she could not get to sleep.

She remembered the discontent when it began to be perceived that she did not intend to sing, and how Julia had said, when it came to her to sing, that she did not dare. Julia had fixed her eyes on her, and then everyone seemed to be looking at her. The consumptive man was emboldened to demand "Elsa's Dream," but she had refused to sing for him. She was determined that nothing would induce her to sing that night, but suddenly Monsignor had said—

"I hope you will not refuse to sing, Miss Innes. Remember that I cannot go to the opera to hear you."

"If you wish to hear me, Monsignor, I shall be pleased indeed."

It was impossible for her to refuse Monsignor; it was out of the question that she should refuse to sing for him. If he had wished it, she would have had to sing the whole evening. All that was quite true, but there seemed to be another reason which she could not define to herself. It had given her infinite pleasure to sing to Monsignor, a pleasure she had never experienced before, not at least for a very long while, and wondering what was about to happen, she fell asleep.

CHAPTER NINETEEN

The music-room had seemed haunted with Owen's voice, and yesterday she had asked Ulick to walk with her in the lanes so that she might escape from it. But to-day half-pleased, half-perplexed by her own perversity, she could not resist taking him to the picture gallery—she wanted to show him "The Colonnade."
The picture was merged in shadow, and no longer the picture she remembered; but when the sun shone, all the rows quickened with amorous intrigue, and the little lady held out her striped skirt (she had lost none of her bland delight), and the gentleman who advanced to meet her bowed with the mock humility of yore, and the beautiful perspectives of the colonnade floated into the hush of the trees, and the fountain warbled.
For a reason which eluded her, she was anxious to know how this picture would strike Ulick, and she tried to draw from him his ideas concerning it.
"Their thoughts," he said, "are not in their evening parade; something quite different is happening in their hearts...." And while waiting for her parasol and his stick, he said—
"I can see that you always liked that picture; you've seen it often before."
She had been longing to speak of Owen. He seemed always about them, and in phantasmal presence he seemed to sunder them, to stand jailor-like. It was only by speaking of Owen that his interdiction could be removed, and she said that she had often been to the gallery with him. Having said so much, it was easy to tell Ulick of the story of the three days of hesitation which had preceded her elopement.
"The Colonnade," and "The Lady playing the Virginal," had seemed to her symbols of the different lives which that day had been pressed upon her choice. Ulick explained that Fate and free will are not as irreconcilable as they seem. For before birth it is given to us to decide whether we shall accept or reject the gift of life. So we are at once the creatures and the arbiters of destiny. These metaphysics excited and then eluded her perceptions, and she hastened to tell him how she had stood at the corner of Berkeley Square, seeing the season passing under the green foliage, thinking how her life was summarised in a single moment. She remembered even the lady who wore the bright irises in her bonnet; but she neglected to mention her lest Ulick should think that it was memory of this woman's horses that had decided her to the choice of her pair of chestnuts. She told him about the journey to France, the buying of the trousseau, and the day that Madame Savelli had said, "If you'll stay with me a year, I'll make something wonderful of you." She told him how Owen had sent her to the Bois by herself, and the madness that had risen to her brain: and how near she had been to standing up in the carriage and asking the people to listen to her. She told the tale of all this mental excitement fluently, volubly, carried away by the narrative. Suddenly she ceased speaking, and sat absorbed by the mystery.
She sat looking into that corner of the garden where the gardener on a high ladder worked his shears without pausing. The light branches fell, and she thought of how she had grown up in this obscure suburb amid old instruments and old music. She remembered her yearning for fame and love; now she had both, love and fame. But within herself nothing was changed; the same little soul was now as it had been long ago, she could hear it talking, living its intense life within her unknown to everyone, an uncommunicable thing, unchanged among much

change. She remembered how Owen, like Siegfried, had come to release her, and all the exhausting passion of that time. She had sat with him under this very tree. She was sitting there now with Ulick. Everything was changed, yet everything was the same.... She was going to fall in love with another man, that was all.

She awoke with a start, frightened as by a dream; and before she had time to inquire of herself if the dream might come true, she remembered the girl with whom Ulick used to play Mozart in a drawing-room hung with faded tapestries. She feared that he would divulge nothing, and to her surprise he told her that it had happened two years ago at Dieppe, where he had gone for a month's holiday. At that time when he was writing "Connla and the Fairy Maiden." He had composed a great deal of the music by the sea-shore and in sequestered woods; and to assist himself in the composition of the melodies, he used to take his violin with him. One day, while wandering along the dusty high road on the look out for a secluded, shady place, he had come upon what seemed to be a private park. It was guarded by a high wall, and looking through an iron gate that had been left ajar, he was tempted by the stillness of the glades. "A music-haunted spot if ever there was one," he said to himself; and encouraged by the persuasion of a certain melody which he felt he could work out there, and nowhere but there, he pushed the gate open, and entered the park. A perfect place it seemed to him, no one but the birds to hear him, and the sun's rays did not pierce the thick foliage of the sycamore grove. Never did place correspond more intimately with the mood of the moment, and he played his melody over and over again, every now and then stopping to write. Her step was so light, and he was so deep to his music, that he did not hear it.... She had been listening doubtless for some time before he had seen her. He spoke very little French, and she very little English, but he easily understood that she wished him to go on playing. A little later her father and mother had come through the trees; she had held up her hand, bidding them be silent. Ulick could see by the way they listened that they were musicians. So he was invited to the villa which stood in the centre of the park, and till the end of his holiday he went there every day. The girl—Eliane was her beautiful name—was an exquisite musician. They had played Mozart in the room hung with faded tapestries, or, beguiled by the sunshine, they had walked in the park. When Evelyn asked him what they said, he answered simply, "We said that we loved each other." But when he returned to Dieppe three months later, all was changed. When he spoke of their marriage she laughed the question away, and he perceived that his visits were not desired; on returning to England, all his letters were returned to him.... Soon after she married a Protestant clergyman, and last year she had had a baby.

He sat absorbed in the memory of this passion, and Evelyn and the garden were perceived in glimpses between scenes of youthful exaltations and romantic indiscretions. He remembered how he had threatened to throw himself from her window for no other reason except the desire of romantic action; and while he sat absorbed in the past, Evelyn watched him, nervous and irritated, striving to read in his face how much of the burden had fallen from him, and how free his heart might be to accept another love story.

As he sat in the garden under the calm cedar tree he dreamed of a reconciliation with Eliane. He even speculated on the effect that the score of his opera would have upon her if he were to send it—all that music composed in her honour. But which opera? Not "Connla and the Fairy Maiden," for a great deal of it was crude, thin, absurd. No; he could not send it. But he might send "Grania." Yes, he would send "Grania" when he had finished it. To arrive suddenly from England, to cast himself at her feet—that might move her. Then, with a sigh, "These are things we dream of," he thought, "but never do. Only in dreams do men set forth in quest of the ideal."

He looked up, Evelyn's eyes were fixed on him, and he felt like Bran returning home after his voyage to the wondrous isles.

They saw the footman coming across the green sward. He had come to tell her that Mr. Innes was waiting for her. She was taking him to St. Joseph's. But there was not room in the victoria for three, and Ulick would have to go back to London by train.

"But you will come and see me soon? You promised to go through the 'Isolde' music with me. Will you come to-morrow?"

Her clear, delightful eyes were fixed upon him; he felt for the first time the thrill of her personality; their light caused him to hesitate, and then to accept her invitation eagerly. He heard her remind her father that he had promised to come to-night to hear her sing Elizabeth. He would be there too. He would see her to-night as well, and he stood watching the beautiful horses bearing father and daughter swiftly away. The shady Dulwich street dozed under a bright sky, and the bloom of the flowering trees was shedding its fine dust. He thought of Palestrina and Wagner, and a delicious little breeze sent a shower of bloom about his feet, as if to remind him of the pathos of the passing illusion of which we are a part. He stood watching the carriage, and the happiness and the sorrow of things choked him when he turned away.

She was happy with her father, and she felt that he loved her better than any lover. The unique experience of taking him to St. Joseph's in her carriage, and the event of singing to him that night at Covent Garden, absorbed her, and she dozed in her happiness like a beautiful rose. Never had she been so happy. She was happier than she merited. The thought passed like a little shadow, and a moment after all was brightness again. Her father was the real love of her life; the rest was mere excitement, and she wondered why she sought it; it only made her unhappy. Monsignor was right.... But she did not wish to think of him.

On the steps of St. Joseph's, she bade her father good-bye, and remained looking back till she could see him no more. Then she settled herself comfortably under her parasol, intent on the enjoyment of their reconciliation. The two days she had spent with him looked back upon her like a dream from which she had only just awakened. As in a dream, there were blurred outlines and places where the line seemed to have so faded that she could no longer trace it. The most distinct picture was when she stood, her hand affectionately laid on his shoulder, singing Ulick's music. She had forgotten the music and Ulick himself, but her father, how near she was to him in all her sympathies and instincts! Another moment, equally distinct, was when she had looked up and seen him in the choir loft conducting with calm skill.

He was coming to-night to hear her sing Elizabeth; that was the great event, for without his approval all the newspapers in the world were as nothing, at least to her. She hummed a little to herself to see if she were in voice. To convince him that she sang as well as mother was out of the question, but she might be able to convince him that she could do something that mother could not have done. It was strange that she always thought of mother in connection with her voice; the other singers did not seem to matter; they might sing better or worse, but the sense of rivalry was not so intimate. The carriage crossed Westminster Bridge, and as she looked down the swirling muddy current, her mother's face seemed to appear to her. In some strange way her mother had always seemed more real than her father. Her father lived on the surface of things, in this life, whereas her mother seemed independent of time and circumstance, a sort of principle, an eternal essence, a spirit which she could often hear speaking to her far down in her heart. Since she had seen her mother's portrait, this sensation had come closer; and Evelyn drew back as if she felt the breath of the dead on her face, as if a dead hand had been laid upon hers. The face she saw was grey, shadowy, unreal, like a ghost; the eyes were especially distinct, her mother seemed aware of her; but though Evelyn sought for it, she could not detect any sign of disapproval in her face. She looked always like a grey shadow; she moved like a shadow. Evelyn was often tempted to ask her mother to speak. Her prayer had always been a doubting, hesitating prayer, perhaps that was why it had not been granted. But now, sitting in her carriage in a busy thoroughfare, she seemed to see over the brink of life, she seemed to see her mother in a grey land lit with stars. She recalled Ulick's tales of evocation, and wondered if it were possible to communicate with her mother. But even if she could speak with her, she thought that she would shrink from doing so. She thought of what Ulick had said regarding the gain and loss of soul, how we can allow our soul to dwindle, and how we can increase it until communion with the invisible world is possible.

She felt that it were a presumption to limit life to what we see, and Owen's argument that ignorance was the cause of belief in ghosts and spirits seemed to her poor indeed. Man would not have entertained such beliefs for thousands of years if they had been wholly false.

Ulick was coming to-morrow. But he was going to read through Isolde's music with her, and she could hardly fail to learn something, to pick up a hint which she might turn to account.... Her conduct had been indiscreet; she had encouraged him to make love to her. But in this case it did not matter; he was a man who did not care about women, and she recalled all he had said to convince herself on this point. However this might be, the idea of her falling in love with him was out of the question. A second lover stripped a woman of every atom of self-esteem, and she glanced into her soul, convinced that she was sincere with herself, sure or almost sure that what she had said expressed her feelings truthfully. But in spite of her efforts to be sincere, there was a corner of her soul into which she dared not look, and her thoughts drew back as if they feared a lurking beast.

Immediately after, she remembered that she had vowed in church that she would ask Owen to marry her. Owen would say yes at once, he would want to marry her at the end of the week; and once she was married, she would have to leave the stage. She would not be able to play Isolde.... But she knew the part! it would seem silly to give up the stage on the eve of her appearance in the part. It would be such a disappointment to so many people. All London was looking forward to seeing her sing Isolde. Mr. Hermann Goetze, what would he say? He would be entitled to compensation. A nice sum Owen would have to pay for the pleasure of marrying her. If she were to pay the indemnity—could she? It would absorb all her savings. More than all. She did not think she could have saved more than six or seven thousand pounds. The manager might claim twenty. Her thoughts merged into vague calculations regarding the value of her jewellery.... Even Owen would not care to pay twenty thousand pounds so that he might marry her this season instead of next. Next year she was going to sing Kundry! Her face tightened in expression, and a painful languor seemed to weaken and ruin all her tissues. He might ask her why she had so suddenly determined to accept what she had often avoided, put aside, postponed. She would have to give some reason. If she didn't, he would suspect—what would he suspect? That she was in love with Ulick?

She might tell Owen that she wished to be married on account of scruples of conscience. But she had better not speak of Monsignor. Any mention of a priest was annoying to him. In that respect he was even more arbitrary, more violent than ever. But a sudden desire to see him arose in her, and she told the coachman to drive to Berkeley Square.

The trees wore their first verdure, and there was a melody among the boughs, and she took pleasure in the graceful female figure pouring water from the long-necked ewer. She lay back in her carriage, imitating the lady she had seen six years ago, regretting that she would not know her if she were to meet her; she might be one of her present friends.

Owen's house had been freshly painted that spring, its balcony was full of flowers chosen by herself, and arranged according to her taste ... and a pleasant look of recognition lit up in the eyes of the footmen in the hall, and the butler, whom Evelyn remembered since the first day she came to Berkeley Square, was sorry indeed that Sir Owen was out. But he was sure that Sir Owen would not be long. Would she wait in Sir Owen's room, or would she like lunch to be served at once? She said she would wait in Sir Owen's room, and she walked across the hall, smiling at the human nature of the servants' admiration. If their master had a mistress, they were glad that he had one they could boast about. And picking up two songs by Schubert, and hoping she was in good voice, she sat down at the piano and sang them. Then, half aware that she was singing unusually well, she sang another. The third song she sang so beautifully that Owen stood on the threshold loth to interrupt her, and when she got up from the piano he said—

"Why on earth don't you sing like that on the stage?"

"Ah, if one only could," she said, laughing, and taking him by the hand, she led him to the sofa and sat beside him as if for a long talk.

"Yes," she said, "I've seen him. It's all right."

"I'm so glad. I hope you said something in my favour. I don't want him to think me a brute, a villainous seducer, the man who ruined his daughter?"

"No, there was nothing of that kind."

She began at first very gravely, but her natural humour overcame her, and she made him laugh, with her account of her wooing of her father, and the part the new harpsichord had played in their reconciliation delighted him. He was full of pleasant comments, gay and sympathetic; he was interested in her account of Ulick, and said he would like to know him. This pleased her, and looking into Owen's eyes, she wondered if she should ask him to marry her. They talked of their friends, of the performance that night at the opera, and Evelyn thought that perhaps Owen ought not to go there lest he should meet her father, and she remembered that she had only to ask him to marry her in order to make it quite easy for him to meet her father. Every moment she thought she was going to ask him; she determined to introduce the subject in the first pause in the conversation, but when the pause came she didn't or couldn't; her tongue did not seem to obey her. She talked instead things that did not interest either her or him—the general principles of Wagner's music, or some technicality, whether she should insist on the shepherd's song being played on the English horn. At last she felt that she could not continue, so fictitious and strained did the conversation seem to her.

"Are you going already? I've not seen you for four days. We are dining to-morrow at Lady Merrington's."

Owen hoped that she would sing there the three songs which she had just sung so well, but she answered instantly that she did not think she would, that she wanted to sing Ulick's songs. She knew that this second mention of Ulick's name would rouse suspicion; she tried to keep it back, but it escaped her lips. She was sorry, for she did not think that she wished to annoy. She would not stop to lunch, though she could not urge any better reason than that Lady Duckle was waiting for her, and when he wished to kiss her, she turned her head aside; a moody look collected in her eyes, an ugly black resentment gathered in her heart; she was ashamed of herself, for there was nothing to warrant her being so disagreeable, and to pass the matter off, she described herself as being aggressively virtuous that morning.

On her singing nights she dined at half-past five, and the interval after dinner she spent in looking through her part, humming bits of it to herself, but to-day Lady Duckle was quick to remark the score of "Tannhäuser" in her hand. She sat with it on her knees, looking at it only occasionally, for she was thinking how the music would appeal to her father, and how her mother would have sung it. But she had to abandon these vain speculations. She must play the part as she felt it, to tamper with her conception would be to court failure. To please herself was her only chance of pleasing her father; if he did not like her reading of the part, if her singing did not please him, it was very unfortunate, but could not be helped. And when the carriage came to take her to the theatre, she was not sure that she would not be glad to receive a telegram saying that he was prevented from coming. She was very nervous while dressing, and on coming downstairs she stood watching the stage-box where he was sitting. She could distinguish his handsome, grave face through the shadows, and the orchestra was playing that rather rhetorical address to the halls which neither she nor Ulick cared much about. She waited, forgetful of her entrance, and she had to hurry round to the back of the stage.

But the moment the curtain went up, she became the mediæval German princess; her other life fell behind her, and her father was but a little shadow on her brain. Yet he was the inspiration of her acting, and that night the whole theatre consisted for Evelyn of one stage-box. Her eyes never wandered there, but she knew that there sat her ultimate judge, one whom no excess or trick could deceive. He would not judge her by the mere superficial appearance she presented on the stage, by the superficial qualities of her voice or her acting; he would see to the origin of the idea, whence it had sprung, and how it had been developed.

He did not know this particular opera, but he knew all music, and would judge it and her not according to the capricious taste of the moment, but in its relation and her relation to the immutable canons of art, from the plain chant to Palestrina, from Palestrina to Bach and Beethoven. Her singing of every phrase would be passed as it were through the long tradition of the centuries; it would not be accepted as an isolated fact, it would be judged good, indifferent or bad, by learned technical comparison. That she was his daughter would weigh not a hair's weight in the scale, and the knowledge of this terrible justice raised her out of herself, detached her more completely from the superficial and the vulgar. She sang and acted as in a dream, hypnotised by her audience, her exaltation steeped in somnambulism and steeped in ecstasy.

The curtain was raised several times, but that night the only applause or censure she was minded to hear awaited her in her dressing-room. She sent her maid out of the room, and waited for some sound of footsteps in the corridor, and at the first sound she rushed to the door and flung it open. It was her father, Merat was bringing him along the corridor, and they stood looking at each other; her clear, nervous eyes were trembling with emotion. His face seemed to tell her that he was pleased; she read upon it the calm exaltation of art, yet she could not however summon sufficient courage to ask him, and they sat down side by side. At last she said—

"Why don't you speak? Aren't you satisfied? Was I so bad?"

"You are a great artist, Evelyn. I wish your mother were here to hear you."

"Is that really true? Say it again, father. You are satisfied with me. Then I have succeeded."

He told her why she had sung well, and he knew so well. It was like walking with a man with a lantern; when he raised the light, she could see a little farther into the darkness. But she had still the prayer to sing to him. She wanted to know what he would think of her singing of the prayer. The voice of the call-boy interrupted them. She sang the prayer more purely than ever, and the flutes and clarionettes led her up a shining road, and when she walked up the stage she seemed to disappear amid the palpitation of the stars.

Her father was waiting for her, and on their way to the station she could see that he was absorbed in her art of singing. His remarks were occasional and disparate, but she guessed his train of thought, supplying easily the missing links. His praise was all inferential, and this made it more delicate and delicious. On bidding him good-night he asked her to come to choir practice. She would have liked to, but her accompanist was coming at half-past ten.

There were few days when she was not singing at night that she dispensed with her morning's work. She considered herself like a gymnast, bound to go through her feats in private, so as to assure herself of her power of being able to go through them in public. Even when she knew a part, she did not like to sing it many times without studying it afresh. She believed that once a week was as often as it was possible to give a Wagner opera, and even then an occasional rehearsal was indispensable if the first high level of excellence was to be maintained.

With her morning's work she allowed no one to interfere. Owen was often sent away, or retained for such a time as his criticism might be of use. But to-day she was expecting Ulick; he had promised to go through the music with her; so when Merat came to tell her that the pianist had arrived, she hesitated, uncertain whether she should send him away. But after a moment's reflection she decided not to forego her serious study of the part. She only wished to talk to Ulick about the music, to sing bits of it here and there, to question him regarding certain readings, to get at his ideas concerning it. All that was very interesting and very valuable in a way, but it was not hard work, and she felt, moreover, that hard work was just what she wanted before the rehearsals of "Tristan" began; there were certain passages where she was not sure of herself. She thought of the cry Isolde utters in the third act when Tristan falls dead. The orchestra comes in then in a way very perplexing for the singer, and she had not yet succeeded in satisfying herself with those few bars.

"Tell the young man that I shall be with him in half an hour."

And when she had had her bath and her hair was dressed, she tied a few petticoats round her waist and slipped on a morning wrapper; that was enough, she paid no heed to her accompanist, treating him as if he were her hairdresser. She sang sitting close to his elbow, her arm familiarly laid upon the back of his chair, a little grey woollen shawl round her shoulders. In the passages requiring the whole of her voice, she got up and sang them right through, as if she were on the stage, listened to by five thousand people. Owen, accustomed as he was to her voice, sometimes couldn't help wondering at the power of it; the volume of sound issuing from her throat drowned the piano, threatening to break its strings. Her ear was so fine that it detected any slightest tampering with the text. "You have given me a false chord," she would say; and sure enough, the pianist's fingers had accidentally softened some harshness. Sometimes he ventured a slight criticism. "You should hold the note a little longer." Then she would sing the passage again.

After singing for about two hours she had lunch. That day she was lunching with Lady Ascott, and did not get away until after three o'clock. Owen came to fetch her, and they went away to see pictures. But more present than the pictures were Ulick's dark eyes, and Owen noticed the shadow passing constantly behind her eyes. Twice she asked him what the time was, and she told him she would have to go soon.

At last she said, "Now I must say good-bye."

She could see he was troubled, and that she grieved him, and at one moment it was uncertain whether she would not renounce her visit and send Ulick a telegram. But she remembered that he had probably seen her father, and would be able to tell her more of what her father thought of her Elizabeth. It was that feeble excuse that sufficed to decide her conduct, and she bade him good-bye.

Standing on the threshold of her drawing-room, Evelyn admired its symmetry and beauty. The wall paper, a delicate harmony in pale brown and pink roses, soothed the eye; the design was a lattice, through which the flowers grew. An oval mirror hung lengthwise above the white marble chimney piece, and the Louis XV. clock was a charming composition of two figures. A Muse in a simple attitude leaned a little to the left in order to strike the lyre placed above the dial; on the other side, a Cupid listened attentive for the sound of the hour, presumably his hour. There was a little lyrical inevitableness in the lines of this clock, and Owen could not come into the room without admiring it. On the chimney piece there were two bowls filled with violets, and the flowers partly hid the beautiful Worcester blue and the golden pheasants. And on either side of the clock were two Chelsea groups, factitious bowers made out of dark green shell-like leaves, in which were seated a lady in a flowered silk and a beribboned shepherd playing a flute.

They had spent long mornings seeking a real Sheraton sofa, with six or eight chairs to match. For a long time they were unfortunate, but they had happened upon two sofas, certainly of the period, probably made by Sheraton himself. A hundred and twenty years had given a beautiful lustre to the satinwood and to the painted garlands of flowers, and the woven cane had attained a rich brown and gold; and the chairs that went with the sofa were works of art, so happy were the proportions of their thin legs and backs, and in the middle of the backs the circle of harmonious cane was in exquisite proportion.

For a long while the question for immediate decision had become what carpet should be there. Evelyn had happened upon an old Aubusson carpet, a little threadbare, but the dealer had assured her that it could be made as good as new, and she had telegraphed to Owen to go to see its pale roses and purple architecture. He had written to her that its harmony was as florid, and yet as classical as an aria by Mozart. He was still more pleased when he saw it down, and he had spent hours thinking of what pictures would suit it, would carry on its colour and design. The Boucher drawing which he had bought at Christie's had seemed to him the very thing. He had brought it home in a cab.

She was proud of her room, but she was doubtful if it would please Ulick, and was curious to hear what he would think of it. She remembered that Owen had said that such exquisite exteriorities were only possible in a pagan century, when man is content to look no farther than this strip of existence for the reason of his existence and his birthright. And while waiting for Ulick she wondered what his rooms were like, and if she would ever go there. She expected him about five, and she sat waiting for him by her tea-table amid the eighteenth century furniture, a little to the right of the Boucher.

She watched him as he came towards her, expecting and hoping to see him cast a quick glance at the picture. He shook hands with her vaguely, and sat down on a Sheraton chair and fixed his eyes on the Aubusson carpet. She thought for some time that he was examining it, but at last the truth dawned; he did not see it at all, he was maybe a thousand years away, lost in some legendary past. Had she not seen him before pass from such remote mood and become suddenly animated and gay, she would have despaired of any pleasure in his visit. Above everything else she was minded to ask him if he had seen her father, and if her father had spoken to him about her Elizabeth. But shyness prevented her, and she spoke to him about ordinary things, and he answered her questions perfunctorily, and without any apparent reason he got up and walked about the room; but not looking at any object, he walked about, with hanging head, absorbed in thought. "If he won't look at me he might look at my room, I'm sure that is pretty enough," and she sat watching him with smiling eyes. When she asked him what he thought of the Boucher, he said that no doubt it was very graceful, but that the only art he took interest in, except Michael Angelo and Leonardo da Vinci and some German Primitives, was Blake. Then he seemed to forget all about her, and she had begun to think his manner more than usually unconventional, and, having made all the ordinary remarks she could think of, she asked him suddenly if he had seen her father, and if he had said anything to him about her Elizabeth.

"I went to Dulwich on purpose to hear."

She blushed, and was very happy. It was delicious to hear that he was sufficiently interested in her to go to Dulwich on purpose to inquire her father's opinion of her Elizabeth.

"I wonder if he will like my Isolde as well."

He did not answer, and his silence filled her with inquietude.

"I have been thinking over what you said regarding your conception of the part."

She waited for him to tell her what conclusion he had come to, but he said nothing. At last he got up, and she followed him to the piano. When she came to the passage where Isolde tells Brangäne that she intended to kill Tristan, he stopped.

"But she is violent; hear these chords, how aggressive they are. The music is against you. Listen to these chords."

"I know those chords well enough. You don't suppose I am listening to them for the first time. I admit that there are a few places where she is distinctly violent. The curse must be given violently, but I think it is possible to make it felt that her violence is a sexual violence, a sort of wish to go mad. I can't explain. Can't you understand?"

"Yes, I think I do; you want to sing the first part of the act languidly. There is more in the music which supports your reading than I thought. In the passage where Isolde says to Brangäne, but really to herself, 'To die without having been loved by that man!' the love motive appears here for the first time, but more drawn out, broader than elsewhere."

She declared that Wagner had emphasised his meaning in this passage as if he had anticipated all the misreadings of this first act, and was striving to guard himself against them. She grew excited in the discussion. She had merely followed her instinct, but she was glad that Ulick had challenged her reading, for as they examined the music clause by clause, they found still further warrant for her conception.

"Ah, the old man knew what he was doing," she said; "he had marked this passage to be sung gloomily, and by gloomily he meant infinite lassitude." But this intention had not been grasped, and the singers had either sung it without any particular expression, or with a stupid stage expression which meant if possible something less than nothing. "Then, you see, if I sing the first half of the first act as wearily as the music allows me, I shall get a contrast—an

Isolde who has not drunk the love potion. The love potion is of course only a symbol of her surrender to her desire."

Ulick would have liked to have gone through the whole of the music of the act with her. It was only in this way that he could get an idea of how her reading would work out. But in that moment each read in the other's eyes an avowal of which they were immediately ashamed, and which they tried to dissimulate.

"I am tired. We won't have any more music this evening."

His thoughts seemed to pass suddenly from her, and then, without her being aware how it began, she found herself listening intently to him. He was talking in that strange, rhythmical chant of his about the primal melancholy of man, and his remote past always insurgent in him. Although she did not quite understand, perhaps because she did not quite understand, she was carried away far out of all reason, and it seemed to her that she could listen for ever. Nor could she clearly see out of her eyes, and she felt all power of resistance dissolve within her. He might have taken her in his arms and kissed her then; but though sitting by her, he seemed a thousand miles away; his remoteness chastened her, and she asked him of what he was thinking.

"When your father used to speak of you, I used to see you; sometimes I used to fancy I heard you. I did hear you once sing in a dream."

"What was I singing? Wagner?"

"No; something quite different. I forgot it all as I awoke except the last notes. I seemed to have returned from the future—you seemed in the end to lose your voice.... I cannot tell you—I forget."

"It is very sad; how sad such feelings are."

"But I never doubted that I should meet you, that our destinies were knit together—for a time at least."

She wanted to ask him by what signs do we recognise the moment that we are destined to meet the one that is more important to us than all the world. But she could find no way of asking this question that would not betray her. She could not put it so that Ulick would fail to read some application of the question to herself, and to himself. So it seemed strange indeed that he should, as if in answer to her unexpressed thought, say that the instinct of man is to consult the stars. She remembered the evenings when she used to go into the patch of black garden and gaze at the stars till her brain reeled. She used even to gather the daffodils and place them on the wall in homage to the star which she felt to be hers. She could not refrain from this idolatrous act; but in her bed at night, thinking of the flowers and the star, she had believed herself mad or very wicked; for nothing in the world would she have had anyone know her folly, and she remembered the agony it had been to her to confess it. But now she heard that she had been acting according to the sense of the wisdom of generations. As he had said, "according to the immortal atavism of man."

With her ordinary work-a-day intelligence, she felt that the stars could not possibly be concerned in our miserable existence. But deep down in her being someone who was not herself, but who seemed inseparable from her, and over whom she had no slightest control, seemed to breathe throughout her entire being an affirmation of her celestial dependency. She could catch no words, merely a vague, immaterial destiny like distant music; and her ears filled with a wailing certitude of an inseverable affinity with the stars, and she longed to put off this shameful garb of flesh and rise to her spiritual destiny of which the stars are our watchful guardians. It was like deep music; words could not contain it, it was a deep and indistinct yearning for the stars—for spiritual existence. She was conscious of the narrowness of the prison-house into which Owen had shut her, and looking at Ulick, she felt the thrill of liberation; it was like a ray of light dividing the dark. Looking at Ulick, she was startled by the conviction of his indispensability in her life, and the knowledge that she must repel him was an acute affliction, a desolate despair. It seemed cruel and disastrous that she might not love him, for it was only through love that she could get to understand him, and life without knowledge of him seemed failure.

"I'm very fond of you, Ulick, but I mustn't let you kiss me. Can't we be friends?"

He sat leaning a little forward, his head bent and his eyes on the carpet. He represented to her an abysmal sorrow—an extraordinary despair. She longed to share this sorrow, to throw her arms about him and make him glad. Their love seemed so good and natural, she was surprised that she might not.

"Ulick."

"Yes, Evelyn."

He looked round the room, saw it was getting late, and that it was time for him to go.

"Yes, it is getting late. I suppose you must go. But you'll come to see me again. We shall be friends, promise me that ... that whatever happens we shall be friends."

"I think that we shall always be friends, I feel that."

His answer seemed to her insufficient, and they stood looking at each other. When the door closed after him, Evelyn turned away, thinking that if he had stayed another moment she must have thrown herself into his arms.

CHAPTER TWENTY

Dreams was the first of the five, but the music that haunted belonged to the third song. She could not quite remember a single phrase, nor any words except "pining flowers." She had thought of sending for it, but such vague memory suited her mood better than an exact text. If she had the song she would go to the piano, and she did not wish to move from the Sheraton sofa, made comfortable with pale blue cushions. But again the music stirred her memory like wind the tall grasses, and out of the slowly-moving harmonies there arose an invocation of the strange pathos of existence; no plaint for an accidental sorrow, something that happened to you or me, or might have happened, if our circumstances had been different; only the mood of desolate self-consciousness in which the soul slowly contemplates the disaster of existence. The melancholy that the music exhales is no querulous feminine plaint, but an immemorial melancholy, an exalted resignation. The music goes out like a fume, dying in remote chords, and Evelyn sat absorbed, viewing the world from afar, like the Lady of Shallott, seeing in the mirror of memory the chestnut trees of the Dulwich street, and a little girl running after her hoop; and then her mother's singing classes, and the expectation she had lived in of learning to sing, and being brought upon the stage by her mother. If her mother had lived, she would have been singing "Romeo and Juliet" and "Lucia." ... Her father would have deemed her voice wasted; but mother always had had her way with father. Then she saw herself pining for Owen, sick of love, longing, hungry, weak, weary, disappointed, hopeless. Her thoughts turned from that past, and her mother's face looked out of her reverie, grey and grave and watchful, only half seen in the shadows. She seemed aware of her mother as she might be of some idea, strangely personal to herself, something near and remote, beyond this span of life, stretching into infinity. She seemed to feel herself lifted a little above the verge of life, so that she might inquire the truth from her mother; but something seemed to hold her back, and she did not dare to hear the supernatural truth. She was still too thrall to this life of lies, but she could not but see her mother's face, and what surprised her was that this grey shadow was more real to her than the rest of the world. The face did not stir, it always wore the same expression. Evelyn could not even tell if the expression of the dim eyes was one of disapproval. But it needs must be—she could have no doubt on that point. What was certain and sure was that she seemed in a nearer and more intimate, in a more essential communication with her mother, than with her father who was alive. Nothing seemed to divide her from her mother; she had only to let her soul go, and it could mingle with her mother's spirit, and then all misunderstandings would be at an end.

She was tempted to free herself from this fettering life, where all is limitation and division. Its individualism appeared to her particularly clear when she thought of Owen. They had clasped and kissed in the hope to become part of the other's substance. They had sought to mingle, to become one; now it was in the hope of a union of soul that Owen sought her, his kisses were for this end. She had read his desire in his eyes. But the barrier of the flesh, which at first could barely sunder them, now seemed to have acquired a personal life, a separate entity; it seemed like some invisible force thrusting them apart. The flesh which had brought them together now seemed to have had enough of them; the flesh, once gentle and persuasive, seemed to have become stern, relentless as the commander in "Don Juan." She thought of it as the forest in "Macbeth"; of something that had come out of the inanimate, angry and determined—a terrible thing this angry, frustrated flesh. Like the commander, it seemed to grasp and hurry her away from Owen, and she seemed to hear it mutter, "This vain noise must cease." The idea of the flesh was not their pleasure, but the next generation; the frustrated flesh was now putting them apart. She hummed the music, and the life she had lived continued to loom up and fall back into darkness like shapes seen in a faded picture. She had loved Owen, and sung a few operas, that was all. She remembered that everything was passing; the notes she sang existed only while she sang them, each was a little past. A moment approaches; it is ours, and no sooner is it ours than it has slipped behind us, even in the space of the indrawing of a breath. No wonder, then, that men had come to seek reality beyond this life; it was natural to believe that this life must be the shadow of another life lying beyond it, and she leaned forward, pale and nervous, in the pale grace of the Sheraton sofa. Her depression that morning was itself a mystery. What did it mean? Whence did it proceed? She had not lost her voice. Owen did not love her less. Ulick was coming to see her; but within her was an unendurable anxiety. It proceeded from nothing without; it was her own mind that frightened her. But just now she had been exalted and happy in the memory of that deeply emotional music. She tried to remember the exact moment when this strange, penetrating sorrow had fallen upon her. Whence had it come, and what did it mean? A few minutes ago it was not with her. She knew that it would not always be with her, yet it did not seem as if it would ever leave her. She could not think of herself as ever being happy again. But Ulick would distract this misery from her brain. She would send him to the piano, and the exalted sorrow in the music, which she could but faintly remember, would raise her above sorrow, would bear her out of and above the circle of personal despondency. Ulick might help her; she could not help herself. She was incapable of going to the piano, though she was fully conscious that her mood would pass away in music. She walked across the room, her eyes contracted with suffering, and she stretched herself like one who would rid herself of a burden.

She felt as if she could resign with a little smile the part that she had to play in life. Not the past, that was no longer hers either to preserve or to blot out; she could not wish herself different from what she had been; but the future—was that to be the same as the past? Then, with an apparent contradiction to what she had been thinking a few moments before regarding the worthlessness of life, she began to think that her unhappiness was possibly the result of her eccentric life. She had lived in defiance of rules, governed by individual caprice. Apparently it had succeeded, but only apparently. Underneath the surface of her life she had always been unhappy. All her talent, all her intelligence had not been able to save her. And Owen? All that pride of intelligence had resulted in unhappiness in his case as in hers. Both had disobeyed the law which we feel to be right when we look into the very recesses of our soul, and that these laws seem foolish and illogical when criticised by the light of reason does not prove their untruth. There is something beyond reason, and to become concentric, to enter into the conventions, seemed to her in a vague and distant manner to be indispensable. She was weary of living in the inhospitable regions outside of prejudice and authority.... She felt that it was prejudice and authority that gave a meaning, or a sufficient semblance of a meaning, to life as it was; she was a helpless atom tossed hither and thither by every gust of passion as a leaf in a whirlwind, and she longed to understand herself and her mission in life. In her present attitude towards life, nothing mattered except the present reality, the satisfaction of the moment; her present conception of life only counselled sacrifice of personal desires for the sake of larger desires. But these larger satisfactions did not differ in kind from the lesser, and all went the same way, the pleasure we take in a bunch of violets, or that which a love story brings, and both pass, but one leaves neither remorse nor bitterness behind. A thought told her that she was, while in the midst of these moral reflections, preparing herself to be Ulick's mistress. She denied the thought and put it behind her angrily, attributing its intrusion to her nerves, and to separate herself from it she allowed thoughts on the mutability of things to again exclusively occupy her. If she were to get up from the sofa she would create another division in her life, and to-morrow she would not remember her mood of to-day; it would have vanished as if it had never been. She asked, What do we live for? and rose nervously from the sofa, and then stood still. That half-hour was now behind her; again her place in life had been shifted. Yesterday, too, was gone, and with it the pleasure of her walk with Ulick. She had walked with him yesterday in the Green Park, in the still crystal evening. She could almost see the two figures, she could see them at one spot, but if she looked too long they disappeared from her eyes. She remembered nothing of what they had said, only that the colour of the evening was pale blue, with a little east wind in it, and that was yesterday! They had talked and walked, and been tremulously interested in each other; but she remembered nothing that had been said until they turned to go home. Then arose an exact vision of herself and Ulick walking under the graceful trees which overhung the Piccadilly railings. There the park had been shaped into little dells, and it had reminded her of the picture in the Dulwich Gallery. There his pleading was more passionate. He had begged her to go away with him, and she had had to answer that she could not give Owen up. She had felt that it was better to speak frankly, though she was sorry to have to say things that would give him pain. She had told him the truth, and was glad she had done so, but she liked him very much, and had said it was a pity they had not met earlier. "I missed you by about a year," he answered. His words came back to her, and she wondered if there was a cause for the accident, and if it could have been predicted. They had walked slowly up the pathways, and seeing the young summer in the sky and trees, they had walked as upon air, borne up by the sadness of finding themselves divided. They had thought of what forms and colours their lives would have taken if she had waited a few months, if she had not gone away with Owen; or, better still, if she had never met Owen. She was conscious that such thoughts amounted to an infidelity, and she knew that she did love Ulick as she loved Owen. But the temptation was cruelly intense, and she could not wrench herself out of its grip. Their voices had fallen, they suffocated in the silence. Ulick had mentioned Blake's name, and she had accepted an artistic discussion as an escapement, but their hearts were overloaded, and it was in answer to his own thoughts that Ulick had spoken of the eighteenth-century mystic. For the question had arisen in him whether the passions of the flesh are not destructive of spiritual exaltation, and he told her that exaltation was the gospel according to Blake. We must seek to exalt ourselves, to live in the idea; sexual passion was a merely inferior state, but mean content was the true degradation.

"Then passion is the highest plane to which the materialist can rise?" asked Evelyn, thinking of Owen.

"Yes; I don't think I'm wrong in admitting that, in the main, that is Blake's contention."

But at this point he had broken off his discourse, and told an anecdote in his half-witty, half-wistful way about an article which he had written on Blake and which had somehow strayed into the hands of a man and his wife living in Normandy. This couple were at the time engaged in continuing the tradition of Bastien Lepage. They laboriously copied what they saw in the fields—grey days, hobnailed boots and the rest of it. His article had, however, awakened them to the vanity of realism; and they had taken their pictures to a neighbouring tower, and at the top of it made a holocaust of all their abominable endeavour. And a few days after, two faded human beings had presented themselves at Ulick's lodgings in Bloomsbury, seemingly at once unhappy and excited, and professing their complete willingness to accept the gospel of life according to Blake. It was the man who did the talking, the woman, who was dressed in olive-green garments, acquiesced in what he said. They were tired of materialism; they had trudged that bleak road till they were weary, and now they desired Blake, submission to Blake, and were therefore disappointed when Ulick explained that Blake's doctrine was not subordination to Blake, but the very opposite, the development of self, the cultivation of personal will.

"It was clear to me," Ulick said, "that the woman had abased herself before the man, that she ate what he ate, drank what he drank, thought what he thought, so I decided that we should begin with first principles; that the woman should decide for herself, without referring to her husband, what she should eat for dinner. But after some efforts to attain sufficient personal will, she confessed her incapacity, and I therefore proposed to the husband that she should be kept in her room until she had regained her will. They went away hopeful, but he called a few days after to tell me that the experiment had failed. For after striving for many hours to decide between soles and plaice, she had burst into tears, and I felt I could not advise him further."

It had seemed a pity to ask Ulick how much of this story was true, how much invention; and it was a remembrance of the will-less lady in the olive-green gown that caused Evelyn's face to light up into smiles as she stood at the window watching for his coming.

Her excuse for not marrying Owen was that she would have to retire from the stage. But she was not convinced that that was the real reason. There seemed to be another reason at the back of her mind which her reason could not drag out. She tried again and again, but it eluded her, and it was frightening to find that she had so little knowledge of the motives that had determined her life. Feeling that she must change her thoughts, she asked herself what a man like Ulick, of spiritual temperament, but uninfected with religious dogma, would think of her relations with Owen. "Ah, that was the front door bell!" She waited in a delicious tremble of expectation, and the servant announcing Sir Owen awoke her, and with a shock as painful as if she had been struck on the nape of the neck.

CHAPTER TWENTY-ONE

On account of the numerous rehearsals demanded by Evelyn for the production of "Tristan and Isolde," Mr. Hermann Goetze's opera season was limited to four nights a week. But the hours she spent in the theatre were only a small part of the time she devoted to her idea. Her entire life was lived in or about the new incarnation, her whole life seemed to converge and rush into an ultimate channel, and Lady Ascott sought her in vain. She avoided social distractions, and the friends she saw were those who could talk to her about her idea. But while listening she forgot them, and absorbed in her dream strayed round the piano. She meditated journeys to Cornwall and Brittany; and one day when Owen called he heard that she had gone to Ireland, and was expected back to-morrow evening. She read Isolde into the morning paper, receiving hints from the cases that came up before the magistrates. She found Isolde in every book, all that happened seemed extraordinarily fortuitous, the light of her idea revealing significance in the most ordinary things. Her life was ransacked like an old workbox, all kinds of stages of mentality, opinions, beliefs, prejudices, trite and conventional enough, came up and were thrown aside. But now and then the memory of an emotion, of a feeling, would prove to be just what she wanted to add a moment's life to her Isolde; the memory of a gesture, of a look was sufficient, and she sank back in her chair, her eyes dilated and moody, thinking how she could work this truth to herself into the harmony of the picture she was elaborating.

Evelyn had seen Rosa Sucher play the part, and had admired her rendering as far as we can admire that which is not only antagonistic, but even discordant to our own natures. She admitted it to be very sweeping, triumphant and loud, a fine braying of trumpets from the rise to the fall of the curtain. Rosa Sucher had no doubt attained an extraordinary oneness of idea, but at what price? Her Isolde was a hurricane, a sort of avalanche; and the woman was lost in the storm. She had missed the magic of the woman who, personal to our flesh and dream, breaks upon our life like the Spring; and this was just what Evelyn wanted to out on the stage. There was plenty of breadth, but it was breadth at the price of accent. There was a great frame and a sort of design within the frame, but in Evelyn's sense the picture was wanting. There was an extraordinary and incomprehensible neglect of that personal accent without which there is no life. And the difference between the Isolde who has not drunk, and the Isolde who has drunk the love potion which she, Evelyn, was so intent upon indicating, had never occurred to Rosa Sucher, or if it had, it had been swept aside as a negligible detail. After all, Isolde has to be a woman a man could be in love with, and that is not the impact and the shriek of a gale from the south-west. No doubt Rosa Sucher's idea of the part was Wagner's idea at one moment of his life. Wagner was a man with hundreds of ideas; he tried them all, retaining some and discarding others. Some half-dozen have fixed themselves immutably in certain minds, and an undue importance is given to them, an importance that Wagner would never have allowed. The absurd idea, propounded in the heat of controversy, that all the arts were to wax to one art in the music drama, that even sculpture was to be represented by attitudes of the actors and actresses! Wagner had written this thing in order to confound his enemies and bring the weak-kneed to his side, or maybe, it was merely written to make himself clear to himself. For it was impossible that a man of genius should be so seriously wanting in appreciation of sculpture as to think with the centre of his brain, that an actor standing, his hand on his hip, could fill the place hitherto occupied in the mind by, let us say, the Hermes of Praxiteles. Yet this idea still obtained at Bayreuth, and Rosa Sucher walked about, her arms raised and posed above her head, in the conventional, statuesque attitude designed for the decoration of beer gardens.

"It really is very sad," Evelyn said, her eyes twinkling with the humour of the idea, "that anyone should think that such figuration could replace sculpture."

"But you will not deny that the actor and the actress can supply part of the picturesqueness of a dramatic action."

"No, indeed; but not by attitudinising, but by gestures that tell the emotion that is in the mind."

By some obscure route of which they were not aware, these artistic discussions wound around the idea which dominated their minds, and they were led back to it continually. The story of "Tristan and Isolde" seemed to be their own story, and when their eyes met, each divined what was passing in the other's mind. The music was afloat on the currents of their blood. It gathered in the brain, paralysing it, and the nervous exhaustion was unbearable about six, when the servant had taken away the tea things; and as the afternoon drooped and the beauty of the summer evening began in the park, speech seemed vain, and they could not bring themselves to argue any longer.

It was quite true that she had begun to feel the blankness of the positivist creed, if it were possible to call it a creed. There seemed nothing left of it, it seemed to have shrivelled up like a little withered leaf; true or false, it meant nothing to her, it crushed up like a dried leaf, and the dust escaped through her fingers. Then without any particular reason she remembered a phrase she had heard in the theatre.

"As I always says, if one man isn't enough for a woman, twenty aren't too many."

The homeliness of this speech seemed to accentuate the moral truth, and making application of it to herself, she felt that if she were to take another lover she would not stop at twenty. Her face contracted in an expression of disgust at this glimpse of her inner nature which had been flashed upon her; and looking into herself she could discover nothing but a talent for singing and acting. If she had not had her voice, God only knows what she would have been, and she turned her eyes from a vision of gradual decadence. If she were not to sink to the lowest, she must hold to her love of Owen, and not yield to her love of Ulick. This low nature which she could distinguish in herself she must conquer, or it would conquer her. "If one man isn't enough for a woman, twenty are not too many." The humble working woman who had uttered these words was right.... If she were to give way she would have twenty and would end by throwing herself over one of the bridges.

She felt that she must marry Owen, and under this conclusion she stopped like one who has come face to face with a blank wall. But did she love him well enough to marry him? She loved him, but was her present love as intense as the love that had obsessed her whole nature in Paris six years ago? She tried to think that it was, and found casual consolation in the thought that if she were not so mad about him now as she was then, her love was deeper; it had become a part of herself, and was founded on such knowledge of his character that nothing could change or alter it. She knew now that in spite of all his faults she could trust him, and that was something; she knew that his love for her was enduring, that it was not a mere passing passion, as it easily might have been. He had given her fame, wealth, position—everything a woman could desire. Some might blame him for having taken her away from her home, but she did not blame him, for she knew that she could not have remained with her father at that time. If she had not gone away with Owen she might have killed herself; something had given way within her, she had to do what she had done.

But did she love Owen, or was she getting tired of him? It was so easy to ask and so difficult to answer these questions. However closely we look into our souls, some part of the truth escapes us. One always slurred something or exaggerated something.... She remembered that Owen had been very tiresome lately; his egoism was ceaseless; it got upon her nerves, and she felt that, no matter what happened to her, she could not endure it. There were his songs! How tired she was of talking about his songs, the long considerations whether this chord or the other chord, this modulation or another, were the better. He could not compose a dozen bars without having them engraved and sending copies to his friends. He wished the whole world to be occupied about him and his affairs. He was so childish about his music. Other people said, "Oh, yes, very pretty," but she had to sing it. If she refused, it meant unpleasantness, and though he did not often say so, a charge of ingratitude, for, of course, without him she wouldn't have been able to sing at all. The worst of it was that he did not see the ridiculous side.

When singing some of his songs, she had caught a look in people's eyes, a pitying look, and she could not help wondering if they thought that she liked such commonplace, or worse still, if they thought that she was obliged to sing it. But when she had remembered all he had done for her, it seemed quite a disgrace that she should hate to sing his songs. It was the one thing she could do to please him, and she reflected on her selfishness. She seemed to have no moral qualities; the idea she had expressed to Ulick regarding the necessity of chastity in women returned, and she felt sure that in women at least every other virtue is dependent on that virtue. But when Owen was ill she had travelled hundreds of miles to nurse him; she had not hesitated a moment, and she might have caught the fever. She wouldn't have done that if she did not love him.... She was always thinking how she could help him, she would do anything for him. But he was such a strange man. There were times when there was no one kinder, gentler, more affectionate, but at other times he turned round and snapped like a mad dog. The desire to be rude took him at times like a disease; this was his most obvious fault. But his worst fault, at least in her eyes, was his love of parade; his determination to appear to the world in the aspect which he thought was his by birth and position. Notwithstanding a seeming absence of affection and candour, he was always acting a part. True that he played the part very well; and his snobbery was never vulgar.

Thinking of him profoundly, looking into his nature with the clear sight of six years of life with him, she decided that the essential fault was an inability to forego the temptation of the moment. For him the temptation of the moment was the greatest of all. He was the essential child, and had carried all the child's passionate egoism into his middle age. One gave way because everything seemed to mean so much more to him that it could to oneself. He could not be deprived of his toy; his toy came before everything. But why did he make himself offensive to many people by speaking against Christianity? It was so illogical to love art as he did and to hate religion.... He had listened much more indulgently to Ulick than she had expected, and seemed to perceive the picturesqueness of the gods, Angus and Lir. It was Christianity that irritated and changed him to the cynic he was not, and forced him into arguments which she hated: "that when you went to the root of things, no one ever acted except from a selfish motive" and his aphorism, "I don't believe in temptations that one doesn't yield to." Her thoughts went back over years, to the very day he had said the words to her for the first time.... It was true in a way, but it was not the whole truth. But to him it was the whole truth, that was the unfortunate part of it, and his life was a complete exemplification of this theory, and the result was one of the unhappiest men on the face of the earth. He would tell you he had the finest place in the world, and the finest pictures in the world, yet these things did not save him from unhappiness. He could not understand that happiness is attained through renunciation. He had never renounced anything, and so his life was a mere triviality. The clearness of her vision surprised her; she paused a moment and then continued. He must always be amused, he could not bear to be alone. Distraction, distraction, distraction was his one cry. She had to combat the spectre of boredom and save the man from himself. Hitherto she had done this, it had been her pleasure, but if she married him it would become her mission, her duty, her life. Could she undertake it? Her heart sank. He had worn her out, she could do no more. She grew frightened, life seemed too much for her; and then she bit her lips, and vowed that whatever it cost her she would marry him if he wished her to.... If she did not mean to take the consequences, she ought not to have gone away with him. To be Owen's wife was perchance her mission.

It had always been arranged that they were to be married when she left the stage. But he wished her to remain on the stage till she had played Kundry; but if she were going to leave the stage she did not care to delay, nor did she care for the part of Kundry. The meaning of the part escaped her.... So the time had come for her to offer herself to Owen. Whatever his desires might be, his honour would force him to say Yes. So there was no escape. Fate had decreed it so, she was to be his wife; but one thing she need not endure, and that was unnecessary suspense. She had decided to go to Lady Ascott's ball.... But she wouldn't see him there. He was kept indoors by the gout. He had written asking her to come and pass the evening with him.... She might call to see him on her way to the ball; yes, that is what she would do, and she sat down at once and wrote a note.

And she laughed and talked during dinner, and was surprised when Lady Duckle remarked how pale and ill she was looking, for she thought she was making a fine outward show of high spirits. She and Lady Duckle were dining alone, and she tried to devise a plan for going to Berkeley Square without taking Lady Duckle into her confidence. The horrible scene with Owen flitted before her eyes while talking of other things. And so the evening dragged itself out in the drawing-room.

"Olive, I want to make a call before going to Lady Ascott's; I will send the carriage back for you."

"But we need not get there until a quarter to one. There will be plenty of time."

"Very well," Evelyn answered, as unconcernedly as she could. "I'll be here a little after twelve." In the carriage she remembered that she was going to the same house to tell him that she would be his wife as she had gone to tell him she would be his mistress.

"Sir Owen has been very bad to-day, miss," the butler said in a confidential undertone. "It has taken him again in his right toe;" and he leaned forward to open the door of Owen's private sitting-room.

She passed in, the door closed softly behind her, and she saw her lover lying in a large, chintz-covered arm-chair, full of cushions, deep like a feather bed. He held his book high, so that all the light of the electric lamp fell upon it, and the small, wrinkled face seemed to have suddenly grown older behind the spectacles, and the appearance at that moment was of a man just slipping over the years that divides middle from old age.

In the single second that elapsed before they spoke, Evelyn felt and understood a great deal. Never had Owen seemed so like himself; the old age which so visibly had laid its wrinkles and infirmities upon him was clearly his old age, and the old age of his fathers before him. He was in his own old room, planned and ordered by himself. Even his arm-chair seemed characteristic of him. With whatever hardships he might put up in the hunting field or the deer forest, he believed in the deepest arm-chair that upholstery could stuff when he came home. In this room were his personal pictures, those he had bought himself. They, of course, included a beautiful woman by Gainsborough, and a pellucid evening sky, with a group of pensive trees, by Corot. There were beautiful painted tables and chairs, and marble and ormolu clocks, the refined and gracious designs of the best periods; and the sight of Owen sitting amid all these attempts to capture happiness, revealed to her the moral idea of which this man was but a symbol; and the thought that life without a moral purpose is but a passing spectre, and that our immortality lies in our religious life, occurred to her again. His first remark, too, about his gout, that it wasn't much, but just enough to make life a curse—could she tell him what end was served by torturing us in this way?—laid, as it were, an accent upon the thoughts of him that were passing in her mind.

It was that crouching attitude in the arm-chair that had made him seem so old. Now that he had taken off his spectacles, and was standing up, he did not look older than his age. He wore a silk shirt and a black velvet smoking suit, and had kept his figure—it still went in at the waist. She admired him for a moment and then pitied him, for he limped painfully and pulled over one of his own chairs for her. But she declined it, choosing a less comfortable one, feeling that she must sit straight up if she were to moralise. She had imagined that the subject would introduce itself in the course of conversation, and that it would develop imperceptibly. She had imagined that they would speak of the first performance of "Tristan and Isolde," now distant but a couple of days, or of Lady Ascott's ball, at which she had promised to appear. But Owen had spoken of a song which he had re-written that afternoon, not having anything else to do. He believed he had immensely improved it, and wished that she would try it over. To sing one of his songs, to decipher manuscript, was the last thing she felt she could do, and the proposal irritated her. Her whole life was at stake; it had cost her a great deal to come to the decision that she must either marry him or send him away. Partly on purpose, and partly because she could not help it, her face assumed a calm and fixed expression which he knew well.

"Evelyn, you're going to say something disagreeable. Don't, I've had enough to worry me lately; there's my mother's health, and this, miserable attack of gout."

"I hope you won't think what I've come to say disagreeable, but one never knows." He waited anxiously, and after some pause she said, though it seemed to her that she had come to the point much too abruptly, "Owen, was it not arranged that we should marry when I left the stage?" She had not been able to lend herself to the diplomatic subtleties which she had been considering all the evening, and had stumbled in the first step. But the mistake had been made, they were face to face with the question—it was for her not to give way. She had noticed the look that had passed between his eyes, and she was not surprised at the slight evasion of his answer, "But you are going to sing Kundry next year?" for she knew him to be naturally as averse to marriage as she was herself.

"I don't think I should succeed as Kundry. I don't know what the part means."

"But she's a penitent. You like penitents; your Elisabeth—"

"Elizabeth is different. Elizabeth is an inward penitent, Kundry is an external, and you know I can do nothing with externalities."

He did not understand, and it was impossible to explain without entering into a complete exposition of Ulick's idea regarding "Parsifal." The subject of "Parsifal" had always been disagreeable to him, but he had not been able to find any argument against the art of it. So the criticism "revolting hypocrisy," "externality," and the statement that the prelude to "Lohengrin" was an inspiration, whereas the prelude to "Parsifal" was but a marvellous piece of handicraft, delighted him. He had always known these things, but had not been able to give them expression. He wondered how Evelyn had attained to so clear an understanding, and then, unconsciously detecting another mind in the argument, he said—

"I wonder what Ulick Dean thinks of 'Parsifal?' Something original, I'm sure."

She could not explain that she had not intended to deceive; she could not tell him that she was so pressed and obsessed by the question of her marriage that she hardly knew what she was saying, and had repeated Ulick's ideas mechanically. She already seemed to stand convicted of insincerity. He evidently suspected her, and all the while he spoke of Ulick and "Parsifal," she suffered a sort of trembling sickness, and that he should have perceived whence her enlightenment had come embittered her against him. Suddenly he came to the end of what he had to say; their eyes met, and he said,—

"Very well, Evelyn, we'll be married next week; is that soon enough?"

The abruptness of his choice fell upon her so suddenly, that she answered stupidly that next week would do very well. She felt that she ought to get up and kiss him, and she was painfully conscious that her expression was the reverse of pleased.

"I don't want to limp to the altar; were it not for the gout I'd say to-morrow.... But something has happened, something has forced you to this?"

He did not dare to suggest scruples of conscience. But his thoughts were already back in Florence.

"Only that you often have said you'd like to marry me. One never knows if such things are true. It may have been mere gallantry on your part; on the other hand, I am vain enough to believe that perhaps you meant it." Then it seemed to her that she must be sincere. "As I am determined that our present relations shall cease, there was no help for it but to come and tell you."

Her eyes were cast down; the expression of her face was calm resolution, whereas his face betrayed anxiety, and the twitching and pallor of the eyes a secret indecision with which he was struggling.

"Then I suppose it is scruples of conscience.... You've been to Mass at St. Joseph's."

"We won't enter into that question. We've talked it for the last six years; you cannot change me."

The desire to please was inveterate in her, and she felt that she had never been so displeasing, and she was aware that he was showing to better advantage in this scene than she was. She wished that he had hesitated; if he had only given her some excuse for—She did not finish the sentence in her mind, but thought instead that she liked him better when he wasn't so good; goodness did not seem to suit him.

She wore a beautiful attractive gown, a mauve silk embroidered with silver irises, and he regretted his gout which kept him from the ball. He caught sight of her as she passed down the glittering floor, saving with a pretty movement of her shoulders the dress that was slipping from them, he saw himself dancing with her.... They passed in front of a mirror, and looking straight over her shoulder his eyes followed the tremulous sparkle of the diamond wings which she wore in her hair. Then, yielding to an impulse of which he was not ashamed, for it was as much affection as it was sensual, he drew over a chair—he would have knelt at her feet had it not been for his gout—and passing his arm about her waist, he said—

"Dearest, I'm very fond of you, you know that. It is not my fault if I prefer to be your lover rather than your husband." He kissed her on her shoulders, laying his cheek on her bosom. "Don't you believe that I am fond of you, Evelyn?"

"Yes, Owen, I think you are."

"Not a very enthusiastic reply. It used to be you who delighted to throw your arms about my neck. But all that is over and done with."

"One is not always in such humours, Owen."

Watching each other's eyes they were conscious of their souls; every moment it seemed as if their souls must float up and be discovered; and, while fearing discovery, there came a yearning to stand out of all shadow in the full light. But they could not tell their souls; words fell back abortive; and they recognised the mortal lot of alienation; and rebelling against it, he held her face, he sought her lips, but she turned her face aside, leaving him her cheek.

"Why do you turn your lips away? It is a long time since I've kissed you ... you're cold and indifferent lately, Evelyn."

A memory of Ulick shot through her mind, and he would have divined her thought if his perception had not been blinded by the passion which swayed him.

"No, Owen, no. We're an engaged couple; we're no longer lovers."

"And you think that we should begin by respecting the marriage ceremony?"

She seemed to lose sight of him, she perceived only the general idea, that outline of her life which he represented, and which she could in a way trace in the furniture of the room. It was in this room she had said she would be his mistress. It was from this room she had started for Paris. Her eyes lighted on the harpsichord. He had bought it in some vague intention of presenting it to her father, some day when they were reconciled; the viola da gamba he had bought for her sake; it was the poor little excuse he had devised for coming to see her at Dulwich.

She saw the Gainsborough: how strange and remote it seemed! She looked at the Corot, its sentimentality was an irritation. In the Chippendale bookcases there were many books she had given him; and the white chimney piece was covered with her photographs. There he was, a tall, thin man, elegant and attractive notwithstanding the forty-five years, dressed in a silk shirt and a black smoking suit. Their eyes met again, she could see that he was thinking it over; but it was all settled now, neither could draw back, and the moments were tense and silent; and as if confronted by some imminent peril, she wondered.

"You arranged that I should leave the stage when I married, and you say that we are to be married next week. You don't want me to throw up my engagement at Covent Garden? I should like to play Isolde."

"Of course you must play Isolde; I must hear you sing Isolde."

She felt that she must get up and thank him, she felt that she must be nice to him; and laying her hand on his shoulder, she said—

"I hope I don't seem ungrateful; you have always been very good to me, Owen. I hope I shall make a good wife."

"I think I am less changed than you; I don't think you care for me as you used to."

"Yes, I do, Owen, but I am not always the same. I can't help myself."

He watched her face; she had forgotten him, she was again thinking of herself. She had tried to be sincere, but again had been mastered by her mood. No, she did not dislike him, but she wished for an interval, a temporary separation. It seemed to her that she didn't want to see him for some weeks, some months, perhaps. If he would consent to such an alienation, she felt that she would come back fonder of him than ever. All this did not seem very sane, but she could not think otherwise, and the desire of departure was violent in her as a nostalgia.

"We have been very fond of each other. I wonder if we shall be as happy in married life? Do you think we shall?"

"I hope so, Owen, but somehow I don't see myself as Lady Asher."

"You know everyone—Lady Ascott, Lady. Somersdean, they are all your friends, it will be just the same."

"Yes, it'll be just the same."

He did not catch the significance of the repetition. He was thinking of the credit she would do him as Lady Asher. He heard his friends discussing his marriage at the clubs. She was going to Lady Ascott's ball, and would announce her engagement there. To-morrow everyone would be talking about it. He would like his engagement known, but not while she was on the stage. But when he mentioned this, she said she did not see why their engagement should be kept a secret. It did not matter much; he was quite ready to give way, but he could not understand why the remark should have angered her. And her obstinacy frightened him not a little. If he were to find a different woman in his wife from the woman he had loved in the opera singer!

"Evelyn, you have lived with me in spite of your scruples for the last six years; why should we not go on for one more year? When you have sung Kundry, we can be married."

"Owen, do you think you want to marry me? Is not your offer mere chivalry? *Noblesse oblige*?" That he was still master of the situation caused a delicious pride to mount to his head. For a moment he could not answer, then he asked if she were sure that she had not come to care for someone else, and feeling this to be ineffective, he added—

"I've always noticed that when women change their affections, they become a prey to scruples of conscience."

"If I cared for anyone else, should I come to you to-night and offer to marry you?"

"You're a strange woman; it would not surprise me if the reason why you wish to be married is because you're afraid of a second lover. That would be very like you."

His words startled her in the very bottom of her soul; she had not thought of such a thing, but now he mentioned it, she was not sure that he had not guessed rightly.

How well he understood one side of her nature; how he failed to understand the other! It was this want in him that made marriage between them impossible. She smiled mysteriously, for she was thinking how far and how near he had always been.

"Tell me, Evelyn, tell me truly, is it on account of religious scruples, or is it because you are afraid of falling in love with Ulick Dean, that you came here to-night and asked me to marry you?"

"Owen, we can live in contradiction to our theories, but not in contradiction to our feelings, and you know that my life has always seemed to me fundamentally wrong."

For a moment he seemed to understand, but his egotism intervened, and a moment after he understood nothing, except that for some stupid morality she was about to break her artistic career sharp off.

He strove to think what was passing behind that forehead. He tried to read her soul in the rounded temples, the bright, nervous eyes. His and her understanding of life and the mystery of life were as wide apart as the earth and the moon, and he could but stare wondering. No inkling of the truth reached him. As he strove to understand her mind he grew irritated, and turned against that shadow religion which had always separated them. Without knowing why—almost in spite of himself—he began to argue with her. He reminded her of her inconsistencies. She had always said that a lover was much more exciting than a husband. If it had not been for her religion, he did not believe they would have thought of marriage, they would have gone on to the end as they had begun. The sound of his voice entered her ears, but the meaning of the words did not reach her brain, and when she had said that she had come to him not on account of Ulick, but on account of her conscience, she sat perplexed, trying to discover if she had told the truth.

"You're not listening, Evelyn."

"Yes, I am, Owen. You said that I had always said that a lover was much more exciting than a husband."

"If so, why then—"

They stared blankly at each other. Everything had been said. They were engaged to be married. What was the use of further argument? She mentioned that it was getting late, and that Lady Duckle was waiting for her.

"She will tell her first," he thought, "and she'll tell Lady Ascott. They'll all be talking of it at supper. 'So Owen has gone off at last,' they'll say. I'll hear of it at the club to-morrow."

"I wonder what Lady Ascott will think?" he said, as he put her into the carriage.

"I don't know.... I shall not go to the ball. Tell him to take me home."

She lay back in the blue shadows of the brougham, striving to come to terms with herself, to arrive at some plain conclusion. It seemed to her that she had been animated by an honest and noble purpose. She had gone to Owen in the intention of marrying him if he wished to marry her, because it had seemed to her that it was her duty to marry him. But everything had turned out the very opposite of what she had intended, and looking back upon the hour she had spent with him, it seemed to her that she had certainly deceived him. She certainly had deceived herself.

She could not believe that she was going to marry Owen. She felt that it was not to be, and before the presentiment her her soul paused. She asked herself why she felt that it was not to be. There was no reason; but she felt quite clear on the point, and could not combat the clear conviction. She began thinking the obvious drama—Owen discovering her with Ulick, declining ever to see her again, her suicide or his, etc. But she could not believe that Owen would decline ever to see her again even if—but she was not going to go wrong with Ulick, there was no use supposing such things, And again her thoughts paused, and like things frightened by the dark, withdrew silently, not daring to look further.

She met Ulick every night at the theatre, and she had him to sit with her in her dressing-room during the entr'actes.... She remembered the pleasure she had taken in these conversations, and the strange, whirling impulse which drew them all the while closer, until they dreaded the touching of their knees. She had taken him back in the carriage and he had kissed her; she had allowed him to kiss her the other night, and she knew that if she were alone with him again that she would not be able to resist the temptation. Her thoughts turned a little, and she considered what her life would be if she were to yield to Ulick. Her life would become a series of subterfuges, and in a flash of thought she saw how, after spending the afternoon with Ulick, she would come home to find Owen waiting for her: he would take her in his arms, she would have to free herself, and, feeling his breath upon her cheek, save herself somehow from his kiss. He would suspect and question her. He would say, "Give me your word of honour that Ulick Dean is not your lover;" and she heard herself pledge her word in a lie, and the lie would have to be repeated again and again.

Until she had met Ulick, she had not seen a man for years whose thoughts ranged above the gross pleasure of the moment, the pleasure of eating, of drinking, of love-making ... and she was growing like those people. The other night at dinner at the Savoy she had looked round the table at the men's faces, some seven or eight, varying in age from twenty-four to forty-eight, and she had said to herself, "Not one of these men has done anything worth doing, not one has even tried." Looking at the men of twenty-four, she had said to herself, "He will do all the man of forty-eight has done,—the same dinners, the same women, the same racecourses, the same shooting, the same tireless search after amusement, the same life unlit by any ideal." She was no better, Owen was no better. There was no hope for either of them? He had surrounded her with his friends, and she thought of the invitations ahead of her. Her profession of an opera singer chained her to this life.... She felt that a miracle would have to happen to extricate her from the social mire into which she was sinking, sinking.

To give up Ulick would only make matters worse. He was the plank she clung to in the shipwreck of all her convictions. She could not tell how or why, but the conviction was overpowering that she could not give him up. Happen what might happen, she must see him. If Owen were to go for a sea voyage.... In three or four months she would have acquired that something which he could give her and which was necessary to complete her soul. She seemed to be quite certain on this point, and she lay back in the brougham lost in vague wonderment. Her thoughts sank still deeper, and thoughts came to her that had never come before, that she had never dared to think before. Even if she were not done with Ulick when Owen returned, it seemed to her that she could make them and herself very happy; they both seemed necessary to her happiness, to her fulfilment; and in her dream, for she was not responsible for her thoughts, the enjoyment of this double love seemed to her natural and beautiful....

But she awoke from her dream frightened, and feeling like one who has lost the clue which was to lead her out of the labyrinth.

Instead of sending the footman to tell Lady Duckle that the carriage was waiting, Evelyn got out and went up to the drawing-room.

"I'm sorry to have kept you waiting, Olive, but I can't go with you. Tell Lady Ascott I am very sorry. Good-night, I'm going to my room."

"Oh, my dear Evelyn, not going ... and now that you're dressed."

Evelyn allowed herself to be persuaded. If she went to bed now she would not sleep. She went to the ball with Lady Duckle, and as she went round in the lancers, giving her hand first to one and then to the other, she heard a voice crying within her, "Why are you doing these things? They don't interest you at all."

CHAPTER TWENTY-TWO

"Eternal night, oh, lovely night, oh, holy night of love." Rapture succeeded rapture, and the souls of the lovers rose, nearer to the surface of life. In a shudder of silver chords he saw them float away like little clouds towards the low rim of the universe.

But at that moment of escape reality broke in upon the dream. Melot had betrayed them, and Ulick heard King Mark's noble and grave reproaches like a prophecy, "Thou wert my friend and didst deceive me," he sang, and his melancholy motive seemed to echo like a cry along the shore of Ulick's own life. Amid calm and mysteriously exalted melodies, expressive of the terror and pathos of fate fulfilled, Tristan's resolve took shape, and as he fell mortally wounded, the melancholy Mark motive was heard again, and again Ulick asked what meaning it might have for him. He heard the applause, loud in the stalls, growing faint as it rose tier above tier. Baskets of flowers, wreaths and bouquets were thrown from the boxes or handed up from the orchestra, the curtain was rung up again, and her name was called from different parts of the theatre. And when the curtain was down for the last time, he saw her in the middle of the stage talking to Tristan and Brangäne. The garden scene was being carried away, and to escape from it Evelyn took Tristan's hand and ran to the spot where Ulick was standing. She loosed the hand of her stage lover, and dropping a bouquet, held out two small hands to Ulick covered with violet powder. The hallucination of the great love scene was still in her eyes; it still, he could see, surged in her blood. She had nearly thrown herself into his arms, seemed regardless of those around; she seemed to have only eyes for him; he heard her say under her breath," That music maddens me," then with sudden composure, but looking at him intently, she asked him to come upstairs with her.

For the last few days he had been engaged in prediction, and last night he had been visited by dreams, the significance of which he could not doubt. But his reading of her horoscope had been incomplete, or else he had failed to understand the answers. That he was a momentous event in her life seemed clear, yet all the signs were set against their marriage; but what was happening had been revealed—that he should stand with her in a room where the carpet was blue, and they were there; that the furniture should be of last century, and he examined the cabinets in the corners, which were satinwood inlaid with delicate traceries, and on the walls were many mirrors and gold and mahogany frames.

"Merat!" The maid came from the dressing-room. "You have some friends in front. You can go and sit with them. I sha'n't want you till the end." When the door closed, their eyes met, and they trembled and were in dread. "Come and sit by me." She indicated his place by her side on the sofa. "We are all alone. Talk to me. How did I sing to-night?"

"Never did the music ever mean so much as it did to-night," he said, sitting down.

"What did it mean?"

"Everything. All the beauty and the woe of existence were in the music to-night."

Their thoughts wandered from the music, and an effort was required to return to it.

"Do you remember," she said, with a little gasp in her voice, "how the music sinks into the slumber motive, 'Hark, beloved;' then he answers, 'Let me die'?"

"Yes, and with the last note the undulating tune of the harps begins in the orchestra. Brangäne is heard warning them."

They sat looking at each other. In sheer desperation she said—

"And that last phrase of all, when the souls of the lovers seemed to float away."

"Over the low rim of the universe—like little clouds."

"And then?"

He tried to speak of his ideas, but he could not collect his thoughts, and after a few sentences he said, "I cannot talk of these things."

The room seemed to sway and cloud, and her arms to reach out instinctively to him, and she would have fallen into his arms if he had not suddenly asked her what had been decided at Sir Owen Asher's.

"Let me kiss you, Evelyn," he said, "or I shall go mad."

"No, Ulick, this is not nice of you. I shall not be able to ask you to my room again."

He let go her hand, and she said—

"I'm not going to marry Sir Owen, but I must not let you kiss me."

"But you must, Evelyn, you must."

"Why must I?"

"Do you not feel that it is to be?"

"What is to be?"

"I do not know what, but I have been drawn towards you so long a while—long before I saw you, ever since I heard your name, the moment I saw that old photograph in the music-room, I knew."

"What did you know?"

"When I heard your name it called up an image in my mind, and that image has never wholly left me—it comes back often like a ghost."

"When you were thinking of something different?"

"I am your destiny, or one of your destinies."

Her eyes were fixed eagerly upon him; his darkness and the mysteries he represented attracted her, and she even felt she could follow. At the same moment his eyes seemed the most beautiful in the world, and she desired him to make love to her. While enticing, she resisted him, now more feebly, and when he let go her hands she sat looking at him, wondering how she was to get through the evening without kissing him.... She spoke to him about his opera. He asked her if she were going to sing it, and she looked at him with vague, uncertain eyes. He said he knew she never would. She asked him why he thought so, and again a great longing bent him towards her. She withdrew her hands and face from his lips, and they had begun to talk of other things when he perceived her face close to his. Unable to resist he kissed her cheek, fearing that she would order him from the room. But at the instant of the touching of his lips, she threw her arm about his neck, and drew him down as a mermaiden draws her mortal lover into the depths, and in a wondering world of miraculous happiness he surrendered himself.

"Dearest, dearest," he said, raising himself to look at her.

"Ulick, Ulick," she said, "let me kiss you, I've longed such a while."

He thought he had never seen so radiant a face. What disguise had fallen? And looking at her, he strove to discover the woman who had denied him so often. This new woman seemed made all of light and love and transport, the woman of all his divinations, the being the old photograph in the old music-room had warned him of, the being that the voice of his destiny had told him he was to meet. And as they stood by the fireplace looking into each other's eyes, he gradually became aware of his happiness. It broke in his heart with a thrill and shiver like an exquisite dawn, opal and rose; the brilliancy of her eyes, the rapture of her face, the

magnetic stirring of the little gold curls along her forehead were so wonderful that he feared her as an enchanter fears the spirit he has raised. Like one who has suddenly chanced on the hilltop, he gazed on the prospect, believing it all to be his. They stood gazing into each other's eyes too eager to speak, and when she called his name he remembered the legended forest, and replied with the song of the bird that leads Siegfried to Brunnhilde. She laughed, and sang the next two bars, and then seemed to forget everything.
"Dearest, of what are you thinking?"
"Only if I ever shall kiss you again, Ulick."
"You will always kiss me!"
She did not answer, and, frightened by her irresponsive eyes, he said—
"But, Evelyn, you must love me, me—only me; you will never see him again?"
She did not answer, and when he spoke, his voice trembled.
"But it is impossible you can ever marry him now."
"I am not going to marry Owen."
"You told him so the other night?"
"Yes, I told him, or very nearly, that I could not marry him."
"You cannot marry him, you love me.... But why don't you answer. What are you thinking of?"
"Only of you, dear.... Let me kiss you again," and in the embrace he forgot for the moment the inquietude her answer had caused him.
"That is my call," she said. "How am I to sing the Liebestod after all this? How does it begin?"
Ulick sang the opening phrase, and she continued the music for some bars.
"I hope I shall get through it all right. Then," she said, "we shall go home together in the brougham."
At that moment a knock was heard, and Merat entered. "Mademoiselle, you have no time to lose."
The call boy's voice was heard on the stairs, and Evelyn hastened away. Ulick followed, and the first thing he heard when he got on the stage was Tristan's death motive. He listened, not so much to the music itself as to its occult significance regarding Evelyn and himself. And as Isolde's grief changed from wild lament for sensual delight to a resigned and noble prayer, the figure of ecstasy broke with a sound as of wings shaking, and Ulick seemed to witness a soul's transfiguration. He watched it rising in several ascensions, like a lark's flight. For an instant it seemed to float in some divine consummation, then, like the bird, to suddenly quench in the radiance of the sky. The harps wept farewell over the bodies of the lovers, then all was done, and he stood at the wings listening to the applause. She came to him at once, as soon as the curtain was down.
"How did I sing it?"
"As well as ever."
"But you seem sad; what is it?"
"It seemed to mean something—something, I cannot tell what, something to do with us."
"No," she said, looking at him. "I was only thinking of the music. Wait for me, dear, I shall not keep you long."
He walked up and down the stage, and in his hand was a wreath that some admirer had kept for the last. For excitement he could hardly bid the singers good-night as they passed him. Now it was Tristan, now Brangäne, now one of the chorus. The question raged within him. Was it fated that she should marry him? So far as he understood the omens she would not; but the readings were obscure, and his will threw itself out in opposition to the influence of Sir Owen. But he was not certain that that was the direction whence the danger was coming. He could only exert, however, his will in that direction. At last he saw her coming down the steep stairs, wrapped in a white opera cloak. They walked in silence—she all rapture, but his happiness already clouded. The brougham was so full of flowers that they, could hardly find place for themselves. She drew him closer, and said—

"What is the matter, dear? Am I not nice to you?"

"Yes, Evelyn, you're an enchantment. Only—"

"Only what, dear?"

"I fear our future. I fear I shall lose you. All has come true so far, the end must happen."

She drew his arm about her waist, and laid his face on her bare shoulder.

"Let there be no foreboding. Live in the present."

"The future is too near us. Say you'll marry me, or else I shall lose you altogether. It is the one influence on our side."

She was born, he said, under two great influences, but each could be modified; one might be widened, the other lessened, and both modifications might finally resolve into her destiny. So far as he could read her future, it centred in him or another. That other, he was sure, was not Sir Owen, nor was it himself, he thought; for when she and he had met in the theatre, she had experienced no dread, but he had dreaded her, recognising her as his destiny. He had even recognised her as Evelyn Innes before she had been pointed out to him.

"But you had seen my photograph?"

"But it was not by your photograph that I knew you."

"And you knew that I should care for you?"

"I knew that something had to happen. But you did not feel that I was your destiny. You said you experienced no dread, but when you met Sir Owen did you experience none?"

"I suppose I did. I was afraid of him. At first I think I hated him."

"Ah, Evelyn, we shall not marry—it is not our fate. You see that you cannot say you will marry me. Another fate is beckoning you."

"Who is it who beckons me? Have I already met him?"

He fell to dreaming again, and Evelyn asked him vainly to describe this other man.

"Why are you singing that melancholy Mark motive?"

"I did not know I was singing it." He returned to his dream again, but starting from it, he seized her hands.

"Evelyn," he said, "we must marry; a reason obliges us. Have you not thought of it?" And then, as if he had not noticed that she had not answered his question, he said, "On your father's account, if he should ever know. Think what my position is. I have betrayed my friend. That is why the Marie motive has been singing in my head. Evelyn, you must say you will marry me. We must marry at once, for your father's sake. I have betrayed him, my best friend.... I have acted worse than that other man."

"Ulick, dear, open the window; the scent of these flowers is overpowering.... That is better. Throw some of those bouquets into the street. We might give them to those poor men, they might be able to sell them.... Tell the coachman to stop."

The chime of destiny sounded clearer than ever in their ears; it seemed as if they could almost catch the tune, and with a convulsive movement Evelyn drew her lover towards her.

"Every hour threatens us," he said. "Can you not hear? Do not go to Park Lane—Park Lane threatens; your friend Lady Duckle threatens. I see nothing but threats and menaces; all are leagued against us."

"Dearest, we cannot spend the night driving about London."

He sighed on his mistress's shoulder. She threw his black hair from his forehead.

"There is no hope. We shall be separated, scattered to different winds."

"Why do you think that? How do you know these things, Ulick?"

"Evelyn, in losing you I lose the principle of my life, but you will lose nothing in losing me. So it is written. But you are not listening; I am wearying you; you're clinging to the present, knowing that you will soon lose it."

She threw herself upon him, and kissed him as if she would annihilate destiny on his lips, and until they reached Park Lane there was no future, only a delirious present for both of them.

"I won't ask you in; I am tired. Good-bye, dearest, good-bye. I'll write."

"Remember that my time is short," and there was a strange accent in his voice which she did not hear till long after. She had locked herself into the sensual present, and, lulled in happy sensations of gratified sense, she allowed Merat to undress her. She thought of the soft luxury of her bed, and lay down, her brain full of floating impressions of flowers, music and of love.

CHAPTER TWENTY-THREE

And when Merat called her in the morning, she was dreaming of love. She turned over, and, closing her eyes, strove to continue her dream, but it fled like moonshine from her memory, and was soon so far distant that she could not even perceive the subject of it. And she awoke in spite of herself, and sat up in bed sipping her chocolate; and then lay back upon the pillow with Ulick for the inner circle of her thought. It seemed that she could think of him for hours; the romance of his personality carried her on and on. At one moment she dwelt on the gold glow in his dark eyes, the paint-like blackness of his hair, and his long thin hands. At another her fancy liked to evoke his superstitions. For him the past, present and future were not twain, but one thing. And every time she saw him, she was more and more interested. Every time she discovered something new in him—he did not exist on the surface of things, but deep in himself; and she wondered if she would ever know him.

Her thoughts paused a moment, and then she remembered something he had said. It had struck her at the time, but now it appeared to her more than ever interesting. Catholicism, he had said, had not fallen from him—he had merely learnt that it was only part of the truth; he had gone further, he had raised himself to a higher spirituality. It was not that he wanted less, but more than Catholicism could give him. In religion, as in art, there were higher and lower states. We began by admiring "Faust," and went on to Wagner, hence to Beethoven and Palestrina. Catholicism was the spiritual fare of the multitude; there was a closer communion with the divine essence. She had forgotten what came next.... He held that we are always warned of our destiny and it had been proved that in the hypnotic sleep, when the pulse of life was weakest, almost at pause, there was a heightening of the powers of vision and hearing. A patient whose eyes had been covered with layers of cotton wool had been able to read the newspaper. Another patient had been able to tell what was passing in another mind, and at a distance of a mile. The only explanation that Charcot could give of this second experiment was that the knowledge had been conveyed through the rustling of the blood in the veins, which the hypnotic sleep had enabled the patient to hear. And Ulick submitted that this scientific explanation was more incredible than any spiritual one. There was much else. There was all Ulick's wonderful talk about the creation of things by thought, and his references to the mysterious Kabbala had strangely interested her. But suddenly she remembered that perchance his spiritualism was allied to the black art of the necromancers; and her Catholic conscience was mysteriously affrighted, and she experienced the attraction of terror. Was it possible that he believed that all the accidents, or what we suppose are accidents, have been earned in a preceding life? Did he really believe that lovers may tempt each other life after life, that a group of people may come together again?

"Mademoiselle, it is half-past ten."

"Very well, Merat, I will get up. I will ring for you when I have had my bath."

"Lady Duckle has gone out, and will not be home for lunch."

There was not even a letter, and the day stretched out before her. Ulick might call, but she did not think he would. She thought of a visit to her father, but something held her back, and Dulwich was a long way. After breakfast she went to the piano and sang some of Ulick's music; stopping suddenly in the middle of a bar, she thought she would send him a note asking him to come to lunch. But what should she do till two o'clock? it was now only eleven. Suddenly it struck her that she might take a hansom and go and see him. She had never seen his rooms, and to visit him there would be more amusing than for him to come to Park Lane; and she imagined his surprise and delight at seeing her. Her thoughts went to the frock she would wear—a new one had come home yesterday—this would be an excellent opportunity to wear it. She would take him to lunch with her at some restaurant! She was in excellent humour. Her thoughts amused her, and she reflected that she had done well to choose the pale shot silk with green shades in it. It was trimmed with black lace, and she selected a large black hat with black ostrich feathers to wear with it.

And seeing the people in the streets as she drove past, she wondered if they were as happy as she was. She speculated on their errands, and wondered if many of the women were going, like her, to their lovers. She wondered what their lovers were like, and she laughed at her thoughts. Seeing that she was passing through a very mean street, she hoped that Ulick's rooms were not too Bohemian, and felt relieved when she found that the street she dreaded led into a square. A square, she reflected, always means a certain measure of respectability. And the faded, old-fashioned neighbourhood pleased her. Some of the houses seemed as if they had known more fashionable days; and the square exhaled a tender melancholy; it suggested a vision of dreamy lives—lives lived in ideas, lives of students who lived in books unaware of the externality of things.

But the cabman could not find the number, and Evelyn impatiently inquired it from the vagrant children. There were groups of them on the wide doorstep, and Evelyn imagined the interior of the house, wide passages, gently-sloping staircase, its heavy banisters. It surprised and amused her to find that she had imagined it quite correctly; and when she reached the landing to which she had been directed, she stopped, hearing his voice. He was only talking to himself; she pushed the door and called to him.

"Oh, it is you?" he said; "you have come sooner than I expected."

"Then you expected me, Ulick?"

"Yes, I expected you."

"Expected me ...to-day! But, Ulick, what were you saying when I came in?"

"Only some Kabbalistic formula," he replied, quite naturally.

"But you don't really believe in such superstitions, and it surely is very wrong."

He looked at her incredulously, as he might at some beautiful apparition likely at any moment to vanish from his sight, then reverentially drew her towards him and kissed her. Her hand was laid on his shoulder, and in a delicious apprehension she stood looking at him.

"Where shall we sit?"

He threw some books and papers from a long cane chair, and she lay down in it. He sat on the arm, and then tried to talk.

"Let me take your hat."

She unpinned it, and he placed it on the piano.

His room was lighted by two square windows looking on the open space in front of the square, where the vagrant children gathered in noisy groups round a dripping iron fountain. The floor was covered with grey-green drugget, and near the fireplace, drawn in front of the window, was a large oak table covered with papers of various kinds. Against the end wall there was a bookcase, and there were shelves filled with books. There were two arm-chairs, a piano, and some prints of Blake's illustrations to Dante on the wall. The writing table, covered with manuscript music, roused Evelyn's curiosity. She glanced down a page of orchestration, and then picked up the first pages of an article, and having read them she said—

"How severe you are in your articles. You are gentler in your music, more like yourself; but I see your servant does not waste her time dusting your books ...and that is your bedroom, may I see it?"

He looked at her abashed. "I am afraid my room will seem to you very unluxurious. I have read of prima donnas' bed-rooms."

But the bare simplicity of the room did not displease her; it seemed to her more natural to sleep in a low, narrow bed like his, than in fine linen and eiderdown quilts, and she liked the scant, bleak furniture, the two chairs, the iron wash-hand stand, and the window curtained with a bit of Indian muslin. They stood talking, hardly knowing what they were saying. Her eyes embarrassed him, and she stopped in the middle of a sentence.

"Now, Ulick," she said, turning towards the door, "I want you to take me to lunch. We'll go to the Savoy."

He had to admit he had not sufficient money. Three shillings and sixpence were what remained until he received the cheque from one of his newspapers.

"But I am not going to have you pay for my lunch, Ulick. I am asking you. Be nice, don't refuse; what does it matter? What does money matter to me? It comes in so fast that I don't know what to do with it."

It was at the end of the season, and there were not many people in the low-ceilinged dining-room. All the waiters knew Evelyn, and she was conducted ceremoniously to a table. And as she passed up the room, she wondered what was being thought of Ulick. He was so different from the exquisite, foppish elegance of the man she was usually seen with. He was strange-looking, but Ulick was as distinguished as Owen, only the distinction was of another kind.

He always remembered how at the end of lunch she took out her gold knitted purse, and emptied its contents on the tablecloth. And he was astonished at the casualness with which she spent money in every shop that caught her fancy. The afternoon included a visit to the saddler's, where she had to make inquiries about bits and bridles. She called at two jewellers, where she had left things to be mended. She ordered a dozen pair of boots, and purchased a large quantity of stationery after a long discussion about dies, stamps and monograms. And when all this was finished, she proposed they should have tea in Kensington Gardens.

Ulick knew very little of London. He knew Victoria Station, for he took the train there to Dulwich; the Strand, for he went there to see editors; and Bloomsbury, because he lived there. But he had never been to the park, and seemed puzzled when Evelyn spoke of the Serpentine and the round pond. It was surprising, he said, to find forest groves in the heart of London. They had tea at a little table set beneath huge branches, and after tea they sat on a sloping lawn facing the long water. She wondered if he were aware of the beauty of things, the wonder of life, the blue of the sky, the romance of the clouds. But she was bent on hearing of the invisible world apparently always so visible to him, and she tried to win his thoughts away from the park, and to lead him to speak of his visions. She did not know if she believed in them, but she pined for exaltation, for, an unloosening of the materialistic terror in which Owen had tied her, and in this mood Ulick's dreams floated up in her life, like clouds in a cloudless sky. He sat talking, lost in his dreams, and she sat listening like one enchanted. Now their talk had strayed from the descriptions of visions beheld by folk who lived in back parlours in Bloomsbury squares to the philosophy of his own belief; and she smiled for delight at seeing the Druid in him. The ancient faiths had survived in him, and it seemed natural and even right that he should believe that after death men pass to the great plain of the land over the sea, the land of the children of Dana. Men lived there, he said, for a while, enjoying all their desires, and at the end of this period they are born again. Man lives between two desires—his desire of spiritual peace and happiness, and his desire of earthly experience.

"Oh, how true that is!"

"Man's desire of earthly experience," Ulick continued, "draws him to re-birth, and he is born into a form that fits his nature as a glove fits a hand; the soul of a warrior passes into the robust form of a warrior; the soul of a poet into the most sensitive body of a poet; so you see how modern science has only robbed the myths of their beauty."

He spoke of the old Irish legend of Mongan and the Bard, and Evelyn begged of him to tell it her.

"Mongan," he said, "had been Fin MacCool two hundred years before. When he was Fin he had been present at the death of a certain king. The bard was singing before Mongan, and mis-stated the place of the king's death. Mongan corrected him, and the Bard was so incensed at the correction that he threatened to satirise the kingdom so that it should become barren. And he would only agree to withhold his terrible satire if Mongan would give him his wife.

"Mrs. Mongan?"

"Yes, just so," Ulick replied, laughing. "Mongan asked for three days' delay to consider the dreadful dilemma in which the Bard's threat had placed him. And during that time Mongan sat with his wife consoling her, saying, "A man will come to us, his feet are already upon the western sea." And at the time when the Bard stood up to claim the wife, a strange warrior came into the encampment, holding a barbless spear. He said that he was Caolte, one of Fin's famous warriors, that the king whose place of death was in dispute was killed where Mongan had said, that if they dug down into the earth they would find the spear-head, that it would fit the shaft he held in his hand, that it was the spear-head that had killed the king."

"Go on, and tell me some more stories. I love to listen to you—you are better than any play." And she wondered if he were indeed an ancient Druid come to life again, and that the instinct of the ancient rites lingered in him. However this might be, he could answer all her questions, and she was much interested when at the end of another tale he told her of Blake's visions and prophetic books. She knew little about Blake, and listened to Ulick's account of his visions and prophecies. Evelyn thought of Owen, and to escape from the thought she spoke of a legend which Ulick had once mentioned to her.

"You did not tell it to me, only the end; the very last phrase is all I know of it, 'and the further adventures of Bran are unknown.'"

"Bran, the son of Feval, is the story of a man who went to the great plain, the land over the sea, the land of the children of Dana. He was sitting in his court when a beautiful woman appeared, and she told him to man his ship and sail to the land of the Gods, the land where no one dies, where blossoms fall for ever.... I have forgotten the song, what a wonderful song it is. Ah, I remember, 'Where music is not born, but continually is there, where' ... no, I can't remember it. Bran sails away, and after sailing for some days he meets a man driving a chariot over the waves. This man says, 'To my eyes you are sailing over the tops of a forest,' and in many other ways makes clear to him that all things are but appearances, and change with the eye that sees them."

"How true that is. At Lady Ascott's ball I was enjoying myself, delighted with the brilliancy of the dresses, the jewellery and the flowers, and in a moment they all passed away; I only saw a little triviality and heard a voice crying within me, 'Why are you here, why are you doing these things? This ball means nothing to you.'"

"That was the voice of your destiny; your life is no longer with Owen."

"With whom is it, Ulick? Tell me, you can see into the future."

"I know no more than I told you last night. I am your destiny for to-day."

They looked at each other in fear and sadness—and though both knew the truth, neither could speak it.

"Then what happens to Bran, the son of Feval?"

"Bran visits many islands of many delights, but wishing to see his native land once more, he sails away, but the people of those islands have told him that he must not set foot on any earthly shore, or he will perish. So he sails close to his native land, but does not leave the ship. The inhabitants ask him who he is; he tells them, and they reply, 'The voyage of Bran, son of Feval, is among our most ancient stories.' One man swims ashore, and the moment his foot touches earth he becomes a heap of dust. Bran sails away, and the story ends with a phrase which you already know—'The further adventures of Bran are unknown.'"

"How true! how true! the stories of our lives are known up to a certain point, and our further adventures are unknown."

They were glad of a little silence, and Evelyn sat striving to read her own destiny in the legend. Bran visited many islands of many delights, but when he wished to return to his native land he was told that he must do no more than to sail along its coast, that if he set foot on any earthly shore he would perish. But what did this story mean, what meaning had it for her? She had visited many islands of many delights, and had come home again! What meaning had this story for her? why had she remembered the last phrase? why had she been impelled to ask Ulick to tell her this story? She looked at him—he sat with his eyes on the ground absorbed in thought, but she did not think he was thinking of the legend, but of how soon he would lose her, and she shuddered in the warm summer evening as from a sudden chill. It was now nearly seven o'clock—she would soon have to go home to dress for dinner. They were dining out, she and Lady Duckle, and she would meet once more Lady Ascott, Lady Summersdean, those people whose lives she had begun to feel had no further concern for her.

The hour was inexpressibly calm and alluring; the blue pallor of the sky and the fading of the sunset behind the tall Bayswater houses raised the soul with a tingling sense of exalted happiness and delicious melancholy? She did not ask herself if she loved Ulick better than Owen; she only knew that she must act as she was acting—that the moment had not come when she would escape from herself. They walked by the water's edge, their souls still like the water, and like it, full of calm reflections. They were aware of the evening's sad serenity, and the little struggling passions of their lives. Very often Nature seemed on the very point of whispering her secret, but it escaped her ears like an echo in the far distance, like a phantom that disappears in the mist.

"Will you come and see me to-morrow?" he asked suddenly.

"We had better not see each other every day," she said; "still, I don't see there would be any harm if you came to see me in the afternoon."

Her conscience drowsed like this heavy, somnolent evening, and a red moon rose behind the tall trees.

"The time will come," he said, "when you will hate me, Evelyn."

"I don't think I shall be as unjust as that. Good-bye, dear, the afternoon has passed very pleasantly."

CHAPTER TWENTY-FOUR

Owen had telegraphed to her and she had come at once. But how callous and unsympathetic she was. If people knew what she was, no one would speak to her. If Owen knew that she had desired his mother's death ... But had she? She had only thought that, if Lady Asher were not to recover, it were better that she died before she, Evelyn, arrived at Riversdale. As the carriage drove through the woods she noticed that they were empty and silent, save for the screech of one incessant bird, and she thought of the dead woman's face, and contrasted it with the summer time.

The house stood on the side of some rising ground in the midst of the green park. Cattle were grazing dreamily in the grass, which grew rich and long about a string of ponds, and she could see Owen walking under the colonnade. As the carriage came round the gravel space, his eyes sought her in the brougham, and she knew the wild and perplexed look on his face.

"No, don't let's go into the house unless you're tired," he said, and they walked down the drive under the branches, making, they knew not why, for the open park. "This is terrible, isn't it? And this beautiful summer's day too, not a cloud in the sky, not a wind in all the air. How peaceful the cattle are in the meadow, and the swans in the pond. But we are unhappy. Why is this? You say that it is the will of God. That is no answer. But you think it is?"

Fearing to irritate him, she did not speak, but he would not be put off, and she said—

"Do not let us argue, Owen, dear. Tell me about it. It was quite unexpected?"

"She had been in ill-health, as you know, for some time. Let us go this way."

He led her through the shrubbery and through the wicket into the meadows which lay under the terrace, and, thinking of the dead woman, she wondered at the strange, somnolent life of the cattle in the meadows and the swans on the pond. The willows, as if exhausted by the heat, seemed to bend under the stream, and their eyes followed the lines of the woods and

looked into the burning blue of the sky, striving to read the secret there. A rim of moist earth under their feet, and above their heads the infinite blue! The stillness of the summer was in every blade of grass, in every leaf, and the pond reflected the sky and willows in hard, immovable reflections. An occasional ripple of the water-fowl in the reeds impressed upon them the mystery of Nature's indifference to human suffering.
"In that house behind that colonnade she lies dead. Good God! isn't it awful! We shall never see her. But you think we shall?"
"Owen, dear, let as avoid all discussion. She was a good woman. She was very good to me."
"I haven't told you that it was by her wish that I sent for you. She wanted to ask you to promise to marry me.... I told her that I had asked you, and that in a way we were engaged. I could not say more. You seemed unsettled, you seemed to wish to get out of your promise—is not that so?"
Evelyn thought of the scene by Lady Asher's bedside that an accident had saved her from. Marriage was more than ever impossible. What should she have said if Lady Asher had not died before she arrived? The dying woman's eyes, the dying woman's voice! Good heavens! what would she have said? But she had considered nothing. After glancing at the telegram, she had told Merat to pack a few clothes, and had rushed away. She pondered the various excuses she might have sent. She might have said she was not in when the telegram came, she had only just caught the train as it was; if she had not got the telegram before eleven o'clock she would have been safe. But all that was past now, Lady Asher had died before she arrived. It were better that she had died—anything were better rather than that scene should have taken place; for she could not have promised to marry Owen. What would she have done? Refused while looking into her dying eyes, or run out of the room?
"You don't answer me, Evelyn."
"Owen, don't press me. Enough has been said on that subject. This is no time to discuss such questions."
"But it is Evelyn—it was her dearest wish.... Is it then impossible? Have you entirely ceased to care?"
"No, Owen, I'm very fond of you. But you don't really want to marry me, it is because your mother wished it."
His face changed expression, and she knew that he was not certain on the point himself.
"Yes, Evelyn, I do, indeed I do;" and convinced for the moment that what he said was true, he took her hands, and looking at her he added, "It was her wish, and if what you believe be true, she is listening now from behind that blue sky."
Both were trembling, and while the swans floated by, they considered the depth of blue contained in the sky. He was taken with a little dread, and was surprised to find in himself a vague, haunting belief in the possibility of an after life. Suddenly his self-consciousness fell from him, was merged in his instinct of the woman.
"Evelyn, if I don't marry you I shall lose you. I cannot lose you, that would be to lose everything. I don't ask any questions, whether you like Ulick Dean, nor even what your relations are. I only want to know if you will marry me."
He read in her eyes that the tale of their love was ended, and heard his future life ring hollow. It seemed strange that at such a moment the serene swans should float about them, that the water-fowl should move in and out of the reeds, and that the green park and the cloudless sky were like painted paper.
"Then everything is over, everything I had to live for, all is a blank. But when you sent me away before, you had to take me back; you're not a woman who can live without a lover."
"It is difficult, I know."
"What has come between us, tell me? This fellow Ulick Dean or religious scruples?"
"I have no right to talk about religious scruples."

"Then it is this man. You love him, you've ceased to care for me, and you ask me to barter my right to kiss you, to take you in my arms, so that I may remain your friend." "Why, Evelyn, have you got tired of me?"
"But I have not got tired of you, Owen. I am very fond of you."
"Yes, but you don't care any more for me to make love to you."
"Of course it is not the same as it was in the beginning, but there is affection."
"When passion is dead, all is dead, the rest is nothing."
It seemed so shameful that he should suffer like this, and she strove to rouse herself out of her stony determination. She was like one upon a rampart; she could see the surrounding country, but could not escape to it; this rampart was the instinct, in which Nature had shut her soul. But she could not bear to see him cry.
"Oh, Evelyn, this cannot be."
Then, feeling that the reality was too brutal, she yielded to the temptation to disguise the truth.
"I don't know what I shall do, Owen; there would be no use making promises."
"Then you do love me a little, Evelyn?"
"Yes, Owen, you must never doubt that. I shall always be fond of you; remember that, whatever happens."
"Yes, I know, as a friend. Look round! the earth and the sky are quiet, and one day we shall be quiet too, only that is sure."
As they walked towards the house, their self-consciousness rose to so high a pitch that the park and house seemed to them like a thin illusion, a sort of painted paper reality, which might fall to pieces at any moment. He thought how little were the hours between the present moment and the moment when she would be taken from him. Whereas she was thinking that these hours would never pass. She realised the long hours before the sunlight waned. She thought of their lonely dinner and their evening after it. All that while she would witness his grief for the love that had gone from her, a love which she could no more give than she could once withhold. The great green park lay before their eyes, they strayed through the woods talking of her Isolde. He had not seen the performance. He had been called away the day she played it, but his pockets were full of the articles that had been written about her. The leaves of the beech trees shimmered in the steady sunlight, and they could see the green park through the drooping branches. She often detected a sob in his voice, and once, while sitting under a cedar tree at the edge of the terrace, he had to turn aside to hide his tears, and the sadness of everything made her sick and ill.
They had tea in the west hall. Owen had ceased to complain, and she had begun to think that she could not give him up entirely.
The day had passed somehow; dinner was over. Around the green park the last light of the sunset grew narrower, and the cattle faded mysteriously into the gathering gloom. Owen held converse with himself, but with recognition of the fact that he was listened to by the second subject of his discourse, and that they themselves were his ideas, the figuration of his teaching, endowed his philosophy with a dramatic intensity.
"How you used to hang round my neck and listen with eager nervous eyes. You always had the genius of exaltation. You were wonderful; I watched you, I understood you, I appreciated you; you were a marvellous jewel I had found, and of which I was excessively proud. I hardly lived at all for myself. You were my life; my life lived in you. Every time I went to see you, every appointment was a thrill, a wonder, a mystery. But it was not until you took me back after that separation at Florence that I sank into the depths of love. Then I became like a diver in the deep sea. What I had known before were but the shallows of passion. What I felt after Florence was the translucid calm of the ocean's depth. I lived in the light of an inner consciousness, seeing you always, your face always before me, and my whole being held in a rapt devotion, a self-sufficiency, an exaltation beyond the reach of words. Oh, Evelyn, I have been extraordinarily in love. But all this is nothing to you; it even bores you."

"No, Owen, no, but you don't understand."

The desire to tell him the truth came up in her throat, but the moment she sought to express it in words it became untruth, and it was to save herself from falsehood that she remained silent.

"I knew my mistake, but the temptation was irresistible. I wanted so to tell you that I loved you. I could not deny myself, effusion, tears, aspiration. I gained two very wonderful years, and so I lost you. I wonder if any lover would have the courage to forswear these joys so that he might retain his mistress? Would any mistress be worthy of the sacrifice? 'Better fifty years of Europe than a cycle of Cathay.'"

"Owen, dear, you're very cruel. Why do you speak like that? I shall never cease to love you. Owen, dear, you don't hate me?" she said, turning towards him.

The silence was intense. It seemed to enter her ears and eyes like water or fire, and with dim sight and a dissolution of personal control of her body, she was moved towards him, and without any sort of thrill of desire she was drawn, almost thrown at his feet.

She accepted his kisses wearily. There was a strange look in her eyes which he could not interpret, and she could not confide her secret, and there was an inexpressible sadness in these last kisses, and Owen's heart seemed to stand still when he said,—

"Her last wish was our marriage; she would be glad if she could see us."

Evelyn hid her face on his shoulders several times. He thought she was weeping, but her eyes remained dry. He came to her room that evening, and now that they were lovers again, it seemed to him impossible that she could refuse to marry him. But she stood looking at him, absorbed, in the presence of her future life, her eyes full of a strange farewell. He could extort no words from her, and her eyes retained their strange melancholy till her departure; his last memory of her visit was their melancholy.

CHAPTER TWENTY-FIVE

The forces within her were at truce. She was conscious of a suspension of hostilities. The moment was one in which she saw, as in a mirror, her poor, vague little soul in its hopeless wandering through life. She drew back, not daring to see herself, and then was drawn forward by a febrile curiosity. She felt towards them so differently that she could not think of herself as the same person when she was with Owen as she was when she was with Ulick. She remembered what she had heard the "dresser" say, and she remembered the sin. But apart from the deception she practised upon both men, there was the wrong-doing. Her conscience did not assail her now; but she knew that she would suffer to-morrow or next day. That sense of sin which she could not obliterate from her nature would rise to her lips like a salt wave, and poison her life with its bitterness, and she asked herself vain questions: Why had she left her father? Why had she two lovers? Why did she rise to seek things that made her unhappy? She thought of yesterday's journey to see a dying woman, and of to-night's performance of "Tristan and Isolde." What an unhappy, maddening jingle. The bitter wave of conscience, which rose to her lips and poisoned her taste, forced from her an avowal that she would mend her life. She foresaw nothing but deception, and easily imagined that not a day would pass without lies. All her life would be a lie, and when her nature rose in vehement revolt, she looked round for means to free herself from the fetters and chains in which she had locked herself. Thinking of Owen, she vowed that it must not happen again. But what excuse would she give? Should she tell him that Ulick was her lover? That was the only way, only it seemed so brutal. Even so she would have a lover; and strictly speaking, she ought to send them both away. Very probably that is what she would do in the end.... In the meantime, she would keep them both on! Her face contracted in an expression of terror and disgust. Had her moralising, then, ended in such miserable selfishness as this?

To escape from her thoughts she looked out at the landscape, hoping it would distract her. But she could take no interest in it. Yesterday it had seemed so beautiful, but to-day it was all reversed, and the light was different. She preferred to remember it. She thought that they must be nearing the river, and she remembered how in one place it ran round a field, making a silver horse shoe in the green land, they had crossed it twice in the space of a quarter of a mile; then it followed the railway, placid, docile, reflecting the trees and sky. Then like a child it was soon taken with a new idea; it ran far away out of sight, and Evelyn thought it would never return. But it came back again, turbulent and shallow; and with woods on the steep hillside, and spanned by a beautiful stone bridge. A little later its wanderings grew still more perplexing, and she was not sure that it had not been joined in some strange way by another river. But flowing round a low-lying field, coming suddenly from behind a bend in the land, it had seemed in that place like a pond. One bank was lined with bushes, the other lay open to a view of a treeless plain divided by ditches. Three ladies had held their light boat in the deep current, and she had wondered who they were, and what was their manner of living and their desires, and though she would never know these things, the image of these ladies in their boat had fixed itself in her mind for ever.

Soon after the train began to slacken speed, and nervously she awaited her destiny.

For she was uncertain whether she would send Ulick a telegram, telling him to come to Park Lane, or whether she would drive straight to his lodgings. At the bottom of her heart she knew that when she arrived at St. Pancras she would tell the cabman, "Queen's Square, Bloomsbury." And an hour later, nervous with expectation, she sat in the cab, seeing the streets pass behind her. She was beginning to know the characteristics of the neighbourhood, and in the afternoon light they awoke her out of a trembling lethargy. She recognised the old iron gateway, the open space, the thirsty fountain and the troop of neglected children. She liked the forlorn and rusty square. She experienced a sort of sinking anguish while waiting on the doorstep, lest he might not be at home. But when the servant girl said Mr. Dean was upstairs, she liked her dirty, good-natured smile, and she loved the stairs and banisters—it was all wonderful, and she could hardly believe that in a few moments more she would catch the first sight of his face. She would have to tell some part of the truth; and since Lady Asher was dead, he could not fail to believe. He would never think of asking her—she put the ugly thought aside, and ran up the second flight.

In the pauses of their love-making, they often wandered round the walls participating in the mystery of the Wanderers, and the sempiternal loveliness of figures who stood with raised arms, by the streams of Paradise. It seemed a profanation to turn from these aspirations to the enjoyment of material love, and Evelyn looked at Ulick questioningly. But he said that life only became wrong when it ceased to aspire. In an Indian temple, it had once been asked who was the most holy man of all. A young saint who had not eaten for ten days had been pointed out, but he said that the holiest man who ever lived stood yonder. It was then noticed that the man pointed to was drunk ... Ulick explained that the drunkenness did not matter; it was an unimportant detail in the man's life, for none aspired as he did; and laughing at the story, they stood by the dusty, windy pane, her hand resting on his shoulder, and they always remembered that that day they had seen the foliage in the square.

Lady Duckle had gone to Homburg; Owen had been obliged to go to Bath on account of his gout; and Evelyn was free to abandon herself to her love of Ulick and to her love of her father, and she begged him not to spoil her happiness, but to come to Dulwich with her. His scruples were easily argued away. She urged that he had not taken her away, he had brought her back to her father. This last argument was convincing, and the happiest time in their lives was the week they spent in Dulwich. They sat down together to dinner under the lamp at the round table in the little back room, and their evenings were passed at the harpsichord and the clavichord; and amid the dreams and aspirations of great men they attained their sublime nature. The music that had been given and that was to be given at St. Joseph's furnished a never-failing subject of discussion, and Mr. Innes told them stories of Italy in the sixteenth century. How almost every Sunday there was a festival in some church where the most beautiful music was heard. Along the nave were eight choirs, four on one side and four on the other, raised on stages eight to ten feet high, and facing one another at equal distances. Each choir had a portable organ, and the *maître composateur* beat the time for the principal choir. And Mr. Innes's eyes lighted up when he spoke of the admirable *style recitatif* in the oratory of St. Marcellus when there was a congregation of the Brothers of the Holy Crucifix. This order was composed of the chief noblemen of Rome, who had therefore the power of bringing together the rarest musicians Italy could produce. The voices began with a psalm in motet form, and then the instruments played a symphony, after which the voices sang a story from the Old Testament. Each chorister represented a personage in the story, etc. He spoke of the great organist at St. Peter's, and the wonderful inventions he is said to have displayed in his improvisations. No one since had played the harp like the renowned Horatio, but there was no one who could play the lyre like the renowned Ferrabosco in England. Evelyn leaned across the table, transported three centuries back, hearing all this music, which she had known from her earliest years, performed by virtue of her father's description in Italy, in St. Peter's, in the oratory of St. Marcellus and in the church of Minerva. Sometimes her father and Ulick began an argument, her sympathies alternated between them; she spoke very little, preferring to listen, not liking to side with either, agreeing with them, sometimes angering her father by her neutrality. But one evening he was a little too insistent, and Evelyn burst into tears, and ran upstairs to her room. The two men looked at each other, and Mr. Innes begged Ulick to tell him if he had been unkind, and then besought him to go upstairs and try to induce Evelyn to come down. Her face brightened into merry laughter at her own folly, and it called from her many entertaining remarks, so Ulick was tempted to set them one against the other, and to do so he had only to ask if Evelyn could sing such light soprano parts as Zerlina or Rosetta as well as her mother.

In the mornings Evelyn and Ulick lingered in the shade of the chestnut trees or loitered in the lanes. At one moment they were telling each other of the fatality of their passion; in the next, by some transition of which they were not aware, they found themselves discussing some musical question. They went for long drives; and Richmond Park, not more than eight or ten miles distant, was at this season a beautiful, plaintive languor. There was a strange stillness in the air and a tender bloom upon the blue sky which spoke to the heart as no words, as only music could. The shadows moved listlessly among the bracken, and every vista was an enticement. Soft rain had allayed the dust of the road, and the distant hillsides seemed in the morning mists extraordinarily blue and romantic. There were wide prospects suggesting some great domain, and about the large oaks which stood in these open spaces herds of deer browsed, themselves the colour of the approaching month. About a sudden hillside, brilliantly blue, the evanescent mist hung over the heavy fronds, going out in the sunlight that was breaking through a grey sky. Ulick exclaimed, "How beautiful," and at the same moment Evelyn said, "Look at the deer, they are going to jump the railings." But the deer ran underneath, and galloped down the sloping park between a line of massive oaks; and the white and the tan hinds and fawns expressed in their life and beauty something which thrilled in the heart, and perforce Evelyn and Ulick remained silent. The park was wreathed that morning in sunlight and mist, it seemed to invite confidences, and the lovers dreamed of a perfect union of soul. The carriage was told to wait for them, and they took a path leading under a long line of trees toward high ground. Carts had passed there, and the ruts were full of water, but the earth about them was a little crisp, as if there had been frost during the night. They had brought with them a score of "Parsifal," for it was not yet certain that Evelyn would not play the part of Kundry. Notwithstanding Ulick's criticism, she thought she would like to act in the third act. But they were too interested in each other to open the score, and they were excited by the wonder of Nature in the still morning. The sky was all silver, and a very little distance bathed the hillsides in beautiful blue tones. The leaves of the oak trees hung languidly, as if considering the lowly earth to which they must soon return. Yet the blood was hot and the nerves were highly strung, and life seemed capable of great things in this moody, contemplative morning. There was a wonder in the little wren that picked her way among the fronds, and a thrill in the scurry of the watchful rabbit; and when they reached the crest of the upland and saw an open expanse of park, with the deer moving away through the mist, their souls dilated, and in happy ecstasy they looked upon Nature with the same innocent wonderment as the first man and woman.

The morning seemed to inspire adventure, and the little tale that Evelyn was telling was just what was required to enhance its suggestion. By some accident in the conversation she had been led to speak of how she had been nearly captured by pirates in the Mediterranean. They were becalmed off the African coast, and a boat had rowed out with fruits and vegetables. The suspicious countenances of this boat's crew did not strike them at the time. But they were a reconnoitring party, and next day about four in the afternoon they noticed a vessel propelled by sails and oars steering straight for them, as if in the intention of running them down. It paid no attention to the cries of the captain, but came straight at them, and would have succeeded in its design if the yacht had not been going through the water faster than the pirates supposed, so they fell astern, and no one thought any more of them till they tacked, and they had almost overtaken the yacht, they were hardly distant more than fifty yards, when their intention was suspected. The captain put the *Medusa's* head up to the wind, and she soon began to leave her pursuer behind.

"We had no arms on board, they were fifty to twenty; the men would have been massacred, and I should have finished my days in a harem."

Ulick had brought his violin with him, and they walked under the drooping boughs, she singing and he playing old-world melodies by Lulli and Rameau. Sometimes a passer-by stopped, and peering through, discovered them in a hollow sitting under an oak. A snake crawled out of its hole, and Ulick was about to rush forward to kill it, but Evelyn laid her hand upon his, and said—

"Let it listen, poor thing. No living thing should meet its death for its love of music."

"You're no longer the Evelyn Innes that loved Owen Asher."

"I think I have changed a great deal. I was very young when I knew him first."

She spoke of the influence he had exercised over her, but now his ideas meant as little as he did himself—it was all far away. Only a little trick of speech and a turn of phrase remained to recall his passage through her life. When they returned home she found a letter from him on the table, and her face clouded as she read his letter, for it announced an intention to call when he came to town, and to avoid his visit she thought she would stop in Dulwich. But if she stayed over Saturday, she would have to go to Mass on Sunday. Last Sunday she escaped by pleading indisposition. She wondered which she would prefer, to face Owen or to brave the effect that she knew Mass would produce upon her.

CHAPTER TWENTY-SIX

She was in the music-room, looking through the first act of "Grania," and thinking that perhaps after all she might remain on the stage and create the part. Her father had gone to St. Joseph's for choir practice, Ulick had gone to London for strings for her viola da gamba; and all the morning she had been uneasy and expectant. The feeling never quite left her that something was about to happen, that she was to meet someone—someone for whom she had been waiting a long while. So she started on hearing the front door bell ring. She could think of no one whom it might be unless Owen. If it were, what would she say? And she waited, eager for the servant to announce the visitor. It was Monsignor Mostyn.

She was dressed in a muslin tea-gown over shot green silk, and was conscious of her triviality as she stood before the tall, spare ecclesiastic. She admired the calm, refined beauty of his face, the bright, dark eyes and the thin features, steadfast and aloof as some saints she had seen in pictures.

"I called to see your father, Miss Innes, but he is not in, and hearing that you were, I asked to see you. For my business is really with you, that is, if you can spare the time?"
"Won't you sit down, Monsignor?"
"I have come, Miss Innes, to remind you of a promise that you once made me."
The colour returned to her cheeks, and a smile to her lips. But she did not remember, and was slightly embarrassed.
"Did I make you a promise?"
"Have you forgotten my speaking to you about some poor sisters who might be driven from their convent if they failed to pay the interest on a mortgage?"
"Ah, yes, on the night of the concert."
"They have paid the interest and kept a roof over their heads, but in doing so they have exhausted their resources; and not to put too fine a point upon it, I am afraid they often have not enough to eat. Something must be done for them. I thought that a concert would be the quickest way of getting them some money."
"You want me to sing?"
"It really would be a charitable action."
"I shall be delighted to sing for them. Where is this convent?"
"At Wimbledon."
"My old convent! The Passionist Sisters!"
"Your old convent?"
"Yes," Evelyn replied, the colour rising slightly to her cheeks. "I made a retreat there, long ago, before I went on the stage."
She was grieved to hear that the Reverend Mother she had known was dead; she had died two years ago, and Mother Margaret was dead too. Monsignor could tell her nothing about Sister Bonaventure. Mother Philippa was the sub-prioress; and in the midst of her questions he explained how the financial difficulties had arisen. They were, he said, the result of the imprudences of the late Reverend Mother, one of the best and holiest of women, but unfortunately not endowed with sufficient business foresight. He was quite prepared to admit that the little wooden chapel which had preceded the present chapel was inadequate, and that she was justified in building another, but not in expending nearly one thousand pounds in stained glass. The new chapel had cost ten thousand pounds, and the interest of this money had to be paid. There were other debts—
"But there is no reason why I should weary you with an exact statement."
"But you do not weary me, Monsignor; I am, on the contrary, deeply interested."
"The convent owes a great deal to the late Reverend Mother, and the last thing I wish to express is disapproval. We do not know the circumstances, and must not judge her; we know that she acted for the best. No doubt she is now praying to God to secure the safety of her convent."
Evelyn sat watching him, fascinated by the clear, peremptory, ecclesiastical dignity which he represented. If he had a singing voice, she said to herself, it would be a tenor. He had allowed the conversation to wander from the convent to the concert; and they were soon talking of their musical preferences. There was an impersonal tenderness, a spiritual solicitude in his voice which enchained her; no single idea held her, but wave after wave of sensation passed, transforming and dissolving, changeable as a cloud. Human life demands hope, and the priest is a symbol of hope; there is always a moment when the religionist doubts, and there is also a moment when the atheist says, "Who knows, perhaps." And this man had done what she had not been able to do: he had put aside the paltry pleasures of the world, he placed his faith in things beyond the world, pleasures which perchance were not paltry. An entirely sensual life was a terrible oppression; hers often weighed upon her like a nightmare; to be happy one must have an ideal and strive to live up to it. Her mind flickered and sank, changing rapidly as an evening sky, never coming to anything distinct enough to be called a thought. She desired to hear him speak, she felt that she must speak to him about religion; she wanted to

know if he were sure, and how he had arrived at his certitudes.... She wanted to talk to him about life, death and immortality. She had tried to lead the conversation into a religious discussion, but he seemed to avoid it, and just as she was about to put a definite question, Ulick came into the room. He stood crushing his grey felt hat between his hands, a somewhat curious figure, and she watched him talking to Monsignor, thinking of the difference of vision. As Ulick said, everything was in that. Men were divided by the difference of their visions. She was curious to know how the dogmatic and ritualistic vision of Monsignor affected Ulick, and when the prelate left she asked him.

He was as ingenuous and unexpected on this subject as he was on all subjects. If the antique priest, he said, clothed himself in purple, it was to produce an exaltation in himself which would bring him closer to the idea, which would render him, as it were, accessible to it. But the vestments of the modern priest had lost their original meaning, they were mere parade. This explanation was very like Ulick; she smiled, and was interested, but her interest was passing and superficial. The advent of the priest had moved her in the depths of her being, and her mind was thick with lees of ancient sentiment, and wrecks of belief had floated up and hung in mid memory. She knew that the beauty of the ritual, the eternal psalms, the divine sacrifice, the very ring of the bell, the antiquity of the language, lifted her out of herself, and into a higher, a more intense ecstasy than the low medium of this world's desires. And if she did not believe that the bread and wine were the true body and blood of God, she still believed in the real Presence. She was aware of it as she might be of the presence of someone in the room, though he might be hidden from her eyes. Though the bread and wine might not be the body and blood of Christ, still the act of consecration did seem to her to call down the spirit of God, and it had seemed to her to inhabit the church at the moment of consecration. It might not be true to Owen, nor yet to Ulick, but it was true to her—it was a difference of vision.... She sat buried in herself. Then she walked to the window confused and absorbed, with something of the dread of a woman who finds herself suddenly with child. When Ulick came to her she did not notice him, and when he asked her to do some music with him she refused, and when he put his arms about her she drew away sullenly, almost resentfully.

A few days after she was in Park Lane. She had gone there to pay some bills, and she was going through them when she was startled by the front door bell. It was a visitor without doubt. Her thoughts leaped to Monsignor, and her face lighted up. But he did not know she was at Park Lane; he would not go there.... It was Owen come up from Bath. What should she say to him? Good heavens! It was too late to say she was not at home. He was already on the stairs. And when he entered he divined that he was not welcome. They sat opposite each other, trying to talk. Suddenly he besought her not to throw him over.... She had to refuse to kiss him, and that was convincing, he said. Once a woman was not greedy for kisses, the end was near. And his questions were to the point, and irritatingly categorical. Had she ever been unfaithful to him? Did she love Ulick Dean? Not content with a simple denial, he took her by both hands, and looking her straight in the face, asked her to give him her word of honour that Ulick Dean was not her lover, that she had never kissed him, that she had never even desired to kiss him, that no idea of love making had ever arisen between them. She pledged her word on every point, and this was the second time that her *liaison* with Ulick had obliged her to lie, deliberately in so many words. Nor did the lying even end there. He wanted her to stay, to dine with him; she had to invent excuses—more lies.

She was returning to Dulwich in her carriage, and until she arrived home her thoughts hankered and gnawed, pestered and terrified her. Never had she felt so ashamed, so disgusted with herself, and the after taste of the falsehoods she had told came back into her mouth, and her face grew dark in the beautiful summer evening. Her brows were knit, and she resolved that if the occasion happened again, she would tell Owen the truth. This was no mock determination; on this point she was quite sure of herself. Looking round she saw the mean streets of Camberwell. She saw them for a moment, and then she sank back into her reverie.

She was deceiving Owen, she was deceiving her father, she was deceiving Ulick, she was deceiving Monsignor—he would not have thought of asking her to sing at the concert if he knew what a life was hers. Nor would those good women at the convent accept her aid if they knew what kind of woman she was. And the strange thing was that she did not believe herself to be a bad woman; at the bottom of her heart she loved truth and sincerity. She wished to have an ideal and to live up to it, yet she was doing the very opposite. That was what was so strange, that was what she did not understand, that was what made her incomprehensible to herself. She sighed, and at the bottom of her heart there lay an immense weariness, a weariness of life, of the life she was leading, and she longed for a life that would coincide with her principles, and she felt that if she did not change her life, she would do something desperate. She might kill herself.

It is true that man is a moral animal, but it is not true that there is but one morality; there are a thousand, the morality of each race is different, the morality of every individual differs. The origin of each sect is the desire to affirm certain moral ideas which particularly appeal to it; every change of faith is determined by the moral temperament of the individual; we prefer this religion to that religion because our moral ideas are more implicit in these affirmations than in those.

The restriction of sexual intercourse is the moral ideal of Western Europe; it is the one point on which all Christians are agreed; it is the one point on which they all feel alike. So inherent is the idea of sexual continence in the Western hemisphere that even those whose practice does not coincide with their theory rarely impugn the wisdom of the law which they break; they prefer to plead the weakness of the flesh as their excuse, and it is with reluctance that they admit that without an appeal to conscience it would be impossible to prove that it is wrong for two unmarried people to live together. It is not perceived that the fact that no material proof can be produced strengthens rather than weakens the position of the moralist. To do unto others as you would be done unto, to love your neighbour as yourself, are practical moralities which may be derived from social necessities, but the abstract moralities, that sexual intercourse is wrong except between married people, and that it is wrong to tell a lie, even if the lie be a perfectly harmless one, exist of themselves. That we cannot bring abstract moralities into the focus of our understanding is no argument. As well deny the stars because we cannot understand them. That abstract moralities impose on us should be a sufficient argument that they cannot be the futilities that Owen would argue them to be—not them, he only protested against one.... (She had not thought of that before—Owen was no more rational than she.) That the idea of chastity should persist in spite of reason is proof of its truth. For what more valid argument in favour of a chaste life than that the instinct of chastity abides in us? After all, what we feel to be true is for us the greatest truth, if not the only real truth. Ulick was nearer the truth than Owen. He had said, "A sense which eludes all the other senses and which is not apprehensible to reason governs the world, all the rest is circumstantial, ephemeral. Were man stripped one by one of all his attributes, his intelligence, his knowledge, his industry, as each of these shunks was broken up and thrown aside, the kernel about which they had gathered would be a moral sense."

Evelyn remembered that when she had sent Owen away before, he had said, "Sexual continence at best is not the whole of morality; from your use of the word one would think that it was." But for her the sexual conscience was the entire conscience—she had no temptation to steal. There was lying, but she was never tempted to tell lies except for one reason; she could not think of herself telling a lie for any other. To her the sexual sin included all the others. She turned her head aside, for the bitterness of her conscience was unendurable, and she vowed that, whatever happened, she would speak the truth if Owen questioned her again. She could never bring herself to tell such horrible falsehoods again.

These revulsions of feeling alternated with remembrances of Owen's tenderness; fugitive sensations of him tingled in her veins, and ill-disposed her to Ulick. She spoke little, and sat with averted eyes. When he asked her if he should come to her room, she answered him peremptorily; and he heard her lock her door with a determined hand.

As she lay in bed, conscious of the inextricable tangle of her life, it was knotting so closely and rapidly that her present double life could not endure much longer, the odious taste of the lies she had told that afternoon rose again to her lips, and, as if to quench the bitterness, she vowed that she would tell Owen the truth ... if he asked her. If he did not ask her she would have to bear the burden of her lies. She tried not to wish that he might ask her. Then questions sallied from every side. She could not marry Owen without telling him about Ulick. She could not marry Ulick without telling him that she had been unfaithful to him with Owen. Should she send away Owen and marry Ulick, or would it be better to send away Ulick and marry Owen—if he would marry her after he had heard her confession? It was unendurable to have to tell lies all day long—yes, all day long—of one sort or another. She ought to send them both away.... But could she remain on the stage without a lover? Could she go to Bayreuth by herself? Could she give up the stage? And then?

She awoke in a different mood—at least, it seemed to her that her mood was different. She was not thinking of Owen, of the lies she had told him; and she could talk gaily with Ulick about the concert she had promised to sing at. She seemed inclined to take the whole responsibility of this concert upon her own shoulders. As Ulick said, it was impossible for her to take a small part in any concert.

They were driving in Richmond Park, not far from the convent. The autumn-tinted landscape, the vicissitudes of the woods, and the plaintive air brought a tender yearning into her mood, and she contrasted the lives of those poor, holy women with her own life. Ulick did not intrude himself; he sat silent by her, and she thought of Monsignor. Sometimes he was no more than a little shadow in the background of her mind; but he was never wholly absent, and that day all matters were unconsciously referred to him. She was curious to know what his opinions were of the stage; and as they returned home in the short, luminous autumn evening, she seemed to discover suddenly the fact that she was no longer as much interested in the stage as she used to be. She even thought that she would not greatly care if she never sang on the stage again. Last night she had put the thought aside as if it were madness, to-day it seemed almost natural. Thinking of the poor sisters who lived in prayer and poverty on the edge of the common, she remembered that her life was given up to the portrayal of sensual emotion on the stage. She remembered the fierce egotism of the stage—an egotism which pursued her into every corner of her life. Compared with the lives of the poor sisters who had renounced all that was base in them, her life was very base indeed. In her stage life she was an agent of the sensual passion, not only with her voice, but with her arms, her neck and hair, and every expression of her face, and it was the craving of the music that had thrown her into Ulick's arms. If it had subjugated her, how much more would it subjugate and hold within its sensual persuasion the ignorant listener—the listener who would perceive in the music nothing but its sensuality. Why had the Church not placed stage life under the ban of mortal sin? It would have done so if it knew what stage life was, and must always be. She then wondered what Monsignor thought of the stage, and from the moment her curiosity was engaged on this point it did not cease to trouble her till it brought her to the door of the presbytery. The ostensible object of her visit was to make certain proposals to Monsignor regarding the music she was to sing at the concert.

She was shown into a small room; its one window was so high up on the wall that the light was dim in the room, though outside there was brilliant sunshine. The sadness of the little room struck cold upon her, and she noticed the little space of floor covered with cocoa-nut matting, and how it grated under the feet. The furniture was a polished oak table, with six chairs to match. A pious print hung on each wall. One was St. Monica and St. Augustine, and the rapt expression of their faces reminded her that she might be bartering a divine inheritance for a coarse pleasure that left but regret in the heart. And it was in such heartsick humour that Monsignor found her. He seemed to assume that she needed his help, and the tender solicitude with which he wished to come to her aid was in itself a consolation. She was already an incipient penitent as she told him of her project to bring an orchestra at her own expense to Wimbledon, and give the forest murmurs with the Bird Song from "Siegfried." Monsignor left everything to her; he placed himself unreservedly in her hands. After a long silence she pushed a cheque for fifty pounds across the table, begging him not to mention the name of the giver. She was singing for them, that was sufficient obligation. He approved of her delicacy of feeling, thanked her for her generosity, and the business of the interview seemed ended.

"I'm so much obliged to you, Monsignor Mostyn, for having come to me, for having given me an opportunity of doing some good with my money. Hitherto, I'm ashamed to say, I've spent it all on myself. It has often seemed to me intolerably selfish, and I often felt that I must do something, only I did not know what to do."

Then, feeling that she must take him into her confidence, she asked him what proportion of our income we should devote to charity. He said it was impossible to fix a precise sum, but he knew many deserving cases, and offered to advise her in the distribution of whatever money she might decide to spend in charity. Suddenly his manner changed; he even seemed to wish her to stay, and the conversation turned back to music. The conversation was mundane as possible, and it was only now and then, by some slight allusion to the Church, that he reminded Evelyn, and perchance himself, that the essential must be distinguished from the circumstantial.

Again and again the temptation rose up, it seemed to look out from her very eyes, and she was so conscious of this irresistible desire to speak to him of herself that she no longer heard him, and hardly saw the blank wall with the pious print upon it.

"I have not told you, Monsignor," she said at last, "that I am leaving the stage."

She knew that he must ask her what had induced her to think of taking so important a step, and then she would have an opportunity of asking his opinion of the stage. Of course neither Ulick's nor Owen's name would be mentioned.

"As at present constituted, the stage is a dangerous influence. Some women no doubt are capable of resisting evil even when surrounded by evil. Even so they set a bad example, for the very knowledge of their virtue tempts others less sure of themselves to engage in the same life, and these weak ones fall. The virtuous actress is like a false light, which instead of warning vessels from the rocks entices them to their ruin."

He did not indite the Oberammergau Passion Play, but he could not accept "Parsifal." He had heard Catholics aver, while approving of the performance of "Parsifal," that they would not wish to see the piece performed out of Bayreuth. But he failed to understand this point of view altogether. It seemed to assume that a parody of the Mass was unobjectionable at Bayreuth, though not elsewhere. If there was no parody of the Mass, why should they say that they would not like to see the piece performed elsewhere? He had read the book and knew the music, and could not understand how a great work of art could contain scenes from real life. Whether these be religious ceremonies or social functions, the artistic sin is the same. He asked Evelyn why she was smiling, and she told him that it was because the only two whom she had heard disapprove of "Parsifal" were Monsignor Mostyn and Ulick Dean. It seemed strange that two such extremes should agree regarding the profligacy of "Parsifal." Monsignor was interested for a moment in Ulick Dean's views, and then he said—

"But was it with the intention of consulting me, Miss Innes, that you introduced the subject? I hear that you are going to play the principal part next year—Kundry."

"Nothing is settled. As I told you just now, Monsignor, I am thinking of leaving the stage, and your opinions concerning it do not encourage me to remain an actress."

"My dear child, you have had the good fortune to be brought up in holy Church. You have, I hope, constant recourse to the sacraments. You have confided the difficulties of your stage life to your confessor. How does he advise you?"

Raising her eyes, Evelyn said in a sinking voice—

"Even if one has doubts about the whole doctrine of the Church, it is still possible to wish to lead a good life. Don't you think so, Monsignor?"

"There are many Protestants who lead excellent lives. But I have always noticed that when a Catholic begins to question the doctrine of the Church, his or her doubts were preceded by a desire to lead an irregular life."

And in the silence Evelyn became aware of the afternoon sun shining through the window above their heads, enlivening the dark parlour. It seemed strange to sit discussing such subjects in the sunshine. The ray that fell through the window lighted up the priest's thin face till it seemed like one of the wood carvings she had seen in Germany. When he resumed the conversation it was to lead her to speak of herself and the reasons which had suggested an abandonment of her stage career. The tender, impersonal kindness of the priest drew her out of herself, and she told him how she had begun to perceive that the stage had ceased to interest her as it had once done; she spoke of vulgarity and parade, yet that was not quite what she meant; it had come to seem to her like so much waste, as if she were wasting her time in doing things that did not matter, like grown people would feel if they were asked to pass the afternoon playing with dolls. Shrugging her shoulders hysterically, she said she could not explain.

"But have you an idea of what life you wish to lead?"

"No, I don't think I have; I only know that I am not happy in my present life."

"I believe you see a good deal of Sir Owen Asher. He helped you, did he not, in your musical education?"

"Yes," she answered under her breath. "He is an intimate friend." In a moment of unexpected courage, she said, "Do you know him, Monsignor?"

"I have heard a good deal about him, and nothing, I regret to say, to his credit. He is, I believe, an avowed atheist, and does not hesitate to declare his unbelief in every society, and to make open boast of an immoral life. He has read and tried to understand a little more than the people with whom he associates. I suppose the doubts you entertain regarding the doctrine of the Church are the result of his teaching?"

With a little pathetic air, Evelyn admitted that Owen had used every possible argument to destroy her faith. She had read Huxley, Darwin, and a little Herbert Spencer.

"Herbert Spencer! Miserable collections of trivial facts, bearing upon nothing. Of what value, I ask, can it be to suffering humanity to know that such and such a fact has been observed and described? Then the general law! rubbish, ridiculous rubbish!"

"The scientists fail to see that what we feel matters much more than what we know."

"True, quite true," he said, turning sharply and looking at her with admiration. Then, recollecting himself, he said, "But God does not exist because we feel He exists. He exists not through us, but through Himself, from all time and through all eternity. To feel is better than to observe, to pray is better than to inquire, but indiscriminate abandonment to our feelings would lead us to give credence to every superstition. You have, I perceive, escaped from the rank materialism of Sir Owen's teaching, but whither are you drifting, my dear child? You must return to the Church; without the Church, we are as vessels without a rudder or compass."

He walked up and down the room as though debating with himself. Evelyn held her breath, wondering what new turn the conversation would take. Suddenly she lost her courage, and overcome with fear got up to go, and Monsignor, considering that enough had been said, did not attempt to detain her. But as he bade her good-bye at the door, his keen eye fixed upon her, he added, "Remember, I do not admit your difficulties to be intellectual ones. When you come to realise that for yourself, I shall be glad to do all in my power to help you. God bless you, my child!"

If only she could put the whole thing aside—refuse to bother her head any more, or else believe blindly what she was told. She hated wobbling, yet she did nothing else. Suddenly she felt that if she were to believe at all, it must be like Monsignor. The magnetism of his faith thrilled her, and, in a moment, it had all became real to her. But it was too late. She could never do all her religion asked. Her whole life would have to come to pieces; nothing of it would remain, and she entirely lost heart when she considered in detail the sacrifices she would have to make. She saw herself at Dulwich with her father, giving singing lessons, attending the services, and living about St. Joseph's. She saw herself singing operas in every capital, and always a new lover at her heels. Both lives were equally impossible to her. As she lay back in her carriage driving through the lazy summer streets, she almost wished she had no conscience at all. What was the use of it? She had just enough to spoil her happiness in wrong-doing, yet not enough to prevent her doing what deep down in her heart she knew to be wrong.

That evening she wrote a number of letters, and begged a subscription of every friend—Owen was out of the question and she hesitated whether she should make use of Ulick. She would have liked to have left him out of this concert altogether, and it was only because she had no one else whom she could depend upon that she consented to let him go off in search of the necessary tenor. But to take him to the concert did not seem right.

She dipped her pen in the ink, and then laid it down, overcome by a sudden and intolerable melancholy. She could have cried, so great was her weariness with the world, so worthless did her life seem. She had begged her father's forgiveness; he had forgiven her, but she had not sent away her lover.... She had told Monsignor that, in consequence of certain scruples of conscience, she intended to give up the stage, but she had not told him that she had taken another lover and brought him to live with her under her father's roof. Whether there was a God and a hereafter, or merely oblivion, such conduct as hers was surely wrong. She walked to and fro, and came to a resolution regarding her relations with Ulick, at all events in her father's house.

Then life seemed perfectly hopeless, and she wished Monsignor had not come to see her. What could she do to shake off this clammy and unhealthy depression which hung about her? She might go for a walk, but where? The perspective of the street recalled the days when she used to stand at the window wondering if nothing would ever happen to her. She remembered the moment with singular distinctness when she heard the voice crying within her? "Will nothing ever happen? Will this go on for ever?" She remembered the very tree and the very angle of the house! Dulwich was too familiar; it was like living in a room where there was nothing but mirrors. Dulwich was one vast mirror of her past life. In Dulwich she was never living in the present. She could not see Dulwich, she could only remember it. One walk more in that ornamental park! She knew it too well! And the picture gallery meant Owen—she would only see him and hear his remarks. Her thoughts reverted to his proposal of marriage and her acceptance. Not for the whole world! Why, she did not know. He had been very good to her. Her ingratitude shocked her. She shrugged her shoulders hysterically; she could not help it—that was how she felt.

But Ulick? Should she marry him and accept the Gods? That would settle everything.

But a sense of humour solves nothing, and at that moment the servant brought her a small brown paper parcel. It looked like a book. It was a book. She opened it. Monsignor had sent her a book. As she turned the leaves she remembered the parcels of books from Owen which she used to open in the same room, sitting in the same chair. *Sin and its Consequences*! She began reading it. On one point she was sure, that sin did exist.... If we felt certain things to be wrong, they were wrong; at least they were wrong for those who thought them wrong, and she had never been able to feel that it was right to live with a man to whom she was not married. Everyone had a moral code. Owen would not cheat at cards, and he thought it mean to tell lies—a very poor code it was, but still he acted up to it. She did not know how Ulick felt on such matters; his beliefs, though numerous and picturesque, supplied no moral code, and she could not live on symbols, though perhaps they were better than Owen's theories. Her mistake from the beginning was in trying to acquire a code of morals which did not coincide with her feelings. But the teaching in this book did coincide with her feelings. Could she follow it? That was the point. Could she live without a lover? Owen thought not. She laughed and then walked about the room, unable to shake off a dead weight of melancholy. Though the Church was all wrong, and there was no God, she was still leading a life which she felt to be wrong; and if the Church were right, and there was a resurrection, her soul was lost. She took up the book and read till her fears became so intense that she could read no more, and she walked up and down the room, her nerves partially unstrung. In the evening she talked a great deal and rapidly, apparently not quite aware of what she was saying, or else her face wore a brooding look; sometimes it awakened a little, and then her eyes were fixed on Ulick. The next day was Friday, and as the train service seemed complex and inconvenient, and as she had not at Dulwich a suitable dress to wear at the concert, she decided to sleep at Park Lane and drive to Wimbledon in the afternoon. She left her father, promising to return to him soon, and she had told Ulick that she thought it better he should return by train. She saw that he had noticed the book in her hand, and she knew that he understood her plea that she did not wish to be seen driving with him to mean that she was going to call on Monsignor on her way home. She had thought of calling at St. Joseph's, but, unable to think of a sufficient excuse for the visit, had abandoned the idea. She knew the time was not opportune. Monsignor would be hearing confessions. But as the carriage turned out of Camberwell, she remembered that it would be polite to thank him for the book, and leaning forward she told the coachman to drive to St. Joseph's.... So after all she was going there.... Ulick was right.

The attendant told her that Monsignor was hearing confessions, and would not be free for another half-hour. She drew a breath of relief, for this second visit had frightened her. The attendant asked her if she would wait. She thought she would like to wait in church. She desired its collectedness, its peace. But the thought of Monsignor's confessional frightened her, and she thanked the attendant hurriedly, and went slowly to her carriage.

When Ulick came in that evening she was seated on the corner of the sofa near the window. The moon was shining on the breathless park, and a moth whirled between the still flames of the candles which burned on the piano. He noticed that her mood was subdued and reflective. She liked him to sit by her, to take her hand and tell her he loved her. She liked to listen to him, but not to music; nor would she sing that evening, and his questions as to the cause remained unanswered. Her voice was calm and even, and seemed to come from far away. There was a tremor in his, and between whiles they watched and wondered at the flight of the moth. It seemed attracted equally by darkness and light. It emerged from the darkness, fluttered round the perilous lights and returned again to its natural gloom. But the temptation could not be resisted, and it fell singed on the piano.

"We ought to have quenched those candles," Evelyn said.

"It would have found others," Ulick answered, and he took the maimed moth on to the balcony and trod it out of its misery. They sat there under the little green verandah, and in the colour of the clear night their talk turned on the stars and the Zodiacal signs. Ulick was born under the sign of Aquarius, and all the important events of his life began when Aquarius was rising. Pointing to a certain group of stars, he said—

"The story of Grania is no more than our story, your story, my story, and the story of Sir Owen Asher, and I had written my poem before I saw you." Then, as a comment on this fact, he added, "We should be careful what we write, for what we write will happen. Grania is the beautiful fortune which we will strive for, which chooses one man to-day and another to-morrow."

The idea interested her for a moment, but she was thinking of her project to find out if, like Owen, he thought that the virtue of chastity was non-essential in women, or if the other virtues were dependent upon it. But how to lead the conversation back to this question she did not for the moment know. At last she said—"You ask me to love you—but to be my lover you would have to surrender all your spiritual life, that which is most to you, that which makes your genius. Do you think it worth it?"

He hesitated, then answered her with some vague reference to destiny, but she guessed the truth. As free as Owen himself from ethical scruples, he still felt that we should overcome our sexual nature. She asked herself why: and she wondered just as Owen wondered when confronted by her religious conscience. They looked at each other long and gravely, and he told her of the great seer who had collected in her own person all the cryptic revelation, all the esoteric lore of the East. He admitted that she had allowed carnal intercourse to some of her disciples while forbidding it to others.
"Evidently judging chastity to be in some cases essential to the other virtues."
She heard him say that a sect of mystics to which he belonged, or perhaps it was whose society he frequented, advised the married state but with this important reservation, that instead of corporal possession they should endeavour to aid each other to rise to a higher spiritual plane, anticipating in this life a little the perfect communion of spirit which awaited them in the next. But such theories did not appeal to Evelyn. She could only understand the renunciation of the married state for the sake of closer intimacy with the spiritual life; and she was more interested when he told her of the cruelties, the macerations and the abstinences which the Indian seers resorted to, so that the opacity of the fleshly envelope might be diminished and let the soul through. In modern, as in the most ancient ages, with the scientist as with the seer, marvels and prodigies are reached through the subjugation of the flesh; as life dwindles like a flame that a breath will quench, the spirit attains its maximum, and the abiding and unchanging life that lies beyond death waxes till it becomes the real life.
"Is this life, then, not real?"
"If reality means what we understand, could anything be more unreal?"
"Then you do believe in a future state?"
"Yes, I certainly believe in a future state.... So much so that it seems impossible to believe that life ends utterly with death."
But to Evelyn's surprise, he seemed to doubt the immortality of this future state, and fell back on the Irish doctrine which holds that after death you pass to the great plain or land under the sea, or the land over the sea, or the land of the children of the goddess Dana.
"Even now my destiny is accomplishing."
The true Celt is still a pagan—Christianity has been superimposed. It is little more than veneer, and in the crises of life the Celt turns to the ancient belief of his race. But did Ulick really believe in Angus and Lir and the Great Mother Dana? Perhaps he merely believed that as a man of genius it was his business to enroll himself in the original instincts and traditions of his race.
They were as unquiet as cattle before an approaching storm, and when they returned to the drawing-room it seemed to him like a scene in a theatre about to be withdrawn to make way for another part of the story. Even while looking at it, it seemed to have receded a little.
At last it was time for Ulick to go. As they said good-night he asked her if he should come to lunch. She looked at him, uncertain if she ought to take him to the concert at all.

CHAPTER TWENTY-SEVEN

Monsignor, who was waiting for her at the steps of the hall which had been hired for the concert, introduced her to Father Daly, the convent chaplain. She shook hands with him, and caught sight of him as she did so. It was but a passing glance of a small, blonde man with white eyelashes, seemingly too shy to raise his eyes; and she was too stringently occupied with other thoughts to notice him further.
Owing to her exertions and Monsignor Mostyn's, a large audience had been collected, and though the month was September, there were many fashionable, influential and musical people present.
The idea of the band, which Evelyn had thought of bringing down in the intention of giving the Forest Murmurs and the Bird Music, had been abandoned, but the finest exponent of

Wagner on the piano had come to play the usual things: the closing scene of the "Walküre," the overture of the "Meistersinger" and the Prelude of "Tristan." And, mingled with the students and apostles from London, were a goodly number of young men and women from the various villas. Every degree of Wagner culture was present, from the ten-antlered stag who had seen "Parsifal" given under the eye of the master to the skipping fawns eagerly browsing upon the motives. "That is the motive of the Ride; that, dear, is the motive of the Fire; that is the motive of Slumber in the Fire, and that is the motive of Siegfried, the pure hero who will be born to save Valhalla." The class above had some knowledge of the orchestration. "You see," said a young man, pointing to the score, "here he is writing for the entire orchestra." "Three bars farther on he is writing for three violins and a flute. He withdraws his instruments in a couple of bars; it would take anyone else five-and-twenty." At a little distance the old stag who had never missed a festival at Bayreuth was telling the young lady at his side that the "Walküre" is written in the same style as the "Rheingold" and the first two acts of "Siegfried." Another distinct change of style came with the third act of "Siegfried" and the "Dusk of the Gods," which were not composed till some years later. "Ah, that wonderful later style! That scale of half-notes! Flats and sharps introduced into every bar; C, C sharp; D, D sharp; E, F, F sharp; G, G sharp; A, B flat, B, C. In that scale, or what would seem to be that scale, he balances himself like an acrobat, springing on to the desired key without preparation," and so on until the old stag was interrupted by a friend, a lady who had just recognised him. As she squeezed past, she stopped to tell him that Wagner had spoiled her for all other music. She had been to hear Beethoven's "Eroica" Symphony once more, but it had seemed to her like a pious book.

Evelyn sang "Elsa's Dream," "Elizabeth's Prayer" and the "Liebestod," and when she was recalled at the end of the concert, she sang Senta's ballad as a *bonne bouche*, something that the audience had not expected, and would send her friends away more than ever pleased with her.

Her father had not been able to come—that was a disappointment—but Ulick had accompanied her beautifully, following her voice, making the most of it at every moment. When she left the platform, she took both his hands and thanked him. She loved him in that instant as a musician and as a mistress. But the joy of the moment, the ecstasy of admiration, was interrupted by Monsignor Mostyn and Father Daly. They too wished to thank her. In his courtly manner, Monsignor told her of the pleasure her singing had given him. But when Father Daly mentioned that the nuns expected her to tea, her courage seemed to slip away. The idea of a convent frightened her, and she tried to excuse herself, arguing that she had to go back to London.

"If you're engaged for dinner, I'm afraid there will not be time," Monsignor said. She looked up, and, meeting his eyes, did not dare to lie to him.

"No; I'm not dining out, but I promised to take Mr. Dean back in my carriage."

"Mr. Dean will, I'm sure, not mind waiting."

It seemed to Evelyn that Monsignor suspected her relations with Ulick, and to refuse to go to the convent, she thought, would only confirm him in his suspicions. So she accepted the invitation abruptly, and when they turned to go, she said—

"My carriage is here; I'll drive you," and, at the same moment, she remembered that Ulick was waiting. But she felt that she could not drive back to London with him after leaving the convent, and she hoped that Monsignor would not correctly interpret the disappointment which was plain upon his face. No; he must go back by train—no, there would be no use his calling that evening at Park Lane.

She wore a black and white striped silk dress, with a sort of muslin bodice covered with lace, and there was a large bunch of violets in her waistband. The horses were beautiful in the sunshine, and their red hides glistened in the long, slanting rays. She put up her parasol and tried to understand, but she could only see the angles of houses, and the eccentricity of every passer-by. She saw very clearly the thin, facial line, and her eyes rested on the touch of purple at the throat to mark his Roman dignity. Father Daly sat opposite, rubbing his thumbs like one in the presence of a superior. He was not ill-looking, but so shy that his features passed unperceived, and it was some time before she saw his eyes; they were always cast down, and his thin, well-cut nose disappeared in his freckled cheeks. The cloth he wore was coarser than Monsignor's; his heavy shoes contrasted with the finely-stitched and buckled shoes of the Papal prelate.

This visit to the convent frightened Evelyn more than the largest audience that had ever assembled to hear her, and, until they got clear of the town, she was not certain she would not plead some excuse and tell the coachman to turn back. But now it was too late. The carriage ascended the steep street, and, at the top of it, the town ended abruptly at the edge of the common. On one side was a high brick wall, hiding the grounds and gardens of the villas; on the other was the common, seen through the leaves of a line of thin trees. In her nervous agitation, she saw very distinctly—the foreground teeming with the animation of cricket, the more remote parts solitary, the windmill hovering in a corner out of the way of the sunset, and two horsemen and a horsewoman cantering along the edge of the long valley into which the plain dropped precipitously. The sun sank in a white sky, and Evelyn caught the point of one of the ribs of her parasol, so that she could hold it in a better position to shade her eyes, and she saw how the houses stretched into a point, the last being an inn, no doubt the noisy resort of the cricketers and the landscape painters. There was a painter making his way towards the valley, his paint-box on his back. But at that moment the carriage turned into a lane where a paling enclosed the small gardens. She then noticed the decaying pear or apple tree, to which was attached a clothes-line. Enormous sunflowers weltered in the dusty corners. The brick was crumbling and broken, beautiful in colour, "And in every one of these cottages someone is living; someone is laughing; someone will soon be dead. Good heavens, how strange!"

"We are nearly there."

Evelyn started; it was Father Daly speaking to her. "The cottages have spoilt the appearance on this side, but the view is splendid from the other."

The lane ascended and Evelyn remembered how the house stood inside a wall behind some trees, looking westward, the last southern end of the common land as the windmill was the last northern end. There had been iron gates when a great City merchant lived in the Georgian house, which had been gradually transformed to suit the requirements of the sisters. The melancholy little peal of the bell hanging on a loose wire sounded far away, and in the interval Evelyn noticed the large double door, from which the old green paint was peeling. A step was heard within, and the little shutter which closed the grated peephole in the panel of the door was drawn back; the eyes and forehead band of a nun appeared for an instant in the opening; and then with a rattle of keys the door was hastily opened and the little porteress, with ruddy cheeks and a shy smile, stood aside to let Evelyn pass in. She kissed the hand of Monsignor as he turned to her with a kindly word of salutation. "The Reverend Mother is expecting you," she said, her agitation being due to the importance of the occasion.

"No doubt they have been praying that I might sing well, poor dears," Evelyn thought, as she followed the nun up the paved, covered way. Through the iron frame-work, woven through and through with creepers and monthly roses, she caught glimpses of the partly-obliterated carriage drive, and of the neatly-kept flower beds filled with geraniums and tall, white asters. In the hall an Adam's ceiling radiated in graceful lines from a central medallion, and before a statue of the Sacred Heart a light was burning. Evelyn remembered how the poor lay sisters laboured to keep the stone floor spotless, and it was into the parlour on the left, which Evelyn remembered to be the best parlour, that Sister Angela ushered them.

In the old days, before a sudden crisis on the Stock Exchange had obliged the owner to sell the house for much less than its true value to the little community of sisters of the Passion who were then seeking a permanent house, this room, round which Evelyn and the two priests were looking for seats, had been used as a morning-room. Three long French windows looked out on the garden, and the flowers and air made it a bright, cheerful room, in spite of the severe pictures on the walls. She recognised at once the engraving of Leonardo's "Last Supper" which hung over the solid marble chimney piece a little above the statue of Our Lady of Lourdes and the two blue vases, and also the pale, distempered walls, and the coloured, smiling portrait of the Pope, and a full-length photograph of Cardinal Manning, signed in his own clear, neat handwriting.

Evelyn and the priests, still undecided where they should sit, looked at the little horsehair sofa. Monsignor brought forward for her one of the six high, straight-backed chairs, and they sat at the circular table laid out with severe books; a volume of the *Lives of the Saints* lay under her hand, and she glanced at a little box for contributions. She looked at the priests and then round the room, striving to penetrate the meaning which it vaguely conveyed to her—an indescribable air of scrupulous neatness and cleanliness, a sense of virginal dulness. But suddenly a startling sense of the incongruity came upon her, that she, the opera-singer, Owen Asher's mistress, should be admitted into a convent, should be received, the honoured guest of holy women. And she got up, leaving the two priests to discuss the financial results of the concert, and stood gazing out at the window. There was the rosery with the lilac bushes shutting out the view of the green fields beyond; and this was the portion of the garden given up to visitors and boarders. She used to walk there during the retreat. Away to the right was the big, sunny garden where the nuns went for their daily recreation. By special permission she had once been allowed there; she remembered the sloping lawns, the fringe of stately elms, and over them the view westward of Richmond Park. She thought of the nuns walking under their trees, half ghost-like, half sybil-like they used to seem in their grey habits with their long grey veils falling picturesquely, their thoughts fixed on an infinite life, and this life never seeming more to them than a little passing shadow.

Evelyn returned slowly to the table. The priests were talking of the convent choir; Monsignor turned to address a question to her, but before he spoke, the door opened and two nuns entered, hardly of this world did they seem in their long grey habits.

The Reverend Mother, a small, thin woman, with eager eyes and a nervous, intimate manner, hastened forward. Evelyn felt that the Reverend Mother could not be less than sixty, yet she did not think of her as an old woman. Between her rapid utterances an expression of sadness came upon her face, instilled through the bright eyes, and Evelyn contrasted her with Mother Philippa, the sub-prioress. Even the touch of these women's hands was different. There was a nervous emotion in the Reverend Mother's hand. Mother Philippa's hand when it touched Evelyn's expressed somehow a simpler humanity.

She was a short, rather stout, homely-faced Englishwoman, about thirty-eight or forty, such a woman as is met daily on the croquet lawns in our suburbs, probably one of three plain sisters, and never could have doubted her vocation.

"I cannot tell you how grateful we are, Miss Innes, for what you have done for us. Monsignor will have told you of the straits we are in.... But you are an old friend, I understand of our convent. Mother Philippa, our sub-prioress, tells me you made a retreat here seven or eight years ago."

"I don't think it was more than six years," Mother Philippa said, correcting the Reverend Mother. "I remember you very well, Miss Innes. You left us one Easter morning."

Evelyn liked her plain, matter-of-fact face, a short face undistinguished by any special characteristic, yet once seen it could not be forgotten, so implicit was it of her practical mind and a desire to serve someone.

"That silly Sister Agnes has forgotten the strawberry jam," she said, when the porteress brought in the tea. "I will run and fetch it; I shan't be a moment."

"Oh, Mother Philippa, pray don't trouble; I prefer some of that cake."

"No, no, I've been thinking all the afternoon of this jam; we make it ourselves; you must have some."

The Reverend Mother apologised for having put sugar in Evelyn's tea, for she remembered now that Evelyn had said that she did not like sugar; and Monsignor took advantage of the occasion to reassure the Reverend Mother that the success of the concert had been much greater than he had anticipated.... Thanks to Miss Innes, he hoped to be able to hand her a cheque for more than two hundred pounds. This was more than double the sum she had hoped to receive.

"We shall always pray for you," she said, taking Evelyn's hand. "I cannot tell you what a load you have taken off my shoulders, for, of course, the main responsibility rests upon me."

Evelyn regretted that the nuns could not have tea with her, and wondered whether they were ever allowed to partake of their own excellent home-made cake. She was beginning to enjoy her visit, and to acquire an interest in the welfare of the convent. She had hitherto only devoted her money to selfish ends; but now she resolved that, if she could help it, these poor sisters should not be driven from their convent. Mother Phillippa asked her suddenly why she had not been to see them before. Evelyn answered that she had been abroad. But living abroad meant to the nun the pleasure of living in Catholic countries, and she was eager to know if Evelyn had had the privilege of going to Rome. She smiled at the nun's innocent curiosity, which she was glad to gratify, and told her about the old Romanesque churches on the Rhine, and the hundred marble spires of the Cathedral of Milan. But in the midst of such pleasant conversation came an unfortunate question. Mother Philippa asked if Evelyn had travelled with her father. Any simple answer would have sufficed, but she lost her presence of mind, and the "No," which came at last was so weak and equivocal that the Reverend Mother divined in that moment some part of the truth. Evelyn sat as if tongue-tied, and it was Monsignor who came to her rescue by explaining that she had sung in St. Petersburg, Vienna, Paris, and all the capitals of Europe.

"You must excuse us," the Reverend Mother said, "for not knowing, but these things do not penetrate convent walls."

The conversation dropped, and the Reverend Mother took advantage of the occasion to suggest that they should visit the chapel.

Mother Philippa walked on with the priests in front, leaving Evelyn with the Reverend Mother.

"I am forced to walk very slowly on account of my heart. I hope you don't mind, Miss Innes?"

"Your heart, Reverend Mother? You suffer from your heart? I'm so sorry."

The Reverend Mother said the new chapel had been built by the celebrated Catholic architect, and mentioned how the last three years of the Reverend Mother's life had been given over to this work Evelyn knew that the mouldings and carving and the stained glass had caused the pecuniary embarrassments of the convent, and did not speak of them She was told that the architect had insisted that every detail should be in keeping, and understood that the thirteenth century had proved the ruin of the convent; every minor decoration was faithful to it—the very patterns stitched in wool on the cushions of the *prie-dieu* were strictly Gothic in character.

Only the lower end of the nave was open to the public; the greater part was enclosed within a high grille of gilded ironwork of an elaborate design, through which Evelyn could vaguely discern the plain oak stalls of the nuns on either side, stretching towards the ornate altar, carved in white stone. And falling through the pointed windows, the long rays slanted across the empty chapel; in the golden air there was a faint sense of incense; it recalled the Benediction and the figures of the departed watchers who had knelt motionless all day before the elevated Host. The faintly-burning lamp remained to inspire the mind with instinctive awe and a desire of worship. And as always, in the presence of the Blessed Sacrament, Evelyn's doubts vanished, and she knelt in momentary prayer beside the two nuns.

Then at her request they went into the garden. It was the part of the convent she remembered best. She recognised at once the broad terrace walk extending the full length of the house, from the new wing to the rose garden whence some steps led to the lower grounds. They

were several acres in extent and sloped gently to the south-west. The Reverend Mother and the priests had turned to the left; they had business matters to discuss and were going round the garden by the outer walk. Evelyn and Mother Philippa chose the middle path. The sunset was before them, and the wistfulness of a distant park sinking into blue mist. Evelyn thought that in all her travels she had never seen anything so lovely as the convent garden in that evening light. It filled her soul with an ecstatic sense of peace and joy, and a sudden passionate desire to share this life of calm and happy seclusion brought tears to her eyes. She could not speak, but Mother Philippa, with a single, quick glance, seemed instinctively to understand, and it was in silence that they walked down a grassy path, that led between the narrow beds filled with a gay tangle of old-fashioned flowers, to a little summer-house. Behind the summer-house, at the bottom of the garden, was a broad walk pleasantly shaded by the overhanging branches of the elms.
"We call this St. Peter's path," Mother Philippa said placidly, "and for his feast the novices put up his statue in the summer-house and decorate it with flowers. They always come here for their mid-day recreation."
"Your garden is quite lovely, Mother Philippa; I remember it all so well."
They wandered on, past the apple and plum trees laden with fruit—they made a pretty orchard in one corner; and while the nun passed here and there gathering flowers, Evelyn stood gazing, recalling all her girlish impressions. Almost every turn in the walks recalled some innocent aspiration, some girlish feeling of love and reverence. In every nook there was a statue of the Virgin, or a cross whereby the thoughts of the passer-by might be recalled to the essential object of her life. She remembered how she had stopped one morning before the crucifix which stood on the top of some rocks at the end of the garden. She had stopped as in a dream, and for a long while had stood looking at the face of the dying Redeemer, praying to his Father for pardon for them that persecuted him. She had felt as if crazed with love, and had walked up the pathway feeling that the one thing of worth in the world was to live for him who had died for her. But she had betrayed him. She had chosen Owen!
Mother Philippa added another flower to the bouquet. She looked at it and, regarding it as finished, she presented it to Evelyn.
"I hope I did not say anything that caused you pain in the parlour. If I did you must know that I did not mean it. I I hope your father is quite well."
"Yes, he's quite well. You did not offend me, Mother Philippa," she said, raising her eyes, and in that moment the two women felt they understood each other in some mute and far-off way.
"The day you left us was Easter Sunday. It was a beautiful morning, and you walked round the rose garden with an old lady; she asked you to sing, and you sung her two little songs."
"Yes, I remember; her hair was quite white, and she walked with a stick."
"I am glad you remember; I feared that you had forgotten, as you were so long coming back. I often prayed for you that you might come and see us. I always felt that you would come back, and when one feels like that, it generally happens."
Evelyn raised her eyes, drawing delight from the nun's happy and contented face. She experienced an exquisite idea, a holy intimacy of feeling; there was a breathless exaltation in the heavens and on the earth, and the wild cry of a startled bird darting through the shrubberies sounded like a challenge or defiance. The sunset grew narrower in the slate-coloured sky, and the long plain of the common showed under two bars of belated purple. The priests and the Reverend Mother went up the steps and were about to enter the convent. Evelyn and Mother Philippa lingered by a distant corner of the garden marked by nine tall crosses.
"When I was here there were but six. I remember Sister Bonaventure, thin and white, and so weak that she could not move. She was dying far from all she knew, yet she was quite happy. It was we who were unhappy."

"She was happy, for her thoughts were set upon God. How could she be otherwise than happy when she knew she was going to him?"

A few minutes after, Evelyn was bidding the nuns good-night. The Reverend Mother hoped that when she made another retreat she would be their guest. Mother Philippa was disappointed that they had not heard her sing. Perhaps one day she might sing to them. They would see how it could be arranged: perhaps at Benediction when she came to make another retreat. Evelyn smiled, and the carriage passed into the night.

CHAPTER TWENTY-EIGHT

The dawn crept through her closed eyelids, and burying her face in the pillows, she sought to retain the receding dream.

But out of the gloom which she divined and through which a face looked, a face which she could not understand, but which she must follow, there came a sound as of someone moving. The dream dissolved in the sound, she opened her eyes, and upon her lips there was terror, and she could not move.... Nor did she dare to look, and when her eyes turned towards the doorway she could not see beyond it; she could not remember if she had left the door ajar. Shadows gathered, and again came the awful sound of someone; she slipped under the bedclothes, and lay there stark, frozen with terror. When she summoned sufficient courage, she looked towards the shadowy doorway, but the passage beyond it was filled with nameless foreboding shapes from an under-world; and the thought that the sound she had heard had been caused by her clothes slipping from a chair failed to reassure her. She was as cold as a corpse in a grave. She felt that it was her duty to explore the dark, but to get out of bed to stand in that grey room and look into the passage was more than she dared; she could only lie still and endure the sensation of hands at her throat and breath above her face.

A little later she was able to distinguish the pattern of the wall-paper, and as she followed its design human life seemed black and intolerably loathsome. She strove against the thought, but she saw the creature leer so plainly that there was no way of escaping from the conviction that what she had accepted as life was but a mask worn by a leper. The vision persisted for what seemed a long while, and when it faded it was pictures of her own life that she read upon the wall; her soul cried out against the miserable record of her sins, and turning on her pillow she saw the dawn—the inexorable light that was taking her back to life, to sin, and all the miserable routine of vanity and selfishness which she would have to begin again. She had left her father, though she knew he would be lonely and unhappy without her. She had lived with Owen when she knew it was wrong, and she had acquiesced in his blasphemies, and by reading evil books she had striven to undermine her faith in God. It seemed to her incredible that anyone should be capable of such wickedness, yet she was that very one; she had committed all sins, and in her great misery she wished herself dead, so that she might think no more.

With eyes wide open to the dawn and to her soul she lay hour after hour. She heard the French clock strike six sharp strokes, and unable to endure her hot bed any longer, she got up, slipped her arms into a dressing-gown, and went down to the drawing-room. It was filled with a grey twilight, and the street was grey-blue and silent save for the sparrows. Sitting on the edge of the sofa she remembered the convent. The nuns had thought her a good Catholic, and she had had to pretend she was. Monsignor, it is true, had turned the conversation and saved her from exposure. But what then? She knew, and he knew, everyone knew; Lady Ascott, Lady Mersey, Lady Duckle very probably didn't care, but appearances had to be preserved, and she had to tell lies to them all. Her life had become a network of lies. There was no corner of her life into which she could look without finding a lie. She had been faithful to no one, not even to Owen. She had another lover, and she had sent Owen away on account of scruples of conscience! She could not understand herself; she had taken Ulick to Dowlands and had lived with him there—in her father's house. So awful did her life seem to her that her thoughts stopped, and she became possessed of the desire of escape which takes a trapped animal and forces it to gnaw off one of its legs. She must escape from this life of lies whatever it cost her; she must free herself. But how? If she went to Monsignor he would tell her she must leave the stage, and she had promised to create the part of Grania. She had promised, and she hated not keeping her promise. He would say it was impossible for her to remain on the stage and live a virtuous life; he would tell her that she must refuse to see Owen. She was still very fond of him, and would like to see him sometimes. What reason could she give to her friends for refusing to see him? what reason could she give for leaving the stage?—to do so would set everyone talking. Everyone would want to know why; Lady Ascott, Lady Mersey, all her friends. How was she to separate herself from her surroundings? Wherever she went she would be known. Her friends would follow her, lovers would follow her, temptations would begin again, would she have strength to resist? "Not always," was the answer her heart gave back. A great despair fell upon her, and she walked up the room. Stopping at the window she looked out, and all reform of her life seemed to her impossible. She was hemmed in on every side. If she could only think of it no more! She had adopted an evil life and must pursue it to the end. She must be wretched in this life, and be punished eternally in the next.

Hearing a footstep on the stairs, she drew herself behind the door, and when the sound passed downstairs she tried to reason with herself. After all, the housemaid would have been merely surprised to find her in the drawing-room at that hour. She could not have guessed why she was there. She ran up the stairs, and when she had closed the door of her room she stood looking at the clock. It was not yet seven, and Herat did not come to her room till half-past nine. She must try to get to sleep between this and then. She lay with her eyes closed, and did not perceive that a thin, shallow sleep had come upon her, for she continued to think the same thoughts; fear of God and hatred of sin assumed even more terrifying proportions, and she started like a hunted animal when Merat came in with her bath. "I hope Mademoiselle is not ill?" "No, I am not ill, only I have not slept at all."

In order to distract her thoughts, she went for a walk after breakfast in the park, but any casual sight sufficed to recall them to the one important question. She could not see the children sailing their toy boats without thinking her ambitions were as futile, and a chance glimpse of a church spire frightened her so that she turned her back and walked the other way. In the afternoon she tried to interest herself in some music, but her hands dropped from the keys, so useless did it appear to her. At four she was dreaming of Owen in an armchair. The servant suddenly announced him, and he came in, seemingly recovered from his gout and his old age. His figure was the perfect elegance of a man of forty-three, and in such beautiful balance that an old admiration awakened in her. His "waistcoats and his valet," she thought, catching sight of the embroideries and the pale, subdued, terrified air of the personal servant. The valet carried a parcel which Evelyn guessed to be a present for her. It was a tea-service of old Crown Derby that Owen had happened upon in Bath, and they spent some time examining its pale roses and gilt pattern. She expected him to refer to their last interview, but he avoided doing so, preferring to take it for granted that he still was her lover, and he did so without giving her sufficient occasion to correct him on this point. He was affectionate and intimate; he sat beside her on the sofa, and talked pleasantly of the benefit he had derived from the waters, of the boredom of hotel life, and of a concert given in aid of a charity.

"But that reminds me," he said; "I heard about the Wimbledon concert, and was sorry you did not write to me for a subscription. Lady Merrington told me about the nuns; they spent all their money building a chapel, and had not enough to eat."

"I didn't think you would care to subscribe to a convent."

"Now, why did you think that? Poor devils of nuns, shut up in a convent without enough to eat. Of course I'll subscribe; I'll send them a cheque for ten pounds to-morrow."

This afternoon, whether by accident or design, he said no word that might jar on her religious scruples; he even appeared to sympathise with religious life, and admitted that the world was not much, and to renounce the world was sublime. The conversation paused, and he said, "I think the tea-service suits the room. You haven't thanked me for it yet, Evelyn."

"I don't know that I ought to accept any more presents from you. I have accepted too much as it is."

She was conscious of her feebleness. It would have been better to have said, "I am another man's mistress," but she could not speak the words, and he asked if they might have tea in the new service. She did not answer, so he rang, and when the servant left the room he took her hands and drew her closer to him. "I am another man's mistress, you must not touch me," rang in her brain, but he did not kiss her, and the truth was not spoken.

"Lady Duckle is still at Homburg, is she not?" he asked, but he was thinking of the inexplicable event each had been in the other's life. They had wandered thus far, now their paths divided, for nothing endures. That is the sadness, the incurable sadness! He was getting too old for her; in a few more years he would be fifty. But he had hoped that this friendship would continue to the end of the chapter. And while he was thinking these things, Evelyn was telling him that Lady Duckle had met Lady Mersey at Homburg, and had gone on with her to Lucerne, where they hoped to meet Lady Ascott.

"You are going to shoot with Lord Ascott next month?" she said, and looking at him she wondered if their relations were after all no more than a chance meeting and parting. While he spoke of Lord Ascott's pheasant shooting, she felt that whatever happened neither could divorce the other from his or her faults.

"How beautiful the park is now, I like the view from your windows. I like this hour; a sense of resignation is in the air."

"Yes," she said, "the sky is beautifully calm," and she experienced a return of old tendernesses, and she had no scruple, for he did not make love to her, and did not kiss her until he rose to leave. Then he kissed her on the forehead and on the cheek, and refrained from asking if they were reconciled.

Never had he been nicer than he had been that afternoon, and she dared not look into her heart, for she did not wish to think that she would send him away. Why should she send him away? why not the other? She could not answer this question; she only knew that the choice had fallen upon Owen. She must send him away, but what reasons should she give? She felt that her conduct that afternoon had rendered a complete rupture in their relations more difficult than ever. It was as she lay sleepless in bed long after midnight that the solution of the difficulty suddenly sounded in her brain. She must write to him saying that he might come to see her once more, but that it must be for the last time. This was the way out of her difficulty, and she turned over in her bed, feeling she might now get to sleep. But instead of sleep there began the very words of this last interview, and her brain teemed with different plans for escape from her lover. She saw herself on ocean steamers, in desert isles, and riding wild horses through mountain passes. Barred doors, changes of name, all means were passed and reviewed; each was in turn dismissed, and the darkness about her bed was like a flame. There was no doubt that she was doomed to another night of insomnia. The bell of the French clock struck three, and, quite exhausted, she got up and walked about the room. "In another hour I shall hear the screech of the sparrow on the window-sill, and may lie awake till Merat comes to call me." She lay down, folded her arms, closed her eyes and began to count the sheep as they came through the gate. But thoughts of Owen began to loom up, and in spite of her efforts to repress them, they grew more and more distinct. The clock struck four, and soon after it seemed to her that the darkness was lightening. For a long while she did not dare to open her eyes. At last she had to open them, and the grey-blue light was indescribably mournful. Again her life seemed small, black and evil. She jumped out of bed, passed her arms into a tea-gown, and paced the room. She must see Owen. She must tell him the truth. Once he knew the truth he would not care for her, and that would make the parting easier for both. She did not believe that this was so, but she had to believe something, and she went down to the drawing-room and wrote—

"DEAR OWEN—You may come and see me to-morrow if you care to. I am afraid that your visit will not be a pleasant one. I don't think I could be an agreeable companion to anyone at present, but I cannot send you away without explaining why. However painful that explanation may be to you, there is at all events this to be said, that it will be doubly painful to me. I am not, dear Owen, ungrateful; that you should think me so is the hardest punishment of all, and I am sorry I have not made you happier. I know other women don't feel as I do, but I can't change myself. I feel dreadfully hypocritical writing in this strain. I, less than anyone have a right to do so, especially now. But you will try to understand. You know that I am not a hypocrite at heart. I am determined to tell you all, and you will then see that no course is open to me but to send you away. Even if you were to promise that we should be friends we must not see each other, but I don't think that you would care to see me on those terms. I should have stopped you yesterday when you took my hand, when you kissed me, but I was weak and cowardly. Somehow I could not bring myself to tell you the truth. I shall expect you in the afternoon, and will tell you all. I am punishing myself as well as you. So please don't try to make things more difficult than they are.—Yours very sincerely, EVELYN INNES."

Leaving this letter with directions that it should be posted at once, weary, and with her brain as clear as crystal, she threw herself upon her bed. Folding her arms, she closed her eyes, and strove to banish thoughts of Owen and the confession she was to make that afternoon. But when sleep gathered about her eyes, the memory of past sins, at first dense, then with greater clearness, shone through, and the traitor sleep moved away. Or she would suddenly find herself in the middle of the interview, the entire dialogue standing clear cut in her brain, she could almost see the punctuation of every sentence. Once more she counted the sheep coming through the gate; she counted and counted, until her imagination failed her, and in spite of herself, her eyes opened upon the dreaded room. She heard the clock strike nine. Merat would knock at her door in another half-hour, and she lay waiting, fearing her arrival. But at last her face grew quieter, she seemed to see Monsignor vaguely, she could not tell where nor how he had come to her, but she heard him saying distinctly that she must never sing Isolde again. He seemed to bar her way to the stage, and the music that was to bring her on sounded in her ears, yet she could see the shape of her room and its furniture. A knock came at the door, and she was surprised to find that she had been asleep.

Her brain was a ferment; it seemed as if it were about to fall out of her head; she feared the day, its meal times and the long hours of morning and evening sunshine. The idea of the coming interview with Owen was intolerable. Her brain was splitting, she could not think of what she would say. But her letter had gone! After breakfast she felt a little rested, and went into the park and remained there till lunch time, dimly aware of the open air, the waving of branches, the sound of human voices. Beyond these, and much more distinct, was a vision of her evil life, and the cold, stern face of the priest watching her. She wandered about, and then hastened back to Park Lane. Owen had been. He had left word that he would call again about three o'clock. He would have stayed, but had an engagement to lunch with friends. She lunched alone, and was sitting on the corner of the sofa, heavy-eyed and weary, but determined to be true to her resolutions, when the servant announced him. He came in hurriedly, his hat in his hand, and his eyes went at once to where she was sitting. He saw she was looking ill, but there were more important matters to speak of.

"I came at once, the moment I got your letter. I should have waited, but I was lunching with Lady Merrington. Such terribly boring people were there. It was all I could do to prevent myself from rushing out of the room. But, Evelyn, what are you determined to tell me? I thought we parted good friends yesterday. You have been thinking it over.... You're going to send me away." He sat beside her, he held his hat in both hands, and looked perplexed and

worried. "But, Evelyn"—she sat like a figure of stone, there was no colour in her cheeks nor any expression in her eyes or mouth—"Evelyn, I am afraid you are ill, you are pale as a ghost."
"I did not sleep last night, nor the night before."
"Two nights of insomnia are enough to break anyone up. I am very sorry, Evelyn, dear—you ought to go away." Her silence perplexed him, and he said, "Evelyn, I have come to ask you to be my wife. Don't keep me in suspense. Will you give up the stage and be my wife? Why don't you answer? Oh, Evelyn, is it—are you married?"
"No, I am not married, Owen. I don't suppose I ever shall be. If you had wished to marry me—"
"I know all that, that if I wanted to marry you I ought to have done so long ago. But you said you were determined to tell me something—what is it?" The expression of her face did not change; her lips moved a little, she cast down her eyes, and said, "I've got another lover."
He felt that he ought to get very angry, and that to do so was in a way expected of him. He thought he had better say something energetic, lest she should think that he did not care for her. But he was so overcome by the thought of his escape—it was now no longer possible for her to send him away—that he could think of nothing. It even seemed to him that everything was happening for the best, for he did not doubt that she would soon tire, if she were not tired already, of this musician, and then he would easily regain his old influence over her. Even if she did marry this musician, she'd get tired of him, and then who knows — anything was better than that she should go over to that infernal priest. While rejoicing in the defeat of his hated rival, he was anxious that Evelyn should not perceive what was passing in his mind, and, afraid to betray himself, he said nothing, leaving her to conjecture what she pleased from his silence.
"I don't intend to defend my conduct; it is indefensible.... But, Owen, I want you to believe that I did not lie to you. Ulick was not my lover when I went to see you that evening in Berkeley Square."
It was necessary to say something, and, feeling that any unguarded word would jeopardise his chances, he said—
"I think I told you that night that you liked Ulick Dean. I can quite understand it; he is a nice fellow enough. Are you going to marry him?"
"No, I am not in love with him—I never was. I liked him merely."
"I can understand; all those hours you spent with him studying Isolde."
"Yes, it was that music, it gets on one's nerves.... But, Owen, there is no excuse."
"We'll think no more about it, Evelyn. I am glad you do not love him. My greatest fear was to lose you altogether."
She was touched by his kindness, as he expected she would be, and he sat looking at her, keeping as well as he could all expression from his face. He thought that he had got over the greatest difficulty, and he congratulated himself on his cleverness. The question now was, what was the next move?
"You are not looking very well, Evelyn. You don't sleep—you want a change. The *Medusa* is at Cowes; what do you say for a sail?"
"Owen, dear, I cannot go with you. If I did, you know how it would end, I being what I am, and you being what you are. There would be no sense in my going yachting unless I went as your mistress, and I cannot do that."
"You love that fellow Ulick Dean too much."
"I don't love him at all.... Owen, you will never understand."
"Understand!" he cried, starting to his feet, "this is madness, Evelyn. I see! I suppose you think it wrong to have two lovers at the same time. Grace has come to you through sin. You are going to get rid of both of us."
Evelyn sat quite still as if hypnotised. She was very sorry for him, but for no single moment did she think she would yield.

Suddenly he asked her why he should be the one to be sent away, and he pleaded the rights of old friendship, going even so far as to suggest that even if she liked Ulick better she should not refuse to see him sometimes.

"I have no right to seem shocked at anything you may say. I told you Ulick was my lover, but I did not say he was going to remain my lover."

"Then what are you going to do? Will that priest get hold of you? I know him—I was at Eton with him. He always was—" and Owen muttered something under his breath. "Surely, Evelyn, you are not thinking of going to confession. After all my teaching has it come to this? My God!" he said, as he walked up the room, "I'd sooner Ulick got you than that damned hypocritical fool. You are much too good for God," he said, turning suddenly and looking at her, remarking at that moment the pretty oval of her face, the arched eyebrows, the clear, nervous eyes. "You'll be wasted on religion."

"From your point of view, I suppose I shall be."

They talked on and on, saying what they had said many times before. Sometimes Evelyn seemed to follow his arguments, and thinking that he was convincing her, he would break off suddenly. "Well, will you come for a cruise with me in the *Medusa*? I'll ask all your friends—we'll have such a pleasant time."

"No, Owen, no, it's impossible, you don't understand. I don't blame you—you never will understand."

And they looked at each other like wanderers standing on the straits dividing two worlds. The hands of the clock pointed to five o'clock. The servants had taken the tea-service away. Owen had urged Evelyn not to abandon the stage; he had urged the cause of Art; he had urged that her voice was her natural vocation; he had spoken of their love, and of the happiness they had found in each other—the conversation had drifted from an argument concerning the authenticity of the Gospels to a lake where they had spent a season five years ago. She saw again the reedy reaches and the steep mountain shores. They had been there in the month of September, and the leaves of the vine were drooping, and the grapes ready for gathering. They had been sweethearts only a little while, and the drives about the lake was one of his happiest memories.

"Evelyn, you cannot mean that you will never see me again?"

His eyes filled with tears, and she turned her head aside so that she might not see them.

"Life is very difficult, Owen; try not to make it more difficult."

"Evelyn, I had hoped that our friendship would have continued to the end. I never cared for any other woman, and when you are my age and look back, you will find that there is one, I don't say I shall be the one, who—" His voice trembled, and he passed his hand across his eyes.

"It's very sad, Owen, and life is very difficult.... There is this consolation for you, that I am not sending you away on account of anyone else. Ulick must go too."

"That does not make it any better for me. By God, I'd sooner that he got you than that infernal religion. Evelyn, Evelyn, it is impossible that an idea, a mere idea, should take you from me. It is inhuman, unnatural, I can't realise it!"

"Owen, you must go now."

"Evelyn, I don't understand. It is just as if you told me you were tallow, and would melt if there was a fire lighted. But never mind, I'll accept your ideas—I'll accept anything. Let us be married to-morrow."

She was frightened in the depths of her feelings, and seemed to lose all control of her will.

"Owen, I cannot marry you. Why do you ask me? You know it is now more than ever impossible."

His face changed expression, but he was urged forward by an irresistible force that seemed to rise up from the bottom of his being and blind his eyes.

"You don't love him, it was only a caprice; we'll think no more about it."

She sought the truth in her soul, but it seemed to elude her. She was like a blind person in a vague, unknown space, and not being able to discover the reason why she refused him, she insisted that Ulick was the reason.
"Are you going to marry him?"
"No, I don't think so."
"Don't you wish to? He is your father's friend."
She shrugged her shoulders.
"Destiny, I suppose."
The question was too profound for discussion, and they sat silent for a long while. A chance remark turned their talk upon Balzac, and Owen spoke about *Le Lys dans la Vallèe*, and she asked him if he remembered the day he had first spoken to her about Balzac.
"It was the day you took me to the races, our first week in Paris."
"And a few days afterwards I took you to Madame Savelli's. She told you that you had the most beautiful voice she had ever heard. You could not speak; you were so excited that I was obliged to send you off for a drive in the Bois. Do you remember?"
"Yes, I remember.... You were always very good to me."
They talked on and on, conscious of the hands of the clock moving on towards their divided lives. When it struck seven, she said he must go, but he begged to be allowed to stay till a quarter past, and in this last period he urged that their separation should not be final. He pleaded that a time should be set on his alienation, and ended by extracting from her a sort of half promise that she would allow him to come and see her in three months. But he and she knew that they would never meet again, and the sad thought floated up into their eyes as they said good-bye. She went to the window, wondering if he would stay a moment to look back. He stood on the edge of the pavement, and she watched him unmoved. She was thinking of Monsignor, and of how he would approve of her conduct. He would tell her that what she liked and disliked was no longer the question. Owen still stood on the kerb, but she did not even see him. Her eyes looked into the sunset, and she was thrilled with a mysterious joy, a joy that came from the heart, not from passions, and it was exquisitely subtle as the light that faded in the remote west.

CHAPTER TWENTY-NINE

He walked up Park Lane, staring now and then at the quaint balconies from a mere habit of admiration. But all were indifferent to him, even the one supported by the four Empire figures. It did not seem that anything in the world could interest him again, and he wondered how he would get through the years that remained to him to live. He was tired of hunting and shooting; he had seen everything there was to be seen; he had been round the world twice; it did not seem to him that he would ever care for another woman, and he reflected with pride that he had been faithful to Evelyn for six years. "But I shall never see her again," his heart wailed; "in three months she'll be a different woman; she won't want to see me, she'll find some excuse. That infernal priest will refuse his absolution if—" Owen stopped suddenly. Far away a little pink cloud dissolved mysteriously. "In another second," he thought, "it will be no more." In the Green Park the trees rocked in the soft autumn air, and he noticed that now and then a leaf broke from its twig, fluttered across the path, and fell by the iron railings.
"Well, Asher, how is it that you are in town at this time of year?"
It was a club acquaintance, one of the ordinary conventional men that Owen met by the dozen in every one of his clubs, a man whose next question would surely be, "How are your two-year-olds?"

"I should like to hear that they had all broken their legs," Owen answered through his teeth, and the colour mounted in his cheeks.

"Asher always was mad ... now he seems madder than ever. What did he mean by saying he wished his two-year-olds had all broken their legs?"

Owen lingered on the kerb, inveighing against the stupidity of his set. He had thought of dining at the Turf Club, but after this irritating incident he felt that he dared not risk it; if anyone were to speak to him again of his two-year-olds, he felt he would not be able to control himself. Suddenly he thought of a friend. He must speak to someone.... He need mention no names. He put up his stick and stopped a hansom. A few minutes took him to Harding's rooms.

The unexpectedness of the visit, and the manner in which Owen strode about the room, trying to talk of the things that he generally talked about, while clearly thinking of something quite different, struck Harding as unusual, and a suspicion of the truth had just begun to dawn upon him, when, breaking off suddenly, Owen said—

"Swear you'll never speak of what I am going to say—and don't ask for names."

"I'll tell no one," said Harding, "and the name does not interest me."

"It's this: a woman whom I have known many years—a friendship that I thought would go on to the end of the chapter—told me to-day that it was all finished, that she never wanted to see me again."

"A friendship! Were you her lover?"

"What does it matter? Suffice it to say that she was my dearest friend, and now I have lost her. She has been taken from me," he said, throwing his arms into the air. It was a superb gesture of despair, and Harding could not help smiling.

"So Evelyn has left him. I wonder for whom?" Then, with as much sympathy as he could call into his voice, he asked if the lady had given any reason for this sudden dismissal.

"Only that she thinks it wrong; we've been discussing it all the afternoon. It has made me quite ill;" and he dropped into a chair.

Harding knew perfectly well of whom they were speaking, and Owen knew that he knew, but it seemed more decorous to refrain from mentioning names, and Evelyn's soul was discussed as if it were an abstract quantity, and all indication of the individual incarnation was avoided. Owen admitted that, notwithstanding many seeming contradictory appearances, Evelyn had always thought it wrong to live with him, and yet, notwithstanding her being very fond of him, she had never shown any eagerness to be married. "Of course it is very wrong," she would say in her own enchanting way, "but a lover is very exciting, and a husband always seems dull. I don't think you'd be half as nice as a husband as you are as a lover." The recital of the Florence episode interested Harding, but it was the opposition of the priest and the musician that made the story from his point of view one of the most fascinating he had ever heard in his life.

They dined together in an old-fashioned club, in a room lighted by wax candles in silver candlesticks. Tall mirrors in gold frames reflected the black mahogany furniture. In answer to Owen, who lamented that Evelyn was sacrificing everything for an idea, Harding spoke, and with his usual conscious exaltation, of the Christian martyrs, the Spanish Inquisition, and then Robespierre seemed to him the most striking example of what men will do for an idea. He mentioned a portrait by Greuze in which Robespierre appears as a beautiful young man. "Such a face," he said, "as we might imagine for a lover or a poet, a sort of Lucien de Rubempré, but in his brain there was a cell containing the pedantic idea, and for this idea he cut off a thousand heads, and would have cut off a million. The world must conform to his idea, or it was a lost world."

Towards the end of dinner, the head waiter interrupted their conversation. He lingered about the table, anxious to hear something of Lord Ascott's two-year-olds; but, in the smoking-room over their coffee, they returned to the more vital question—the sentimental affections.

They were agreed that the pleasure of love is in loving, not in being loved, and their reasons were incontrovertible.

"It is the letters," said Harding, "that we write at three in the morning to tell her how enchanting she was; it is the flowers we send, the words of love that we speak in her ear, that are our undoing. So long as we are indifferent, they love us."

"Quite true. At first I did not care for her as much as she did for me, and I noticed that as soon as I began to fall in love—"

"To aspire, to suffer. Maybe there is no deep pleasure in contentment. In casting you out she has given you a more intense life."

Owen did not seem to understand. His eye wandered, then returning to Harding, he said—

"We cannot worship and be worshipped; is that what you mean? If so, I agree with you. But I'd sooner lose her as I have done than not have told her that I loved her.... There never was anyone like her. Sympathy, understanding, appreciation and enthusiasm! it was like living in a dream. Good God! to think that that priest should have got her; that, after all my teaching, she should think it wrong to have a lover! I don't know if you know of whom we are speaking. If you suspect, I can't help it, but don't ask me. I shouldn't speak of her at all; it is wrong to speak of her, even though I don't mention her name, but it is impossible to help it. If you are proud of a woman you must speak of her—and I was so proud of her. It is very easy to be discreet when you are ashamed of them," he added, with a laugh. "When I had nothing to do, I used to sit down and think of her, and I used to say to myself that if I were the king of the whole world I could not get anything better. But it is all over now."

"Well, you've had six years, the very prime of her life."

"That's true; you're very sympathetic, Harding. Have another cigarette. I was faithful to her for six years—you can't understand that, but it is quite true, and I had plenty of chances, but, when I came to think of it, it always seemed that I liked her the best."

At the same moment Evelyn stood on her balcony, watching the evening. The park was breathless, and the sky rose high and pale, and calm as marble. But the houses seemed to speak unutterable things, and she closed the window and stood looking across the room. Then walking towards the sofa as if she were going to sit down, she flung herself upon it and buried her face among the cushions. She lay there weeping, and when she raised her face she dashed the tears from her streaming cheeks, but this pause was only the prelude to another passionate outbreak, and she wept again, finding in tears fatigue, and in fatigue relief. She sobbed until she could sob no more, and so tired was she that she no longer cared what happened; very tired, and her head heavy, she went upstairs, eager for sleep. And closing her eyes she felt a delicious numbing of sense, a dissolution of her being into darkness....

But in her waking there was a consciousness, a foreboding of a nameless dread, of a heavy weight upon her, and when the foreboding in her ears grew louder, she seemed to know that an irreparable calamity had happened, and trying to fathom it, she saw the wall-paper, and it told her she was in her own room. She seemed to be trying to read something on it, but what she was trying to read and understand seemed to move away, and her brain laboured in anxious pursuit. Her eyes opened, and she remembered her interview with Owen. She had sent him away, she understood it all now, she had sent Owen away! She had told him that Ulick was her lover, so even if he were to come back it never could be the same as it was. Why had she told him about Ulick? It was bad enough to send him away, but she had degraded his memory of her, and the thought that she had not deceived him, but had told him what he otherwise might never have known, did not console her just then. She lay quite still, face to face with, seeing as it were into the eyes of the Irreparable. Never again would a man hold her in his arms, saying, "Darling, I am very fond of you!" Take love out of her life, and what barrenness, what weariness! After all, she was only seven-and-twenty, and the thought came upon her that she might have waited until she was a little older. The word "never" rang in her ears, and she realised as she had not done before all that a lover meant to her—romance, adventure, the brilliancy and sparkle of life. What was life without the delightful excitement of the chase, the delicious doubts regarding the hidden significance of every look and word, then the rapture of the final abandonment? She tried to think that the life she proposed to relinquish had not brought her happiness, but she could not put back memory of the enchanting days she had spent with her lovers. Oh, the intense hours of anticipation! and the wonderful recollections! rich and red as the heart of a flower! Such rapture seemed to her to be worth the remorse that came after, and the peace of mind that a chaste life would secure, a poor recompense for dreary days and months. She realised the length and the colour of the time—grey week after grey week, blank month after blank month, void year after void year! And she always getting a little older, getting older in a drab, lifeless time, in a lifeless life, a weary life filled with intolerable craving! She had endured it once, a feeling as if she wanted to go mad.... She picked up her letters.

Among the letters she received that morning was one from Ulick. He was still in Paris, and would not be back for another week or ten days. He had been lonely, he had missed her, and looked forward to their meeting. He told her about the opera, the people he had met, and what they had said about his music. But the tender affection of his letter was not to her mind. Why did he not say that he longed to take her in his arms and kiss her on the lips? Knitting her brows, she tried to think that if he had written more passionately she would have taken the train and gone to him. She had sent Owen away on account of scruples of conscience, and a life of chastity extended indefinitely before her. But who was this woman to whom Ulick had shown his music, and who had said that if anything happened to prevent Evelyn Innes from singing the part, she hoped that Ulick would give it to her? Why should she have thought that something would happen to prevent Evelyn Innes from creating Grania? Had Ulick suggested it to her? But how could Ulick know? She tried to think if she had ever told him she was tired of the stage. Perhaps he had consulted the stars and had divined her future. This woman seemed to know that something might happen, and something was happening, there could be no doubt about that.

There was no doubt that she was tired of the stage, but perhaps that was on account of hard work, perhaps she required a rest; in two or three months she might return eagerly to the study of Grania; for the sake of Ulick, she might remain on the stage till she had established the success of his opera. This might be if she and Ulick were not lovers. She had promised Owen that she would not keep him for her lover, but that did not mean that she would not sing his opera. If she didn't, another woman would, some wretched singer who did not understand the music, and it would be a failure. Ulick would hate her; he would believe that her refusal to sing his opera was a vile plan to do him an injury. He did not know what conscience meant—he only understood the legends and the Gods! She laughed, and a moment afterwards was submerged in difficulties. Her conduct would seem more incomprehensible to him than it did to Owen; she did not wish him to hate her, but he would hate her, and to avoid seeing her he would not go to Dowlands, and so she would rob her father of his friend—the friend who had kept him company when she deserted him. There was another alternative. If she liked him well enough to be his mistress, she should like him well enough to be his wife. But knowing that she would not marry him, she took up her other letters and began reading them.

Lady Duckle liked Homburg; everyone was there, and she hoped Evelyn would not be detained in London much longer. The Duke of Berwick had proposed to Miss Beale, and Lady Mersey was always about with young Mr. So-and-So. Evelyn didn't read it all. She lay back thinking, for this letter, about things that interested her no longer, had led her thoughts back to self, and she inquired why in the midst of all her enjoyments she had felt that her real life was elsewhere, why she had always known that sooner or later the hour would come when she would leave the things which she enjoyed so intensely. The idea of departure had never quite died down in her, and she had always known that she would be one day quite a different woman. She had often had glimpses of her future self and of her future life, but the moment she tried to distinguish what was there, the vision faded. Even now she knew that she would not marry Ulick, and this not because she would refuse her father anything, but merely because it was not to be. Her eyes went to the piano, but on the way there she stopped to ask herself a question. Why was she in London at this time of year? She knew why she did not care to go to Homburg—because she was tired of society. But why did she not go to some quiet seaside place where she could enjoy the summer weather? She would like to sit on the beach and hear the sea. Her soul threatened to give back a direct answer, and she dismissed the question.

She paced the empty alley facing the Bayswater Road. No one was there except a nursemaid and a small child, and she and they shared the solitude. She could see the omnibuses passing, and hear the clank of the heavy harness, and seated on one of the seats she drew diagrams on the gravel with her parasol. Owen said there was no meaning in life, that it was no more than an unfortunate accident between two eternal sleeps. But she had never been able to believe that this was so; and if she had sought to disbelieve in God, it was as Monsignor had said, because she wished to lead a sinful life. And if she could not believe in annihilation, there could be no annihilation for her, that was Ulick's theory. The name of her lover brought up the faded Bloomsbury Square, the litter of manuscript and the books on magic! She had tried to believe in readings of the stars. But such vague beliefs had not helped her. In spite of all her efforts, the world was slipping behind her; Owen and Ulick and her stage career seemed very little compared with the certainty within her that she was leading a sinful life, and she was only really certain of that. The omnibuses in the road outside, the railways beyond the town, the ships upon the sea, what were these things to her—or yet the singing of operas? The only thing that really mattered was her conscience.

Then, almost without thinking at all, in a sort of stupor, she walked over the hill and descended the slope, and leaning over the balustrade she looked at the fountains. But the splashing water explained nothing, and she turned to resume her walk; and she reflected that to send away her lovers would avail her nothing, unless she subsequently confessed her sins and obtained the priest's absolution. Monsignor would tell her that to send away her lovers was not sufficient, and he would refuse his absolution unless she promised him not to see them any more. That promise she could not give, for she had promised Ulick that she would sing Grania, and she had promised Owen to see him in three months. It seemed to her both weak and shameful to break either of these promises. The spire of Kensington Church showed sharp as a needle on a calm sky, and it was in a sudden anguish of mind that she determined that her repentance must be postponed. She had considered the question from every point of view, and could not at once reverse her life; the change must come gradually. She had sent Owen away; that was enough for the present.

The numerous pea-fowls had gathered in a bare roosting tree on an opposite hillside, and the immense tails of the cock-birds swept the evening sky. Owen would have certainly compared it to a picture by Honderhoker. The ducks clambered out of the water, keeping their cunning black eyes fixed on the loitering children whom the nursemaid was urging to return home. In Kensington Gardens, the glades were green and gold, and for some little while Evelyn watched the delicate spectacle of the fading light, and insensibly she began to feel that a life of spiritual endeavour was the only life possible to her, and that, however much it might cost her, she must make the effort to attain it. Even to feel that she was capable of desiring this ideal life was a delicious happiness, and her thoughts flowed on for a long while, unmindful of practical difficulties. Suddenly it came upon her like a sudden illumination, that sooner or later she would have to make all the sacrifices that this ideal demanded, that she would not have any peace of mind until she had made them. But even at the same moment the insuperable difficulties of the task before her appeared, and she despaired. The last obstacle was money. As she crossed the road dividing Kensington Gardens from Hyde Park, she understood that the simple fact of owing a few thousand pounds rendered her immediate retirement from the stage impossible. She had insisted that the money she required to live in Paris and study with Madame Savelli should be considered as a debt, which she would repay out of her first earnings. But Owen had laughed at her. He had refused to accept it, and he would never tell her the rent of the house in the Rue Balzac; he had urged that as he had made use of the house he could not allow her to pay for it. In the rough, she supposed that a thousand pounds would settle her debt for the year they had spent in Paris.

Since then she had, however, insisted on keeping herself, but now that she came to think it out, it did not seem that she had done much more than pay her dressmaker's bills. She grew alarmed at the amount of her debt, which seemed in her excited imagination so large that all her savings, amounting to about six or seven thousand pounds, would not suffice to pay it off. Most of her jewellery had been given to her by Owen; there was the furniture, the pictures and the china in Park Lane! She would have to return all these, and the horses, too, if she wished to pay everything, and the net result would be that she would mortally offend the man who had done everything for her. She knew he would not forgive her if she sent back the presents he had made her, nor could she blame him, and she decided that such complete restitution was impossible. But, for all she knew, Monsignor might insist upon it. If he did? She felt that she would go mad if she did not put aside these scruples, which she knew to be in a measure fictitious, but which she was nevertheless unable to shake off. And she could not help thinking, though she knew that such thoughts were both foolish and unjust, that Owen had purposely contrived this thraldom. Then there was only one thing for her to do, to go to Paris after Ulick.... A moment after there came a sinking feeling. She knew that she could not. But what was she to do? All this uncertainty was loosening her brain.... She might go to Monsignor and lay the whole matter before him and take his advice. But she knew if she went to him she must confess. Better that, she thought, than that the intolerable present should endure.

Mental depression and sleepless nights had produced nervous pains in her neck and arms. She could hardly drag herself along for very weariness. The very substance of her being seemed to waste away; that amount of unconsciousness without which life is an agony had been abstracted, leaving nothing but a fierce mentality.

She slept a little after dinner, and awakening about eleven, she foresaw another night of insomnia. The chatter of her conscience continued, tireless as a cricket, and she had lost hope of being able to silence it. The hysterical tears of last night had brought her four hours of sleep, but there was no chance of any repetition of them. It would be useless to go upstairs. She sang through the greater part of "Lohengrin," and then took up the "Meistersinger," and read it till it fell from her hands. ... It was three o'clock; and feeling very tired, she thought that she might be able to sleep. But all night long she saw her life from end to end. Her miserable passage through this life, the weakness of her character and the vileness of her sins were shown to her in a hideous magnification. She was exhibited to herself like an insect in a crystal, and she perceived the remotest antennae of her being.

CHAPTER THIRTY

One night it occurred to her that she might ring for Merat and send her to the chemist's for a sleeping draught. But it was four o'clock in the morning, and she did not like to impose such a task on her maid. Moreover, she might get to sleep a little later on, so she wrote on a piece of paper that Merat was not to come to her room until she rang for her, and she lay down and folded her arms, and once more began to count the sheep through the gate. But that night sleep seemed further than ever from her eyes, and at eight she was obliged to ring.

"Merat, I have not closed my eyes all night."

"Mademoiselle ought to have a sleeping draught."

"Yes, I'll take one to-night Get me some tea. Another night like this will drive me mad."

Late in the afternoon she slept for an hour in an armchair, and, a little rested, went to walk in the park. She was not feeling so dazed; her brain was not so light, and the sense of whiteness was gone; the pains in the neck and arms too had died down; they were now like a dim suggestion, a memory. But the greatest relief of all was that she was not thinking, conscience was quiescent and in the calm of the evening and the gentleness of the light, life seemed easier to bear. If she could only get a night's sleep! Now she did not know which was the worst—the reality, the memory, or the anticipation of a sleepless night. She had wandered round the park by the Marble Arch, and had continued her walk through Kensington Gardens, and sitting on the hillside by the Long Water, with the bridge on her left hand and the fountains under her eyes, she looked towards Kensington. There an iridescent sky floated like a bubble among the autumn-tinted trees. She was then thinking of her music and her friends; she hardly knew of what she was thinking, when a thought so clear that it sounded like a bell spoke within her, and it said that the things of which she was thinking were as nothing, and that Life was but a little moment compared with Eternity, and she seemed to see into the final time which lay beyond the grave. "There and not here are the true realities," said the voice, and she got up and walked hurriedly down the hillside, fearing lest the fierce conflict of conscience should begin again in her. She walked as fast as she was able, hoping to extinguish in action the conscience that she dreaded, but she was weak and almost helpless, and had to pause to rest. She stood, one hand on the balustrade, not daring to turn her head lest she should see the spire of the Kensington Church.

She walked across the gardens, through the great groves, and sat down. The grass was worn away about the roots of the trees and through the gnarled trunks she could see the keeper's cottage covered with reddened creeper. Perhaps it was the calm and seclusion that called her thoughts to the convent garden, and she reflected that if she had not accepted the nuns' invitation to tea, her life might have continued without deviation. She was impressed with the slightness of the thread on which our destiny hangs, and then by the inevitableness of our lives. We perceive the governing rule only when we look back. The present always seems chaos, but when we look back, we distinguish the reason of every action, and we recognise the perfect fulfilment of what must be. Her visit to the convent—how little it was when looked at from one side, when looked at from another how extraordinary! If she had known that Monsignor was going to ask her to go there, she would have invented a plausible excuse, but she had had no time to think; his kind eyes were fixed upon her, and he seemed so ready to believe all she said, that her courage sank within her, and she could not lie to him. Perhaps all this was by intention, by the very grace of God! The Virgin might have interceded on her behalf, for is it not said that whoever wears the scapular of Our Lady of Mount Carmel cannot lose his soul? But for the last two years, for more than two years, she has not worn her scapular. The strings had broken, and they had not been mended. She had intended to buy another, but had not been able to bring herself to do so, so hypocritical did it seem.

It might be that these dreadful nights of insomnia had been sent so that she might have an opportunity of realising the wickedness of her life, and the risk she incurred of losing her immortal soul. She dare not have recourse to the sleeping draught, and must endure perhaps another sleepless night. If they had been sent, as she thought they were, for a purpose, she must not dare to hush, by artificial means, the sense God had awakened in her; to do so would be like flying in the face of Providence. She had never suffered from sleeplessness before, and could not think that this insomnia was accidental. No, she dare not have recourse to sleeping draughts, at least not till she had been to confession. If afterwards she did not get to sleep, it would be different. The fear arose in her of taking too much, of dying in her sleep. If she were to awake in hell! And that evening, when Merat reminded her of the draught, she said it was to be left on the table, and that she would take it if she required it.

The darkness could not hide the slim bottle corked with a slim blond cork, and so clear was the vision that she could read the label through the darkness. It was only partially gummed on the bottom, and she could read the pale writing. "To be taken before bedtime." The temptation struck through the darkness, sweet and dreamily seductive it entered her brain. She was tempted as by a dark, dreamless river; hushed in an unconscious darkness she would be upon that river, floating through a long, winding night towards a dim, very distant day. If she were to drink, darkness would sink upon her, and all this visible world, the continual sight of which she felt must end in lunacy, would pass from her. So great was the temptation that she did not dare to get out of bed and put the bottle away—if she did she must drink it, so she lay quite still, her face turned against the wall, trying to find courage in the thought that God had imposed the torture of these sleepless nights upon her in order that she might be saved from the eternal sleeplessness of hell.

Mistakes are made in the preparation of medicines, but if no mistake had been made, a change in her health might unfit her for so large a dose, and if through either of these chances she were to die in her sleep, there was no question that she must awake in hell. She did not dare to go to the draught, but lay quite still, her head close against the wall, praying for darkness, crying for relief from this too fierce mentality; it seemed to be eating up the very substance of her brain.

On the following evening she sat in her armchair watching the clock. It had struck eleven—that was the time for her going to bed, but the hour had become a redoubtable one. Bedtime filled her with fear, and the thought of another sleepless night deprived her of all courage. She did not dare to go upstairs. She sat in her armchair as if in terror of a mortal enemy. She had hidden the bottle, but her maid had ordered another. There were now two, sufficient to procure death, said her conscience, and since dinner the temptation to commit suicide had been growing in her brain; like a vulture perched upon a jag of mountain rock, she could see the temptation watching her. She tried not to see, but the thought grew blacker and larger—its beak was in her brain, and she was drawn, as if by talons, tremblingly from her chair. She was so weak that she could hardly cross the room; but the thought of death seemed to give her courage, and without it she thought she never would have had the strength to get upstairs. The attraction was extraordinary, and her powerlessness to resist it was part of the fascination, and she looked round the room like a victim looking for the knife. She could not see the bottle on her dressing-table, and accepting this as a favourable omen, she undressed and lay down.

After all, she might sleep without having recourse to death; but, lying on the pillow, she could think of nothing but the slim bottle and the slim blond cork, and a thick white liquid, and the dark river into which she would sink, the winding darkness on which she would float, and she had not strength to think whither it led. Her only thought was not to see this world any more; her only desire not to think of Ulick or Owen, and to be tortured no longer by doubt of what was right and what was wrong. She was aware that she was losing possession of her self-control, and would be soon drawn into the dreaded but much-desired abyss; and in this delirium, produced by long insomnia, she began to conceive her suicide as an act of defiance against God, and she rejoiced in her hatred of God, who had afflicted her so cruelly—for it was hatred that had come to her aid, and would enable her to secure a long, long sleep. "Out of the sight of this world"—she muttered the words as she sought the chloral—"I'll sleep, I'll sleep, I must sleep. Sleep or death, one or the other, so long as I am out of the sight of this world." But in her frenzy of desire for sleep she overlooked the slim bottle with the slim blond cork. Yet it stood on the toilet-table amid other bottles, right under her eyes, but over and over again she passed it by, until, frightened at not finding it, she opened drawer after drawer, and rushed to her wardrobe thinking it might be there. She sought for it, throwing her things about, and, not finding it anywhere, a cold sweat broke over her forehead. Another sleepless night and she must go mad. If she did not find it, she must find another way out of this agony, and the thought of cutting her throat, or throwing herself out of the window, flashed across her mind. "Sleep I must have—sleep, sleep, sleep!" she muttered, as with fearing fingers she emptied out the contents of her little workbox, where odds and ends collected. It was her scapular that came up under her hand, and at the sight of it, all her mad revolt was hushed, and a calm settled upon her. "A miracle, a miracle," she murmured, "the Virgin has done this; she interceded for me;" and at the same moment, catching sight of the chloral right under her very eyes, she could no longer doubt the miraculous interposition of the Virgin. For how otherwise could that bottle have escaped her notice? She had looked at the very place where it stood many times, and had not seen it; she had moved the other bottles and she had not seen it. The Virgin had taken it away—she was sure it was not there five minutes ago—or else the Virgin had blinded her eyes to it. A miracle had happened; and in a quivering peace of mind and an intense joy of the heart, she mended the strings of her broken scapular. Then she hung it round her neck, and kneeling by the bedside, she said the prayers that it enjoined; and when she got into bed she saw a light shining in one corner of the room, and, sure that it was the Virgin who had come in person to visit her, she continued her prayers till she fell asleep.

CHAPTER THIRTY-ONE

A knock came at her door, and Merat was glad to hear that Mademoiselle had slept. She noticed that the sleeping-draught had not been taken, and picking up the various things that Evelyn had scattered in her search, she wondered at the disorder of the room, making Evelyn feel uncomfortable by her remarks. Evelyn knew it would be impossible for Merat to guess the cause of it all. But when she hesitated about what dress she would wear, declaring against this one and that one, her choice all the time being fixed on a black crepon, Merat glanced suspiciously at her mistress; and when Evelyn put aside her rings, selecting in preference two which she did not usually wear, the maid was convinced that some disaster had happened, and was ready to conclude that Ulick Dean was the cause of these sleepless nights.

Evelyn had chosen this dress because she was going to St. Joseph's or because she supposed she was going there. It did not seem to her that she could confess to anyone but Monsignor. But why he? one priest would do as well as another. She was too tired to think.

Her brain was like one of those autumn days when clouds hang low, and a dimness broods between sky and earth. True that there were the events of last night—her search for the chloral, the finding of her scapular, her belief in a special interposition of Providence, and then her resolution to go to confession. It was all there; she knew it all, but did not want to think about it. She had been thinking for a week, and this was the first respite she had had from thought, and she wished this stupor of brain to continue till four o'clock. That was the time she would have to be at St. Joseph's. He was generally there at that time.

She had lain down on the sofa after breakfast, hoping to sleep a little; if she didn't, the time would be very long; but as she dozed, she began to see the thin, worn face and the piercing eyes, and the intonation of his voice began to ring in her ears. As she thought or as she dreamed, the striking of the clock reminded her of the number of hours that separated them. Only four hours and she would be kneeling at his feet! Then she felt that she had advanced a stage, and was appreciably nearer the inevitable end, and lay staring at the sequence of events. She saw the hours stretching out reaching to him, and she, all the while, was moving through the hours automatically. All kind of similes presented themselves to her mind. She asked herself how it was that Monsignor had come into her life. She had not sought him; she had not wanted him in her life, but he had come! She remembered the first time she saw him—that Sunday morning when she went to St. Joseph's to meet her father's choir—and could recall the exact appearance of the church as he walked across the aisle to the pulpit. It was illuminated by a sudden ray of sunlight falling through one of the eastern windows, and she remembered how it had lighted up the thin, narrow face, bringing a glow of colour to the dark skin till it seemed like one of the carved saints she had seen in Romanesque churches on the Rhine. She remembered the shape of the small head, carried well back, and how she had been impressed by the slow stride with which he crossed the sanctuary. Then her thoughts passed to the moment when, standing in the pulpit, he had looked out on the congregation, seeming to divine the presence of some great sinner there. She had felt that he was aware of her existence, for in that moment the thin grey eyes seemed to see her, even to think her, and they had frightened her, they were so clear, so set on some purpose—God's or the Church's. She had met him that evening at a concert, and how well she remembered her father introducing him! He had spoken to her several minutes; everyone in the room was looking at them, and she recalled the scene—all the girls, their dresses, and the expression of their eyes. But she could not recall what Monsignor had said, only her impressions; the same strange fascination and fear which she had experienced when Owen came to the concerts long ago—that loud winter's night, harsh and hard as iron. Owen had stood talking to her too, and she had been fascinated.... He had admired her singing, and Monsignor had admired her singing; but she was determined not to sing until Monsignor had asked her to sing, and when he has asked her to go to the convent she had gone. It was very strange; she could not account for it. It was all beyond herself, outside of her, far away like the stars, and she felt now as she did whenever she looked at the stars. Was her character essentially weak, and was she liable to all these influences, these facile assimilations? Was there nothing within her, no abiding principle, nothing that she could call her own? She walked up the room, and tried to understand herself—what was she, bad or good, weak or strong? If she only knew what she was, then she would know how to act.

There were her sins against faith. She had striven to undermine her belief in God. She had read Darwin and Huxley for this purpose, and not in the least to obtain knowledge. As Monsignor has said, "When a Catholic loses his faith, it is because he desires to lead a loose life," and she hardly dared to look into her soul, knowing that she would find confirmation of this opinion. She had not been to Mass, because at the Elevation she believed in spite of herself; so she had been as insincere in her unfaith as in her faith. Then there were the sins of the flesh, and their number and their blackness terrified her. There were sins that she strove to put out of her mind at once, sins she was even ashamed to think of; and the thought of confessing them struck her down, and once more it seemed that she could never raise herself out of the slough into which she had fallen. She had all along taken it for granted that a general admission that she had lived with Owen as his wife would be sufficient. But now it seemed to her that she would have to tell Monsignor how gross her life had been.

In a corner of the room her sins crowded, and covering her face with her hands, she was convinced that she could not go to confession.

Before she went away with Owen she had had no sins to confess, or only venial sins; that she had been late for Mass through her own fault; that she had omitted her evening prayers. Her worst sin was the reading of a novel which she thought she ought not to have read, but now her life was all sin. If the priest questioned her she could not answer, she must refuse to answer. So there seemed no hope for her. She could not confess everything, and the conviction suddenly possessed her that God had deserted her, and she could not hope for redemption from her present life. For she could not confess all her sins; her heart would fail her, she would be tempted to conceal something, and then to her other sins she would add the sin of a bad confession.

Nervous pains began again in her arms and neck, and she experienced the same wasting away of the very substance of her being, of the protecting envelope of the unconscious. She was again a mere mentality, and she looked round the room with a frightened, distracted air. On the table was the book Monsignor had given her, *Sin and Its Consequences*. But she turned from it with a smile. She did not need anyone to tell her what were the consequences of sin—and the familiar proverb of bringing coals to Newcastle rose up in her mind. At the same moment she caught sight of the clock; it was half-past twelve, and she remembered that in about three hours and a half it would be time to go to St. Joseph's. Then like a flash the question came, was it Monsignor's influence that had induced this desire of a pure life in her? She could not deny to herself that she was attracted by his personality. So the question was, how far his personality accounted for the change that had come over her life? Was it the mere personal influence of the prelate, or an inherent sense of right and wrong that compelled her to send her lovers away and change her life? If it were the mere personal influence of Monsignor, her desire of a pure life would not last, and to attain something that was not natural to her she would have ruined her life to no purpose. Owen's influence had died in her; how did she know that Monsignor's would continue even so long? She had lived an evil life for six years; would she lead a good one for the same time? If she knew this she would know how to act. But not only for six years would she have to lead a good life, but till the very end of her life. If she did not persevere till the very end, all this present struggle and the years of self-denial which she was was about to enter on would be useless. She might just as well have had a good time all along. A good time! That was just it. She could not have a good time. She dare not face the agony, the agony which she was at present enduring, so she must go to confession, she must have inward peace.

"So my life is over and done," she said, "and at seven-and-twenty!"

She twisted in her fingers a letter which she had received that morning from Mademoiselle Helbrun. She was staying at the Savoy Hotel, and had just returned from Munich. Evelyn felt she would like to hear about her success as Frika, and how So-and-So had sung Brunnhilde, and the rest of the little gossip about the profession. She would like to lunch with Louise in the restaurant, at a table by the window. She would like to see the Thames, and hear things that she might never hear again. But was it possible that she was never going to join again in the tumult of the Valkyrie? She remembered her war gear, the white tunic with gold breastplates. Was it possible that she would never cry their cry from the top of the rocks; and her favourite horse, the horse that Owen had given her for the part, what would become of him? What would become of her jewellery, of her house, of her fame, of everything? She attempted a last stand against her conscience. Her scruples were imaginary. Owen had said it could not matter to God whether she kissed him or not. But she did not pursue this train of reasoning. She felt it to be wrong. But she could not confess—she could not explain everything, and again she was struck with a sort of mental paralysis. Why Monsignor—why not another priest? No, not another. She could not say why, but not another; he was the one. But perhaps she only wanted to tell someone, a woman—Louise, for instance. If she were to tell Louise—she put the idea out of mind, feeling it to be vain, and trying to think that there was no need why she should leave the stage, and uncertain whether she should stay on the stage if Monsignor forbade her, or if she wanted to even if he allowed her, she put on her hat and went to lunch with Louise. It would help her to pass the time; it would save her from thinking. She must speak to someone. But the Savoy was on her way to St. Joseph's. It was half-way there. A little overcome by the coincidence, she told her servant to call a hansom, and as she drove to the hotel she wondered why she had thought of going to see Louise.

She met her in the courtyard, and the vivacious little woman cried, "My dear, how glad I am to see you!" and she stretched out both hands. Evelyn was more pleased to see her friend than she expected to be, and while listening to her she envied her for being so happy, and she wondered why she was so happy; and while asking herself these questions she noticed her dress. Mademoiselle Helbrun's plump figure was set off to full advantage in a black and white check silk dress, and she wore a wonderful arched hat with flowing plumes of the bird of paradise. She was a prima-donna every inch of her, standing on the steps of her hotel, whereas the operatic stage could hardly be distinguished at all in Evelyn's dress. With the black crepon skirt she wore a heliotrope blouse, and she stood, one foot showing beyond the skirt, in a statue-like attitude, her pale parasol held negligently over one shoulder.

"My dear," she said, "I have come to ask you to let me lunch with you."

"But I shall be enchanted, my dear. I wrote on the chance, never thinking that you would be in town this season."

"Yes, it is strange. I don't know why I am here. There's no one in town."

"Where would you like to lunch? In my room or in the restaurant?"

"It will be gayer in the restaurant. I haven't seen a soul for nearly a week."

"My dear!"

Louise gave her a sharp look, in which the passing thought that Evelyn might be in want of money was dismissed as ridiculous. Louise thought of some unhappy love affair, and when they sat down to lunch she noticed that Evelyn avoided answering a question regarding herself, and turned the conversation on to the Munich performance. The evident desire of Evelyn not to talk about herself clouded Louise's pleasure in talking of herself, and she paused in her account of the Wotan, the Brunnhilde, the conductor and the Rhine Maidens to tell Evelyn of the inquiries that had been made about her—all were looking forward to her Kundry next year. Madame Wagner had said that there never had been such a Brunnhilde.

"I daresay she said so, but at the bottom of her heart she did not like my Brunnhilde. It was against her ideas. She always thought I was too much woman. She said that I forgot that I was a Goddess. And she was right. I never could remember the Goddess. I never remember anything on the stage. 'Tisn't my way. I simply live it all out. I was enthusiastic when Siegfried came to release me, because I should have been enthusiastic about him." Evelyn's thoughts went back to Owen, and she remembered how he had released her from the bondage of music lessons with a kiss.

"But when I came to tell you about the ruined Valhala and the poor fallen Gods you were sorry?"

"Yes, I was sorry for father."

"The All-Father?"

Evelyn laughed.

"No, my own father. That's my way. I think of what has happened to me and I act that. But tell me about the Munich performances."

While Mademoiselle Helbrun told of the different points in which they excelled, Evelyn thought and thought of the strange charm of the woman who had so ably continued the Master's work. She recalled the tall, bending figure, she saw the alley of clipped limes, she remembered the spacious rooms, and then his study, the walls lined with bookcases, books of legends and philosophical works, the room in which he had written "The Dusk of the Gods" and "Parsifal." Thinking of the studious months she had spent in that house, a vivid memory of one night shot across her brain. It was a heavy, breathless night, without star or moon. She had wandered into the dark garden; she had found her way to the grave, and standing by the Master's side she had listened to the music and seen the guests passing across the lighted windows. The warble of the fountain had seemed to her like the pulse of Eternity. All that was three years ago. "It is very wonderful, very wonderful," she thought, and she awoke with a start, and Mademoiselle Helbrun saw she had not been listening. She answered Louise's subsequent remarks, and was glad that what had been had been. She was giving it all up, it was true, but it was not as if she had not known life.

The sun was shining on the great brown river, and out of the smoke-dimmed sky white creamy clouds were faintly rising. Evelyn's eyes had wandered out there, and she seemed to see a thin face and hard, cold eyes, and she asked Louise abruptly what the time was, for she had forgotten her watch. It was only just three o'clock. She returned to the Munich performances, but Louise could see that Evelyn was all the time struggling against an overmastering fate. The only thing she could think of was that Evelyn was being forced into a marriage or an elopement against her will. Once or twice she thought that Evelyn was going to confide in her. She waited, afraid to say a word lest she should check the confidences that her friend seemed tempted to entrust her with. Evelyn's eyes were dull and lifeless. Louise could see that they did not see her, and it was with an effort that Evelyn said, "I am sorry I did not see your Frika;" and once started she rattled on for some time, hardly knowing what she was saying, arguing about the music and expressing opinions about everything and everybody. Stopping abruptly, she again asked her friend what time it was. Louise said that she must not go, and then tried to induce her to come for a drive with her; but Evelyn shook her head—she was engaged. There was no trace of colour in her face, and when Louise asked when they should meet again, she said she did not know, but she hoped very soon. She might be obliged to go to Paris to-morrow, and she had to pay some visits to Scotland at the end of the month. Louise did not like to question her, for she was sure that some momentous event was about to happen. As she drove away Louise said, "I should not be surprised if she did not play Kundry next year."

While wondering at the grotesque movement of the trotting horse, Evelyn tried once more to save herself from this visit to St. Joseph's. She thought of what it would cost her—her present life! Her lovers were gone already, and Monsignor would tell her that she must give up the stage. But these considerations did not alter the fact that she was going to St. Joseph's. She was rolling thither, like a stone down a hill. She saw the streets and people as she passed them, as a stone might if it had eyes. All power of will had been taken from her; it was the same as when she went to meet Owen at Berkeley Square, and in a strange lucidity of mind, she asked herself if it were not true that we are never more than mere machines set in motion by a master hand, predestined to certain courses, purblind creatures who do not perceive their own helplessness, except in rare moments of heightened consciousness. As if to convince herself on this point, she strove to raise her hand to open the trap in the roof of the hansom, and her fear increased on finding that she could not. To acquire the necessary strength, she reminded herself that she was wrecking her whole life for an idea, for, perhaps, nothing more than a desire to confess her sins. Again she tried to raise her hand, and she looked round, feeling that nothing short of some extraordinary accident could save her, nothing except an accident to the horse or carriage could save her artistic life. Some material accident, nothing else.... Monsignor might not be at St. Joseph's. Perhaps he had left town. Nobody stayed in town in September, and for a moment it seemed hardly worth while to continue her drive. Her thoughts came to a standstill, and, as in a nervous vision, Evelyn saw that the whole of her future life depended on her seeing Monsignor that day. She foresaw that if she were turned away from the door of St. Joseph's, she would never come back; never would she be able to bring herself to the point again. She would find Owen waiting for her; wherever she went, she would meet him; sooner or later the temptation to return to him would overcome her. Then, indeed, she would be lost; then, indeed, her tragedy would begin.... Ah! if she could only cease to think for a little while; only for a little while. She had tried to escape from him once before, and had not succeeded because there was no one to help her. Now there was Monsignor. The reflection cheered her, and a few minutes were left to discover how much of her conversion was owing to her original nature, and how much to Monsignor's influence. It seemed to her that if she were certain of this point, she would know whether she should go forward or back. But her heart gave back no answer, and she grew more helpless, and terrified, like a bird fallen into the fascination of a serpent. She was uncertain if she could lead a good life. She no longer desired anything. She was conscious of no sensation, except that she was rolling independent of her own will, like a stone. A moment after, the gable of the church appeared against the sky, and she recognised the poor, ridiculous creature in the tattered black bonnet, whose stiff, crooked appearance she had known since childhood. She had changed little in the last twenty years. She walked with the same sidling gait her hands crossed in front of her like a doll. Her life had been lived about St. Joseph's; the church had always been the theatre and centre of her thoughts. Doubtless she was on her way to Benediction, and the temptation to follow her arose, but was easily resisted. Evelyn paid the cabman his fare, and in an increasing tremor of nervous agitation, she crossed the gravelled space in front of the presbytery. The attendant showed her into the same bare room, where there was nothing to distract her thoughts from herself except the four prints on the walls. She had recourse to them in the hope of stimulating her religious fervour, but as she gazed at St. Monica and St. Augustine she remembered the poor woman she had just seen. There had been scorn of her ridiculous appearance in her heart, and pride that she, Evelyn, had been given a more beautiful body, more perfect health, and a clearer intelligence. So she was overcome with shame. How dare she have scorned this holy woman. If she had been more richly gifted by Nature, to what shameful usage had she put her body and her talents? And Evelyn thought how much more lovely in God's eyes was this poor deformed woman. To sin is the common lot of humanity; but she had done more than commit sins, she had committed *the* sin, she had striven to tear out of her heart that sense of right and wrong which God had planted there. She had denied the ideal as the Jews had denied Christ. Owen had not done that; he lived up to his principles, such as they were. But she had not thought she was acting right, she had always known that she was doing wrong, and she had gone on doing wrong, stifling her conscience, hoping always that it would be the last time.

That poor woman whose appearance had raised a contemptuous thought in her heart had never sinned against her faith. She had not sought to raise doubts in her heart concerning God and morals; she had lived in ardent belief and love, never doubting that God watched her from his heaven, whither he would call her in good time. Almighty God! She was struck with fear lest she did not believe all that this poor woman believed. Did she believe that she, Evelyn Innes, would appear at the final judgment and be assigned a place for ever and ever in either eternal bliss or torment? She did not know if she believed this. Last night she was sure she believed, but to-day she did not know.... She did not know that heaven was as this poor woman imagined it. She asked herself if she believed in a future life of any sort? She was not sure, she did not know; she was only sure that whether there be a future life or none, our obligation to live according to the dictates of our conscience remains the same. But Monsignor might not deem this sufficient, and might refuse her absolution. She strove to convince herself, hurriedly, aware that the moments were fleeting, that she had a soul. That sense of right and wrong which, like a whip, had driven her here could be nothing else but the voice of her soul; therefore there was a soul, and if there was a soul it could not die, and if it did not die it must go somewhere; therefore there was a heaven and a hell. But in spite of her desire to convince herself, remembrance of Owen's arguments whistled like a wind through her pious exhortations, and all that she had read in Huxley and Darwin and Spencer; the very words came back thick and distinct, and like one who finds progress impossible in the face of the gale, she stopped thinking. "We know nothing ... we know nothing," were the words she heard in the shriek of the wind, and revealed religion appeared in tattered, miserable plight, a forlorn spectre borne away on the wind. So distinct was the vision, so explicit her hearing, that she could not pretend to herself that she was a Christian in any but a moral sense, and this would not satisfy Monsignor. Then question after question pealed in her ears. What should she say when he came? Was it not better for her to leave at once? But then? She took one step towards the door. However thin and shallow her belief might be, she must confess her sins. She felt that she must confess her sins even if she did not believe in confession. Her thoughts paused, and she was terrified by the mystery which her own existence presented to herself.

The door opened, and the priest stood looking at her. She could see that he divined the truth. In the first glance he read that Evelyn had come to confession, and it was for him a moment of extraordinary spiritual elation.

Monsignor Mostyn and Sir Owen had been at school together, and though they had not met since, they frequently heard of each other. Owen's ideas of marriage and religion were well known to the priest. He had heard soon after she had gone away that she had gone with Asher, his old schoolfellow. He knew the pride that Asher would take in destroying her faith, and this diabolic project he had determined to frustrate; and every year when he returned from Rome, he asked if Evelyn was expected to sing in London that season. As year after year went by, his chance of saving her soul seemed to grow more remote; but at the bottom of his heart he believed that he was the chosen instrument of God's grace. That night at the concert in her father's house, the first words—something in her manner, the expression in her eyes, had led him to think that the conversion would be an easy one. But it had come about quicker than he had expected. And as he stood looking at her, he was aware of an alloy of personal vanity and strove to stifle it; he thought of himself as the humble instrument selected to win her from this infamous, this renegade Catholic, and the trouble so visible in her was confirmation of his belief that there can be no peace for a Catholic outside the pale of the Church.

"I have wanted to see you so much," she began hurriedly. "There is a great deal I want to tell you. But perhaps you have no time now."

"My dear child, I have ample time, I am only too pleased to be of service to you. I am afraid you are in trouble, you look quite ill."

The kindness of the voice filled her eyes with tears, and she understood in a moment the relief it would be to tell her troubles to this kind friend; to feel his kind advice allaying them one by one, and to know that the sleepless solitude in which she had tried to grapple with them was over at last. To give her time to recover herself, Monsignor spoke of a letter he had received that morning from the Superior of the Passionist Convent.

"I will not trouble you with her repeated thanks for what you have done for her. She begs me to tell you that she and the sisters unite in inviting you to spend a few days with them. They suggest that you should choose your own time."

"Oh, Monsignor, how can I go and stay with them! I thought I should have died of shame when I went there after the concert with you. Mother Philippa asked me if I had travelled with my father when I went abroad. You must remember, for you came to my assistance."

"I turned the conversation, seeing that it embarrassed you."

"But you must have guessed."

"On account of your father's position at St. Joseph's, I had heard of you.... I had heard of your intimacy with Sir Owen Asher, and the life of an opera singer is not one to which a good Catholic can easily reconcile herself."

As they sat on either side of the table, Evelyn was attracted, and then absorbed, by the distinctive appearance of the priest. His mind was in his face. The long, high forehead, with black hair growing sparely upon it; the small, brilliant eyes, and the long, firm line of the jaw, now distinct, for the head was turned almost in profile. The face was a perfect symbol of the mind behind it; and the intimate concurrence of the appearance and the thought was the reason of its attractiveness. It was the beauty of unity; here was a man whose ideas are so deeply rooted that they express themselves in his flesh. In him there was nothing floating or undecided; and in the line of the thin, small mouth and the square nostrils, Evelyn divined a perfect certainty on all points. In this way she was attracted to his spiritual guidance, and desired the support of his knowledge, as she had desired Ulick's knowledge when she was studying Isolde. Ulick's technical knowledge had been useful to her; upon it she had raised herself, through it she had attained her idea. And in the same way Monsignor's knowledge on all points of doctrine would free her from doubt. Then she would be able to rise above the degradation of earthly passion to that purer and higher passion, the love of God. Doctrine she did not love for its own sake as Monsignor loved it. She regarded it as the musician regards crotchets and quavers, as a means of expression; and she now felt that without doctrine she could not acquire the love which she desired; without doctrine she could not free herself from the bondage of the flesh, and every moment the temptation to give her soul into his keeping grew more irresistible. Rising from her chair, she said—

"Will you hear my confession now, Monsignor?"

"The priest looked at her, his narrow, hard face concentrated in an ardent scrutiny.

"Certainly, my child, if you think you are sufficiently prepared."

"I must confess now; I could not put it off again;" and glancing round the room, she slipped suddenly upon her knees.

The priest put on his stole and murmured a Latin prayer, making the sign of the Cross over the head of his penitent.

"I fear I shall never remember all my sins. I have been living in mortal sin so many years."

"I remember that you spoke to me of intellectual difficulties—concerning faith. You see now, my dear child, that you were deceiving yourself. Your real difficulties were quite different."

"I think that my doubts were sincere," Evelyn replied tremblingly, for she felt that Monsignor expected her to agree with him.

"If your doubts were sincere, what has removed them? What has convinced you of the existence of a future life? That, I believe, was one of your chief difficulties. Have you examined the evidence?"

Evelyn murmured that that sense of right and wrong which she had never been able to drive out of her heart implied the existence of God.

"But savages, to whom the Scriptures are unknown, have a sense of right and wrong. Those who lived before the birth of Christ—the Greeks and Romans—had a sense of right and wrong."

Knowing that the priest's absolution depended upon her acceptance of the doctrine of a future life, she strove to believe as a little child. But it was her sins of the flesh that she wanted to confess, and this argument about the Incarnation had begun to seem out of place. Suddenly it seemed to hear inexpressibly ludicrous that she should be kneeling beside the priest. She could not help wondering what Owen would think of her. She remembered his pointing out that it is stated in the Gospel that the Messiah should be descended from David. Now, Mary was not of royal blood, so it was through Joseph, who was not his father, that Christ was descended from David. But these discrepancies did not matter. She felt the Church to be necessary to her, and that its teaching coincided with her deepest feeling seemed to her enough. But Monsignor was insistent, and he pressed dogma after dogma upon her. All the while the cocoa-nut matting ate into her knees, and she was perplexed by remembrances of sexual abandonments. How to speak of them she did not know, and she was haunted and terrified by the idea of concealing anything which would invalidate her confession. So she hastily availed herself of the first pause to tell him that she had lived with Owen Asher for the last six years. The priest did not trouble to inquire further, and she felt that she could not leave him under the impression that she had lived with Owen the moderate, sexual life which she believed was maintained between husband and wife.

"My life during the last six years," she said, interrupting him, "has been so abandoned. There are few—there are no excesses of which I have not been guilty."

"You have said enough on that point," he answered, to her great relief. But at that moment she remembered Ulick, and she felt that she must mention him. To do so she had again to interrupt the priest.

"But I must tell you—Sir Owen was not the only one"—she bowed her head—"there was another." Then, yielding to the temptation to explain herself, she told Monsignor how it was this second sin that had awakened her conscience. She had tried to look upon Sir Owen as her husband. "But one night at the theatre, during a performance of 'Tristan and Isolde,' I sinned with this second man."

"And this showed you, my dear child, the impossibility of a moral life for one who was born a Catholic except when protected by the doctrine and the sacraments of our Holy Church. And that brings us back to the point from which we started—the necessity of an unquestioning acceptance of the entire doctrine, and, I may add, a general acquiescence in Catholic belief. It seems strange to you that I am more anxious about your sins against faith than your sins of the flesh. It is because I know that without faith you will fall again. It is because I know the danger, the seduction of the theory that even if there be neither hell nor heaven, yet the obligation to lead a moral life exists. Such theory is in essence Protestantism and a delicious flattery of the vanity of human nature. It has been the cause of the loss of millions of souls. You yourself are a living testimony of the untrustworthiness of this shelter, and it is entirely contrary to the spirit of the teaching of the Church, which is that we must lead a moral life in order to gain heaven and avoid the pain of hell."

She leaned heavily on the table to relieve her knees from as much weight as possible, and she thought of the possibility of getting her handkerchief out of her pocket and placing it under her. But when her confession turned from her sins against faith to her sins of the flesh, she forgot the pain of her knees.

"There is one more question I must ask you. You have lived with this man as his mistress for six years, you have spoken of the excesses to which you abandoned yourself, but more important than these is whether you deliberately avoided the probable consequences of your sin—I mean in regard to children?"

"If we sin we must needs avoid the consequences of our sin. I know that it is forbidden—but my profession—I had to think of others—my father—"

"Your answer, my dear child, does not surprise me. It shows me into what depths you have fallen. That you should think like this is part of the teaching of the man whose object was to undermine your faith; it is part of the teaching of Darwin and Huxley and Spencer. You were persuaded that to live with a man to whom you were not married differed in no wise from living with your husband. The result has proved how false is such teaching. The sacrament of marriage was instituted to save the weak from the danger of temptation, and human nature is essentially weak, and without the protection of the Church it falls. The doctrine of the Church is our only safeguard. But that you should have proved unfaithful to this man—this second sin which shocked you so much, and which I am thankful awakened in you a sense of sin, is not more important than to thwart the design of Nature. It is important that you should understand this, for an understanding on this point will show you how false, how contradictory, is the teaching of the naturalistic philosophy in which you placed your trust. These men put aside revealed religion and refer everything to Nature, but they do not hesitate to oppose the designs of Nature when it suits their purpose. The doctrine of the Church has always been one wife, one husband. Polygamy and polyandry are relatively sterile. It is the acknowledged wife and the acknowledged husband that are fruitful; it is the husband and wife who furnish the world with men and heaven with souls, whereas the lover and the mistress fulfil no purpose, they merely encumber the world with their vice, they are useless to Nature, and are hateful in God's sight; the nations that do not cast them out soon become decrepid. If we go to the root of things, we find that the law of the Church coincides very closely with the law of Nature, and that the so-called natural sciences are but a nineteenth century figment. I hope all this is quite clear to you?"

Evelyn acquiesced. Her natural instinct forbade her the original sin—what happened after did not appeal to her; she could feel no interest in the question he had raised. But she was determined to avoid all falsehood—on that question her instinct was again explicit—and when he returned again in his irritation at her insubordination to his ideas, and questioned her regarding her belief as to a future life, her answer was so doubtful that after a moment's hesitation he said—

"If you are not convinced on so cardinal a point of dogma, it is impossible for me to give you absolution."

"Do not deny me your absolution. I cannot face my life without some sign of forgiveness. I believe—I think I believe. You probe too deeply. Sometimes it seems to me that there must be a future life, sometimes it seems to me—that it would be too terrible if we were to live again."

"It would be too terrible indeed, my dear child, if we were to live again unassoiled, unpurified, in all our miserable imperfections. But these have been removed by the priest's absolution, by the sinner's repentance in this world and by purgatory in the next. Those who have the happiness to live in the sight of God are without stain."

"I only know that I must lead a moral life, and that religion will help me to do so. I try to speak the truth, but the truth shifts and veers, and in trying to tell the whole truth perhaps I leave an impression that I believe less than I do. You must make allowance for my ignorance and incapacity. I cannot find words as you do to express myself. Do not refuse me absolution, for without it I shall not have strength to persevere.... I fear what may become of me. If you knew the effort it has cost me to come to you. I have not slept for many nights for thinking of my sins."

"There is one promise you must make me before I give you absolution; you must not seek either of these men again who have been to you a cause of sin."

The pain from her knees was expressed in her voice, and it was almost with a cry that she answered—

"But I have promised to sing his opera."

"I thought, my dear child, that you told me you intended to give up the stage. I feel bound to tell you that I do not see how you are to remain on the stage if you wish to lead a new life"

"I have been kneeling a long while," and a cry escaped her, so acute was the pain. She struggled to her feet and stood leaning against the table, waiting for the pain to die out of her limbs. "The other man is father's friend. If I tell him or if I write to him that he may not come to the house, father will suspect. Then I have promised to sing his opera. Oh, Monsignor—"

"These difficulties," said Monsignor, as he rose from his chair, "appear to you very serious. You are overcome by their importance because you have not adequately realised the awfulness of your state in the sight of God. If you were to die now, your soul would be lost. Once you have grasped this central fact in its full significance, the rest will seem easy. I will lend you a book which I think will help you."

"But, Monsignor, are you going to refuse me your absolution?"

"My dear child, you are in doubt regarding the essential doctrine of the resurrection, and you are unable to promise me not to see one of the men who have been to you a cause of sin."

Her clear, nervous vision met the dry, narrow vision that was the priest, and there was a pause in the conflict of their wills. He saw that his penitent was moved to the depth of her being, and had lost control of herself. He feared to send her away without absolution, yet he felt that she must be forced into submission—she must accept the entire doctrine of the Church. He could not understand, and therefore could not sympathise with her hesitation on points of doctrine. If the penitent accepted the Church as the true Church, conscience was laid aside for doctrine. The value of the Church was that it relieved the individual of the responsibility of life. So it was by an effort of will that he retained his patience. He was determined to reduce her to his mind, but he was instinctively aware of the danger of refusing her absolution; to do so might fling her back upon agnosticism. He was contending with vast passions. An unexpected wave might carry her beyond his reach. The stakes were high; he was playing for her soul with Owen Asher. He had decided to yield a point if necessary, but his voice was so kind, so irresistibly kind, that she heard nothing but it. However she might think when she had left him, she could not withstand the kindness of that voice; it seemed to enter into her life like some extraordinary music or perfume. He could see the effect he was producing on her; he watched her eyes growing bright until a slight dread crossed his mind. She seemed like one fascinated, trembling in bonds that were loosening, and that in the next moment would break, leaving her free—perhaps to throw herself into his arms; he did not dare to withdraw his eyes. An awful moment passed, and she turned slowly as if to leave the room. But at the moment of so doing a light seemed to break upon her brain; where there was darkness there was light. He saw her walk suddenly forward. She threw herself upon her knees at the table, and like one to whom speech had suddenly come back, she said—

"I believe in our holy Church and all that she teaches. Father, I beseech you to absolve me from my sins."

So striking was the change that the priest himself was cowed by it, and his personal pride in his conquest of her soul was drowned in a great awe. He had first to thank God for having chosen him as the instrument of his will, and then he spoke to Evelyn of the wonder and magnitude of God's mercies. That at the very height of her artistic career he should have roused her to a sense of her own exceeding sinfulness was a miracle of his grace.

His presence by her at that moment was a balm. She heard him say that life would not be an easy one, but that she must not be discouraged, that she must remember that she had made her peace with God, and would derive strength from his sacraments. An extraordinary sweetness came over her, she seemed borne away upon a delicious sweetness; she was conscious of an extraordinary inward presence. She did not dare to look up, or even to think, but buried herself in prayer, experiencing all the while the most wonderful and continuous sensation of delight. She had been racked and torn, and had fallen at his feet a helpless mass of suffering humanity. He had healed her, and she felt hope and life returning to her again, and sufficient strength to get up and continue her way. Never again would she be alone; he would be always near to guide her. She heard him tell her that she must recite daily for penance the hymn *veni sanctus spiritus*, and the thought of this obedience to him refreshed her as the first draught of spring water refreshes the wanderer who for weeks has hesitated between the tortures of thirst and the foul water of brackish desert pools. She was conscious that he was making the sign of the cross over her bowed head, the murmured Latin formula sounded strangely familiar and delicious in her ears, with the more clearly enunciated "*Ego te absolvo*" towards the close. In that supreme moment for which she had longed, the last traces of Owen's agnostic teaching seemed to fall from her, and she was carried back to the days of her girlhood, to the days of her old prayer-book, a "Garden of the Soul" bound in ivory; and she rose from her knees, weak, but happy as a convalescent.

"I hope you will sleep well to-night," said Monsignor, kindly, noticing the signs of physical exhaustion in Evelyn as she stood mechanically drawing down her veil and putting on her gloves. "A good conscience is the best of all narcotics." Evelyn smiled through her tears, but could not trust herself to speak. "But I don't really like you living alone in Park Lane. It is too great a strain on your nerves. Could you not go to your father's for a time?"

"Yes, perhaps, I don't know. Dear father would like to have me."

He told her that the Mass he was to say to-morrow he would offer up for her; and as she drove home her joy grew more intense, and in a sort of spiritual intoxication she identified herself with the faith of her childhood. Life again presented possibilities of infinite perfection, and she was astonished that the difficulties which she had thought insuperable had been so easily overcome.

All that evening she thought of God and his sacraments, and remembering the moment when his grace had descended upon her and all had become clear, she perforce believed in a miracle—a miracle of grace had certainly happened.

She looked forward to the moment when her maid would leave the room, and she would throw herself on her knees and lose herself in prayer, as she had lost herself when she knelt beside Monsignor, and he absolved her from sin. But when the door closed she was incapable of prayer, she only desired sleep. Her whole mind seemed to have veered. She had exaggerated everything, conducted herself strangely, hysterically, and her prayers were repeated without ardour, almost indifferently.

CHAPTER THIRTY-TWO

But the next day she could not account to herself for the extraordinary relief she had derived from her confession. For years she had battled with life alone, with no light to guide her, blown hither and thither by the gusts of her own emotions. But now she was at peace, she was reconciled to the Church; she would never be alone again. The struggle of her life still lay before her, and yet in a sense it was a thing of the past. She felt like a ship that has passed from the roar of the surf into the shelter of the embaying land, and in the distance stretched the long peacefulness of the winding harbour.

The solution of her monetary obligations to Sir Owen still perplexed her. She regretted not having laid the matter before Monsignor, and looked forward to doing so. She could hear his clear, explicit voice telling her what she must do, and guidance was such a sweet thing. He would say that to try to calculate hotel bills and railway fares was out of the question; but if she had said that the money Sir Owen had advanced her to pay Madame Savelli was to be considered as a debt, she must offer to return it. She knew that Owen would not accept it. It would be horrid of him if he did, but it would be still more horrid of her if she did not offer to return it.

She had not really begun to make money till the last few years, and as there had been no need for her to make money, she had sacrificed money to her pleasure and to Owen's. She had refused profitable engagements because Owen wanted her to go yachting, or because he wanted to go to Riversdale to hunt, or because she did not like the conductor. So it happened that she had very little money—about five thousand pounds, and her jewellery would fetch about half what was paid for it.

If she were to remain on the stage another year she could perhaps treble the amount, and to leave the stage she would have to provide herself with an adequate income. There was the tiara which the subscribers to the opera in New York had presented her with—that would fetch a good deal. It didn't become her, but it recalled a time of her life that was very dear to her, and she would be sorry to part with it. But from the point of view of ornament, she liked better the band of diamonds which a young Russian prince had sent to her anonymously. A few nights after, she had been introduced to him at a ball. His eyes went at once to the diamonds, a look of rapture had come into his face, and she had at once suspected he was the sender. They had danced many times, and retired for long, eager talks into distant corners. And the following evening she had found him waiting for her at the stage door. He had begged her to meet him in a park outside the city. He was attractive, young, and she was alone. Owen was away. She had thought that she liked him, and it was exciting to meet him in this distant park, their carriages waiting for them below the hill. She could still see the grey, lowering sky and the trees hanging in green masses; she had thought all the time it was going to rain. She remembered his pale, interesting face and his eager, insinuating voice. But he had had to leave St. Petersburg the next day. It was one of those things that might have, but had not, happened. How strange! She might have liked him. How strange; she never would see him. And she sat dreaming a long while.

Owen had given her a clasp, composed of two large emerald bosses set with curious antique gems, when she played Brunnhilde. The necklace of gem intaglios, in gold Etruscan filigree settings, he had given her for her Elsa—more than her Elsa was worth. For Elizabeth he had given her ropes of equal-sized pearls, and the lustre of the surfaces was considered extraordinary. For Isolde he had given her strings of black pearls which the jewellers of Europe had been collecting for more than a year. Every pearl had the same depth of colour, and hanging from it was a large black brilliant set in a mass of white brilliants. He had hung it round her neck as she went on the stage, and she had had only time to clasp his hands and say "dearest." These presents alone, she thought, could not be worth less than ten thousand pounds.

She kept her jewels in a small iron safe; it stood in her dressing-room under her washhand stand, and Merat surprised her two hours later sitting on her bed, with everything, down to the rings which she wore daily, spread over the counterpane. The maid gave her mistress a sharp look, remarking that she hoped Mademoiselle did not miss anything. In her hand there was a brooch consisting of three large emeralds set with diamonds; she often wore it at the front of her dress, it went particularly well with a flowered silk which Owen always admired. She calculated the price it would fetch, and at the same time was convinced that Monsignor's permission to sing on the concert platform, and possibly to go to Bayreuth to sing Kundry, would not affect her decision. She wanted to leave the stage. Half-measures did not appeal to her in the least. If she was to give up the stage, she must give it up wholly. It must be a thing over and done with, or she must remain on the stage and sing for the good of Art and her lovers. Since that was no longer possible, she preferred never to sing a note again in public. The worst wrench of all was her promise to Monsignor not to sing Grania, and since she had made that sacrifice, she could not dally with lesser things. Then, resuming her search among her jewellery, she selected the few things she would like to keep. She examined a cameo brooch set in filigree gold, ornamented with old rose diamonds, and she picked up a strange ring which a man whom Owen knew had taken from the finger of a mummy. It was a large emerald set in plain gold. A man who had been present at the unswathing of this princess, dead at least three thousand years, had managed to secure it, and Owen had paid him a large sum for it. She put it on her finger, and decided to keep a dozen other rings, the earrings she wore, and a few bracelets. The rest of her jewellery she would sell, if Owen refused to have them back. Of course there would be her teaching; she could not live in Dulwich doing nothing, and would take up her mother's singing classes....

Her mother had lost her voice in the middle of her career, and her daughter had abandoned the stage at the moment of her greatest triumph! Looking at her jewels scattered all over the bed, Evelyn wondered what was going to happen to her. Was she really going to leave the stage? She—Evelyn Innes? When she thought of it, it seemed impossible. If religion were only a craze. If she were to go back to Owen, or to other lovers? How strange it was; it seemed strange to be herself, and yet it was quite true. Remembering that on Sunday she would partake of the Body and Blood which her Saviour had given for the salvation of sinners, her soul suddenly hushed, and catching sight of the jewels which symbolised the sacrifice she was making, it seemed to her that she could afford much greater sacrifices for what she was going to receive....

She saw lights dying down in the distance, and the world which had once seemed so desirable seemed to her strangely trivial and easily denied. Already she could look back at the poor struggling ones, struggling for what to-morrow will be abandoned, forgotten, passing illusions; and she wondered how it was that she had not always thought as she thought to-day. Her thoughts passed into reveries, and she awoke, remembering that Monsignor had told her that he did not like her living alone in Park Lane. But in Dulwich she would be with her father, whom she had long neglected, and she would be near St. Joseph's and her confessor. At the same moment she remembered that she could not write to her lovers from Park Lane. She put her jewels back in the safe, and told Merat to pack sufficient things for a month, and to follow her with them to Dulwich. Merat asked for more precise instruction, but Evelyn said she must use her good sense; she was going away at once, and Merat must follow by a later train.

"Then Mademoiselle does not want the carriage?"

"No, I shall go by train."

She found her father in the workroom, and the sight of him in his cap and apron mending an old musical instrument caused many home scenes to flash across her mind, and she did not know whether it was from curiosity or a desire to please him that she asked the name of the strange little instrument he was repairing. It looked like an overgrown concertina, and he explained that it was a tiny virginal, and pointed out the date; it was made in 1631, in Roman notation.

"Father," she said, "I have come back to you; we shall never be separated any more—if you'll have me back."

"Have you back, dear! What has happened now?"

He stood with a chisel in his hand, and she noticed that he dug the point nervously into the soft deal plank. She sat down on a small wooden stool, and kicking the shavings with her feet, she said—

"Father, a great deal has happened. I have sent Owen away ... I shall never see him again; I'm sorry to have to speak about him to you; you mustn't be angry; he was very good to me, and he asked me to marry him; he did everything—I'm afraid I've broken his heart."

"You're very strange, Evelyn, and I don't know what answer to make to you.... Why did you send him away, and why did you refuse to marry him?"

"I sent him away because I thought it wrong to live with him, and I refused to marry him—well, I don't know, father, I don't know why I refused to marry him. It seemed to me that if he had wished to marry me he ought to have done so long ago."

"Is that the only reason you can give?"

"It is the only reason I know. You seem sorry for him, father, are you? I hope you are. He has been very good to me. I've often wished to tell you; it has often been in my heart to tell you that you should not hate him. He was very good to me, no one could have been kinder; he was very fond of me, you must not bear him any ill will."

"I never said that I bore him ill will. He made you a great singer, and you say he was very kind to you and wanted to marry you."

"Yes, and he was most anxious to see you, and he went with me to St. Joseph's the Sunday you gave the great Mass of Pope Marcellus. He was distressed that he could not see you to tell you about the choir."

"They sang better that Sunday than the Sunday you heard the 'Missa Brevis.' I have got two new trebles. One has an exquisite voice. I wish I could get a few good altos. It was the altos that were wrong when you heard the 'Missa Brevis.' But you didn't hear they were out of tune. That piano has falsified your ear, but it will come back to you."

"Dear father, how funny you are! If nothing were more wrong than my ear ..."

They glanced at each other hastily, and to change the subject he mentioned that he had had a letter that morning from Ulick. He had finished scoring the second act of Grania, and thinking that he was on safe ground, Mr. Innes told her that Ulick hoped to finish his score in the autumn. The third act would not take him long; he had a very complete sketch of the music, etc. "I shall enjoy going through his opera with him."

"Father, I don't know how to tell you. Will you ever forgive me or him. Ulick must not come back here—at least not while I am here. Perhaps I had better go."

The chisel dropped from his hand, and he stood looking at his daughter. His look was pitiful, and she could not bear to see him shake his head slowly from side to side.

"Poor father is wondering why I am like this;" and to interrupt his reflections she said—

"I don't know why I am like this; that's what you're thinking, father, but henceforth I'll be like mother and my aunts. They were all good women ... I have often wondered why I am like this." Their eyes met, and seized with a sudden dread lest he should think (if such were really the case) that he was the original cause—she seemed to read something like that in his eyes—she said, "You must forgive me, whatever I am; you know that we've always loved each other, and we always shall. Nothing can come between us; you must be sorry for me, and kiss me, and love me more than ever, for I've been very unhappy. I haven't told you all I have given up so that I might be a good woman; it is not easy to make the sacrifices I have made, but I am happier now that I have made them. Ulick—Ulick must not come here while I'm here, but you'll want to see him—I had better go. Father, dear, it is hard to say all these things. I've done nothing but bring you trouble. Now I've robbed you of your friend. For I've promised not to see Ulick again. If I stay here, father, he must not come—I'm ashamed to ask you this, but what am I to do? I bring trouble. Later on, perhaps, but for a long while he and I must not meet."

Mr. Innes stood looking at his daughter, and a peculiar puzzled expression had begun in his eyes, and had spread over his face. He suddenly shrugged his shoulders; the movement was like Evelyn's shrug, it expressed the same nervous hopelessness.

"I promised Monsignor that I would not see either."

"You went to confession—to him?"

Evelyn nodded.

"But how about Grania?"

"I'm not going to sing Grania. I've left the stage for good."

"Left the stage?"

"Yes, father, I've left the stage, and I could not go back even if Monsignor were to permit me. But you must not argue with me; I argued with myself until I nearly went mad. Night after night went by sleepless; I was mad one night, and should have poisoned myself if I had not found my scapular. But you mustn't question me. Some day when it is all far away I'll tell you the whole story. I cannot speak of it at present, it is all too near. Suffice it to say that I have repented, and have come to ask you if you'll have me back to live with you?"

"You're my daughter, and you must do as you like. You were always different from anyone else, I cannot cope with you. So you have left the stage, left the stage! What will people think?"

"I could not be a good woman and remain on the stage, that's what it comes to." In spite of the gravity of the scene, a smile trickled round Evelyn's lips, for she could not help seeing her father like a hen that has hatched out a duckling. He stood looking at her sadly. She had come back—but what new pond would she plunge into? "I am a very unsatisfactory person, I know that. I can't make people happy; but there it is, it can't be otherwise. If I don't sing on the stage, I can sing at your concerts. Come downstairs and let's have some music. We've talked enough.

"What shall we play—a Bach sonata? Ah, I remember this," she said, catching sight of the harpsichord part of a suite by J.P. Rameau, for the harpsichord and viola da gamba. "Where is the viola da gamba part?"

"In the bottom of that bookcase, I think; don't you remember it?"

"Well, it is some time since I've played it," she said, smiling, "but I'll try."

It seemed to her that she remembered it all wonderfully well, and she was surprised how every phrase came up correctly under her bow. But she stopped suddenly.

"I don't remember what comes next."

Mr. Innes played the phrase, she played it after him, but she broke down a little further on, and it took some time to find the music. "No, not in that shelf," cried Mr. Innes, "the next one; not that volume, the next."

"Ah, yes, I remember the volume, about the middle?" When she found the place she said, "Oh, yes, of course," and he answered—

"Ah, it seems simple enough now," and they went on together to the end.

"I've not lost much of my playing, have I?"

"A little stiffness, perhaps, and you've lost your sense of the old forms. Now let's play this rondeau of Marais."

When they had finished, it was dinner-time, and after dinner they had more music. Before going upstairs, Evelyn asked Agnes if there was any ink in her room. She had to ask her father for some writing paper, she would have avoided doing so if she could have helped it. She feared he would guess that she was writing to her lovers. She smiled—so odd did her scruples seem to her—she was writing to send them away. Her father's house was surely the right place. If it were to make appointments, that would be different. It was long past midnight when she read over her letter to Owen.

"Dear Owen,—A great deal has happened since we last met, and I am convinced that it would be unwise for me to see you in three months as I promised. My confessor is of the same opinion; he thinks three months too soon, and I must obey him. I have taken the step which I hope you will take some day, for you too are a Catholic. In going to confession and resolving not to see you again, I had a long struggle with my feelings; but God gave me grace to overcome them. You know me well enough by this time, and can have no doubt that I could not live with you again as your mistress, and as I do not feel that I could marry you, no course is open to me but to beg of you not to write to me, or to try to see me. Owen, I feel that all this is horrid, that I am horrid looked at from your side. I cannot seem anything else. I hate it all, but it has to be done. Perhaps one of these days you will see things as I do.

"I owe you—I do not know how much, but I owe you a great deal of money. I remember saying that Savelli's lessons were to be considered as a debt, also the expenses of the house in the Rue Balzac. You never would tell me what the rent of that house was, but as well as I can calculate, I owe you a thousand pounds for that year in Paris." (Evelyn paused. "It must be," she thought, "much more, but it would be difficult for me to pay more.")

"You have," she continued, "paid for a hundred other things besides Savelli's lessons and the house in the Rue Balzac, but it would be impossible to make out a correct account, I feel, too, that you gave me the greatest part of my jewellery thinking that one day I would be your wife; you would not have given me so much if you had not thought so. Therefore I feel it is only just to offer you the whole of it back. I will only ask you to allow me to keep a few trifles—the earrings you bought for me the day we arrived in Paris, the mummy's ring, etc., not more than half-a-dozen things in all. I should like to keep these in memory of a time which I ought to forget, but which I am afraid I shall never have the courage even to try to forget. Dear Owen, I cannot tell you why I cannot marry you, I only know that I cannot. I am obeying an instinct far stronger than I, and I cannot struggle against it any longer.

"One day perhaps we may meet—but it may not be for years, until we are both quite different.

"Sincerely yours,

"EVELYN INNES."

The moment she had written the address, she threw the pen aside, and she sat striving against an uncontrollable sense of misery. At last her pent-up tears ran over her eyelids. She flung herself on her bed, and lay weeping, shaken by short, choking sobs. All her courage of the morning had forsaken her; she could not face her new life, she could not send away Owen. Her inmost life rose in revolt. Why was this new sacrifice demanded of her? Why was her life to be made so hard, so impossible for her to endure? She felt she could not live in the life which she foresaw awaited her. Then she felt that she was being tried beyond the endurance of any woman. But the storm did not last, her sobs died away. She sat up, mopping her eyes with a soaking pocket handkerchief, and utterly exhausted by the violence of her emotions, she began to undress. She felt the impossibility of saying her prayers, her one longing was for sleep, oblivion; she wished herself dead, and was too worn out to put the thought from her, though she knew it was wrong.

In the morning the first thing she saw was the letter to Owen. There it was! And every word and letter sank into her brain. "Sir Owen Asher, Bart., Riversdale, Northamptonshire." She would have to post it, and never again would she see him. She questioned the right of the priest in obtaining from her a promise not to see him, so long as she did not sin. But Owen was an approximate cause of mortal sin....

Ashamed of her instability, and feeling herself unworthy and no longer pure as absolution had made her, she went that afternoon to St. Joseph's, and in confession laid the matter before Monsignor Mostyn. Regarding the money question, he approved of what she had written to Sir Owen, and he was far more indulgent regarding her breakdown than she had dared to hope. He had expected some such mental crisis. It was extraordinary the strength it gave her even to see his stern, grave face; she was thrilled by his certainty on all points, and it no longer seemed difficult to send the letter she had written, or to write a similar letter to Ulick, which he advised her to send by the same post. She began it the moment she got home, and she wrote in perfect confidence and courage, the words coming easily to her, so easily that there were times when she seemed to hear Monsignor speaking over her shoulder.

"Dear Ulick,—A very great event has happened in my life since I saw you. The greatest event that can happen in any life—Grace has been vouchsafed to me. Now I understand how sinful my life has been, as much from a human as a religious point of view. I deserted my dear father, I left him alone to live as best he could. I was not even faithful to my lover. From a worldly point of view I owed him everything, yet for the sake of my passion for you I encouraged myself for a while to dwell on his faults, to see nothing in him but the small and the mean. I strove to degrade him in my eyes so that I might find some excuse for loving you. You were nice, Ulick, you were kind, you were good to me, and I was enthusiastic about your genius. One of my greatest troubles now is that I shall not be able to sing your opera. For a long while this very thing prevented my repentance. I said to myself, 'It is impossible, I cannot, I have promised, I must do what I said I would do. He will think me hateful if I do not create the part.' But these hesitations between what is certainly right and what is certainly wrong existed in me because I did not then perceive how very little the things of this world are, compared with eternal things, and that nothing matters compared with the necessity of saving our souls. All this is now quite clear to me, and it would therefore be madness for me to remain on the stage, recognising as I do that it is a source of grave temptation to me. You will try to understand, dear Ulick, you will try to look at things from my point of view. You will see that it is impossible for me to act otherwise.

"I am living now with my father, and must not see you when you return to London. I have promised my confessor not to see you. One of these days, in years to come, when you and I are different beings, we may meet, but we must not see each other at present. I must beg of you not to write or to try to see me. My resolve is unalterable, and any attempt on your part to induce me to return to my old life will be useless. It as already far away and inconceivable to me. I know that by asking you not to come to Dulwich I am robbing my father of his friend. I have never brought happiness to anyone, not to father, not to Sir Owen, not to you, not to myself. If other proof were wanting, would not this fact be enough to convince me that my life has been all wrong? What it will be in the future I don't know, I have confidence in the goodness of God and in the wisdom of my spiritual adviser.—Sincerely yours,
"EVELYN INNES."

"*P.S.*—In course of conversation with my father, I mentioned inadvertently that you were my lover; I begged him not to be angry with you, but I know that I should not have mentioned your name. I must ask you to forgive me this too."

The next day and the day following were lived within herself, sometimes viewing God far away, as if at one end of a great plain, and herself kneeling penitent at the other. She was filled with thoughts of his infinite goodness and mercy, and of the miraculous intercession of the Virgin at the moment when she was about to commit a crime that would have lost her her soul for ever. She went to Mass daily, and took peculiar delight in reciting the hymn which Monsignor had given her for a penance. She regretted it was not more. It seemed to her such a trivial penance, and she reflected on the blackness of her sins, and the penances which the saints had imposed upon themselves. But her chief desire was to keep herself pure in thought, and she read pious books when she was alone, and encouraged her mind to dwell on the profound mystery in which she was going to participate, and to believe in the marvellous change it would produce in her.

It was on Friday morning that Agnes handed her Ulick's letter. She did not read it at once, it lay on the table while she was dressing, and she was uncertain whether it would not be better to put off reading it until she came back from St. Joseph's.

"Alas, from our first meeting, and before it, we were aware of the fate which has overtaken us. We heard it in our hearts, that numb restlessness, that vague disquietude, that prophetic echo which never dies out of ears attuned to the music of destiny ... Love you less, you who are the source of all joy to me? Evelyn, my heart aches and my brain is light with grief, but the terrible certitude persists that we are being drawn asunder. I see you like a ship that has cleared the harbour bar, and is already amid the tumult of the ocean.... We are ships, and the destiny of ships is the ocean, the ocean draws us both: we have rested as long as may be, we have delayed our departure, but the tide has lifted us from our moorings. With an agonised heart I watched the sails of your ship go up, and now I see that mine, too, are going aloft, hoisted by invisible hands. I look back upon the bright days and quiet nights we have rested in this tranquil harbour. Like ships that have rested a while in a casual harbour, blown hither by storms, we part, drawn apart by the eternal magnetism of the sea. I would go to you, Evelyn, if I could, and pray you not to leave me. But you would not hear: destiny hears no prayers. In the depths of our consciousness, below the misery of the moment, there lies a certain sense that our ways are different ways, and that we must fare forth alone, whither we know not, over the ocean's rim; and in this sense of destiny we must find comfort. Will resignation, which is the highest comfort, come to us in time? My eyes fall upon my music paper, and at the same time your eyes turn to the crucifix. Ours is the same adventure, though a different breeze fills the sails, though the prows are set to a different horizon. God is our quest—you seek him in dogma, I in art.

"But, Evelyn, my heart is aching so. How awful the word never, and the years are filled with its echoes. And the wide ocean which lies outside the harbour is so lonely, and I have no heart for any other joy. 'May we not meet again?' my heart cries from time to time; 'may not some propitious storm blow us to the same anchorage again, into the same port?' Ah, the suns and the seas we shall have sailed through would render us unrecognisable, we should not know each other. Last night I wandered by the quays, and, watching the constellations, I asked if we were divided for ever, if, when the earth has become part and parcel of the stars, our love will not reappear in some starry affinity, in some stellar friendship.—Yours,
"ULICK DEAN."

The symbol of the ships seemed to Evelyn to express the union and the division and the destiny that had overtaken them. She sat and pondered, and in her vision ships hailed each other as they crossed in mid-ocean. Ships drew together as they entered a harbour. Ships separated as they fared forth, their prows set towards different horizons. She sat absorbed in the mystery of destiny. Like two ships, they had rested side by side in a casual harbour. They had loved each other as well as their different destinies had allowed them. None can do more. She loved him better—in a way—but he was less to her than Owen. She felt that, and he had felt that.... As he said, if they were to meet again they would not recognise each other, so different were the suns that would shine upon them and the oceans they would travel through. She understood what he meant, and a prevision of her future life seemed to flicker up in her brain, like the sea seen through a mist; and through vistas in the haze she saw the lonely ocean, and her bark was already putting off from the shore. All she had known she was leaving behind. The destiny of ships is the ocean.

Owen's letter she received in the evening about six o'clock. She changed colour at the sight of it, and her hand trembled, and she tore the envelope across as she opened it.

"You ask me to make no attempt to save you. You ask me to stand on the bank while you struggle and are dragged down by the current. Evelyn, I have never disobeyed your slightest wish before, but I declare my right to use all means to save you from a terrible fate. I return to London to do so. God only knows if I shall succeed.... In any case I hope you will never allude again to any money questions. What I gave, I gave, and unless you want to kill me outright, never speak again of returning my presents.—As ever,
OWEN ASHER."

Her eyes ran through the lines, and her heart said, "How he loves me." But the temptation to see him quenched instantly in remembrance of her Communion, and she tore the letter hastily into two pieces, as if by destroying it she destroyed the difficulty it had created for her. She must not see him. But how was she to avoid meeting him? To-morrow be would be waiting in the street for her, and she walked about the room too agitated to think clearly. He seemed like the devil trying to come between her and God. She must not see him, of that she was quite sure. She would lock herself in her room. But then she would miss Holy Communion, and her heart was set on the Sacrament; the Sacrament alone could give her strength to persevere. To see him and to hear him would ruin her peace of mind, and peace of mind was essential to the reverent reception of the Sacrament. It was lost already, or very nearly. She stopped in her walk, she looked into her soul, she asked herself if any thought had crossed her mind which would render her unfit for Communion ... and on the spot she resolved to go straight to Monsignor and consult him. He would advise her, he would find some way out of the difficulty. But it was now six; she could not get to St. Joseph's before seven. It was late, but she did not think he would refuse to see her; he would know that it was only a matter of the greatest moment that would bring her to inquire for him at that hour.

It was as she expected. Monsignor did not receive anyone so late in the evening.

"Yes, I know, but I think Monsignor Mostyn will see me. Tell him—tell him that my business does not admit delay."

She was shown into the same waiting-room. This seemed to her a favourable presage, and she offered up a prayer that Monsignor would not refuse to see her; everything depended on that. She listened for his step; twice she was mistaken; at last the door opened. It was he, and he guessed, before she had time to speak, what had happened.

"One of those men," he said, "has come again into your life?"

She nodded, and, still unable to speak, she searched in her pocket for their letters.

"I received these letters to-day—one this morning, the other, Sir Owen's, just now. That was why I came. I felt that I had to see you."

"Pray sit down, my child, you are agitated." He handed her a chair.

"You remember you said I might go to Communion on Sunday, and if I were to meet him to-morrow it would—there is no temptation, I don't mean that—but I do not wish to be reminded of things which you told me I was to try to forget."

The priest stood reading the letters, and Evelyn sat looking into space, absorbed in the desire to escape from Owen. All her faith was in Monsignor, and she believed he would be able to save her from Owen's intrusion.

"I don't think you need fear anything from Mr. Dean."

"No, not from him."

Monsignor continued to read Ulick's letter. Evelyn wished he would read Owen's; Ulick's interested her not in the least.

"Mr. Dean seems a very extraordinary person. Does he believed in astrology, the casting of horoscopes, or is it mere affectation?"

"I don't know; he always talks like that. He believes, or says he believes, in Lir and the great Mother Dana, in the old Irish Gods. But, Monsignor, please read Sir Owen's letter. I want to know what I am to do."

He walked once across the room, and when he returned to the table he said half to himself, as if his thoughts had long out-stripped his words—

"I am glad I advised you to leave Park Lane, for of course he will go there first."

"He will easily find out I'm at Dulwich, he need not even ask—he will guess it at once."

"Yes, to be sure."

"If I am not to meet him I must go away—but where? All my friends and acquaintances are his friends. You would approve of none of them Monsignor," she said, smiling a little.

He did not seem to hear her. Suddenly he said, "I think you had better go and spend a few days at the Passionist Convent. The Reverend Mother sent you an invitation through me, you remember, so we need have no hesitation in proposing it. Indeed, I feel confident that they will receive you with the greatest pleasure. It will do you a great deal of good. You will have peace and quiet, my child; you will find yourself in an atmosphere of faith and purity which cannot but be helpful to you in your present unsettled state."

It seemed to Evelyn that that was what she had wanted all the time, only she had not been able to say so. Yes; to spend a week with those dear nuns, to sit in the convent garden, to kneel before the Blessed Sacrament in the convent church, it would be a real spiritual luxury.

"Yes, I should love to go," she said. "I feel it is just what I need. I have so much to think out, so much to learn, and at home there are a hundred things to distract me."

"Very well, then, that is settled. I will send the Reverend Mother word to-morrow; but there is no necessity, you can write yourself, and say you are coming in the afternoon; she will only have to get your room ready."

"But, Monsignor, my Communion? I had forgotten it was from you I was to receive Holy Communion. Of course I know it doesn't really make any difference, but still, you heard my confession, and I would far rather receive Communion this first time from you than from anyone else. I don't think it could be quite the same thing—if it weren't from you."

"And I should be sorry too, my child, as by God's grace I have been the means of bringing you thus far, not to complete your reconciliation to him. But I think we can manage that too without much difficulty. I say Mass to-morrow at nine o'clock, and will give you Communion then, and you can go to the convent for your retreat early in the afternoon. Will that suit you?"

And Evelyn could not find words to express her gratitude.

That evening she sat with her father. He was busy stringing a lute, and they had not spoken for some time; they often spent quite long whiles without speaking, and only occasionally they raised their eyes to see each other. The sensation of the other's presence was sufficient for their happiness.

CHAPTER THIRTY-THREE

It being Saturday, there was choir practice at St. Joseph's, and when Evelyn returned her father had left, and she breakfasted alone. After breakfast she sat absorbed in the mysteries of the Sacrament she had received. But in the middle of her exaltation doubt intervened, and Owen's arguments flashed through her mind. She strove to banish them; it was terrible that she should think such things over again, and on the morning of her Communion. Her spiritual joy was blighted; she could only hope that these dreadful thoughts were temptations of the devil, and that she was in no wise responsible. She stood in the middle of the room, asking herself if she had not in some slight measure yielded to them. No direct answer came to her question, but the words, "When I'm a bad woman I believe, when I'm a good woman I doubt," sounded clear and distinct in her brain, and she remained thinking a long while.

Her father came in after lunch. And while she spoke about his trebles and his altos, she was thinking how she should tell him that she was going away that afternoon.

"You're very silent."

"I was at Holy Communion this morning."

"This morning? I thought you were going to Communion on Sunday?"

"Yes, so I was, but I received a letter from Owen Asher saying he intended to see me. I took it to Monsignor; he said it was necessary that I should not see Owen, and he advised me to go and stay with the Sisters at Wimbledon. That is why I went to Communion this morning; I wanted Monsignor to give me Communion. Father, I cannot remain here, I should be sure to meet him."

"He will not come here."

"No, but he'll be waiting in the street."

"When are you going?"

"This afternoon," she answered, and handed him Owen's letter. He glanced at it, and said—

"He seems very fond of you."

The answer shocked her, and nothing more was said on the subject. A little later she asked him about the trains. She did not know how she was to get from Dulwich to Wimbledon. Neither were very apt in looking out the trains, and eventually it was Agnes who discovered the changes that would have to be made. She would have to go first to Victoria, and then she would have to drive from Victoria to Waterloo, and this seemed so complicated and roundabout that she decided to drive all the way in a hansom. Dulwich and Wimbledon could not be more than ten miles apart.

"I must go upstairs now, father, and pack my things."

Her father followed her and stood by, while she hesitated what she should take. Smiling, she rejected a tea-gown as unsuitable for convent wear, and put in a black lace scarf which she thought would be useful for wearing in church; it would look better in the convent chapel than a hat. Instead of a flowered silk she chose a grey alpaca. Then she remembered that she must take some books with her. It would be useless to bring pious books with her, she would find plenty of those in the convent.

"Have you any books, father? I must have something to read."

"There are a few books downstairs; you know them all."

"You don't read much, father?"

"Not much, except music. But Ulick brings books here, you may find something among them."

She returned with Berlioz's *Memoirs*, Pater's *Imaginary Portraits*, and Blake's *Songs of Innocence and Experience*.

"I suppose these books belong to Ulick. I don't know if I ought to take them."

"I cannot advise you; you must do as you like. I suppose you'll bring them back?"

"Oh, yes, of course I shall bring them back."

"Evelyn, dear, is it quite essential that you should go?"

"Yes, father, yes, it is quite; but I don't know how I am to get away."

"How you're to get away! What do you mean?"

"Well," she answered, laughing, "you see in his letter he says he's coming to watch me. Father, I can see that you pity him; you're sorry for him, aren't you?"

"Well, Evelyn, he offered to marry you, he made you a great singer, and you say he'd do anything for you. I suppose I am sorry for him."

They stood looking out of the window.

"You know I'd like to stop with you; it can't be helped; but I shall come back."

"Do you think you'll come back?"

"Of course I shall come back. Where should I go if I did not come back?"

At that moment Agnes drove up in a hansom; she ran up the little garden, and carried out Evelyn's bag and placed it in the hansom.

"I must go now, father; good-bye, darling. I shan't be away more than seven or eight days."

A moment after her dear father was behind her, and she was alone in the hansom, driving towards the convent. About her were villas engarlanded with reddening creeper. On one lawn a family had assembled under the shade of a dwarf cedar, and miles of this kind of landscape lay before her. It seemed to her like painted paper, an illusion that might pass away at any moment. Her truth was no longer in the external world, but in her own soul. Her soul was making for a goal which she could not discern. She was leaving a life of wealth and fame and love for a life of poverty, chastity and obscurity. All the joy and emulation of the stage she was relinquishing for a dull, narrow, bare life at Dulwich, giving singing lessons and saying prayers at St. Joseph's. Yet there was no question which she would choose, and she marvelled at the strangeness of her choice.

The road lay through fields and past farmhouses, but the suburban street was never quite lost sight of. Its blue roofs and cheap porticos appeared unexpectedly at the end of an otherwise romantic prospect, and so on and so on, until the driver let his horse walk up Wimbledon hill. When they reached the top she craned her neck, and was in time to catch a glimpse of the windmill far away to the right. The inn was in front of her, the end of a long point of houses stretching into the common, and the hansom rolled easily on the wide, curving roads. She anticipated the choked gardens, the decaying pear trees, the gold crowns of sunflowers; and a moment after the hansom passed these things and she saw the old green door, and heard the jangling peal. The eyes of the lay sister looked through the barred loop-hole.

"How do you do, sister? I suppose you expected me?"

The cabman put the trunk inside the long passage, and Evelyn said—

"But my luggage."

"If you'll come into the parlour I'll get one of the sisters to help me to carry it upstairs."
Evelyn was sitting at the table turning over the leaves of the Confessions of St. Augustine, when the Reverend Mother entered. She seemed to Evelyn even smaller than she had done on the first occasion they had met; she seemed lost in the voluminous grey habit, and the long, light veil floated in the wind of her quick step.
"I'm glad you were able to come so soon. All the sisters are anxious to meet you, you who have done so much for us."
"I've done very little, Reverend Mother. Could I have done less for my old convent? I hope that your difficulties are at an end."
"At an end, no, but you helped us over a critical moment in the fortunes of our convent."
Her hands were leaned against the edge of the table, her white fingers, white with age, played with the hem of her veil, her blue, anxious eyes were fixed on Evelyn at once tenderly, expectantly, and compassionately. Her voice was the clear, refined voice which signifies society, and Evelyn would not have been surprised to learn that she belonged to an old aristocratic family, Evelyn imagined her to be a woman in whom the genius of government dominated, and who, not having found an outlet into the world, had turned to the cloister. Was that her story? Evelyn wondered, and suddenly seemed to forsee a day when she would hear the story which shone behind those clear blue eyes, and obliterated age from the white face.
They went up the circular staircase, at the top of which was a large landing; there were two rooms at the head of the stairs, and the Reverend Mother said—
"These are our guest chambers." Standing on a second landing, one step higher than the first, a solid wooden partition had been erected, and pointing to a door the nun said with a laugh, "That door leads to the sisters' cells. You must not make a mistake."
Evelyn was pleased to see that her room had two windows overlooking the garden. There was a table covered by a cloth at which she could write, and she bent over the bowl of roses and wondered which kind nun had gathered them. The Reverend Mother left her, saying that she would be told when supper was ready, and on looking round the room she perceived her portmanteau, which the lay sister had not unstrapped. She would have to unstrap it herself. She remembered that she had brought very few things with her, and yet she was surprised at the smallness of her luggage. For she usually took half-a-dozen dresses with her, now she had only brought one change, a grey alpaca. She thought she might have left her dressing-case behind, a plain brush and comb would have been all she needed. But at the last moment, she had felt that she could not do without these bottles of scent and brushes and nicknacks; they had seemed indispensable. The dressing-case was Owen's influence still pursuing her. She had not known why she was compelled to bring the dressing-case, now she knew—Owen! Never would she be able to wholly separate herself from him. He had become part of her.
As she stood in the convent room noticing the beeswaxed floor and the two rugs, one by the small iron bed, she remembered a hunting morning three years ago at Riversdale. She had gone to Owen's room to see if he were ready. A multitude of orders were being given there, the valet was searching anxiously in the large wardrobe, piled high with many various coats and trousers; Owen stood before the looking-glass tying a white scarf, and two footmen watched each movement, dreading a mistake. She remembered that she had been amused at the time, and she never recalled the scene without smiling. But she had liked Owen better for the innumerable superfluities, all of which were necessary to his happiness, the breakdown of any one of which made him the most miserable man alive. She remembered how she had secretly imitated him, and how she had gathered about her a mass of superfluous necessities. But they had never become necessities to her, they had always galled her. It was in a spirit of perversity she had imitated him. She had always felt it to be wrong to eat peaches at five francs a piece, and had always been aware of an inward resentment against the extravagance of a reserved carriage on the railway and private saloon on board the boat. She had always desired a simple life; the life of these nuns was a simple life, simpler perhaps than she cared

for. There was no hot water in her room, she wondered how she would wash her hands, and smiling at her philosophical reflections, she thought how Owen would laugh if he could see her in her present situation—in a convent, crying out for a constant supply of hot water and her maid. A religious life with home comforts, that was what she wanted.

She was always a subject of amusement to herself, and she was still smiling when a knock awoke her from her whimsical reveries. She answered "Come in," and an elderly nun told her that supper was ready in the parlour. In this room, furnished with a table and six chairs and four pious prints, Evelyn ate her convent meal, a sort of mixed meal, which included soup, cold meat, coffee, jam and some unripe pears. The porteress took the plates away, and somehow Evelyn could not help feeling that she was giving a good deal of trouble. She could see that the nuns did everything for themselves, and she abandoned hope of ever finding a can of hot water in her room. She remembered that when she made her retreat some years ago, she had not noticed these things. She owed all her wants to Owen. Mother Philippa came in, delighted to see her, and anxious to know if she had everything she wanted.

"I thought you would be sure to be going abroad, and that next Easter, the time you were here before, would be the time to ask you."

"But the Reverend Mother thought that now would be a better time."

"Yes, she said that Easter was a long way off, and that a rest would do you good after singing all the season in London."

Evelyn wondered what idea the phrase "the season in London" awoke in the mind of the nun. A little puzzled look did pass in her eyes, and then she resumed her friendly chatter. Evelyn listened, more interested in Mother Philippa's kind, amicable nature than in what she said. She imagined in different circumstances what a good wife she would have been, and what a good mother! "But she is happier as she is." Evelyn could not imagine any soul-rending uncertainties in Mother Philippa. At a certain age, at seventeen or eighteen, she had felt that she would like to be a nun; very probably she was not any more pious than her sisters; she had merely felt that the life would suit her. That was her story. Evelyn smiled, and looked into Mother Philippa's mild eyes, in which there was nothing but simple kindness, and with a yes and a no she kept the conversation going till the bell rang for Office.

"I do not know if you would care to come to church. Perhaps you are tired after your journey?"

"Journey! I have only driven a few miles."

Evelyn ran upstairs for her hat, and she followed the nun down the cloister which led to the church.

"That is your door, it will take you into the outer church."

The nuns' choir was still empty, but the two candles on the high altar were already lit, ready for Matins and Lauds. Evelyn had only just taken her place, when at that moment a door opened on the other side of the grille, and the grey figures, their heads a little bent, came in couples and took their place in the stalls. They were wonderfully beautiful and impressive, and the idea they represented seemed to Evelyn extraordinary, simple and true. For, once we are convinced that there is a God, and that we are here to save our souls, it were surely folly to think of anything else. Our loves and our ambitions, what are they when we consider him? and Evelyn remembered how he waits for us in an eternity of bliss and love, only asking for our love. These were the wise ones, they thought of the essential and let the ephemeral and circumstantial go by them. Even from a worldly point of view, their life was the wiser, since it produced the greater happiness. Owen was a proof of this. She remembered how he used to say he had the finest place, the most beautiful pictures, and the most desirable mistress in Europe. Yet he was always the unhappiest man she knew. His life had been an unceasing effort to capture happiness, and he had failed because he had sought happiness from without instead of seeking it from within. He lived in externals, he was dependent on a multitude of things, the breakdown of any one of which was sufficient to cause him the acutest misery. The howl of a dog, the smell of a cigar, any trifle was sufficient to wreck his happiness. He had taught her to live in external things, to place her faith in the world instead of in her own conscience. How unhappy she had been; she had been driven to the brink of suicide. Ah, if it had not been for Monsignor. She bent her face on her hands, and did not dare to think further.

When her prayer was finished, she listened to the high monotonous chant of the nuns reciting Matins. It sank into her soul, soothing it, and at the same time inspiring an ardent melancholy. The long, unbroken rhythm flowed on and on, each side of the choir chanting an alternate verse. In the dimness of her sensation, Evelyn lost count of time, nor did she know of what she was thinking. She was suddenly awakened by a sound of shuffling. The nuns had risen to their feet, and in the middle of the floor a sister began the lessons in a shrill voice, keeping always on the same note, never letting her voice fall at the close of the sentences. Evelyn grew more interested; the rite was full of a penetrating mystery. She viewed the lines of grey nuns and heard the Latin syllables. These poor nuns whom she was just now pitying for their ignorance of life could at all events read the Office in Latin.

CHAPTER THIRTY-FOUR

When she opened her eyes and saw the convent room, she remembered how she had come there. Her still dreaming face lighted up with a smile, and she began to wonder what was going to happen next. Soon after, someone knocked. It was the little porteress telling her that it was seven o'clock. Evelyn expected her to come in, pull up the blinds and pour out her bath. But she did not even open the door, and Evelyn lay looking through the strange room, unable to face the discomfort of a small basin of cold water. She would have to do her hair herself, and there was no toilette table. The convent seemed suddenly a place to flee from; she hadn't realised that it would be like this.... But it would never do for her to miss Mass, and she sat on the edge of the bed, unable to think of any solution of her difficulties. The only glass in the room was about a foot square; it had been placed on the chest of drawers, and nothing seemed to Evelyn more inefficient than this wretched glass. Its very position on the top of the chest of drawers was vexatious. She could not even get it into the proper angle, and when she removed the piece of paper that held it in position, it swung round and its back confronted her. That morning it seemed as if she could not dress herself. Her hair had curled itself into many a knot; she nearly broke the comb, and her hand dropped by her side, and then she laughed outright, having caught sight of some part of her dejection. As she hooked on her skirt she reflected on the necessity of not leaving bottles of scent nor too many sponges for the observation of the nuns; and the nightgown she had brought was certainly not a conventual garment.

She hurried downstairs, and was just in time to see the nuns coming into church. They came in by a side door, walking two by two, and Evelyn was again struck by the beauty and mystery of this grey procession. She had seen on the stage the outward show of men who had renounced the world—the pilgrims in "Tannhäuser," the knights in "Parsifal," but this was no outward show. The women she was now witnessing had renounced the world; the life she was witnessing was the life they lived from hour to hour, from day to day, from year to year. She had included lovers amid their renunciations; such inclusion was ridiculous, for of such sins as hers they had not even dreamed. To pass through life without knowing life! To have renounced, to have refused love, friends, art, everything, dinner-parties, conversations, all the distractions which we believe make life endurable, to have refused these things from the beginning—not even to have been tempted to taste, not even to have desired to put life to the test of a fugitive personal experience, but to have divined from the first, by instinct, by the grace of God, the worthlessness of life—that was what was so wonderful. Mother Philippa, that simple nun, had done this, instinct had led her—there was no other explanation. She had arrived at the same conclusion as the wisest of the philosophers and without any soul-searching, by instinct—each of the humble lay sisters, the little porteress had done this.

And Evelyn was filled with shame when she thought of the effort it had cost her to free herself from a life of sin.

In extraordinary beauty of grey habit and veil and solemn procession, the nuns passed to their seats. Now they were kneeling altarwise, and Evelyn was still occupied by the thought that this was not outward show as she had often seen it on the stage, but the thing itself. This was not acting, this was truth, the truth of all their lifetimes.

Suddenly began the plaint of the organ, and some half-dozen voices sang a hymn; and these pale, etiolated voices interested her. It was not the clear, sexless voice of boys, these were women's voices, out of which sex had faded like colour out of flowers; and these pale, deciduous voices wailing a poor, pathetic music, so weak and feeble that it was almost interesting through its very feebleness, interested Evelyn. Tears trembled in her eyes, and she listened to the poor voices rising and falling, breaking forth spasmodically in the lamentable hymn. "Desolate" and "forgotten" were the words that came up in her mind.

They were still kneeling altarwise; their profiles turned from her. Outside of the choir stalls, on either side of the church, were two special stalls, and the Reverend Mother and the sub-prioress knelt apart. Their backs were turned to Evelyn, and she noticed the fine delicate shoulders of the Reverend Mother, and the heavy figure of Mother Philippa. "Even in their backs they are like themselves," she thought. She smiled at her descriptive style, "like themselves," and then, seeing that Mass had begun, she resolutely repressed all levity, and began her prayers. She had not felt especially pious till that moment, and to rouse herself she remembered Monsignor's words, "That at the height of her artistic career she should have been awakened to a sense of her own exceeding sinfulness was a miracle of his grace," and she felt that the devotion of her whole life to his service would not be a sufficient return for what he had done for her. But in spite of her efforts she followed the sacrifice of the Mass in her normal consciousness until the bell rang for the Elevation. When the priest raised the Host she was conscious of the Real Presence. She raised her eyes a little, and the bent figures of the nuns, their veils hanging loose about them, contributed to her exaltation, and with a last effort, holding as it were her life in her hands, she asked pardon of God for her sins.

Then the pale, etiolated voices of the nuns, the wailing of these weak voices—there were three altos, three sopranos—began again. They were singing an Agnus Dei, a simple little music nowise ugly, merely feeble, touchingly commonplace; they were singing in unison thirds and fifths, and the indifferent wailing of the voices contrasted with the firmness of the organist's touch; and Evelyn knew that they had one musician among them. She listened, touched by the plaintive voices, so feeble in the ears of man, but beautiful in God's ears. God heard beyond the mere notes; the music of the intention was what reached God's ears. The music of these poor voices was more favourable in his ears than her voice. Months she had spent seeking the exact rhythm of a phrase intended to depict and to rouse a sinful desire. Though the hymns were ugly—and they were very ugly—she would have done better to sing them; and she sought to press herself into the admission that art which does not tend to the glory of God is vain and harmful. Far better these hideous hymns, if singing them conducts to everlasting life. But every time she pressed her mind towards an inevitable conclusion, it turned off into an obscure bypath. She brought it back like an intractable ass, but the stubborn beast again dodged her, and she had to abandon the attempt to convince herself that art which did not tend to the honour and glory of God should be suppressed—should be at least avoided. Once we were convinced that there was a God and a resurrection, this world must become as nothing in our eyes, only it didn't become as nothing in our eyes; every sacrifice should become easy, but every sacrifice didn't become easy. That was the point; to these nuns, perhaps, not to her. At least not yet.

She had fussed a great deal this morning because she had no hot water to wash with. Seven o'clock had seemed to her somewhat early to get up. But they had been up long before. She had heard of nuns who got up at four in the morning to say the Office. She did not know what time these nuns got up, but she felt that she was not capable of much greater sacrifice than six or seven o'clock. These nuns lived on a little coarse food, and spent the day in prayer. She thought of their aching knees in the long vigils of their adorations. She understood that the inward happiness their life gives them compensates them for all their privations. She understood that they are the only ones who are happy, yet the knowledge did not help her; she felt that she would never be happy in their happiness, and a great sorrow came over her. Mass was over, and again the beautiful procession, with bowed heads and meekly folded veils, glided out of the church. Only the watchers remained.

Last night she had sat watching the stars shining on the convent garden. There were, as Owen said, twenty millions of suns in the Milky Way; beyond the Milky Way there were other constellations of which we know nothing, nebulæ which time has not yet resolved into stars, or stars so distant that time has not yet brought their light hither. But why seek mystery beyond this poor planet? It furnishes enough, surely. That we should see the stars, that we should know the stars, that we should place God above the stars—are not these common facts as wonderful as the stars themselves? That those twenty or five-and-twenty women should give up all the seduction of life for the sake of an idea, accepting Owen's theory that it is but an idea, even so the wonder of it is not less; even from Owen's point of view is not this convent as wonderful as the stars?

On coming out of church, she was told that in half-an-hour her breakfast would be ready in the parlour, and to loosen the mental tension—she had thought and felt a great deal in the last hour—she asked the lay sister who were the nuns who sang in the choir. The lay sister answered her perfunctorily. Evelyn could see that she was not open at that moment to conversation. She guessed that the sister had work to attend to, and was not surprised that she did not come back to take the things away. Although only just begun, the day had already begun to seem long. She proposed to herself some pious reading; and wondered how she was going to get through the day. She would have liked to go into the garden; but she did not know the rules of the convent, and feared to transgress them. However, she was free to go to her room. The books she had brought with her would help her to get through the morning. Berlioz's *Memoirs I* The faded voices she had heard that morning singing dreary hymns were more wonderful than his orchestral dreams. Nor did she find the spiritual stimulus she needed in Pater's *Imaginary Portraits*. Some moody souls reflecting with no undue haste, without undue desire to arrive at any definite opinion concerning certain artistic problems, did not appeal to her. She put the book aside, fearing that she was in no humour for reading that morning; and with little hope of being interested, she took up another book. The size of the volume and the disproportion of the type seemed to drag her to it, and the title was a sort of prophetic echo of the interest she was to find in the book. Her thoughts clouded in a sense of delight as she read; she followed as a child follows a butterfly, until the fluttering colour disappears in the sky. And before she was aware of any idea, the harmony of the gentle prose captivated her, and she sat down, holding in her heart the certitude that she was going to be enchanted. The book procured for her the delicious sensualism of reading things at once new and old. It seemed to her that she was reading things that she had known always, but which she had somehow neglected to think out for herself. The book seemed like her inner self suddenly made clear. All that the author said on the value of Silence was so true. She raised her eyes from the page to think. She seemed to understand something, but she could not tell what it was. The object of every soul is to unite itself to another soul, to be absorbed in another, to find life and happiness in another; the desire of unison is the deepest instinct in man. But how little, the author asked, do words help us to understand? We talk and talk, and nothing is really said; the conversation falls, we walk side by side, our eyes fixed on the quiet skies, and lo! our souls come together and are united in their immortal destiny. She again raised her eyes from the page—now she understood, and she thought a long while. The chapter entitled "The Profound Life" interested her equally. The nuns realised it, but those who live in the world live on the surface of things. To live a life of silence and devotion, illumined not from without but from within, the eternal light that never fails or withers, and to live unconscious of the great stream of things, our back turned to that great stream flowing mysteriously, solemnly, like a river! The chapter entitled "Warnings" had for her a strangely personal meaning. How true it is that we know everything, only we have not acquired the art of saying it. Had she not always known that her destiny was not with Owen, that he was but a passing, not the abiding event of her life? She looked through the convent room, and the abiding event of her life now seemed to murmur in her ear, seemed to pass like a shadow before her eyes. At the moment when she thought she was about to hear and see, a knock came at her door, and the revelation of her destiny passed, with a little ironical smile, out of her eyes and ears.

Her visitor was a strange little nun whom she had not seen before. Over her slim figure the white serge habit fell in such graceful, mediæval lines as Evelyn had seen in German cathedrals; and her face was delicate and childlike beneath the white forehead band. She came forward with a diffident little smile.

"Reverend Mother sent me to you; she is watching now, or she would have come herself, but she thought you might like me to take you round the garden. She will join us there when she comes out of church. But Reverend Mother said you must do just as you liked."

The little nun corresponded to her mood even as the book had done; she seemed an apparition, a ghost risen from its pages. Her face was a thin oval, and the purity of the outline was accentuated by the white kerchief which surrounded it. The nose was slightly aquiline, the chin a little pointed, the lips well cut, but thin and colourless—lips that Evelyn thought had never been kissed, and that never would be kissed. The thought seemed disgraceful, and Evelyn noticed hastily the dark almond eyes that saved the face from insipidity; the black eyebrows were firmly and delicately drawn, her complexion, without being pale, was extraordinarily transparent, and the thin hands and long, narrow fingers, half hidden beneath the long sleeves, were in the same idea of mediæval delicacy.

"I was longing to go out, but I had not the courage. I feared it might be against the rule for me to go into the garden alone. But tell me first who you are."

"Oh, I'm Sister Veronica. I'm only a novice as yet."

Evelyn noticed that, unlike the other nuns she had seen, Sister Veronica wore neither the silver heart on her breast, suspended by a red cord, nor the long straight scapular which gave such dignity to the religious habit. Her habit was held in at the waist by a leather girdle; it looked as though it might slip any moment over the slight, boyish hips, and by her side hung a rosary of large black beads.

Sister Veronica warned Evelyn that she must be careful how she went down the staircase, as it was very slippery. Evelyn said she would be careful; she added that the sisters kept the stairs in beautiful order, and wondered what her next remark would be. She was nervous in the presence of these convent women, lest by some unfortunate remark she should betray herself. And when they reached the garden it was Sister Veronica who was the most self-possessed—she was already confessing to Evelyn that they had all felt very nervous knowing that a "real" singer was listening to them.

"Oh, do you sing?" Evelyn asked eagerly.

"Well, I have to try," Sister Veronica answered, with a little laugh. "Mother Prioress thought perhaps I might learn, so she put me in the choir, but Sister Mary John says I shall never be the least use."

"Is Sister Mary John the sister who teaches you?"

"Yes; it is she who played the organ at Mass. She loves music. She is simply longing to hear you sing, Miss Innes. Do you think you will sing at Benediction this afternoon for us? It would be lovely."

"I don't know, really. You see I haven't been asked yet."

"Oh, Reverend Mother is sure to ask you—at least I hope she will. We all want to hear you so much."

They were sitting in the shadow of a great elm; all around was a wonderful silence, and to turn the conversation from herself, Evelyn asked Sister Veronica if she didn't care for their beautiful garden.

"Oh, yes, indeed I do. I'm glad you like it.... When I was a child my greatest treat was to be allowed to play in the nuns' garden."

"Then you knew the convent long before you came to be a nun yourself?"

"Oh, yes, I've known it all my life."

"So it was not strange when you came here first?"

"No, it was like coming home."

Evelyn repeated the nun's words to herself, "Like coming home." And she seemed to see far into their meaning. Here was an illustration of what she had read in the book—she and Veronica seemed to understand each other in the silence. But it became necessary to speak, and in answer to a question, Sister Veronica told Evelyn that there were four novices and two postulants in the novitiate, and that the name of the novice mistress was Mother Mary Hilda. The novitiate was in the upper storey of the new wing, above the convent refectory.

"And here is Reverend Mother," and Sister Veronica suddenly got up. Evelyn got up too, and they waited till the elderly nun slowly crossed the lawn. Evelyn noticed, even when the Reverend Mother was seated, that Veronica remained standing.

"You can go now, Veronica."

Veronica smiled a little good-bye to Evelyn, and left them immediately.

"Veronica told you, Miss Innes, I was taking my watch?"

"Yes, Reverend Mother."

"I hope she has not been wearying you with the details of our life?"

"On the contrary, I have been very much interested.... Your life here is so beautiful that I long to know more about it. At present my knowledge is confined to the fact that the second storey in the new wing is the novitiate, and that there are four novices and two postulants."

The Reverend Mother smiled, and after a pause Evelyn added—

"But Sister Veronica is very young."

"She is older than she looks, she is nearly twenty. Ever since she was quite a child she wished to be a nun. Even then her mind was quite made up."

"She told me that when she was a child her great pleasure was to be allowed to walk in the convent garden."

"Yes. You don't know, perhaps, that she is my niece. My poor brother's child. She was left an orphan at a very early age. Her's is a sad story. But God has been good: she never doubted her vocation, she passed from an innocent childhood to a life dedicated to God. So she has been spared the trouble that is the lot of those who live in the world."

An accent of past but unforgotten sorrow had crept into her voice; and once more Evelyn was convinced that she had not, like Veronica, passed from innocent childhood into the blameless dream of convent life. She had known the world and had renounced it. In the silence that had fallen Evelyn wondered what her story might be, and whether she would ever hear it. But she knew that in the convent no allusion is made to the past, that there the past is really the past.

"I hope that you will sing for us at Benediction. All the sisters are longing to hear you. It will be such a pleasure to them."

"I shall be very glad ... only I have brought nothing with me. But I daresay I shall find something among the music you have here."

"Sister Mary John will find you something; she is our organist."

"And an excellent musician. I noticed her playing."

"She has always been anxious to improve the choir, but unfortunately none of the sisters except her has any voice to speak of.... You might sing Gounod's 'Ave Maria' at Benediction; you know it, of course, what a beautiful piece of music it is. But I see that you don't admire it."

"Well," Evelyn said, smiling, "it is contrary to all the principles I've been brought up in."
"We might walk a little; we are at the end of the summer, and the air is a little cold. You do not mind walking very slowly? I'm forbidden to walk fast on account of my heart."
They crossed the sloping lawn, and walking slowly up St. Peter's walk, amid sad flutterings of leaves from the branches of the elms, Evelyn told the Reverend Mother the story of the musical reformation which her father had achieved. She asked Evelyn if it would be possible to give Palestrina at the convent and they reached the end of the walk. It was flushed with September, and in the glittering stillness the name of Palestrina was exquisite to speak. They passed the tall cross standing at the top of the rocks, and the Reverend Mother said, speaking out of long reflection—"Have I never heard any of the music you sing? Wagner I have never heard, but the Italian operas, 'Lucia' and 'Trovatore,' or Mozart? Have you never sung Mozart?"
"Very little. I am what is called a dramatic soprano. The only Italian opera I've sung is 'Norma.' Do you know it?"
"Yes."
"I've sung Leonore—not in 'Trovatore,' in 'Fidelio.'"
"But surely you admire 'Trovatore'—the 'Miserere,' for instance. Is not that beautiful?"
"It is no doubt very effective, but it is considered very common now." Evelyn hummed snatches of the opera; then the waltz from "Traviata." "I've sung Margaret."
"Ah."
And as she hummed the Jewel Song she watched the Reverend Mother's face, and was certain that the nun had heard the music on the stage. But at that moment the angelus bell rang. Evelyn had forgotten the responses, and as she walked towards the convent she asked the Reverend Mother to repeat them once again, so that she might have them by heart. She excused herself, saying how difficult was the observance of religious forms for those who live in the world.
After dinner she wrote two letters. One was to her father, the other was to Monsignor, and having directed the letters she imagined the postal arrangement to be somewhat irregular. After Benediction she would ask Veronica what time the letters left the convent. And looking across the abyss which separated them, she saw her passionate self-centred past and Veronica's little transit from the schoolroom to the convent. It seemed strange to her that she never had what might be called a girl friend. But she had arrived at a time when a woman friend was a necessity, and it now suddenly occurred to her that there would be something wonderfully sweet and satisfying in the uncritical love of a woman younger than herself. She felt that the love of this innocent creature who knew nothing, who never would know anything, and who therefore would suspect nothing, would help her to forget her past as Monsignor wished. She felt a sympathy awaken in her for her own sex which she had never known before, and this yearning was confounded in a desire to be among those who knew nothing of her past. Now she was glad that she had refrained from taking the Reverend Mother into her confidence, and she wondered how much Monsignor had told her the day they had walked in the garden; it relieved her to remember that he knew very little except what she had told him in confession.
Someone knocked. She answered, "Come in." It was Mother Philippa and another nun.
"I hope we're not interrupting.... But you're reading, I see."
"No, I was thinking;" and glad of the interruption, she let the book fall on her knees. "Pray come in, Mother Philippa," and Evelyn rose to detain her.
The nuns entered very shyly. Evelyn handed them chairs, and as she did so she remarked the tall, angular nun who followed Mother Philippa, and whose face expressed so much energy.
"Good afternoon, Miss Innes. I hope you slept well last night, and did not find your bed too uncomfortable?"
"Thank you, Mother Philippa. I liked my bed. I slept very well." Evelyn drew two chairs forward, and Mother Philippa introduced Evelyn to Sister Mary John. And while she

explained that she had heard from the Reverend Mother that Miss Innes had promised to sing at Benediction, Sister Mary John sat watching Evelyn, her large brown eyes wide open. Her eagerness was even a little comical, and Evelyn smiled through her growing liking for this nun. She was unlike any other nun she had seen. Nuns were usually formal and placid, but Sister Mary John was so irreparably herself that while the others presented feeble imitations of the Reverend Mother's manner, her walk and speech, Sister Mary John continued to slouch along, to cross her legs, to swing her arms, to lean forward and interrupt when she was interested in the conversation; when she was not, she did not attempt to hide her indifference. Evelyn thought that she must be about eight-and-twenty or thirty. The eyes were brown and exultant, and the eyebrows seemed very straight and black in the sallow complexion. All the features were large, but a little of the radiant smile that had lit up all her features when she came forward to greet Evelyn still lingered on her face. Now and then she seemed to grow impatient, and then she forgot her impatience and the smile floated back again. At last her opportunity came, and she seized it eagerly.

"I'm quite ashamed, Miss Innes, we sang so badly this morning; our little choir can do better than that."

"I was interested; the organ was very well played."

"Did you think so? I have not sufficient time for practice, but I love music, and am longing to hear you sing. But the Reverend Mother says that you have brought no music with you."

"I hear," said Mother Philippa, "that you do not care for Gounod's 'Ave Maria.'"

"If the Reverend Mother wishes me to sing it, I shall be delighted to do so, if Sister Mary John has the music."

Sister Mary John shook her head authoritatively, and said that she quite understood that Miss Innes did not approve of the liberty of writing any melody over Bach's beautiful prelude. Besides, it required a violin. The conversation then turned on the music at St. Joseph's. Sister Mary John listened, breaking suddenly in with some question regarding Palestrina. She had never heard any of his music; would Miss Innes lend her some? Was there nothing of his that they could sing in the convent?

"I do not know anything of his written for two voices. You might play the other parts on the organ, but I'm afraid it would sound not a little ridiculous."

"But have you heard the Benedictine nuns sing the plain chant; they pause in the middle of the verse—that is the tradition, is it not?"

Meanwhile Mother Philippa sat forgotten. Evelyn noticed her isolation before Sister Mary John, and addressed an observation to her. But Mother Philippa said she knew nothing about music, and that they were to go on talking as if she weren't there. But a mere listener is a dead weight in a conversation; and whenever Evelyn's eyes went that way, she could see that Mother Philippa was thinking of something else; and when she looked towards Sister Mary John she could see that she was longing to be alone with her. A delightful hour of conversation awaited them if they could only find some excuse to get away together, and Evelyn looked at Sister Mary John, saying with her eyes that the suggestion must come from her.

"If I were to take Miss Innes to the organ loft and show her what music we have—don't you think so, Mother Philippa?'

"Yes, I think that would be the best thing to do.... I'm sure the Reverend Mother would see no objection to your taking Miss Innes to the organ loft."

Mother Philippa did not see the look of relief and delight that passed in Sister Mary John's eyes, and it was Evelyn who had a scruple about getting rid of Mother Philippa.

"I was so disappointed not to have seen you the day you came here; and what made it so hard was that it was first arranged that it was the Reverend Mother and I who were to meet you. I had looked forward to seeing you. I love music, and it is seven years since I've spoken to anyone who could tell the difference between a third and a fourth. There's no one here who cares about music."

It seemed to Evelyn that the problem of life must have presented itself to Sister Mary John very much as it presents itself to a woman who is suddenly called to join her husband in India. The woman hates leaving London, her friends, and all the habits of life in which she has grown up; but she does not hesitate to give up these things to follow the man she loves out to India.

"I don't know why it was settled that Mother Philippa was to meet you instead of me; it seemed so useless, meeting you meant so little to her and so much to me; I'm always inclined to argue, but that day the Reverend Mother's heart was very bad; she had had a fainting fit in the early morning; we all got up to pray for her."

"Yet she was quite cheerful; I never should have guessed."

"Mother Philippa and Mother Mary Hilda tried to dissuade her. But she would see you."

"Then it is with her heart disease that the Reverend Mother rules the convent," Evelyn thought, as she followed Sister Mary John up the spiral staircase to the organ loft. She looked over the curtained railing into the church. The watcher knelt there, her head bowed, her habit still as sculpture, and Evelyn heard Sister Mary John pulling out her music. She could not find what she wanted, and she sat with her legs apart, throwing from side to side piles of old torn music.

"Never can one find a piece of music when one wants it: I don't know if you have noticed that nothing is so difficult to find as a piece of music. Day after day it is under your hands, it would seem as if there was not another piece in the organ loft, but the moment you want it, it has disappeared. I don't know how it is."

"What are you looking for? Perhaps I can help you."

"Well, I was thinking that you might like"—Sister Mary John looked up at Evelyn—"I suppose you can sing B flat, or even C?"

"Yes, I can sing C;" and Evelyn thought of the last page of the "Dusk of the Gods." "But what are you looking for?"

Sister Mary John did not answer. She threw the music from side to side, every minute growing more impatient. "It is most strange," she said at last, looking up at Evelyn. Evelyn smiled. With all her brusque, self-willed ways, Sister Mary John was clearly a lady born and an intelligent woman.

"I'm afraid I shall not be able to find you anything that you'd care to sing."

"Oh, yes, I shall," Evelyn replied encouragingly.

"It is all such poor stuff. We've no singers here. Do you know, I've never heard a great singer, and I've often wished to. The only thing I regret is not having heard a little music before I came here. But I've heard of Wagner; you sing Wagner, don't you, Miss Innes?"

"Yes, I sing little else. 'Fidelio'—"

"Ah, I know some of the music. Do you sing—"

Sister Mary John hummed a few bars.

"Yes, I sing that."

"Well, I shall hear you sing to-day. I've been wishing to go to St. Joseph's to hear Palestrina. You were brought up on music. You can sing at sight—in the key that it is written in?"

"Yes, I think so."

"But all prima-donnas can do that?"

"No; on the contrary, I think I'm the only one. Singers on the operatic stage learn their parts at the piano."

She could see that to Sister Mary John music was the temptation of her life, and she imagined that her confession must be a little musical record. She had lost her temper with Sister So-and-So because she could not, etc. But time was getting on. If she was to sing that afternoon, she must find something, and seeing that Sister Mary John lingered over some sheets of music, as if she thought that it presented some possibility, Evelyn asked her what it was. It was a Mass by Mozart for four voices, which Sister Mary John had arranged for a single voice.

"The choir and I sing the melody in unison, and I play the entire Mass on the organ."

Evelyn smiled, and seeing that the smile distressed the nun, she was sorry.

"To you, of course, it would sound absurd, it does to me too, but it was a little change, it was the only thing I could think of. We have some pieces written for two voices, but I can hardly get them sung. I have to teach the sisters the parts separately. Till they know them by heart, I can't trust them. It is impossible sometimes not to lose one's temper. If we had a few good voices, people would come to hear them, the convent would be spoken about, and some charitable people would come forward and pay off our mortgages. I've lain awake at night thinking of it; the Reverend Mother agrees with me. But in the way of voices we've been as unlucky as we could well be. I've been here eight years—there was one, but she died six years ago of consumption. It is heartbreaking. I play the organ, I beat the time, and, as I said to them the other day, 'There are five of you, and I'm the only one that sings.'"

Sister Mary John asked Evelyn if she composed. Evelyn told her that she did not compose, and remembering Owen's compositions, she hoped that Sister Mary John had not an "O Salutaris" in manuscript.

"Let me look through the music; we are talking of other things instead of looking."

"So we are.... Let us look." At the bottom of a heap, Sister Mary John found Cherubini's "Ave Maria."

"Could you sing this? It is a beautiful piece of music."

Evelyn read it over.

"Yes," she said, "I can sing it, but it wants careful playing; the end is a sort of little duet between the voice and the organ. If you don't follow me exactly, the effect will be like this," and she showed what it would be on the mute keyboard.

"You haven't confidence in my playing."

"Every confidence, Sister Mary John, but remember I don't know the piece, and it is not easy. I think we had better try it over together."

"I should like to very much, but you will not sing with all your voice?"

"No, we'll just run through it...."

The nun followed in a sort of ecstasy, and when they came to what Evelyn had called the duet, she played the beautiful antiphonal music looking up at the singer. The second time Evelyn was surer of herself, and she let her voice flow out a little in suave vocalisation, so that she might judge of the effect.

"I told you that I had never heard anyone sing before. If you were one of us!"

Evelyn laughed, and then, catching sight of the nun's eyes fixed very intently upon her, she spoke of the beauty of the "Ave Maria," and was surprised that she did not know anything of Cherubini's.

"Gracious, how the time has gone! That is the first bell for vespers."

She hurried away, forgetting all about Evelyn, leaving her to find her way back to her room as best she could. But Evelyn found Sister Mary John waiting for her at the bottom of the stairs. She had come back for her, she had just remembered her, and Sister Mary John apologised for her absence of mind, and seemed distressed at her apparent rudeness. They walked a little way together, and the nun explained that it was not her fault; her absence of mind was an inheritance from her father. Everything she had she had inherited from him— "my love of music and my absence of mind."

She was intensely herself, quaint, eccentric, but she was, Evelyn reflected, perhaps more distinctly from the English upper classes than any of the nuns she had seen yet. She had not the sweetness of manner of the Reverend Mother, her manners were the oddest; but withal she had that refinement which Evelyn had first noticed in Owen, and afterwards in his friends, that style which is inheritance, which tradition alone can give. She had spoken of her father, and Evelyn could easily imagine Sister Mary John's father—a lord of old lineage dwelling in an eighteenth century house in the middle of a flat park in the Midlands. She could see a piece of artificial lake obtained by the damming of a small stream; one end full of thick reeds, in which the chatter of wild ducks was unceasing. But her family, her past, her name—all was lost in the convent, in the veil. The question was, had she renounced the world, or had she refused the world? Evelyn could not even conjecture. Sister Mary John was outside not only of her experience, but also of her present perception of things. Evelyn wondered why one of such marked individuality, of such intense personal will, had chosen a life the very *raison d'être* of which was the merging of the individual will in the will of the community? Why should one, the essential delight of whose life was music, choose a life in which music hardly appeared? Was her piety so great that it absorbed every other inclination? Sister Mary John did not strike her as being especially religious. What instinct behind those brown eyes had led her to this sacrifice? Apparently at pains to conceal nothing, Sister Mary John concealed the essential. Evelyn could even imagine her as being attractive to men—that radiant smile, the beautiful teeth, and the tall, supple figure, united to that distinct personality, would not have failed to attract. God did not get her because men did not want her, of that Evelyn was quite sure.

There were on that afternoon assembled in the little white chapel of the Passionist Sisters about a dozen elderly ladies, about nine or ten stout ladies dressed in black, who might be widows, and perhaps three or four spare women who wore a little more colour in their hats; these might be spinsters, of ages varying between forty and fifty-five. Amid these Evelyn was surprised and glad to perceive three or four young men; they did not look, she thought, particularly pious, and perceiving that they wore knickerbockers, she judged them to be cyclists who had ridden up from Richmond Park. They had come in probably to rest, having left their machines at the inn. Even though she was converted, she did not wish to sing only to women, and it amused her to perceive that something of the original Eve still existed in her. But if any one of these young men should happen to have any knowledge of music, he could hardly fail to notice that it was not a nun who was singing. He would ride away astonished, mystified; he would seek the explanation of the mystery, and would bring his friend to hear the wonderful voice at the Passionist Convent. By the time he came again she would be gone, and his friend would say that he had had too much to drink that afternoon at the inn. They would not be long in finding an explanation; but should there happen to be a journalist there, he would put a paragraph in the papers, and all sorts of people would come to the convent and go away disappointed.

She looked round the church, calculating its resonance, and thought with how much of her voice she should sing so as to produce an effect without, however, startling the little congregation. The sermon seemed to her very long; she was unable to fix her attention, and though all Father Daly said was very edifying, her thoughts wandered, and wonderful legends and tales about a voice heard for one week at the Wimbledon Convent thronged her brain, and she invented quite a comic little episode, in which some dozen or so of London managers met at Benediction. She thought that their excuses one to the other would be very comic.

She was wearing the black lace scarf instead of a hat; it went well with the grey alpaca, and under it was her fair hair; and when she got up to go to the organ loft after the sermon, she felt that the old ladies and the bicyclists were already wondering who she was. Her involuntary levity annoyed her, and she forced a certain seriousness upon herself as she climbed the steep spiral staircase.

"So you have found your way ... this is our choir," and she introduced Evelyn to the five sisters, hurrying through their names in a low whisper. "We don't sing the 'O Salutaris,' as there has been exposition. We'll sing this hymn instead, and immediately after you'll sing the 'Ave Maria'; it will take the place of the Litany."

Then the six pale voices began to wail out the hymn, wobbling and fluctuating, the only steady voice being Sister Mary John's. Though mortally afraid of the Latin syllables, Evelyn seconded Sister Mary John's efforts, and the others, taking courage, sang better than usual. Sister Mary John turned delighted from the organ, and, her eyes bright with anticipation, said, "Now."

She played the introduction, Evelyn opened her music. The moment was one of intense excitement among the five nuns. They had gathered together in a group. The great singer who had saved their convent (had it not been for her they would have been thrown back upon the world) was going to sing. Evelyn knew what was passing in their minds, and was a little nervous. She wished they would not look at her so, and she turned away from them. Sister Mary John played the chord, and the voice began.

Owen often said that if Evelyn had two more notes in her voice she would have ranked with the finest. She sang from the low A, and she could take the high C. From B to B every note was clear and full, one as the other; he delighted especially in the middle of her voice; for one whole octave, and more than an octave, her voice was pure and sonorous and as romantic as the finest 'cello. And the romance of her voice transpired in the beautiful Beethoven-like phrase of Cherubini's "Ave Maria." It was as if he had had her voice singing in his ear while he was writing, when he placed the little grace notes on the last syllable of Maria. The phrase rose, still remaining well within the medium of her voice, and the same interval happened again as the voice swelled up on the word "plena." In the beautiful classical melody her voice was like a 'cello heard in the twilight. In the music itself there is neither belief nor prayer, but a severe dignity of line, the romance of columns and peristyle in the exaltation of a calm evening. Very gradually she poured her voice into the song, and her lips seemed to achieve sculpture. The lines of a Greek vase seemed to rise before the eye, and the voice swelled on from note to note with the noble movement of the bas-relief decoration of the vase. The harmonious interludes which Sister Mary John played aided the excitement, and the nuns, who knelt in two grey lines, were afraid to look up. In a remote consciousness they feared it was not right to feel so keenly; the harmonious depth of the voice entered their very blood, summoning visions of angel faces. But it was an old man with a white beard that Veronica saw, a hermit in the wilderness; she was bringing him vestments, and when the vision vanished Evelyn was singing the opening phrase, now a little altered on the words Santa Maria.

There came the little duet between the voice and the organ, in which any want of precision on the part of Sister Mary John would spoil the effect of the song; but the nun's right hand answered Evelyn in perfect concord. And then began the runs introduced in the Amen in order to exhibit the skill of the singer. The voice was no longer a 'cello, deep and resonant, but a lonely flute or silver bugle announcing some joyous reverie in a landscape at the close of day. The song closed on the keynote, and Sister Mary John turned from the instrument and looked at the singer. She could not speak, she seemed overpowered by the music, and like one more dreaming than waking, and sitting half turned round on her seat, she looked at Evelyn.

"You sing beautifully," she said. "I never heard singing before."

And she sat like one stupefied, still hearing Evelyn's singing in her brain, until one of the sisters advanced close and said, "Sister, we must sing the 'Tantum ergo.'"

"Of course we must. I believe if you hadn't reminded me I should have forgotten it. Gracious! I don't know what it will sound like after singing like that. But you'll lead them?"

Evelyn hummed the plain chant under her breath, afraid lest she should extinguish the pale voices, and surprised how expressive the antique chant was when sung by these etiolated, sexless voices. She had never known how much of her life of passion and desire had entered into her voice, and she was shocked at its impurity. Her singing sounded like silken raiment among sackcloth, and she lowered her voice, feeling it to be indecorous and out of place in the antique hymn. Her voice, she felt, must have revealed her past life to the nuns, her voice must have shocked them a little; her voice must have brought the world before them too vividly. For all her life was in her voice, she would never be able to sing this hymn with the same sexless grace as they did. Her voice would be always Evelyn Innes—Owen Asher's mistress.

The priest turned the Host toward them, and she saw the two long rows of grey-habited nuns leaning their veiled heads, and knew that this was the moment they lived for, the essential moment when the body which the Redeemer gave in expiation of the sins of the world is revealed. Evelyn's soul hushed in awe, and all that she had renounced seemed very little in this moment of mystery and exaltation.

"What am I to say, Miss Innes? I shall think of this day when I am an old woman. But you'll sing again before you leave?"

"Yes, sister, whenever you like."

"When I like? That would be all day. But I did follow you in the duet, I was so anxious. I hope I did not spoil it?"

"I was never better accompanied. You made no mistake."

As they passed by her the other nuns thanked her under their breath. She could see that they looked upon her as a providence sent by God to save them from being cast back upon the world they dreaded, the world from which they had fled. But all this extraordinary drama, this intensity of feeling, remained inarticulate. They could only say, "Thank you, Miss Innes; it was very good of you to come to sing for us." It was their very dumbness that made them seem so wonderful. It was the dumbness of these women—they could only speak in prayer—it was that that overcame her. But the Reverend Mother was different. Evelyn listened to her, thinking of nothing but her, and when the Reverend Mother left her, Evelyn moved away, still under the spell of the authoritative sweetness which her presence and manner exhaled. But the Reverend Mother was only a part of a scheme of life founded on principles the very opposite to those on which she had attempted to construct her life. Even in singing the "Ave Maria," she had not been able to subdue her vanity. Her pleasure in singing it had in a measure sprung out of the somewhat mean desire to proclaim her superiority over those who had attained the highest plane by renouncing all personal pride. They had proclaimed their superiority in their obeisance. It was in giving, not in receiving, praise that we rise above ourselves. This was the lesson that every moment of her convent life impressed upon her. Her thoughts went back to the Reverend Mother, and Evelyn thought of her as of some woman who had come to some terrible crisis in her worldly life—some crisis violent as the crisis that had come in her own life. The Reverend Mother must have perceived, just as she had done, as all must do sooner or later, that life out of the shelter of religion becomes a sort of nightmare, an intolerable torture. Then she wondered if the Reverend Mother were a widow—that appeared to her likely. One who had suffered some great disaster—that too seemed to her likely. She had been an ambitious woman. Was she not so still? Is a passion ever obliterated? Is it not rather transformed? If she had been personally ambitious, she was now ambitious only for her convent: her passion had taken another direction. And applying the same reasoning to herself, she seemed to see a future for herself in which her love passions would become transformed and find their complete expressions in the love of God.

The Reverend Mother again addressed her, and Evelyn considered what age she might be. Between sixty and seventy in point of years, but she seemed so full of intelligence, wisdom and sweetness that she did not suggest age; one did not think of her as an old woman. Her slight figure still retained its grace, and though a small woman, she suggested a tall one; and the moment she spoke there was the voice which drew you like silk and entangled you as in a soft winding web. Evelyn smiled a little as she listened, for she was thinking how the Reverend Mother as a young woman must have swayed men. Presumably at one time it had pleased her to sway men's passion, or at least it pleased Evelyn's imagination to think it had. Not that she thought the Reverend Mother had ever been anything but a good woman, but she had been a woman of the world, and Evelyn attributed no sin to that. Even the world is not wholly bad; the Reverend Mother and Monsignor owed their personal magnetism to the world. Without the world they would have been like Father Daly and Mother Philippa—holy simplicities. She looked at the quiet nun, and her simple good nature touched her. Evelyn went toward her. Sister Mary John broke into the conversation so often that the Reverend Mother had once to check her.

"Sister Mary John, we hope that Miss Innes will sing to-morrow and every day while she is with us. But she must do as she likes, and these musical questions are not what we are talking about now."

But Sister Mary John was hardly at all abashed at this reproof. She was clearly the only one who stood in no awe of the Reverend Mother.

They were sitting on the terrace, and a mauve sunset faded in the grey sky. There was a strange wistfulness in the autumn air and in the dim garden where the gentle nuns were taking their recreation. There was a subtle harmony in the grey habits and floating veils; they blended and mingled with the blue mist that was rising among the trees. And a pale light fell across the faded lawns, and Evelyn looked into the light, and felt the pang that the passing of things brings into the heart. This spectacle of life seemed to her strangely pathetic, and it seemed to mean something which eluded her, and which she would have given a great deal to have been able to express. Music alone could express the yearning that haunted her heart, the plaint of the Rhine Maidens was the nearest to what she felt, and she began to sing their song. Sister Mary John asked her eagerly what she was singing. She would have told her, but the Reverend Mother grew impatient with Sister Mary John.

"You must be introduced to Mother Mary Hilda, our novice mistress, then you will know all the mothers except our dear Mother Christina, who is quite an invalid now, and rarely leaves her cell."

On St. Peter's path a little group of nuns were walking up and down, pressing round a central figure. They were faint grey shadows, and their meaning would not be distinguished in the violet dusk. It was like a half-effaced picture in which the figures are nearly lost in the background; their voices, however, sounded clear, and their laughter was mysterious and far distant, yet distinct in the heart. Evelyn again began to hum the plaint of the Rhine Maidens. But the voices of the novices were more joyous, for they, Evelyn thought, have renounced both love and gold. The Reverend Mother clapped her hands to attract attention, and one of the novices, it was Sister Veronica, ran to them.

"Ask Mother Mary Hilda to come and speak to me, Veronica."

"Yes, Reverend Mother;" and Veronica ran with the message without once looking at Evelyn. Mother Mary Hilda crossed the lawn toward them, and Evelyn noticed her gliding, youthful walk. She was younger than the prioress or even the sub-prioress. And she had that attractive youthfulness of manner which often survives in the cloister after middle age.

"Here is Miss Innes," said the prioress; "I know you wished to make her acquaintance."

"Yes, indeed."

Evelyn noticed the bright eyes and the small, clearly cut nose and the pointed chin, but her liveliest sensation was of Mother Hilda's hand; so small was it and soft that it seemed like a little crushed bird in Evelyn's hand, and Evelyn did not think that hers was a large hand.

"I am sure, Miss Innes, you feel that you have been thanked sufficiently for all you have done for us, but you'll forgive us if we feel that we cannot thank you often enough. Your singing at Benediction to-day was a great pleasure to us all. Whose 'Ave Maria' was it, Miss Innes?"

Evelyn told them, and thinking it would interest the nuns, she admitted that her father would not allow it to be sacred music. This led the conversation on to the question of Palestrina, and how the old music had rescued the Jesuits from their pecuniary embarrassments. A casual mention of Wagner showed her that the Reverend Mother was interested, and she said that she might sing them Elizabeth's prayer. Evelyn spoke of the Chorale in the first act of the "Meistersinger," and this led her into quite a little account of the music she sang on the stage. It pleased her to notice the different effect of her account of her art on the four nuns. The conversation, she could see, carried the prioress back into the past, but she put aside these memories of long ago and affected a polite interest in the stage. Mother Philippa listened as she might to a story, too far removed from her for her to be more than vaguely interested; Sister Mary John listened in the hopes that Evelyn would illustrate her experience with some few bars of the music—with her it was the music and nothing else; Mother Mary Hilda

listened very prettily, and Evelyn noticed that it was she who asked the most questions. Mother Mary Hilda was the most fearless, and showed the least dread in the conversation. Yet for no single moment did Evelyn think that she was the worldliest of the four nuns. Evelyn thought that probably she was the least. Her trivial utterances were the necessity of the unimportant moment, and she seemed to bring to them the enlightenment of her own vivid faith. The holiness that shone out of her eyes inspired the calm, tender smile, and was in her whole manner. "She speaks," Evelyn thought, "of worldly things without affectation, but how clear it is that they lie outside, far outside, of her real life."
Evelyn was saying that it was a long while since she had sung any sacred music, and, referring to the difference of the rule in France and in England, she mentioned that in Paris the opera singers frequently sang in the churches.
"It must be hard on Catholics with beautiful voices like yours that they may not be allowed to sing in church choirs, for there can be nothing so delightful as to bring a great gift to God's service."
It was the prioress who broke off the conversation, to Evelyn's regret.
"Mother Hilda, I am afraid we are forgetting your young charges."
"Yes, indeed, I must run back to my children. Good-bye, Miss Innes, I am so glad that you have come to us;" and the warm, soft clasp of the little hand was to Evelyn a further assurance of friendly welcome.

CHAPTER THIRTY-FIVE

She was ashamed not to be able to follow the Office in chapel, so at the Reverend Mother's suggestion she consented to employ part of her long convent leisure in taking lessons in Latin. Mother Mary Hilda was to be her instructress.
The library was a long, rather narrow room, once the drawing-room of the Georgian mansion. Only a carved Adams' chimney-piece, now painted over in imitation of oak remained of its former adornment; the tall windows were eighteenth century, and with that air they looked upon the terrace. The walls had been lined by the nuns with plain wooden shelves, and upon them were what seemed to be a thousand books, every one in a grey linen wrapper, with the title neatly written on a white label pasted on the back. Evelyn's first thought was of the time it must have taken to cover them, but she remembered that in a convent time is of no consequence. If a thing can be done better in three hours than in one, there is no reason why three hours should not be spent upon it. She had noticed, too, that the sisters regarded the library with a little air of demure pride. Mother Mary Hilda had told her that the large tin boxes were filled with the convent archives. There were piles of unbound magazines—the *Month* and the *Dublin Review*. There was a ponderous writing-table, with many pigeon-holes; Evelyn concluded it to be the gift of a wealthy convert, and she turned the immense globe which showed the stars and planets, and wondered how the nuns had become possessed of such a thing, and how they could have imagined that it could ever be of any use to them. She grew fond of this room, and divided her time between it and the garden. It had none of the primness of the convent parlour, which gave her a little shiver every time she entered it. In the further window there stood a deep-seated, venerable arm-chair, covered in worn green leather, the one comfortable chair, Evelyn often thought, in the convent. And in this chair she spent many hours, either learning to construe the Office with Mother Mary Hilda, or reading by herself. The investigation of the shelves was an occupation, and the time went quickly, taking down book after book, and she seemed to penetrate further into the spirit of the convent through the medium of the convent books.
The light literature of the convent were improving little tales of conversion, and edifying stories of Catholic girls who decline to enter into mixed marriages, and she thought of the

novices reading this artless literature on Sunday afternoons. There were endless volumes of meditations, mostly translations from the French, full of Gallicisms and parenthetical phrases, and Evelyn often began a paragraph a second time; but in spite of her efforts to control her thoughts they wandered, and her eyes, lost in reverie, were fixed on the sunny garden.

She returned the volumes to the shelves, and remembering Mother Mary Hilda's recommendation, she took down a volume of Faber's works. She found his effusive, sentimental style unendurable; and had turned to go to her room for one of the books she had brought with her when her eyes lighted upon Father Dalgairn's *Frequent Communion*. The father's account of the various customs of the Church regarding the administration of the Sacrament—the early rigorism of the African fathers, and the later rigorism of the Jansenists at once interested her, and, lifting her eyes from the book, she remembered that the Sacrament had always been the central light around which the spiritual belief of the church had revolved. Her instinctive religion had always been the Sacrament. When Huxley and Darwin and Spencer had undermined the foundations of her faith, and the entire fabric of revelation was showering about her, her belief in the Divine Presence had remained, burning like a lamp, inviolate among the débris of a temple. She had never been able to resist the Sacrament. She had put her belief in the mystery of transubstantiation to the test, and when the sanctus bell rang, her head had solemnly bowed; softer than rose leaves or snowflakes, belief had rained down upon her choked heart. She had never been able to reason about the Divine Presence—she felt it. She had believed whether she willed it or not. Owen's arguments had made no difference. Her desire of the Sacrament had more than once altered the course of her life, and that she should have unconsciously wandered back to the Passionist Convent, a convent vowed to Perpetual Adoration, seemed to her to be full of significance.

Father Dalgairn's book had made clear to her that wherever she went and whatever she did she would always believe in the Divine Presence. His book had discovered to her the instinctive nature of her belief in the Sacrament, but it had not widened her spiritual perceptions, still less her artistic: the delicious terror and irresistible curiosity which she experienced on opening St. Teresa's *Book of Her Life* she had never experienced before. It was like re-birth, being born to a new experience, to a purer sensation of life. It was like throwing open the door of a small, confined garden, and looking upon the wide land of the world. It was like breathing the wide air of eternity after that of a close-scented room. She knew that she was not capable of such pure ecstasy, yet it seemed to her very human to think and feel like this; and the saint's holy rapture seemed as natural—she thought for a moment—even more natural, even more truly human than the rapture which she had found in sinful love.

Before she had read a dozen pages, she seemed to know her like her own soul, though yet unaware whether the saint lived in this century or a dozen centuries ago. For all she said about the material facts of her life St. Teresa might be alive to-day and in England. She lived in aspiration, out of time and place; and like one who, standing upon a hill top, sees a bird soaring, a wild bird with the light of the heavens upon its wings, Evelyn seemed to see this soul waving its wings in its flight towards God. The soul sang love, love, love, and heaven was overflowed with cries for its Divine Master, for its adorable Master, for its Bridegroom-elect.

The extraordinary vehemence and passion, the daring realism of St. Teresa reminded Evelyn of Vittoria. She found the same unrestrained passionate realism in both; she thought of Belasquez's early pictures, and then of Ribera. Then of Ulick, who had told her that the great artist dared everything. St. Teresa had dared everything. She had dared even to discriminate between the love of God the Father and God the Son. It was God the Father that inspired in her the highest ecstasy, the most complete abandonment of self. In these supreme moments the human form of Jesus Christ was a hindrance, as in a lower level of spiritual exaltation it was a help.

"The moment my prayer began to pass from the natural to the supernatural, I strove to obliterate from my soul every physical obstacle. To lift my soul up, to contemplate, I dared not; aware of my imperfection it seemed over bold. Nevertheless I knew the presence of God to be about me, and I tried to gather myself in him. And nothing could then induce me to return to the sacred humanity of the Saviour."

But how touching is the saint's repentance for this infidelity to the Divine Bridegroom.

"O Lord of my soul, of all my goods, Jesus crucified, I shall never remember without pain that I once thought this thing. I shall think of it as a great treason, and I stand convicted before the Good Master; and though it proceeded from my ignorance, I shall never expiate it with tears."

Just as every variation of habit, of fashion is noticeable to those who live outside themselves, so the changes and complexities in the life of the soul are perceived by them who live within themselves. The saint relates how for many months she refrained from prayer, and as we know that prayer was the source of all her joy, a joy touching ecstasy, often above the earth and resplendent with vision, we can imagine the anguish that these abstinences must have caused her.

"To destroy confidence in God the Demon spread a snare, his most insidious snare. He persuaded me that owing to my imperfections I could not, without being wanting in humility, present myself in prayer to God. This caused me such anguish that for a year and a half I refrained. For at least a year, for the six months following I am not sure of my memory. Unfortunate one, what did I do! By my own act I plunged myself in hell without demons being about to drag me there."

This scruple is followed by others. The saint suspects the entire holiness of her joy in prayer, and she asks if these transports, these ravishments, these moments in which she lies exhausted in the arms of the Beloved Bridegroom, were contrived by the Demon or if they were granted to her by God. Her anxiety is great, and men learned in holy doctrine are consulted. They incline to the belief that her visions proceed from God, and encourage her to persevere. Then she cries to her Divine Master, to the Lord of her soul, to her adorable Master, to the adorable Bridegroom.

"Cannot we say of a soul to whom God extends this solicitude and these delicacies of love that the soul has made for our Lord a bed of roses and lilies, and that it is impossible that this adorable Master will not come, though he may delay, and take his delight with her."

This saint, in whom religion was genius, was one of Ulick's most unqualified admirations. He never spoke of her that his voice did not acquire an accent of conviction, or without alluding to the line of an old English poet, who had addressed her:

'Oh, thou undaunted daughter of desires.'

She recalled with a smile his contempt of the Austins and the Eliots, those most materialistic writers, he would say, whose interest in humanity and whose knowledge of it is limited to social habits and customs. But St. Teresa he placed among the highest writers, among the great visionaries. "Her desire sings," he said, "like the sea and the winds, and it breaks like fire about God's feet." He had said that the soul that flashed from her pages was more intense than any soul in Shakespeare or Balzac. "They had created many, she but one incomparable soul—her own, and in surging drift of vehement aspiration, and in recession of temporal things we hear the singing of the stars, the beating of the eternal pulse."

On Friday she had finished the autobiography, and before going into the garden she took down another of the saint's works, *The Way of Perfection*, intending to look through it in some sunny corner.

She had slipped easily into the early hours of the convent. After breakfast she had the morning to herself, and she divided it between the library and the garden. The leaves were beginning to fall, and in the thinning branches there seemed to be an appearance of spring. From St. Peter's walk she strolled into the orchard, and then into the piece of uncultivated ground at the end of it. Some of the original furze bushes remained, and among these a streamlet trickled through the long grasses, and following it she found that it led her to the fish pond in the shrubbery, at the back of St. Peter's walk. There was there a pleasant, shady place, where she could sit and read. She stood for a moment watching the fish. They were so tame that they would take the bread from the novices' hands. She had brought some bread, but she had to throw it to them. She divided it amongst them, not forgetting to favour the little ones, and she thought it strange that they could distinguish her from the novices. That much they knew of the upper air. The fish watched her out of their beady eyes, stirring in their dim atmosphere with a strange, finny motion.

At that hour of the day the sun was warm enough to sit out; the little shiver in the air was not unpleasant; and sitting on the garden bench, she opened her book in a little tremor of excitement. Her thoughts fluttered, and she strove to imagine what book the saint could have written to justify so beautiful a title. Her expectations were realised. The character of the book is clearly defined in the first pages: she perceived it to be a complete manual of convent life, a perfect compendium of a nun's soul. On its pages lay that shadowy, evanescent and hardly apprehensible thing—the soul of a nun, only the soul, not a word regarding her daily life: any mother-abbess could have written such a materialistic book: St. Teresa, with the instinct of her genius, addressed herself to the task which none but she could fulfil—the evolution of a nun's soul. And as Evelyn read she marked the passages that specially caught her attention.

"Do not imagine, my daughters, that it is useless to pray, as you are constantly praying, for the defenders of the Church: Have a care lest you should share the opinion of certain folk to whom it seems hard that they should not pray much oftener for themselves. Believe me that no prayer is better or more profitable than that of which I am speaking. Perhaps you fear that it will not go to diminish the pains which you will suffer in purgatory: I answer that such prayer is too holy and too pleasing to God to be useless. Even if the time of your expiation should be a little longer—well, let it be so."

"Oh, to be good like that," she thought. And her soul raised its eyes in a little shy emulation....

A few pages further on she read—

"That all may take heed. For neglect of this counsel a nun may find herself in an entanglement from which she may not find strength to free herself. And then, great God! What feebleness, what puerile complaisances this particular friendship may not be the source. It is impossible to say what number, none but an eye-witness may believe. They are but trifles, and I see no reason for specifying them here. I merely add: in whosoever it is found it is an evil, in a superior it is a plague spot....

"An excellent remedy is to be together only at those times enjoined by the rule, on other occasions to refrain from speech, as is now our custom, and to live separately each in her cell as the rule ordains. And, although it be a praiseworthy custom to unite for work in a community room, I desire that the nuns of the convent of St. Joseph shall be freed from this custom, for it is much easier to keep silence if each works in her cell. Moreover, it is of the first importance to accustom oneself to solitude, in order to advance oneself in prayer; and as prayer should be the mortar of this monastery, we should cherish all that which increases the spirit in us."

Glancing down the pages, her eyes were arrested by a passage of even more subtle, more penetrating wisdom.

"Would you know a certain sign, my daughters, by which you may judge of your progress in virtue? Let each one look within herself and discover if she believes herself to be the unworthiest of you all, and if for the benefit of the others she makes it visible by her actions that she really thinks that this is so, that is the certain sign of spiritual advancement, and not delight in prayer, nor ravishment, nor visions, and such like favours which God grants to souls when he is so pleased. We shall only know the value of such favours in the next world. It is not so with humility—humility is a money which is always current, it is safely invested capital, a perpetual income; but extraordinary favours are money which is lent for a time and may at any moment be called in. I repeat, our true treasure is profound humility, great mortification, and an obedience which, seeing God in the superior, submits to his every order."

The saint's delicate yet virile perception, and her power of expressing the shadowy and evanescent, filled Evelyn with admiration; and the saint appeared to her in the light of a great novelist; she wondered if Balzac had ever read these pages.

"The best remedy, in my opinion, that a nun can employ to conquer the imperfect affection which she still bears her parents, is to abstain from seeing them until by patient prayer she has obtained from God the freedom of her soul; when she is so disposed that their visit is a cross, let her see them by all means. For then she will bring good to their souls, and do no harm to her own."

This seemed not a little grim. But how touching is the personal confession which appears on the following page.

"My parents loved me extremely, according to what they said, and I loved them in a way that did not allow them to forget me. Nevertheless I have seen from what has happened to me, and what has happened to other nuns, how little we may count upon their affection for us."

The unselfishness of such conduct seemed open to doubt. But unselfishness is a word that none may speak without calling into question the entire conduct of his or her life. Evelyn remembered that she had left her father for the sake of her voice, and that she had refused to marry Owen because marriage, especially marriage with Owen, did not seem compatible with her soul's safety. Looked at from a certain side, her life did seem self-centred, but allowance, she thought, must be made for the difficulties—the entanglements in which the first false step had involved her. But in any case she must not question the efficacy of prayer, that was a dogma of the Church. The mission of the contemplative orders is to pray for those who do not pray for themselves, and if we believe in the efficacy of prayer, we need not scruple to leave our parents to live in a monastery where, by our prayers, we held them to eternal salvation. We leave them for a little while, but only that we may live with them for ever.

"Believe me, my dear sisters, if you serve him well you will not find better parents than those the Divine Master sends you. I know that it is even so."

"What beauty there is in her sternness," Evelyn thought.

"I repeat that those whose trend is toward worldly things and who do not make progress in virtue, shall leave this monastery; should she persist in remaining a nun let her enter another convent; for if she doesn't she will see what will happen to her. Nor must she complain about me; nor accuse me of not having make known to her the practical life of the monastery I founded. If there is an earthly paradise it is in this house, but only for souls who desire nothing but to please God, who have no thought for themselves; for these the life here is infinitely agreeable."

This passage is one of the very few in which appears the wise, practical woman, the founder of an order and of many monasteries, who lived side by side in the same body, the constant associate of the lyrical saint. Evelyn tried to picture her to herself, and two pictures alternated in her thoughts. She saw deep, eager, passionate eyes, and a frail, exhausted body borne along easily by the soul, and doing the work of the unconquerable soul. In the second picture, there were the same consuming eyes, the same wasted body, but the expression was quite different. The saint's manner was the liveliest, happiest manner, and Evelyn thought of the privilege of such companionship, and she envied those who had walked with her, hearing her speak.

The little pond at her feet was full of fair reflections of the sky and trees, and the idea of convent life lay on the pages of the book even as fair. In itself it was disparate and vague, but on the pages of the book it floated clear and distinct. She asked if any of the Wimbledon nuns lived a life of that intense inward rapture which St. Teresa deemed essential if a sister were to be allowed to remain in the convent of St. Joseph at Avila, and the coincidence of the names gave her pause. This convent's patron saint was St. Joseph, and she sought for some resemblance between the Reverend Mother and St. Teresa. She wondered if she, Evelyn, were a nun, towards which of the nuns would her personal sympathies incline: would she love better Sister Veronica or Sister Mary John? It might be Mother Mary Hilda. It would be one of the three. There was not one among the others likely to interest her in the least. She tried to imagine this friendship: it assumed a vague shape and then dissolved in the distance. But would the Reverend Mother tolerate this friendship, or would it be promptly cut down to the root according to the advice of St. Teresa?

Her thoughts pursued their way, now and then splashing as they leaped out of the soul's dimness. Only the splashing of the fish broke the stillness of the garden, and startled at a sudden gurgling sound, she rose, in time to see a shadowy shape sinking with a motion of fins amid the weeds. That she should be living in a convent, that she should have repented of her sins, that the fish should leap and fall back with strange, gurgling sound, filled her with wonderment. The vague autumn blue expressed some vague yearning, some indistinct aspiration; the air was like crystal, the leaves were falling.... We have perceptions of the outer forms of things, but that is all we know of them. The only thing we are sure of is what is in ourselves. We know the difference between right and wrong. She stood for a long time at the edge of the fish pond, gazing into the vague depths. Then she walked, exalted, overcome by the mystery of things. She seemed to walk upon air, the world was a-thrill with spiritual significances, all was symbol and exaltation. Her past life shrank to a tiny speck, and she knew that she had been happy only since she had been in the convent. Ah, that little chapel, haunted by prayers! it breathed prayer, in that chapel contemplation was never far off. She had prayed there as she had never prayed before, and she wondered if she should attribute the difference in her prayers to the chapel or to herself. She had always felt, in a dumb, instinctive way, that to her at least everything depended on her chastity.... She had been chaste now a long while. The explanation seemed to have come to her. Yes, it is by denial of the sexual instinct that we become religious.

As she passed through the orchard she caught sight of the strange little person whom she had seen in chapel with a pile of prayer books beside her, and who always wore something startlingly blue, whether skirt, handkerchief or cloak. She had met her in the garden before, but she had hurried away, her eyes fixed on the ground. Mother Philippa had spoken of a Miss Dingle, a simple-minded person who had been sent by her family to the convent to be looked after by the nuns, and Evelyn concluded that it must be she. But at that moment other thoughts engaged her attention; and she lingered in the orchard, returning slowly by St. Peter's walk. As she passed the Georgian temple or summer-house, she was taken by a desire to examine it, and there she found Miss Dingle. She was seated on the floor, engaged, so Evelyn thought, in a surreptitious game of Patience. That was only how she could account for Miss Dingle's consternation and fear at seeing her. But what she had taken for cards were pious pictures. Evelyn stood in the doorway, and for the first time had an opportunity of seeing what Miss Dingle was really like. It was difficult to say whether her face was ugly or pretty; the features were not amiss—it was the expression, vague and dim like that of an animal, that puzzled Evelyn.

"Please let me help you to pick up your pictures." Miss Dingle did not answer, and Evelyn feared for a moment that she had offended her. "Won't you let me help you to pick up your pictures?"

"Yes," she said, "you may help me to pick them up, but you must be very quick."

"But why must I be quick? Are you in such a very great hurry?"

Miss Dingle seemed uncertain of her own thoughts, and to reassure her, Evelyn asked her if she would not like to walk with her in the orchard.

"Oh," she said, looking at Evelyn shyly—it was a sort of child-like curiosity, "I dare not go into the orchard to-day.... I brought these pictures to keep him from me. I know that he is about."

"Who is about?"

"I'm afraid he might hurt me."

"But who would hurt you?"

"Well," she said cautiously, "perhaps he'd be afraid to come near me to-day," and she glanced at her frock. "But I'm sure he's about. Did you see any one as you came through the furze bushes?"

"No," Evelyn answered; and trying to conceal her astonishment, she said, "I'm sure there's no one there."

"Ah, he knows it would be useless." She glanced again at her frock. "You see my blue skirt, that has perhaps frightened him away."

"But who has gone away?"

"Oh, the devil is always about."

"But you don't think he would hurt you?"

Miss Dingle looked suspiciously at Evelyn, and some dim thought whether Evelyn was the devil in disguise must have crossed her mind. But whatever the thought was, it was but a flitting thought; it passed in a moment, and Miss Dingle said—"But the devil is always trying to hurt us. That is what he comes for."

"So that is why you surrounded yourself with pious pictures—to keep him away?"

Miss Dingle nodded.

"What a nice dress you have on. I suppose you like blue. I always notice you wear it."

"I wear blue, as much blue as I can, for blue is the colour of the Virgin Mary, and he dare not attack me while I have it on. But I wear sometimes only a handkerchief, sometimes only a skirt, but now that he is about so frequently, I have to dress entirely in blue."

Evelyn asked her if she had lived in the convent long, and Miss Dingle told her she had lived there for the last three or four years, but she would give no precise answer when Evelyn asked if she hoped to become a nun, or whether she liked her home or the convent the better.

"Now," she said, "I must really go and say some prayers in the church."

Evelyn offered to accompany her, but she said she was well armed, and showed Evelyn several rosaries, which in case of need she would wave in his face.

Sister Mary John was digging in the kitchen garden, and Evelyn told her how she had come upon Miss Dingle in the summer-house surrounded by pious pictures. Leaning on her spade, Sister Mary John looked across the beds thinking, and Evelyn wondered of what. She said at last that Miss Dingle thought too much of the devil.

"We should not waste thoughts on him, all our thoughts should be for God; there is much more pleasure and profit in such thoughts."

"But it does seem a little absurd to imagine that the devil is hiding behind gooseberry bushes."

"The devil is everywhere, temptation is always near."

Evelyn saw that the nun did not care for discussion on the subject of the devil's objectivity, and in the pause in the conversation she noticed Sister Mary John's enormous boots. They looked like a man's boots, and she had a full view of them, for Sister Mary John wore her skirt very short, so that she might be able to dig with greater ease.

"One of the disadvantages of convent life are the few facilities it affords for exercise and for music," she added, with her beautiful smile. "I must have exercise, I can't live without it.... It is extraordinary how differently people are constituted. There is Mother Mary Hilda, she had never been for what I should call a good sharp walk in her life, and she does not know what an ache or a pain is."

The nun pointed with admiration to the bed which she had dug up that morning, and complained of the laziness of the gardener: he had not done this nor that, but he was such a good man—since he became a Catholic.

"He and I used to talk about things while we were at work: he said that he had never had it properly explained to him that there should only be one true religion.

"Since he became a Catholic, has he not done as much work as he used to do?"

"No, I'm afraid he has not," Sister Mary John answered. "Indeed, we have been thinking of sending him away, but it would be difficult for him to get another Catholic situation, and his faith would be endangered if he lived among Protestants."

At this moment they were interrupted by a loud caw, and looking round, Evelyn saw the convent jackdaw. The bird had hopped within a few yards, cawing all the while, evidently desirous of attracting their attention. With grey head a-slanted, the bird watched them out of sly eyes. "Pay no attention to him; you'll see what he'll do," said Sister Mary John, and while Evelyn waited, a little afraid of the bird who seemingly had selected her for some purpose of his own, she listened to the story of his domestication. He had been hatched out in the hen-house, and had tamed himself; he had declined to go wild, preferring a sage convent life to the irregularity of the world. The bird hopped about, feigning an interest in the worms, but getting gradually nearer the two women. At last, with a triumphant caw caw, he flew on to Sister Mary John's shoulder, eyeing Evelyn all the while, clearly bent on making her acquaintance.

"He'll come on your shoulder presently," said Sister Mary John, and after some plausive coquetting the bird fluttered on to Evelyn's shoulder, and Sister Mary John said—

"You wait; you'll see what he will do."

Evelyn remained quite still, feeling the bird's bill caressing her neck. When she looked round she noticed a wicked expression gathering in his eyes.

"Pretend," said Sister Mary John, "not to see him."

Evelyn did as she was bidden, and, satisfied that he was no longer observed, the bird plunged his beak into Evelyn's hair, pulled at it as hard as he could, and then flew away, cawing with delight.

"That is one of his favourite tricks. We are so fond of him, and so afraid that one day a cat will take him. But there is Mother Mary Hilda coming to fetch you for your lesson."

Evelyn bade Sister Mary John good-bye, and went forward to meet her instructress.

The morning seemed full of adventure. There were Miss Dingle, her pious pictures, and the devil behind the gooseberry bushes. There was the picturesque figure of Sister Mary John, digging, making ready for the winter cabbages. There was the jackdaw, his story and his humours, and there was her discovery of the genius of St. Teresa. All these things had happened that morning, and Evelyn walked a little elated, her heart full of spiritual enthusiasm. The project was already astir in her for the acquisition of an edition in the original Spanish, and she looked forward to a study of that language as a pleasant and suitable occupation when she returned to London. She questioned Mother Mary Hilda regarding the merits of the English translation; the French, she said, she could read no longer. She described the worthy father's prose as asthmatic; she laughed at his long, wheezy sentences, but Sister Mary Hilda seemed inclined to set store on the Jesuit's pious intentions. The spirit was more essential than the form, and it was with this argument on their lips they sat down to the Latin lesson. The nun had opened the book, and Evelyn was about to read the first sentence, when, raising her eyes and voice, she said—

"Oh! Mother Mary Hilda, you've forgotten ... this is my last lesson, I am going away to-morrow."

"Even so it need not be the last lesson; you will come and see us during the winter, if you are in London. I don't remember that you said that you are going abroad to sing."

"Mother Mary Hilda, I'm thinking of leaving the stage."

The nun turned the leaves of the breviary, and it seemed to Evelyn that she dreaded the intrusion on her thoughts of a side of life the very existence of which she had almost succeeded in forgetting; and, feeling a little humbled, Evelyn applied herself to the lesson. And it was just as Mary Hilda's hand closed the books that the door opened and the Reverend Mother entered, bringing, it seemed, a new idea and a new conception of life into the room. Mother Mary Hilda gathered up her books, and having answered the Reverend Mother's questions in her own blithe voice, each word illuminated by the happy smile which Evelyn thought so beautiful, withdrew like an apparition.

The Reverend Mother took the place that Mother Mary Hilda had left, and by her very manner of sitting down, showed that she had come on some special intention.

"Miss Innes, I have come to ask you not to leave to-morrow. If you are not already tired of our life, it would give us great pleasure if you would stay with us till Monday."

"It is very good of you to ask me to stay, I have been very happy; indeed, I dread returning; it is difficult to return to the life of the world after having seen what your life is here."

"We should only be too happy if you will prolong your stay. You are free to remain as long as you please."

"Thank you, Reverend Mother, it is very good of you, but I cannot live here in idleness, walking about the garden. What should I do if it were to rain?"

"It looks like rain to-day. We have had a long term of fine weather."

The nun's old white hand lay on the table, a little crippled, but still a nervous, determined hand, and the pale, sparkling eyes looked so deep into the enigma of Evelyn's soul that she lost her presence of mind; her breath came more quickly, and she hastily remembered that this retreat now drawing to a close had solved nothing, that the real solution of her life was as far off as ever.

"Then I may take it that you will stay with us till Monday. I will not weary you with our repeated thanks for what you have done for us. You know that we are very grateful, and shall never forget you in our prayers, but you will not mind my thanking you again for the pleasure your singing has given us. You have sung every day. You really have been very kind."

"I beg of you not to mention it, Reverend Mother; to sing for you and all the dear sisters was a great pleasure to me. I never enjoyed singing in a theatre so much."

"I am glad you have enjoyed your stay, Miss Innes. Your room will always be ready. I hope you will often come to see us."

"It will be a great advantage for me to come and stay with you from time to time." Neither spoke for a time, then Evelyn said, "Reverend Mother, is it not strange that I should have come back to this convent, my old convent? I never forgot it. I often wondered if I should come here again. When I was here before, it was just as now; it was in a great crisis of my life. It was just before I left home, just before I went to Paris to learn singing. I don't know if Monsignor has told you that I have decided to leave the stage."

"Monsignor has entrusted you to me, and I should like to count you as one of my children. All the nuns tell me their little troubles. Though I have guessed there must be some great trouble in your life, I should like you to feel that you can tell me everything, if to do so can be the least help to you."

Evelyn's eyes brightened, and, trembling with emotion, she leaned across the table; the Reverend Mother took her hand, and the touch of that old benign hand was a delight, and she felt that she must confide her story.

"I have been several times on the point of speaking to you on the subject of my past, for if I am to come here again I feel that you should know something about me. But how to tell it. I had thought of asking Father Daly to tell you. To-day is your day for confession, but last week I confessed to Monsignor, and do not like to submit myself to another director. Do you understand?"

"Father Daly is an excellent, worthy man, the convent is under the greatest obligations to him, but I could not recommend him as a very enlightened director of souls. That is why the nuns tell me all their troubles. I should like you to feel that you can tell me everything."

"Reverend Mother, if you did not pass from the schoolroom to the convent like Veronica, you will have heard, you must know, that the life of an opera singer is generally a sinful life. I was very young at the time, only one-and-twenty. I knew that I had a beautiful voice, and that my father could not teach me to sing. But it was not for self-interest that I left him; I was genuinely in love with Sir Owen Asher. He was very good to me; he wanted to marry me;

from the world's point of view I was very successful, but I was never happy. I felt that I was living a sinful life, and we cannot go on doing what we feel to be wrong and still be happy. Night after night I could not sleep. My conscience kept me awake. I strove against the inevitable, for it is very difficult to change one's life from end to end, but there was no help for it."

Her story, as she told it, seemed to her very wonderful, more wonderful than she had thought it was, and she would have liked to have told the Reverend Mother all the torment and anguish of mind she had gone through. But she felt that she was on very thin ice, and trembled inwardly lest she was shocking the nun.

It was exciting to tell that it was her visit to the convent that had brought about her repentance; how that very night her eyes had opened at dawn, and she had seen clearly the wickedness of her life, and she could not refrain from saying that it was Owen Asher's last letter, in which he said that at all hazards he would save her from losing herself in religion, that had sent her to Monsignor for advice. She noticed her omission of all mention of Ulick, and it seemed to her strange that she could still be interested in her sins, and at the same time genuinely determined to reform her life. The nun sat looking at her, thinking what answer she should make, and Evelyn wondered what that answer would be.

"We shall pray for you.... You will not fall into sin again; it is our prayers that enable men to overcome their passions. Were it not for our prayers, God would have long ago destroyed the world. Think of the times of persecution and sacrilege, when prayer only survived in the monasteries."

Evelyn could not but acquiesce: a world without prayer would be an intolerable world, as unendurable to man as to God. But if the Reverend Mother's explanation were a true one! If these poor forsakers of the world were in truth the saviours of the world, without whose aid the world would have perished long since!

When she had gone, Evelyn sat thinking, her head leaned on her hand, her eyes fixed on the distant garden, seeing life from afar, strange and distant, like reflections in still waters. She could see distant figures in St. Peter's walk, tending the crosses and the statues of the Virgin placed in nooks, or hanging on the branches. Some four or five nuns were playing at ball on the terrace, and in the plaintive autumn afternoon, there was something extraordinarily touching in their simple amusement; and she had, perforce, to feel how much wiser was their childishness than the vanity of the world.

Ulick had said that their adventure was the same, only their ways were different. He had said that he sought God in art, while she sought him in dogma. But if she accepted dogma, it was only as a cripple accepts a crutch, Catholicism was essential to her, without it she could not walk; but while conforming to dogma, it seemed possible to transcend its narrowness, and to attach to every petty belief a spiritual significance. It is right that we should acquiesce in these beliefs, for they are the symbols by which the faith was kept alive and handed down. God leads us by different ways, and though we may prefer to worship God in the open air, we should not despise him who builds a house for worship. The Real Being is all that we are sure of, for He is in our hearts, the rest is as little shadows. Ulick had quoted an Eastern mystic— 'He that sees himself sees God, and in him there is neither I nor thou.'

And, reflecting on the significance of these words, she turned with pensive fingers the leaves of *The Way of Perfection*.

But she was going back to London on Monday! In London she would meet Owen and all her former life. She knew in a way how she was going to escape him. But her former life was everywhere. She got up and walked about the room, then she stood at the window, her hands held behind her back. She was sorely tried, and felt so weak in spirit that she was tempted, or fancied that she was tempted, to go away with Owen in the *Medusa*. Or she might tell him that she would marry him, and so end the whole matter. But she knew that she would do neither of these things. She knew that she would sacrifice Owen and her career as an opera singer so that she might lead a chaste life. Yet a life of prayer and chastity was not natural to her; her natural preferences were for lovers and worldly pleasures, but she was sacrificing all that she liked for all that she disliked. She wondered, quite unable to account for her choice to herself. Her life seemed very mad, but, mad or sane, she was going to sacrifice Owen and her career. She might sing at concerts, but she did not think such singing would mean much to her and she thought of the splendid successful life that lay before her if she remained on the stage. Again she wondered at her choice, seeking in herself the reason that impelled her to do what she was doing. She could not say that she liked living with her father in Dulwich, nor did she look forward to giving singing lessons, and yet that was what she was going to do. She strove to distinguish her soul; it seemed flying before her like a bird, making straight for some goal which she could not distinguish. She could distinguish its wings in the blue air, and then she lost sight of them; then she caught sight of them again, and they were then no more than a tremulous sparkle in the air. Suddenly the vision vanished, and she found herself face to face with herself—her prosaic self which she had known always, and would know until she ceased to know everything. She was here in the Wimbledon Convent, and Owen was in London waiting for her. She knew she never would live with him again. But how would she finally separate herself from him? How would it all come about? She could imagine herself yielding, but if she did, it would not last a week. Her life would be unendurable, and she would have to send him away. For it is not true that Tannhäuser goes back to Venus. He who repents, he who had once felt the ache and remorse of sin, may fall into sin again, but he quickly extricates himself; his sinning is of no long duration! It was the casual sin that she dreaded; at the bottom of her heart she knew that she would never live a life of sin again. But she trembled at the thought of losing the perfect peace and happiness which now reigned in her heart, even for a few hours. Her face contracted in an expression of terror at the thought of finding herself again involved in the anguish, revolt and despair which she had endured in Park Lane. She recalled the moments when she saw herself vile and loathsome, when she had turned from the image of her soul which had been shown to her. Then, to rid herself of the remembrance, she thought of the joy she had experienced that morning at hearing in the creed that God's kingdom shall never pass away. Her soul had kindled like a flame, and she had praised God, crying to herself, "Thy kingdom shall last for ever and ever." It had seemed to her that her soul had acquired kingship over all her faculties, over all her senses, for the time being it had ruled her utterly; and so delicious was its subjection that she had not dared to move lest she should lose this sweet peace. Her lips had murmured an Our Father, but so slowly that the Sanctus bell had rung before she had finished it. Nothing troubled her, nothing seemed capable of troubling her, and the torrent of delight which had flowed into and gently overflowed her soul had intoxicated and absorbed her until it had seemed to her that there was nothing further for her to desire.

She remembered that when Mass was over she had risen from her knees elated, feeling that she had prayed even as the nuns prayed, and she had retired to her room, striving to restrain her looks and thoughts so that she might prolong this union with God.

To remember this experience gave her courage. For she could not doubt that the intention of so special a favour was to convince her that she would not be lacking in courage when the time came to deny herself to Owen Asher. At the same time she was troubled, and she feared that she was not quite sincere with herself. She would easily resist him now; but in six months' time, in a year? Besides, she would meet other men; her thoughts even now went out towards one. Ah! wretched weakness, abominable sin! She was filled with contempt for herself, and yet at the bottom of her heart, like hope at the bottom of Pandora's box, there was tolerance. Her sins interested her; she would not be herself without them, and this being so, how could she hope to conquer herself?

Saturday and Sunday were monotonous and anxious days. She had begun to wonder what was in the newspapers, and she had written to say that her carriage was to come to fetch her on Monday at three o'clock.

There had not been a gleam of light since early morning, only a gentle diffused twilight, and the foliage in the garden was almost human in its listlessness; a flat grey sky hung about the trees like a shroud. Mother Philippa and Mother Mary Hilda were walking with her about the grass-grown drive. They were waiting for the Reverend Mother, who had gone to fetch a medal for Evelyn. She heard her chestnuts champing their bits ready to take her back to London, and she could not listen to Mother Philippa's conversation, for she had been suddenly taken with a desire to say one last prayer in the chapel. She must say one more prayer in the presence of the Sacrament. So, excusing herself, she ran back, and, kneeling down, she buried her face in her hands. At once all her thoughts hushed within her; it was like bees entering a hive to make honey. Prayer came to her without difficulty, without even asking, and she enjoyed almost five minutes' breathless adoration.

The three nuns kissed her, and as the Reverend Mother hung the medal round her neck, she told her that prayers would be constantly offered up for her preservation. The chestnuts plunged at starting.... If she were killed now it would not matter. But the horses soon settled down into their long swinging trot of ten miles an hour, and all the way to London she reflected. The Reverend Mother had said that the prayers of nuns and monks were the wall and bastion tower which saved a sinful world from the wrath of God, and she thought of the fume of prayer ascending night and day from this convent as from a censer. Men had always prayed, since the beginning of things men had prayed, and as Ulick had said, wisdom was not invented yesterday. He agreed with the naturalistic philosophers that force is indestructible, only objecting that the naturalistic philosophers did not go far enough, the theory of the indestructibility of force being equally applicable to the spiritual world. The world exists not in itself, but in man's thought.... Often an intense evocation has brought the absent one before the seer's eyes, and that there are sympathies which transcend and overrule the laws of time and space hardly admits of doubt. Life is but a continual hypnotism; and the thoughts of others reach us from every side, determining in some measure our actions. It was therefore certain that she would be influenced by the prayers that would be offered up for her by the convent. She imagined these prayers intervening between her and sin, coming to her aid in some moment of perilous temptation, and perhaps in the end determining the course of her life.

THE END

Note from the Editor

Odin's Library Classics strives to bring you unedited and unabridged works of classical literature. As such, this is the complete and unabridged version of the original English text unless noted. In some instances, obvious typographical errors have been corrected. This is done to preserve the original text as much as possible. The English language has evolved since the writing and some of the words appear in their original form, or at least the most commonly used form at the time. This is done to protect the original intent of the author. If at any time you are unsure of the meaning of a word, please do your research on the etymology of that word. It is important to preserve the history of the English language.

Taylor Anderson